MINER'S MONOPOLY

New System, Who Dis?
Volume Two

By

Ryan DeBruyn

Ryan DeBruyn

TABLE OF CONTENTS

<u>FOREWORD</u>

Hello everyone. Ryan DeBruyn here.
I just wanted to start out by thanking everyone who has picked up the book. I'm so thrilled that you are reading it and hope you enjoy it as much as I did writing it.
<u>For anyone reading on Royal Road, or Patreon</u>: Please know that while the story contained in these pages are similar, they are not the same. Only the book you see in front of you now can be considered Canon for the series.
Everything else is just a rough draft.
Still, I hope the people supporting me over on Patreon are enjoying the conclusion to Book Four.
Check in at the end of the book after the bloopers for links to Royal Road or Patreon to continue your journey if you're desperate for more!

<u>RECAP</u>

You're currently following my story. Brodie Flacarrada, AKA Alonzo Mars. AKA Smegma's Slave, hey what the hell dude…

"You have your own brain, you shouldn't repeat everything I say!"

Well then, I'm sorry for him…

"Stop apologizing. You're so Canadian…"

Anyway, this shouldn't take long. Since my story isn't some epic tale. I was Mana Assaulted, and fought off the assailant. That turned into me being tried for Manslaughter even though it was self-defense. The case should be clear cut but—

"Someone powerful is pulling strings and is out to get you!"

Shut up, Smegma!

Where was I? Well, we were also about to start our own company to compete with Jagger and P-Cubed?

Not much else to tell. I don't think…

"What about your epic fight with the Golem?

"Or how you plan to become a Hunter now, instead of a Mana Bank?"

Man, he doesn't stop talking. If I listened to that windbag we'd be here all day. That's probably enough for you to all remember my Lawyer, Sparkle Legion and our new decision to start a new company.

I'll try to keep control of the dickless wonder as we continue on.

"Dude, you know I'm sensitive about that!"

<u>INTERLUDE 1</u>

Another Place—A Different Time

Amty-Oha pored over the reports she'd received. She must have missed one from her Larvae Sect on Crendalar. Surely, it was here—even though this was her ninth to ninetieth look through the pile. It had to be her mistake!

"My sweet Succubi," Lorant-Axe crooned from his own desk, right beside hers. "It is not there. They did not send it."

"But how could they have fought all seven of the Trials and given us nothing to help our chances?" Amty-Oha asked, her voice furious and incredulous. "They would not abandon us!"

"Perhaps they did not have time to send in a report. Maybe the System blocked it. Perhaps we are not as valuable as we thought. There are many reasons they could be missing," Lorant-Axe reiterated, using several of the points he'd made before. Amty-Oha glared at him, and he added, "That does not mean we will not succeed, my tyrannical love!"

She rolled her eyes at his placation. He might be right, but the chances of them succeeding weren't great. Not now; not anymore. Her fist clenched onto the top report, slightly crumpling it before she stopped herself and straightened the paper back out.

She knew the words on it by heart. A report from the Elves—her Larvae Guild members. By all metrics, it was a report of success in the first Trial, but for someone who knew every speck of dust dwelling within her Guild—it spelled a disaster.

Sure, it was only a loss of twenty percent of the raiding party—which was within acceptable limits—but it was the specific members they'd lost that were the problem.

Not a single Tank remained. She'd carefully grown the elite Elves over thousands of years. Her Jaegars had been the strongest reported by any in the Larvae Sect from Crendalar, and amongst them, the Tank Jaegars were the ones she poured the most resources into. Followed closely by the Healers.

How had she done it?

She'd collected the Card Shards like all the other groups that went off-world from Crendalar. She'd paired Shards into sets and discovered new ones—that she'd reported back. Amty had even followed numerous guides and strategies for taking down known Portal Monsters.

But none of those were the reason she'd created the strongest Guild with the best chance to Ascend.

No, Amty had discovered a *secret*—one she doubted any other Crendalar Demon knew. This one secret was what had made it possible for her to hand groom Tanks and Healers in particular but benefits were available for everyone else as well.

Amty-Oha had met an Elven woman who knew of another Demon on Sective Agora. That claim didn't surprise Amty. Many other Sects would have used Portals to establish forces here. Still, wanting to establish diplomatic relations with those of similar goals, Amty had asked to meet the Demon.

Aurora Skysong—the Elve's name—had only seemed to consider for a moment before an Imp had suddenly appeared in the room with them. An Imp, who claimed to be a Felguard-Imp named Greb-Shak, from an 'Abyss Sect' Amty hadn't heard of.

Through their discussions, she'd discovered a few reasons why she'd never heard of them. After inquiries on Crendalar Five, she'd discovered even *more* reasons she'd never shared with Greb-Shak.

Still, how his Sect had *created* two Skills was both fantastical and phenomenal. The idea to sell wares, and use them to collect Mana, was profound. The execution, however, was lacking. Especially in the second candidate she'd found—likely the first Skill version created.

Her surprises weren't finished though; Greb-Shak's or Aurora's Skill grew with the amount of Mana sent back—sent back to where? She and a select few surviving members of the Larvae Sect on Crendalar never discovered. She'd hoped that her spies could find this Treasury, but other than a massive crater, nothing remained of the Abyss Sect's compound.

Still, despite that failure, it didn't mean she wouldn't use the surviving gifts it created. And she had. Lorant and she had used them—well, it—perfectly. Surely, they were the strongest Larvae Guild, with the best chances to Ascend.

There was perhaps a single failure—but it wasn't truly that bad. She'd gotten greedy. No, surely an experiment wasn't greedy. Through other experiments, Amty had been able to pair Legendary Skill combinations together—without having to get lucky with Card Shards. She even sported the most wondrous of those Skills herself. The fact that the Abyss Sect had even created their own Skill, and her race still failed to Ascend infuriated both her and Lorant.

Still, they'd consoled themselves with the fact that now was their time! Now they'd prove themselves and become Elders upon Ascension.

But how in the Deepest Hells had it all gone wrong? Was it when she killed Raylight Cloudbreeze?

No, it couldn't have been. Still, where had that second *Demonic Vault* Skill gone? She'd never even told Lorant about its existence, so surely no one else could have known—could have pulled it from his Heart Deck before she got to him. Even before Raylight died, he claimed to have the Skill…

Maybe she should have tried again with Aurora before—

Between two claws on the page, one name amongst the casualties glared at her accusingly. One name that made it impossible for her to salvage the situation. The same name that had made it all possible—and the likely reason so many of her Elites had died.

Aurora Skysong…

"Surely, we can still salvage this," Lorant said, seeming to read her very thoughts. "There are other Elven Guilds—both Elven and Demonic Sects with strength that we can align with."

That was what the rest of these other reports were. Pages and pages about other Guilds and their personnel. Their backers. She clenched her fangs together, and stated, "None of them can hold a candle to our Larvae Guild!"

Lorant grimaced and looked her right in her purple eyes. "*Could* have held a candle, sweets," he said somberly. "What made us the best is now gone. We have twenty-six days to enter the Second Trial.

"Now!" He shouted the word after a pause, startling her. "Do you want to start working toward Ascending, or will you continue to cry over the useless dead Elves?"

Amty looked at Lorant with wide eyes. He was right about them needing to start preparing for the Second Trial but so wrong about the *useless* Elves. She nodded her head and fished out a report on a Guild called Treewall. It had the best chance to plug the holes in their Larvae Guild.

As she handed it over, she addressed the comment he'd made. "You can't call them *useless*, my love. Without them, there's nothing that we could do. Only the inhabitants of the Ascending Race can come back through the Portal without losing a portion of their power. Even with our strength, if we enter the Trial, only one of us can return—and as an A-Rank at best…"

Lorant scoffed. "We are Universe Powerhouses. Surely it wouldn't degrade us that far!" At Amty's pitying look, the Felguard growled. "Then we should have taken the *Demonic Vault* Skill from Aurora! Why did you leave such a valuable Skill with an *Elf?*"

There were a lot of undertones in that scrutiny of her decision. Primary amongst them was the hint of Lorant's true thoughts. If one of *them* possessed the *Demonic Vault* Skill—then they could enter Portals, downgrade to A-Rank and climb back to S and beyond. Surely he couldn't have been the one who took Raylight's Skill in that case, right? He was idiotic, but Amty didn't correct him— didn't mention that they perhaps couldn't take the Skill. He wasn't always the greatest 'thinker,' and she didn't want to confuse him.

Surely, he'd forgive her for withholding the existence of the second Skill, and her experiments with Raylight, right?

Instead, she focused on the fact that he had questioned her choices. "When we began, we didn't know just how powerful that Skill was! We didn't know it could Evolve as it did. How could we suspect its growth? If I remember correctly, you even called it worthless because Greb-Shak was an Imp and 'how could a Sect with an Imp be powerful!' Right?"

Lorant stood quickly, using clenched fists on his table-top to push his thickly framed body to its feet. The wood was not meant to handle his strength and weight. It splintered and then shattered in a rain of fragmented wood. "You dare speak the name of the Abomination!"

Amty stood and glared at the Felguard, meeting his red eyes, and matching his rage. His race was and always had been a tribe of Warriors. One that believed in the purity of blood. As such, a Felguard procreating with a race so far below them—an Imp—was an affront to Lorant. An 'Abomination.'

She didn't tell him how much she sometimes dreamt of him possessing even a portion of the intelligence of that Felguard-Imp. She loved him for himself by this point…

"You just said how powerful of a Skill that 'Abomination' created!" Amty shouted back. "You sandy hypocrite."

Amty could tell that her words stung and confused Lorant. Partly because if he continued to speak on the Abomination's mixed blood, it would belittle their own pairing. He'd made that mistake in the past, and even though he was more muscle than brains—he wasn't entirely stupid. Still, she'd effectively changed the subject away from their need to take the *Demonic Vault* Skill—as she was somewhat sure they wouldn't have been able to.

Not if no one took Raylight's Skill…

Lorant took a deep breath and looked down to his throne of a chair, before brushing it clean of splinters. He then sat and found the crumpled report on the floor. The one on Treewall she'd handed him before he'd 'raged.'

She took a deep breath and sat down as well. This was their way. They'd fight, and then use the simmering anger to move forward. Lorant began to nod at the choice she'd made. "Ahh, I see your thoughts. Double the number of Tanks and Healers to plug our gaps. It should work."

"Focusing on the front line, to allow our rear line to conquer all!" Amty recited. If only the Larvae Guild had followed her suggestion for its own Ascension Trials.

* * *

Amty looked deeply into Lorant's red eyes. "Even without the help of the Larvae Sect, we can use what we've learned from the first two trials here to Ascend!"

Lorant fought the urge to roll his eyes. This woman infuriated him. Sure, she was intelligent, and all of her plans for Sective Agora seemed the best options when proposed. But surely she could see how her prejudices and hang-ups cost them and the useless Elves?

He didn't say any of that, though. Instead, he stared back into her eyes. Lorant wasn't yet committed to his plans, anyway. He could find a Time Bubble on Sective Agora that contained these Dwarves, a race deemed the strongest of the options they'd found. He could follow her in time. If that was the next S-Ranked Portal off-world, he probably would.

But he couldn't stop the wriggling worm of a thought that blamed her for their failure either. What he did say, though, was, "I will follow you through when the next high-ranked Time Bubble appears. I look forward to seeing the rebirth of the Larvae Guild."

"When you next see me, you will be the weaker one in our pairing. Are you certain you don't want to go through first, my sweet?" Amty-Oha asked.

This question did make him grimace. That was true, and the one part of his plan that held the biggest frayed thread. Thankfully, he'd learned the buttons to push to stop her from pulling on it. "I am but a mace, while you are a sword. I can only destroy things, but despite how deadly you are, you are also useful in other mundane tasks. Such as cooking…"

An Elf had once lamented poetically about a sword to him, and he'd stolen what he could recall of that imbecile's views. He knew he'd butchered it, but thankfully Amty expected him to mix idioms.

She smiled up at him. "And your father said you had a muscle for a brain! You've grown so much."

Lorant flushed with heat, both from anger and embarrassment. Amty thankfully mistook it for the latter and leaned in for a kiss. He returned the kiss deeply, lifting her off the ground, and beginning to pull at her clothes simultaneously.

Amty chuckled with her mouth still latched onto his. She pulled away long enough to say, "A little privacy, please," to the remaining servants of their once powerful Larvae Guild. Then she dove back into Lorant's affection.

He would miss this—if he chose not to follow her to this Uther's Edge…

CHAPTER 1: CHAPTER 53

Friday, April 26th, 2069

"—we don't want juror twelve, but neither will Mr. Varnish. So, that just leaves a few others who could swing either way. Do you think the social media hopefuls will be for or against you due to the sudden surge of success?" Mrs. Stovall whispered.

"I don't know. From my perspective, I love a good success story but do harbor some bitterness when it's just someone flaunting their sexuality."

"So, people of the opposite sex are probably out," Mrs. Stovall marked the box with two x's to convey the two young women who both had some minor success with social media. I frowned at her interpretation of the words until I realized she was somewhat right. Whenever I felt bitter about blatant sexuality use, it was from women.

Thanks to *Mental Fortitude* giving me some context, I realized the reason behind it as well. It was because I was never going to be able to duplicate what they were doing. So, I wasn't bitter at their success but at success that had a road map I couldn't use.

Interesting. That thought brought me to another.

"I'm not sure," I began, also in a whisper. "With how much publicity this trial is going to get thanks to Sparkle, they might actually be on our side?" It was tough to think about the fourteen jurors the way Mrs. Stovall seemed to want me to, but surely if they gained some online clout from being included?

"While you might be right, that also creates a swing," Mrs. Stovall whispered back. "Based on what will be better for followers, they could go against the grain or flow to stand out. But with a closed-door trial, they may mess up and reveal something they shouldn't—which would garner a mistrial. So, Varnish may remove them for us?" She changed the x's to question marks. Her tone conveyed that she was mostly talking to herself toward the end.

With raised eyebrows, I nodded. Those were points I hadn't considered but could immediately see. That was a very popular tactic of successful Swift stars. If you were the voice of 'dissent,' then you were guaranteed to attract like-minded people. However, it was a very dangerous game. Since, if you were in the vast minority of the opinion, you also burned a huge portion of potential followers, and sometimes even current ones.

"We would like to excuse jurors twelve and eight," Mrs. Stovall said as she stood up. I guess she'd fallen on not counting on Mr. Varnish to remove the two young women. I guessed a mistrial only favored the person who was losing—which hopefully wouldn't be us.

As she'd hoped, Mr. Varnish removed juror two but also removed three others, including one we really liked. Well, one that Mrs. Stovall really liked.

It went back and forth like that, with the opposing councils questioning the new jurors, until the final fourteen were assembled. By that point, I was so turned around on who we liked and disliked that the ones up there all looked like snakes in the grass to me. Mrs. Stovall's look of annoyance didn't help much.

Why was she annoyed? My guess was that it was the massive amount of wealth on display from the other side. They had four people at the table with laptops and four others sitting directly behind them in the seats, not seeming to give any direction but passing folders over at request. On our side, there were just three people. John, the assistant or paralegal, Mrs. Stovall, and me.

Still, this was just the beginning of the trial that Mrs. Stovall claimed could stretch as long as a few months, depending on what Mr. Varnish had up his sleeve. Part of that was because we assumed he would attempt to extend it—since he had greater resources. Another part was because we suspected dirty tricks.

The other reason was that the court would take weekends off. Which was good for our budding Mining business. It had been a work-week since the decision was made, and we had our first Contract, which would likely stretch out over the weekend.

It actually started this afternoon, since today would only be juror selection.

There was one big problem with that though…

Unfortunately, Sparkle Legion wasn't going to be able to pull off a miracle until we at least had some footage of the new company. They'd released three other videos, which depicted the firing and then Phoenix-like rise from the ashes, of starting our own Mining company, but we'd discovered that wasn't enough for a big Guild to take note—at least, not yet.

The Guild we had our first contract with was D-Rank, which my father and Jarred assured us wasn't good.

* * *

Watching the members of Mirage gear up was like watching a forty-year-old crime movie. It was both impressive and surreal, as they efficiently velcroed themselves into armor, strapped on harnesses, and began loading themselves up from the trunks of their impressively expensive looking cars.

Still, no matter how impressive the cars were, they didn't compare to the ATVs of Lynx and Snowbird. This Portal was in the center of a public park, and from rumor, only contained Lizardmen, which meant it was F to E-Rank. That would also be the reason Mirage was allowed to tackle it. Lizardmen weren't exactly known for being bullet-proof. In fact, each Lizardkin alone wouldn't amount to more than an Awakened child. The complication with fighting them was that each one did possess a Skill, and they fought in groups.

With the chaotic nature of Skill distribution, you just didn't know what you would get. Either way, according to Mirage, the Dungeon had been cleared and was at the farming stage—so we could enter and handle the Ores and Minerals. My father walked back to our quiet group.

A quick look around told me that we were all nervous, including him.

"Echo-Five says that the Mine is nearly atop the entrance, so we won't have to make much of a trek. I think he's wanting us to bring more gear in, since the haul won't be bad," my dad stated as he pulled even with our small circle. He shrugged and motioned to the five Pickaxes that were either being held in hands or leaning against the cars. "It isn't like we *have* more tools, though."

Dave's head fell and he stared at the ground as his face flushed red. I winced as I noticed most of the others mirrored at least a few signs of his embarrassment. I wished Smegma was here—maybe I could buy a few things—no, he didn't sell sledges and wedges I recalled.

"Guys," I said slowly, giving myself time to think of what to say next. "Smegma doesn't sell anything other than these Pickaxes, which tells me that his Sect didn't think they needed wedges and sledges or anything else, really. Let's be confident and blow the Mirage Guild away!"

That at least perked up Willa and my dad. Jarred and Dave, on the other hand, refused to meet anyone's eyes. I knew the reason for Dave's worry. He had never Mined before and didn't feel like he would fit in. Jarred was a total mystery, though. He probably had as much experience as the other two—so, maybe he had used better tools in the past?

Then I saw his shabby, beat-up Pickaxe in comparison to mine and the others' and winced at myself. It was one stage above driftwood, thanks to him not really getting a single day in with P-Cubed. I placed a hand on his shoulder. "Ours all looked like that to start too. Plus, Dave's is worse."

Dave looked at his mace-like Pickaxe with a frown. "Yeah, why is mine beat into nothing more than a Morningstar?"

"I'll have you know that Pick is a hero. It helped smite a Golem," I mumbled.

"Smite? You mean pummel, surely," Dave retorted, some of his normal cheer returning. My father gave a muted laugh but saw what I was attempting and hiked a thumb over his shoulder to two other groups in the parking lot.

"The Gardeners and Cleaners say they've worked with Mirage before. According to them, they are one of the best militarized Guilds out there. Echo-Five only has a *Communication* Skill and a Mana Pool, so they don't rely on a single-Skilled Guild Leader for their reputation. Even watching them suit up is impressive, compared to what Jarred and I did."

Jarred chuckled then. "You mean when we 'smote' the Monsters with hails of gunfire?"

"Don't forget our copious use of grenades," my dad added. The joking really helped lighten the mood, and we entered the Portal in high spirits. It was a dark green sheet, like thick algae on top of a dying lake. It was a color I hadn't seen before, and I wondered where we were headed. Smegma would probably know.

I checked my Mental Universe and clicked my tongue—the *Classes* Skill looked like it was formed, or at least, had stopped growing. What was keeping the Demon? For that matter, what was keeping my *Classes* sub-Skill from activating?

We passed through the Portal and arrived on the other side in ankle-deep sludge. My first thought was that it was mud, but I quickly changed that descriptor because of the color and smell. I bent down and touched it. Slimy and thick, but definitely not dirt mixed with water. I turned my hand into a cup and pulled some of it up to examine. The water surrounding the green was clear, possibly even drinkable—after a thorough boiling. It just was so filled with algae that it took on the same consistency.

"Oh, come on," Dave complained as he lifted one foot and then the other out of the water. "These were white work boots," he added, responding to everyone's looks. He got no pity from the others, who were all wearing worn Mining gear with nearly ruined work boots. Truly, if mine didn't have Extra Terrestrial Metal forty-one, otherwise known as ETM41, in the toe and sole, they'd probably be in multiple pieces. The metal wasn't even from Portals, at least not originally. It was first found on Mars before the Advent—but it was now also sometimes found in the Portals as well.

Our company, currently unnamed, didn't have the funds to purchase new gear for the five of us just yet—plus, I was holding out hope there might be some in the *Demonic Vault* Shop.

"This way," a group of five heavily armed and nearly identical looking men said as they waded to us. Each one carried a Weapon that was clearly mass produced, but just as clearly made from Portal Ore. Which likely meant that the bullets inside were also of harder Material than simple earthly metals.

My father took the lead, and the trip was extremely short, as Echo-Five had said. The only reason I hadn't seen the rocky hill rising out of the sludge from the entrance was because it was behind the Portal and multiple petrified trees. The step from the sludge to dry land felt amazing. But the climb out of the sludge and up the steep slope to an entrance made me glad we didn't have bags of sledges and wedges to lug up.

I turned on my three-dimensional camera, and then took Sparkle Legion's high-grade Lightstone, currently on loan, out of my pocket. Placing it in the holster, I entered the cave. To my surprise, it wasn't necessary and I hurried to shut it off. The walls glowed with a smooth, verdant light.

The source? Thick banks of glowing moss.

I moved closer and studied the stuff. It was like a carpet, but despite the amount, it looked familiar. I reached out a hand and felt the same texture as the slimy algae outside. Except this one was dry and clearly growing larger. I hurried to catch up to the Mirage Hunters when I realized they had continued moving as I'd stopped to take in the sights.

My dad nodded at me as I jogged up beside him. "Since we only have the two good Lightstones, this is kind of nice."

"We'll all probably be in a single chamber though," I responded.

My dad shook his head. "Nah, this Portal's low Ranked. So, the caverns—" he cut off as we entered the first 'cavern.' What he had been about to say was evident. It was more of a widening in the tunnel than a true cavern.

In that widening space, Crystals carpeted only the floor, and while the walls held a few—they were only poking through between large patches of moss. In fact, I should have already noted another difference in the Mine. The hallways, which in other Portals had been covered with Crystals, were entirely clear of them.

"One of you here," one of the heavily armed men said.

We all looked at Dave, since he was the newest, but at his confused expression, I recalled he hadn't Mined before. With a voice I'd worked on for social media, I confidently explained, "Okay, we've got a Specialist trainee here. What do you think about leaving a second guard here with us for a short while? I'll show our new Specialist the ropes and then move to catch up."

The man who spoke, and I assumed was the leader, motioned at a subordinate with a hand. "Jack, you escort the cocky kid. The rest of us will head further in."

I guess my 'confident' voice needed some work. Willa and my dad held snickers back with the help of hands, even as Jarred chuckled out loud and mouthed 'cocky kid' at me.

Family, I thought. Pretty soon the group was around a bend and out of site. I turned to Dave. "Okay, so I've placed my 'Repair Mark' on your Pickaxe—so all you've got to do is Shard, Dave. The more you do, the more the Pick will repair. Once it's repaired enough for the business end to become roughly pointy," I motioned at my own, "try targeting a few stems."

I saw the two Mirage members look at each other and hurried to continue. "The Pick will repair faster if you Mine whole Crystals. The more it repairs, the more Ore—" I paused then, realizing that with the thick moss on the walls unadorned with Crystals, we couldn't see what Ores were hidden underneath them.

Thankfully, my *Mining* Skill identified at least one in the room. I nodded to myself and then hid the way I cut off speaking by continuing to say, "I guess the first lesson I should teach you is how to clear a place to stand."

That was the first lesson taught to me, after all. Within five minutes, I'd shown Dave how to clear a place to stand, and with a single swing of my Pick, also demonstrated where to find the stem in the lettuce-like lattice Mana Crystals.

Dave looked like he wanted to protest me leaving, but the impatience and disappointment on the faces of the two men convinced him to just try his best. I heard his next swing as Jack and I moved through the tunnel the others had gone down.

We passed Willa in the next 'cavern,' and then Jarred, before we arrived at one with my father. He had just finished clearing a space to stand and motioned me over. "You take this one," he said. "I'll head in deeper."

I shook my head. If anyone should head deeper, it was me. I had an unlocked Stat and—

"You will stay here, or we might as well just cancel this company business right now!" my dad said sternly. It felt a lot like I was a child throwing a tantrum at that moment. One where my parents would threaten to turn the car around if I didn't stop.

Rolling my eyes, I responded, "Yes, Dad."

Sure, I might have made it dramatic, but it got a chuckle from Jack and my father's Guild Guard—so, I figured it was worth it. Plus, only Dave knew about my unlocked Stat, at the moment, so an argument would be a bit hard.

When my dad started walking, his guard—the leader of the Mirage's group down here—followed, and I took up the already cleared spot. My first swing produced another full Crystal, and I heard a grunt from Jack. After another four swings and four stems hit, Jack whistled. I'd noticed a while back that with the addition of the Strength Stat, I could power through the rock easier. Plus, my new Pickaxe seemed to reduce the need for additional force.

"I didn't really believe you were actually a Specialist," he said after the noise of appreciation. "But you're just as fast at taking them out whole as others are at Sharding. Mind if I take a video to show Echo?"

I shrugged. That could only bring us some additional notoriety, surely. I kept working and had soon cleared my way to one wall. I hadn't Sharded a single Crystal, and I could tell from Jack behind me that he was becoming more and more excited by that prospect.

"Are the others as good as you?"

"They have way more experience but are also more likely to stick to the contract. So, they'll probably just Shard."

"Husk, really?" Jack said and then looked up and down the tunnels that led out of the small cavern. "You good here on your own for like ten minutes?" he asked.

My nod seemed to release him, and he hurried up the way we had come. I hoped he was about to negotiate on our behalf, but suspected he was going to tell the others to aim for full Crystals with no thought to increasing our cut. Either way, it worked for me. I was left unattended. I bent down and placed as many full Crystals as I dared into my Necklace of Holding.

By the time Jack returned, I had cleared more than half of the room, all of them full Crystals. He looked at the spoils greedily and then pointed angrily behind himself. "You go tell the others to stop Sharding, dammit."

I shook my head emphatically. "Listen, I'm just a worker. You should go chat with the boss."

My motion down the deeper tunnel released Jack again, and he took off. I smiled. This was going the way we hoped it would. My dad would likely ask to talk to Echo-Five and hopefully negotiate as much as five percent more out of the man. If not, I'd also start Sharding.

With low-rank Crystals, it was always a quantity versus quality debate. Large Guilds like Lynx and SnowBirds simply expected as much Sharded as the 'Normie' Miners could do—when they were in low-rank Mines. That and a few Ores. This way, the Hunting Team could move on to the next Portal. Full Crystals only sold for maybe ten percent more than sharded ones—they just didn't have much use after all.

I know better—

"Holy shit!" a familiar Demon's voice gasped. It was immediately followed by the noise of a sucking breath and then an exaggerated inhalation. "How long was I husking gone?"

I spun to find Smegma gasping in and out lungfuls of air that I was pretty certain he didn't need. I raised an eyebrow but hurriedly said, "Make yourself invisible if you aren't already. Someone will be back in a few minutes."

Smegma nodded but stayed doubled over, seeming to almost be in pain. I wondered again just how real the creature was. The fact that he breathed, and was clearly in pain, spoke to him being more alive than his Skill curator title would insinuate. Sure, he couldn't interact with our plane but that didn't mean he wasn't alive in another, right?

[You were gone a week,] I thought to the Demon. [I was starting to wonder what was taking so long.]

"I was putting together another massive puzzle! With sharp edges! Other than that, no husking clue," he answered, his voice filled with clear frustration. His breathing did begin to come under control as I kept working. Before his reappearance, I was hoping to have finished this small chamber by the time my minder returned.

Thankfully, Smegma didn't continue speaking and instead stared down the tunnel Jack had recently rushed down.

My dad soon strode into view with a large smile. "I'm going to head up and negotiate with Echo-Five. Can you finish my chamber after yours—Sharding only!—until I get back." He morphed his grin into a grimace before my eyes and studied the room, seeming disappointed.

I got the hint and looked to the ground ashamedly.

"I've told you before that we stick to the contract, Son."

"Yes, sir," I answered and schooled my features to try not to smile.

"I'll be back soon—I hope," my dad said.

Jack switched out with the leader of the group as my minder, and I frowned until I realized that the video of me Mining was on his phone. I switched from full Crystals to Sharding and thought I saw a disappointed frown cross the new minder's face under his half mask.

However, that could have been my imagination.

CHAPTER 2: CHAPTER 54

Friday, April 26th, 2069

A week! It felt like hours—What the hell did this Skill do?" Smegma asked. In response, I just paused at the bottom of a Sharding-swing and looked at him pointedly. He blinked his black eyes and then nodded calmly, as if to say, 'Oh! Right! I'm the one that should know.'

A moment later, he was frowning. "You've got to come in here and look. I can't interact with the new Skill-planet in your Mental Universe at all."

Thankfully, Sharding took no concentration at this point. Still, trying to picture my Mental Universe while my eyes were open to track the Pick's next target wasn't easy. With difficulty, I *did* manage it—after about three swings.

The 'planet' was easily half the size of the 'sun' that was the *Demonic Vault* Skill. It was a white that was almost blinding with the backdrop of the void black behind it. Around the planet was a large ring, like Saturn, but on closer inspection it wasn't an asteroid belt. To be honest, I couldn't tell what substance it was, but if I had to compare—it seemed closest to ice.

Mentally, I prodded the planet and 'discovered' that nothing happened. I tried all the tricks I knew—all two of them—like 'flicking' my Mana Pool with mental fingers and trying to pass my hand through it. In both cases, I was rebuffed like the planet was a solid object.

[Mana Conduit?]

"Give it a try," Smegma replied.

I scanned over to my Mana Pool, or maybe it was my *Dragon Heart* Skill? Either way, the small galaxy had fifty stars orbiting around it. I hadn't been able to drain the Mana into *Demonic Vault* while Smegma was away, or this *Classes* sub-Skill was forming. So, fifty was a full Mana Pool. The stars seemed to vibrate as they orbited around a black center, and even mentally approaching the space gave me the sense of an impending static shock.

[What's going on with my Mana Pool?] I asked when I realized the Mana itself also felt electrically charged—alive—or perhaps just poised for something?

"I can't touch your Mana Pool," Smegma reminded me. "What does it feel like? How much are you up to?"

I conveyed the indescribable feeling as best I could and heard the sound of a talon tapping a tooth even as I kept Sharding Crystals. I didn't look at the Imp, too focused on maintaining my dual-focus as it was.

"Fifty is the verge of Evolving to the next level—so maybe it's ready to upgrade or something?"

[But my *Dragon Heart* is already B-Grade, right?]

"True. Still, the Mana Pool looks more like a sub-Skill than the actual function of *Dragon Heart*. So, it won't upgrade the entire Skill, but something involving it will probably create a breakthrough."

[Helpful as always,] I responded dryly as I made the Conduit to the new *Classes* sub-Skill planet.

When I took my finger off the 'straw's' end—like I had with *Demonic Vault*—the planet rejected the Mana, and the uncapped straw began to dump Mana into my Mental Universe. I flushed with heat as a feeling of exhilaration hit—followed nearly instantaneously by nausea. I plugged the straw.

It was my turn to breathe heavily. [What the hell? It didn't take the Mana.]

"Okay, don't sound so aghast. It just means we must activate it in some other way. Still," Smegma said, leaving the word hanging as he tapped talon to fang, "it has to need Mana, Martial Power, or Force, or *something...*" The tapping intensified, seeming to try to match the noise of me Sharding Crystals. "Try creating a Conduit from *Demonic Vault* to it."

Still feeling nauseous, I first tried to figure out what to do with my current Conduit that had a mental thumb plugging it. I floundered, and even stopped Sharding, closing my eyes to try to focus on a solution. My gorge felt like it was slowly rising and forcing up my lunch in the process.

Unfortunately, my stop was noticed by the leader of the minders. "Everything okay?"

"Just taking a quick break," I said, even as I heaved lungfuls of air. Thankfully, Smegma also noticed at that point that something was wrong.

"Create a sort of positive 'pressure' and force the Mana back into the Pool," he coached. "Think about it as low- and high-pressure systems. The Mana will take the path of least resistance..." he kept speaking using idioms that had no meaning in this context but helped all the same.

Eventually, with his help, I succeeded and noticed a side effect of creating a draw, or gravity, around my Mana Pool. The spillage was also sucked back into the Pool faster. The effect happened in reverse as my nausea turned to exhilaration and heat before dissipating entirely. Once I knew the 'straw' was empty, I moved it, placing the unplugged end in *Demonic Vault* and the other side into *Classes*. When I unplugged it, nothing happened, and I opened my eyes.

[Well, it's there,] I said lamely. [Now what?]

"No husking clue, maybe try sending Mana to *Demonic Vault*?" That of course worked but converted it to Mana Coins. Smegma noticed first. "Well, isn't this interesting? Your dad's returning. I'll keep thinking on this."

"Didn't finish this chamber yet?" my dad asked in passing. I realized I only had one or two deposits left, but also realized that behind my father were all the minders and the others from our new company. Even Dave had finished before me...

I started to feel embarrassed but told myself he had the smallest chamber. Still, I turned this into an opportunity and asked, "So, am I Sharding these or...?"

"No more Sharding. We got an extra two-percent if we keep them whole." My dad nodded with a paternal smile, and I quickly tapped the stem of the two deposits left before joining the group. We'd been hoping for five percent but we all knew that the Crystals weren't much more valuable whole. Not low Ranked Crystals…

I could tell the plan was to move deeper, since everyone was here.

"Who's coming to pick up the Shards and Crystals?" I asked as I fell in behind my dad. I also studied Dave and Jarred's Pickaxes—they were both looking much better. Nowhere near as nice as Willa's, mine and my father's, but far better.

"Someone will be down soon with a Bag of Holding," the leader that had been watching me said. He looked slightly disappointed, and I wasn't sure if it was because of the negotiations or my break. Either way, I nodded, and the group went down to the final 'worked' chamber, which my dad had started. He had maybe a quarter left to do, and Dave, with his minder, was left to finish up.

"Do your best to not Shard, but don't worry if you mess up a bit," my father said. "We told him that you were new to the crew. It factored in the negotiations. That and the fact that whole Crystals aren't exactly worth much more than Sharded ones," he said the middle part rather proudly, clearly happy with how the negotiations had gone.

The group continued from that room and passed through two more, leaving Willa, and then Jarred, behind with their gun-toting Hunters. As the leader, my father, Jack, and I continued deeper.

Something noticeably changed as we moved into the next hallway between caverns. I looked around, trying to figure out what my brain had clued into, but not immediately seeing it. Smegma had, though.

"The moss is growing brighter."

I stopped and looked around, trying to figure out what could be causing it. My dad and the other two stopped and took note of the wall, too. The leader asked the obvious question first, "Why is it brighter?"

There was one patch of moss that shone at about three times the lumens of the rest. I found it, thanks in part to Smegma floating near it, and my own eyes slowly clueing in to the odd phenomenon. Smegma made a motion with his hand to brush it aside. It didn't work, but I dutifully dug my fingers in and pulled.

The moss tore away with a bit of effort, and soon I was staring at a shining surface. It almost looked like frozen water. However, it wasn't blue but a metallic yellow. I pulled away more of the moss and the others came over to study what I was revealing. The leader again asked the obvious, "What is it?"

As I pulled off more moss, it became clear that it wasn't a natural deposit. Or I guess it became clear that it was more than just a mineral deposit. There were carvings on it that depicted stick-like humanoids surrounding a massive, coiled creature. The oddity was that, where I would put two legs for a stick figure human, these images instead had one thick line that curled to a point under them.

The creature in the center resembled a snake, the more of it I revealed. Mostly because it was a large coiling figure with the telltale segments I'd come to expect from a snake's underbelly. However, if these humanoids were human-sized, then this creature was hundreds of feet long.

The more of the mural I revealed, the more the story grew. The single-legged humanoids had weapons and were fighting the creature. It was coiled either in defense or between strikes.

"What planet are we on?" Smegma asked, cutting into my thoughts.

"No idea," I responded, meaning it for both the leader and Smegma. I continued mentally to the latter. [Outside, there are petrified trees and about one to two feet of water filled with this same algae-plant thing.]

"Oh, a lost world, then," Smegma said, looking up at the ceiling of the hallway. At my look, he continued, "Likely a world that took its Trials before Crendalar."

[Do you know what the stuff this drawing is made of is?]

"No, but it can store Mana. It probably hasn't had any until the Portal led here and is only now reabsorbing some, since the System created the dome."

I knocked on it with a knuckle, and it gave off a tinkling thud that made me think it was crystalline. Offhandedly to my father, I said, "We think it's storing Mana."

"We?" Jack said, even as the leader narrowed his eyes over his face mask.

"Sorry, I think it's storing Mana," I corrected and didn't have to fake my embarrassment.

"If it's storing Mana, it's value would be astronomical," my dad said.

"The problem is whether it has been modified to store Mana, or if it's a natural property of the materials," Smegma warned. I didn't understand why that distinction would be important so asked for some more information with a mental poke. "Well, if it's natural, you can take it out of here in pieces, dumb-dumb. If it's modified, it's likely that it will only store Mana in its current configuration as essentially an art piece, and you probably need the whole fixture. Husking moron."

Ahhh, he was back. I guess being absent for a week and recovering from popping back into existence could only last so long.

It had been enjoyable while it lasted though…

I conveyed what Smegma said in my own words, adding, "The problem is that it's clearly been modified. So, whether it's the mineral that absorbs the Mana or what these people did with it—"

"People?" all three Hunters in the room said in unison.

"This should just be a piece of decoration created by the Portal, surely," the leader stated derisively.

I looked to my father, trying to convey that what I was about to say wasn't true. "Right, sure. What the Portal did to it. I was just getting caught up in the story the Portal created here. All I'm saying is that we either must take it out of here as one full piece or, if the Mineral is absorbing Mana, it will still be fine in pieces."

"Ahh, right. If it's been modified, then the Enchantment is what's valuable, and if not, it's the material itself," Jack said knowingly. "Smart," he complimented.

Smegma scoffed at the man directing his praise at me but thankfully had begun studying the mural again.

"Clear the edges," he directed, his voice clearly expressing that his words were not a suggestion. They were orders. I conveyed his words, and as a group, we managed to uncover the entire piece of metallic yellow crystal-art.

"Oh," Smegma said once he saw the edges. I studied them too. It was jagged, familiar, almost like—"It's a Fused Mana Crystal! High-grade, at that."

[How high?] I asked.

"No way of knowing. I think it's an old iteration of Crystals, from before Crendalar. Still, the sheen of it leads me to think it's above B."

"I think it's a Mana Crystal…" I said, making sure not to use the collective 'we' again. I then tried to touch the metallic yellow Crystal and sell the Mana inside. I figured that if it dimmed suddenly on my touch, I could claim I didn't know what happened. Still, I needn't have worried because nothing happened, which could be because it was still inside the wall.

"Bullshit, kid," the leader exclaimed. "It's too big, and it's the wrong color."

"No, I think he's right," my dad said and pointed to the edges. "I don't know how it's so big, or why it's yellow—but the lattice edges are definitely Mana Crystalline in design. So, it's either a Crystal or they wanted to make it look like one."

"Either husking way, it's valuable, right?" Jack exclaimed, looking excitedly at the leader.

"Yeah, if our esteemed *Miners* can get it out of the wall in a single piece…" the leader answered while narrowing his eyes at us. I couldn't see his mouth, but I felt the scowl.

Smegma shook his head. "It wasn't designed to be removed. You can get it out of here in pieces, and I might even be able to find the fuse points, so you get some full Crystals, but as a whole piece? Husk no! I doubt any Miner could…"

My father was looking at me, seeming to be hoping for an affirmative answer to the question. I shook my head sadly. "I think the Portal fused a bunch of Crystals together. There isn't a stem and it likely wasn't made to come out in a full piece. We can break it up—maybe even get a few full-sized Crystals—but it would be a ton of work. We'd likely want everyone."

The last part wasn't exactly true, but if we were going to Shard a high-ranked Crystal, I wanted Dave and Jarred's Pickaxes involved for the repair and possible Evolution from the likely vast quantities of residual Mana released from a high Ranked Crystal.

"Figures. That should teach Echo to hire the riff-raff," the leader said scornfully.

My dad gave the man a pointed, tight-lipped smile.

He didn't seem to care. "You stay here with these two, Jack. I'll go get the others." As he walked away, I could hear him muttering, "*Husking waste of good luck, cocking-bullshit.*"

"Don't mind him," Jack said as his leader walked away. "He's in a bad mood." He then waited for the leader to no longer be visible before whispering, "Plus, he's in a ton of debt, so this would have been a huge help."

"It already will be. Whatever grade this thing is, it's up there." I shrugged. "Harvested some D-Ranked Crystals a few days back and they didn't make my hair stand on end anywhere close to how this thing's doing right now. We walked into a D-Ranked Dungeon and will be coming out with Crystals at least a rank above that, so forgive me if I'm a bit unsympathetic that we can't perform *another* miracle." I turned back toward the massive Crystal with a frown. "Still, it does suck to ruin it, I'll admit."

My dad shook his head sadly, and I assumed he was thinking along the same lines I was. *Was everyone other than high-ranked Hunters and celebrities in debt or just scraping by?*

"It's the same on any world that has a hierarchical society," Smegma answered my thought, despite me not needing him to. "The good news is that it falls apart in time, thanks to the System. You just can't maintain something like that when power is so readily available."

[Yeah, I don't think our Systems are acting the same. Plus, I don't know what hierarchies you're thinking of, but societies are built on them. The pre-System ones might fall apart, but new ones just get built in their stead. Even with the System, those power structures won't be based purely on personal power or Rankings. No matter how powerful one person is, capable people can gather many strong people together for a common cause. Being one against the world is all well and good in the movies, but I don't see it ever working out in real life.]

"I think you'd be surprised at how powerful single individuals can get under the System, but you're not entirely wrong, either. It's rare for one to defeat the many. However, the System doesn't care if it's one or many that are strong enough to pass the Trials. It cares about results. If your civilization is one that births a God… well, congratulations. It's the entire goal of the System, as far as us Demons could find. It wants you to become powerful. It wants you to Ascend. The System is made to advance civilizations or…"

[Deem them failures and let them slowly die out,] I finished for him when he cut off. He nodded while pointedly studying the mural.

CHAPTER 3: CHAPTER 55

Friday, April 26th, 2069

With my *Mining* Skill, and Smegma's understanding, I did most of the work to remove the full Crystals and pointed out the places for the others to strike and Shard fused connectors.

"This be deep," Willa said as she carefully chipped out a section to expose another large chunk and the visible Crystal stem. "You still be thinkin' it Crystal, Bro?"

I was mid swing near an edge, cracking away stone to expose a stem for myself when she spoke. I let the Pick slam home, and smelled the ozone as a spark flew, but paused for a moment between swings to answer. "Not sure but relatively confident. If it is, it's likely very old, and that should make it rare. Hopefully, valuable and *rare...*"

"You sure that this won't be confiscated too?" my dad whispered from beside me. I took another swing before glancing at the minders from Mirage. Then shrugged as the stem broke with the sound of the shattering tail of a Rupert's drop. The Crystal didn't fall free, and I began looking for the fuse points that needed to be broken away.

"These edges will give us the most whole pieces of material," I said as if directing the others to focus there. I'd already said something similar a while ago, so it wasn't some great epiphany, and a scoff from one of the five minders made me roll my eyes. I turned to face them and said, "We'll be done in about ten to fifteen minutes. You might want to get that porter down here."

As I spoke, I bent down and pretended to study a full Crystal amongst the Shards. As I picked it up to show the men, I used my other hand to send another to my Necklace of Holding. In my best 'I told you so' tone, I addressed the leader, "It sure looks like a Mana Crystal, doesn't it?"

He snatched the Crystal from me and squinted at it, ignoring my comment—and me. His lackeys crowded close, and I saw another opportunity. I 'pocketed' two more of the basketball-sized B-Ranked or higher Crystals. I didn't dare take any more.

The leader got fed up with the crowd from one excited breath to the next. "Buzz off, ya flies. Jack, go get the porter. Viccar and Etien, go scout the next cavern. We don't all need to watch these men sweat."

"An' ladies!" Willa said pointedly, under her breath. She wasn't usually one to speak quietly in these situations, and I gave her a look. She discreetly motioned to the leader, making it clear she didn't like him and was getting a strange vibe. Like her talking back might somehow be a threat to the group.

Blinking, I simultaneously felt my stomach drop. I hoped she was wrong and that she was just being overly cautious thanks to the rumors and stories Jarred and my dad had told. Still, the asshole was unlikeable.

"I'll follow the two to the next cavern," Smegma said, picking up on my internal thoughts. "See if they discuss anything worrisome."

It took another twenty minutes before we were finished, but to my surprise no one had returned. Neither Jack and the porter, or Etien and Viccar. I studied the metallic yellow Crystals on the floor as I mentally sent, [Everything okay, Smegma?]

The massive 'Imp' popped back into view beside me, and his expression immediately put me on edge. "The next cavern is huge. Larger than any we've been in so far, including the ones with the Lynx or Snowbirds Guilds. It's filled with Crystals, but the two who went to scout got too far away to hear more than them speculating about how much this stuff will be worth. I was waiting for them to come back, but I couldn't see where they went."

"Where the husk are Etien and Viccar?!" the leader asked, seeming to realize that we were done with this section and that his two 'scouts' were missing. The late realization from the leader made me dislike him more. Shouldn't he have noticed before I did…

Slapping feet, from the opposite direction of where the two minders were lost, echoed down the hall to us, and soon Jack arrived at a run. "Echo-Five says that the boss is moving, and he needs us all now! They can't send porters!"

"Husk!" the leader said and looked to the tunnel that led to Etien and Viccar. "Jack, go get those two. Aaron and I will head up. You lot, keep Mining."

"That's not part of our contract. We were guaranteed protect—"

The leader was in my father's face so fast that I stepped back. His hand was on his sidearm at his waist, which was a strange way to create a threat considering he had a strapped AK-47-esque weapon draped in front of him. "Listen, here! This is husking protection! You want the boss to collapse the entrance to this Mine with you lot inside?"

My father didn't flinch back and met the man's steely stare. "You and I both know that's a stretch. We can leave and come back in once the 'all clear' is given. The Portal out is close by."

The click of the holster being released sounded louder than the Picks on stone had moments before. "If I tell you to keep Mining, you keep Mining. Do you understand me, Pooler?"

Willa gasped, and I frowned. That was a particularly offensive name to people who awakened with only the Mana Pool gift. It was rarely spoken anymore in pleasant society. There were just too many of us Mana Pool Awakened—and thus, public opinion was heavily swayed by us.

My frown was because I assumed every Hunter in here would also be classified as a 'Pooler.' So, the insult was even more nuanced. Like a superiority complex against Awakened who didn't strap on weapons like these men did.

My dad's jaw was clenched but he slowly nodded while the leader waited, and intensely met his eyes. After a time, the man re-clipped his holster and strode from the hallway. My dad followed his departing back with eyes that threatened retribution. Still, the leader and Aaron were soon out of sight, and despite not having seen Jack leave, he too was gone.

We were essentially by ourselves, with the threat of Jack, Etien and Viccar returning. I studied each of my group in turn. Willa and my father wore expressions of rebellion, where Jarred and Dave both stared silently down to the ground. I, for one, was somewhat happy with this turn of events, and said, "You do realize that being left alone means we can sell more Crystals to *Demonic Vault*, right?"

"We talked about this, Brodie," my dad instantly answered, his voice hard. "This isn't a race! We work our way up—*you* slowly work your way up. Remember?!"

It was my turn to look at the ground.

"Then what are we going to do?" I asked as I studied the metallic yellow carpet of Shards and Crystals.

"Once Viccar, Etien and Jack come back and leave, we're also going to go. Then we will never be working with Mirage again," my dad said.

"Wait, we decided they were the best of the offers Legion could get for us? Plus, won't that stop us from getting a good reference from them?" Dave asked as his head popped up.

"Better be livin', and workin' to better da reputation, than be dead," Willa countered.

Jarred nodded, while Dave and I looked at each other. I agreed with Dave. We had yet to see a Monster down here—clearly, Mirage had done a good job clearing it out. Surely it was safe enough without minders. We hadn't had Sturdy Jural in the same cavern as us or other Hunters when working with Lynx or Snowbirds. Of course, that reminded me of the King Leeches and the fact that Sturdy Jural had died protecting the deepest cavern.

"Listen to your father, but I do suggest we take as much of this stuff as we can," Smegma said, indicating the carpet of Crystals.

[The Hunters are coming back,] I said, even as I studied the carpet again to see if I could get away with more without it being noticeable. After a moment, I shook my head but did think, [Once they've left us, I'll take a few, maybe…]

"Okay, should we go back to the last couple caverns, though, as we wait?" I said, thinking we could still sell many full Crystals from them.

"Yeah, but we stick together," my dad ordered. We all nodded and moved back up the tunnel.

We were finished with the nearest small cavern, and we still hadn't heard or seen anything from the direction we'd come.

I was up to twenty thousand Mana Coins in the *Demonic Vault*, thanks to my very sticky fingers. One issue did seem apparent, looking at the leftovers. Without Sharding, it was easier to identify my theft. Still, I wasn't too worried— thanks to the moss. A quick brush of the hand covered a great deal of the small visible stems that adorned the walls.

Sure, there weren't many there, but it would definitely help hide the missing Crystals.

"Next cavern?" I asked, but only to break the eerie silence.

"Something is wrong," my dad answered. He was staring back down the hallway with the metallic-yellow-Crystal mural. Everyone nodded.

"Do we go check it out, or get the hell out now?" Jarred asked. I could tell his question was again just meant to be a prompt.

"We're getting out of here," my dad sternly answered. He instantly spun on his heels and started walking—the action and words more than enough to get everyone else to follow.

Dave fell in beside me. "Look how good my Pick looks," he said, brandishing the aforementioned Mining tool. It was even starting to darken in the handle—which was interesting, considering ours only did that after we rang the Golem Heart. Otherwise known as defeating the Rock Golem. "I felt it steering my swings a bit when we were working on the mural. Isn't that annoying?"

"Huh? Why?" I asked.

"Well, I was trying to Shard, and it was clearly wanting me to hit elsewhere."

"Mine didn't do that," Jarred said, butting into the conversation. "I did feel it steer, but it made the swings more precise."

"Ask Dave where he was aiming," Smegma said, still invisible in case the Hunters suddenly popped up.

I conveyed the question and Dave shrugged. "In the general areas you or the others indicated."

"That's why," Smegma answered. "He's not being specific—so the Enchantment is choosing the best spot for him. If you know the best spot and aim for it—it directs the point there. It works on intention."

Again, I conveyed the response from Smegma, and Dave's eyebrows raised. "Is it reading my thoughts, then?"

Smegma started laughing and I couldn't help the smile that broke onto my face. I had something reading my surface thoughts—so, this wasn't a big concern for me. Still, the smile didn't last, because the others' concerned looks instantly sobered me.

Smegma didn't stop laughing but did manage to shake his head as he said, "No, no. It's more experience, I guess. Your father, Willa and Jarred are already aiming at the right spot—so they won't feel much. Only minor corrections. Dave intends to strike a wider spot and thus the Pickaxe corrects further—and if that area has two or three good strike points, it will pick one at random. Thus, the intentions."

My smile was returning as I opened my mouth to correct the meaning from a moment before—

When the ground under my feet rumbled. It happened again, and again, in quick, short bursts.

"Is that an earthquake?" Dave asked before I could.

"No, the husking Hunters are using explosives. It's closer than we thought—we better start running!" My father matched his words as he increased his pace to a jog. The sound of slapping work boots on Crystal piles and stone echoed out of rhythm as each of us moved individually. Right up until everyone planted those feet and slid over the Shard-carpet in unison. We came to a stop as an extremely loud crash echoed down to us. We were just passing through the cavern I'd Mined this morning.

So, the fourth from the exit.

A cloud of dust followed the sound, and I just managed to pull up my mask and avert my gaze before it crashed over us. Some of the others began coughing and cursing, having not been quick enough. I stood still, waiting for the dust to settle. The few peeks I did make showed me nothing but a grayish green haze surrounding me.

Smegma seemed to either be able to see or guessed what happened because he soon said, "The entrance collapsed!"

Everyone made noises of distress—telling me that he had made himself visible, not that they saw him. But they clearly heard him.

CHAPTER 4: CHAPTER 56

Friday, April 26th, 2069

It took long minutes for the dust to settle even a fraction. The first thing I heard was Dave coughing. I knew the sound, since the kid frequently hit his bong when I was over gaming.

"Dave, put your mask up. It will help," I said through the cloud.

"Who said that the entrance collapsed? They made it sound impassible, but how could they know?"

"I said it, you imbecile—and while I can simply float through the debris if Brodie gets close enough, you all won't be able to," Smegma retorted, his voice the equivalent of a sneer—that I felt. In response, my soul wanted to shrivel up, and I hunched my shoulders as if to mirror the desire with my physical body.

"That be Smegma?" Willa asked, having only heard of the Demon to this point. "Do ya be knowin' if there's another entrance?" she quickly asked as a follow up to her rhetorical question.

"Let me just fly off and find one. Poof—I'm right back beside you because I can't go more than a hundred yards from the kid! Idiot," Smegma answered.

"Okay, who be pissin' in ya cheerees? Dickwad!" Willa responded.

"What is with you humans and pissing in your breakfast," Smegma retorted.

"Why is it taking so long for the dust to settle?" my dad asked, interrupting the fight that may have started. Then again with a cloud of thick dust around us, I would hope that at least Willa would have given up. I doubted Smegma would have. I could also hear that my dad was trying to use a commanding voice, and it might have worked for people who didn't know him well. But amongst this group, that only included Dave and Smegma.

I, certainly, could tell how worried he was.

"The airflow from the entrance is probably cut off," Jarred responded stoically. "Goes toward Smegta's point of how bad the collapse was…"

I wasn't sure if he mispronounced the name due to the cloud, his mask, by accident or intentionally, but it did break me out of my inaction. "Smegma, can you try to lead me to the others?"

"Sure thing, oh faithful leader," Smegma said mockingly but did as instructed. I saw a darker shadow amongst the white and gray-green particles of dust, no more than inches from me. As it moved, I hesitantly moved to follow, sometimes taking half steps and returning to the start until I found the right direction. After the first step, it became easier because Smegma stayed on course, and in short order I bumped into Dave, Willa, Jarred, and then my father.

Now holding hands, I said, "Can you bring us—"

"This way," Smegma said from inches away, and I repeated the process, knowing he had read my thoughts and was bringing us to the deeper caverns—where I hoped there was less dusty.

Gradually, the dust did grow thinner, and soon we were out in a hallway with no noticeable stone dust, unless you looked closely down the length of said hallway. We kept moving until we came to the cavern that we'd stolen from before deciding to try an escape. Once there, we stopped and realized we were missing some things.

"I dropped my lunchbox," Dave complained.

"Me too, man," I retorted, looking back up the tunnel. I could really use some food right about now. Jarred and Willa had their coolers still, but a quick look inside and a head-shake told us that they had already finished the portions intended for a mid-afternoon snack.

That would put us on a timer—*wait, does Demonic Vault have anything to eat?*

"Umm, nothing mundane," Smegma answered, but the accompanying bone tap let me know he was thinking. Soon enough, a red screen popped up in front of me. "Cheapest thing we have."

Mana Apple
Low C-Rank

This apple will increase Mana Capacity and Recharge rate by 1% for 240 hours. This effect can stack up to five times and resets with each apple eaten within the time limit. The apple is considered a perfectly balanced meal plan for an entire day but should not be abused.

Cost: 20,000 mC

After I finished reading, Smegma continued, "We have others for Martial Power and Force, but they would be less worthwhile to purchase. Same price."

Twenty thousand mC a day per person, if we were stuck down here long enough to need them. That was one hundred thousand a day, or more if Etien, Viccar and Jack returned. That was also more than five times what I currently had saved. I looked at the Crystals strewn on the floor and quickly walked around selling them.

The way we had come probably had at least another twenty thousand, and the lunchboxes as well. Everyone's eyes followed me, and I looked down the hallway that led deeper, thinking of the metallic yellow Crystals. When I had thought through the options, I said, "I think we'll be okay. I can buy some food from the *Demonic Vault* Shop, and we can survive on one a day.

"Unfortunately, they cost quite a bit of Coins, so we'll need to go back and sell the Crystals and Shards above. I'll try again to sell the metallic yellow ones, but it didn't seem to work before. Smegma thinks the Mana is tainted somehow, but maybe when I don't need to be so discreet?" Smegma shrugged at my words, seeming to say, 'it's worth a try.' Still, I was more concerned about getting out of here, so asked, "Do you all think Mirage will get us out of here quickly, and I should leave the Crystals for them?"

Everyone just stared at me, and I quickly realized my *Mental Fortitude* was working overtime. Jarred did oscillate his eye-daggers between me and Smegma, and I could tell that the Demon's appearance disturbed him, but I dismissed it by thinking of something else.

Willa, for example, was studying the Demon but seemed appreciative of his look. Well, maybe not *appreciative* but not fearful or angry.

Maybe even my *Recovery* was working overtime too—Dave wasn't the only one coughing lightly as their lungs fought to clear stone dust. After an awkwardly long silence, Smegma said, "Seeing as how there were explosives that went off and the result was collapsing the entrance, I'm not even sure the Guild is going to be helping us out at all. Regardless, it won't help to hope. Let's plan for the worst—those guys seemed like assholes anyway."

Jarred shivered, and I winced. I knew that Smegma's appearance was disturbing at first, but since Mrs. Stovall and everyone so far hadn't reacted poorly—I'd kind of figured it wasn't so bad…

I also couldn't help the winces his less-than-thought-out words brought on. I would much rather have hoped for the best and planned for the worst—but now I was sure everyone was thinking that Mirage would abandon them. I had come to terms with that already, but the paling faces of the group told me they hadn't even gotten to that thought yet.

My dad collapsed onto his ass. "I knew we shouldn't have taken a contract with a low Ranked Guild!"

My feet took a step toward him before I could think better of it, but Willa held up a hand and went to him first. "Don't worry—we'll get out of here when they clear the Boss and the Dungeon closes."

She made a 'shooing' motion, directing me to return the way we had come and collect the Crystals and lunchboxes. Feeling my heart disagreeing with my brain, I did so. I knew then that if I went to my father, he would insist on holding me for long minutes, distracting me from further actions.

Smegma obviously joined me, and after the next nearest chamber, was forced to direct me again, making conversation impossible and the work slow going. Still, I had over a hundred thousand points by the time I had the lunchboxes and was turning to head back. The dust had also begun to settle enough that I was able to see Smegma up to five feet away. By the time I got back, I could tell the others had reached a few conclusions.

My dad leveled me with a steely gaze. "We should wait for the dust to settle and return to the entrance."

I blinked at him, even as I lowered the lunchboxes to the ground. Dave immediately snatched his up and dug inside to have a granola bar. I saw the others looking at my father and then me from my peripherals.

"Do you really think Mirage will come to rescue us?"

"Three of their Guild members are down here too, so yes." My dad's voice carried all the assuredness I would need to hear, usually—but this time, I was far too skeptical to believe him.

"Where are those three Guild Members?" I asked, pointedly scanning the room. "Surely, they had some way to communicate or locate members?"

My dad frowned and looked at the walls. "Not down here, they don't."

"So, you're hoping they'll dig out the entrance for Guild members that may or may not be alive? Plus, didn't Willa say we'd get out when the Portal closed?"

"We concluded that they must have beaten the Boss already, and if it hasn't given a closing notification yet—it likely is a Permanent Portal or has another Boss, or Boss Respawn feature, that Mirage will go looking for."

"Okay?" I answered, looking at the others. They all shrugged, accepting my father's decision. I felt my face contort into a scowl. "No," I said softly but then repeated firmly when I felt the building storm that was coming. "No. You haven't come to terms with the situation yet. We can't go back. We can only continue forward for now. If they clear out the entrance, then they'll still come deeper, right?"

"I don't think you've thought it out, Brodie," My dad countered. "Three Hunters delved deeper and haven't returned. Going down there is too dangerous!" My father unleashed that gathering storm, trying to use volume to convey his point.

"We have something they don't," I said, having already considered this.

"What?"

I pointed to the Felguard-Imp Demon, and he smirked before taking a bow.

My father looked at the smug Smegma and then at me. "You've got to be husking kidding, right?"

"You know what else you have that you could have used right after the collapse?" Smegma asked, far too innocently. He didn't even wait for me to respond before crowing, "*Heat Sense*, idiot!"

CHAPTER 5: CHAPTER 57

Friday, April 26th, 2069

Thankfully, Smegma's suggestion of me being an idiot proved partially wrong. *Heat Sense* on my eyes made it so I couldn't distinguish the walls at all, and *Heat Sense* on my body didn't notify me of any heat sources other than my group. So, while it would have helped me find them— navigating would have been impossible.

Or that's what I told myself…

"Are you sure we should be following that thing around?" Jarred asked in a whisper that was easily overheard in the silence of the tunnels. "It could be leading us into the depths of Hell."

I'd momentarily forgotten that Jarred was a somewhat 'reformed' Catholic—his wife being the huge driving force behind it—but this comment brought that little nugget back to me.

Just as I decided to keep quiet and not exacerbate the issue, Smegma said, "Yes, because my only goal in this quasi-life is to drag the pure into my depravity."

Jarred didn't turn around, but I did see his shoulders climb up to his ears and his fists clenched. Mentally, I scolded Smegma, [Leave him alone. He's Catholic.]

Smegma gave me a look that said he didn't care, but he did stop poking the man. I counted that as a win. Soon, we were in front of the pile of yellow Mana Crystals, and I took a deep, steadying breath through my nose. To my surprise, the dusky smell of stale Mine air and algae wasn't as strong. In fact, I thought—

"Do ya be smellin' fresher air?" Willa exclaimed, confirming my thought. I nodded even as the others took testing sniffs. Unfortunately for Dave, that set off a round of coughing, but he managed to nod along with the others. "Well dat be removin' one worry At least we ain't gonna be runnin' out of oxygen down here."

"Perfect," Jarred said skeptically while looking at Smegma Thankfully, my dad interrupted the man from saying anything more with a hand on the shoulder and a pleading look.

Once my father was sure that Jarred wasn't going to antagonize Smegma, he looked to me and the Demon. He gestured at the Crystals scattered across the ground. "Try again to sell those Crystals and see where we're at after."

Mentally I crossed my fingers before bending down. I placed my hand on the nearest full Crystal and willed it to the *Demonic Vault* Skill. The Crystal didn't move, and I looked to Smegma. "Still a problem? Any idea what's going on now that we can do this openly?"

"I don't know," Smegma said. "It's like it doesn't exist, according to the System. Or like you're interacting with something that's… useless?"

Frowning, I tried a few more, and then some Shards, but got the same result. "Well, that's bullshit."

Everyone stared at me, and I could only shrug in response. Smegma had put on his thinking face, and I could tell that he could only speculate as to the reason, but I still asked, "Any idea why this isn't working?"

"Several, but the most likely is that the System doesn't recognize it. It's obsolete."

I checked my total mC and found I was at a hundred and ten thousand—which was both good and bad news. Good because we had a day's worth of food, and bad for the same reason. We only had a day unless we got more Crystals, which meant going deeper. Just a glance at Jarred, Willa, and my father told me that was going to be an argument.

"We've got to go deeper," Dave said, seeing the problem instantly. "If we don't have the funds from these Crystals, we have no choice."

For some reason, my dad glared at me, and so I threw up both of my hands in frustration. "We don't have a choice, Dad."

"There's always a choice, Son," my dad responded. Willa stepped back, indicating she was stepping out of this conversation, but Jarred nodded his agreement and sidled up beside my father—looking like that idiotic friend that would shout affirmatives after anything the leader said.

I rolled my eyes.

"Those are just husking words," I said heatedly. "Sure, we can choose to go back to the cave-in and wait—count on others to dig us out. But what if they don't come?"

"God has a plan for us all," Jarred said, his tone so sanctimonious I felt my eyes roll 'harder.'

"So, 'God' is going to dig us out of here?"

"Believe in the goodness of man," Jarred answered.

"Jarred, that's bullshit. We've already seen that Mirage isn't exactly pure of husking heart. What if god's plan is that we need to fight to survive, and only then he will help us?"

"I can tell you right now that gods from higher realms aren't watching this one. There is only the System, and it only rewards those who push to better themselves," Smegma said, his voice calm but morose. His words carried the weight of his people's failure to Ascend.

Jarred's head fell, and he didn't open his mouth to retort, but my dad did. "Brodie, if we don't take the safest route and something happens, I'd never forgive myself—even if we survive."

"If we take the safer route and then are forced to scramble for resources when we're weak, something *will* happen. And whatever that something is, it's bound to be made worse because of our exhaustion," I countered.

My father and Jarred stood there like walls that couldn't be reasoned with. Neither had a retort to my words, but I could tell they weren't willing to stand down.

I played my final card. "*I'm* going deeper, no matter what you say. You'll have to fight me if you want me to stop. So, would you rather come and keep me safe or stay here?"

My dad's eyes widened and he opened his mouth multiple times, closing it again like a fish gasping for breath.

Jarred's head snapped up at my words, though, and he pointed at me. "Do not be deceived by this hellspawn, Brodie. Having finally seen the 'Demon,' I am now sure that this is a test. If we go back, God will reward us."

I shook my head. "I'm not going back, Jarred."

Jarred looked at me sadly, even as my father studied me. After a time, my father pulled Jarred aside and tried to talk to him. In such a small hallway, I heard everything but tried to ignore it—instead placing the 'obsolete' Crystals and Shards into my Necklace of Holding. They might be useless to Smegma, but earth was a different animal.

In the end—even with Willa's help—Jarred decided to return to the upper caverns. I will admit that his decision made me rethink mine for a fraction of a moment, but whether it was through personal conviction or *Mental Fortitude*-assisted logic, I knew I was right. As the group naturally began to separate, I turned to Jarred. "Here's two Mana Apples, they'll—"

"Have you never read the Bible, Brodie? I will not be tempted by Apples!" Jarred practically shouted.

After the 'confirmation' dance with Smegma, I had purchased two for him and was proffering the bright blue fruits in his direction. I let my hand drop and looked around, seeing Dave's lunch box. "Dave, give him your lunchbox, please."

Dave, who was in the process of slinging it over his shoulder, froze, and then scrunched up his face before walking it over to Jarred. "There is half a sandwich and a few granolas in there. It isn't much."

"Thank you, Dave," Jarred said. He opened his mouth again to add something but seemed to think better of it. Instead, he just turned away and began walking back up the hallway. Just before he was out of earshot, he called back, "It's never too late to make the right decision. God forgives mistakes."

"He does," I agreed, trying to meet him on terms that he understood. "Don't let your pride prevent you from following after us if you're ever in a position where you feel like you made the wrong decision, and I promise I'll do the same, okay, *uncle* Jarred?"

He froze for a moment, his back stiff, before resuming his steady walk.

With that, our party was down to four people and Smegma. The looks I got from Willa and my father pleaded with me to change my mind, but I couldn't. They weren't thinking rationally as far as I was concerned. We either had to find another exit or find a way to survive for multiple days until someone did dig us out. Plus, just like my father had told Jarred in their sidebar—the Hunters from Mirage that had gone to scout might still be in front of us.

Not meeting their eyes, I started walking down the tunnel to the next chamber. It was the one that only Smegma and I knew was massive, and out of place in an F-Ranked Dungeon. It was so big, in fact, that the algae moss stopped effectively lighting the space, and Willa pulled out her Lightstone. As soon as it lit up and everyone saw that this wasn't a normal small cavern like the earlier one— the arguments resumed.

Well, my father and Willa attempted to restart it, but I rather effectively diffused it by ignoring them and continuing, with or without them. The floors and much of the walls were covered in Crystals, which meant we could survive quite some time with some work. Still, we needed something more. The Mana Apples may satiate hunger, but what about thirst?

"We need to explore and find water if it's down here," I said, looking at Smegma. The Demon nodded and floated off. He soon was out of range of the light, and I licked my lips. The cavern was definitely larger than any I'd personally been in before. Even as Willa and my father opened their mouths to start another conversation—I pointed to the Crystals nearest our feet. "Let's Mine these while Smegma scouts."

From the clenched jaws, I could tell that they disagreed, but when Dave shouldered his pick and moved to get to work, they grudgingly did as well.

"No Sharding if you can help it!" I commanded as I joined them.

Smegma returned after about ten minutes, shaking his head. "I made a semi-circle from here, but there isn't anything but more Crystals. Let's move and I'll keep going."

We did so, several more times, and I watched as my mC count climbed to over a hundred and twenty thousand. We had just moved, and I was hoping it would get to one-thirty, when Smegma rushed back before we could even start Mining again.

"Don't make any noise," he whisper-hissed. "There's a White Goblin village in a gorge fifty yards from here."

"What?" my dad hissed.

Smegma just pointed in the direction he'd returned from. "Just over there. Also, they captured at least one of the Hunters."

"What?!" my dad hissed again and Smegma rolled his eyes.

"I'm starting to see where your son got his intelligence," Smegma said dryly. My father's face went red, but whether it was anger or embarrassment, I couldn't tell. Thankfully, if it was anger, he kept his outburst contained.

"Wait—does that mean there's water?" I asked, realizing that if Goblins were surviving down here, then there must be.

"A small stream runs through the town, and there is a cave lake in this direction," Smegma answered.

"Water bottles," I ordered and held out my hands. Dave instantly handed his over, and Willa moved to follow suit before my dad held out a hand to stop her.

"I should go," he said.

"Smegma and I are linked—he can't guide you like he can—"

"I should go," my dad said again, his tone brooking no argument. I stared at him helplessly. *I knew he was stubborn since I have that bone too.*

Thankfully, Smegma said, "Don't worry. It's close enough that I can guide him even if you stay here."

My mouth fell open and I stared at Smegma, who shrugged in response. In explanation, the Demon said, "You literally just thought you couldn't win this argument…"

40

***

Greb-Shak led Gary and his extremely poor-quality Lightstone to the cave lake. It wasn't far, but he also wasn't sure if the White Goblins would have patrols. He tried to convince Gary to turn the stupid beacon light off, but Gary said he needed to see. At least he was willing to wait as Greb-Shak ranged out ahead before coming back and moving again.

One thing that the Demon had thought, but didn't give voice to when pushing for Gary to go in Brodie's stead, was the simple fact that Gary was much more expendable than Brodie himself, even though if things came down to a fight, Greb-Shak had no doubt that Brodie would prove the more capable fighter. That had been made clear in the fight against the Golem days ago. None of that mattered, though. Greb-Shak was a practical Demon. While there was no meaningful connection between himself and his own spawn-donators, he knew that humans had weird concerns about close relatives, so he'd kept his full motivations to himself. Perhaps more importantly though, he needed to set this 'dad' straight on the priorities of survival…

If they had walked the hundred yards straight, it would have been a trip that lasted a few minutes at most, but this way—it had already taken ten. Still, they made it to the water without issues. Gary studied the lake, which was white and cloudy. He then combined the leftover water into two of the bottles before filling up the remaining four with the cloudy stuff.

"Why are you doing that?" Greb-Shak asked quietly.

Gary motioned for them to move away and waited about ten steps before whispering, "Water can have contaminants in it. With the white color, it could have bacteria or hard minerals harmful to humans."

Greb-Shak narrowed his eyes. "The System does not poison water. The White Goblins could have, I suppose, but this is upstream from their village…"

"Maybe Demons can drink this without boiling it first, but humans aren't as resilient," Gary answered as the others came into view.

"Well, that's obvious." Smegma shook his head. "But when was the last time you heard about a human getting sick from water?"

Gary froze for a split second in his walk, and Greb-Shak realized that this behavior was a holdover from before the System.

Despite agreeing that Gary was the best fit for the scouting mission, Greb-Shak knew that Brodie needed to get stronger. With his *Skill Cannibalism* and Goblins' penchant for having a wide variety of Skills, along with the fact that they were humanoid, and the *tiny* issue of survival—he knew that there was a significant chance that Brodie would need to fight. Even if that meant giving the boy a little nudge. He couldn't have parental sentiment getting in the way.

Greb-Shak knew that not only Brodie's survival but his own—and the rest of the humans in the Dungeon—may well come down to how the holder of *Demonic Vault* capitalized on his advantages. The Skill his team had created was a force multiplier, and with the shocking foundation of the boy's *Dragon Heart* Skill, he knew that Brodie Flacarada was his own—and what remained of his Sect's— best chance of survival. Which meant he needed the boy alive, and the best way of remaining alive was becoming *strong*.

Still out of earshot from the other three, he added, "You need to stop thinking of your son as weak, Gary. He's stronger than you and was the best choice for this little mission. Your ideas about your son, like this water, is a mental block, and if you don't start trusting your kid's decisions, then the chances of everyone's survival are going to plummet."

Dave waved to them, likely seeing the Lightstone, but Gary stayed frozen. Finally, he looked at Greb-Shak.

"I'll try…"

CHAPTER 6: CHAPTER 58

Friday, April 26th, 2069

"So, what's the plan?" Dave asked after we had moved to an area in the cavern furthest from the White Goblin village.

"Well, we have to boil—" my dad started to say but was quickly cut off by Smegma.

"I've already told you, that's unnecessary. Moronic ape!"

My eyes widened, and my mouth fell open as Smegma insulted my father. There were two reasons for my surprise. First, my father didn't even want to go deeper, and it had taken a lot to convince him to not join Jarred. So, antagonizing him seemed stupid. Second, he was my father. I would never insult him, and Smegma kind of felt like an extension of me. I started scolding the Demon, mentally explaining why he should stop, but to my shock, I was interrupted. Aloud.

"No, Brodie, I won't spare him because he is family. Act like an idiot and you get treated like a Flesh Demon."

"What kind of idiom is that?" Dave asked under his breath, which at least stopped Smegma's glare at my father.

"Flesh Demons chose to become boneless through a ritual. They believed that it would make them invincible and harder to injure. Now, they are essentially Slimes with vulnerable organs."

Dave made a disgusted face, but I only had eyes for my dad. He gave me an appreciative smile and a shrug. Seeming to say that he and Smegma had already had that conversation. He even went as far to gesture to the cave around us, and I took it to mean, 'plus, where am I going to get fuel for a fire?'

I nodded to him, accepting his gratitude for the implied support I offered. I had mentally scolded Smegma, after all. However, I disagreed with the second part. Mana Crystals could burn—sure, it was like using jet fuel to start a fire, and—oh, that's what he had meant. If we started a fire down here, we may just start an inferno. I nodded at my own misinterpretation. It wasn't like we needed a fire, anyway.

"How 'bout some weapons to be defendin' us?" Willa offered, pointing at Smegma. Everyone understood what she was asking, and I nodded. A bit of Mana pulled up the red windows.

Demonic Vault 4.3.4
Crendalar Five — Abyss Sect's Wares

Skills
Consumables

<Weapons>
Armor
Miscellaneous

Currency: 125,092 mC (Mana Coins)

"What's the cheapest weapons available? Preferably something with range," I asked Smegma, hoping for some direction.

"First, unless someone has a hidden Magic Skill, I wouldn't suggest a ranged weapon. It may be effective against White Goblins, but ranged weapons lose efficacy if you don't have a Skill to support them. Plus, almost all of them require ammunition or Mana supply. Take this one, for example…"

Smegma sent me a window.

Precise Crossbow (1)
Low F-Rank

This Crossbow has the enchantments for precision and self-repair. This weapon is made from D-Rank material and will not be able to Evolve past D-Rank. Ammunition not included.

Cost: 1,000,000 mC

I stared at the screen, taking in the fact that a low F-Rank weapon was unaffordable. "Are you trying to rub in the fact that I can't even afford an F-Rank weapon? Plus, how is a weapon a hundred times more valuable than a Miner's Pick?"

"No, dumb-dumb, that wasn't what I was trying to show you! I was pointing out that you need ammunition, and we don't sell Crossbow Bolts. So, your ranged weapon thought is almost as moronic as boiling water."

"What the husk does that matter if I can't even afford the weapon? Idiot!" I countered.

"Well, if I'm honest, you can't even afford an Evolvable Enchanted Dagger—and the Abyss Sect didn't put in anything more useless than that. The reason they are more expensive is simple if you think about it. Where did we get Card Shards on Crendalar to combine into Skill Cards? Oh—that's right, the husking Monsters. Picks and other Gathering Tools were pretty useful, but only in the sense that we needed Ores and Crystals to keep our society going. We needed Herbs and Fruits for Potions and Pills. We needed Monster meat to eat. So, yeah, we created them, but they're pretty common since we could change out Cards as needed. For example, the Demons would clear a Portal, then flip Cards and strip Mine it. Everyone had Gathering Tools and Skills that were low Ranked, but they were considered relatively useless. Either way, the buying a weapon idea is entirely out the husking window, shit-for-brains. I'm just making a point!"

Pointedly ignoring Smegma, I turned to Willa. "Well, *we* can't buy any weapons to defend ourselves," I said very dryly. Willa put a hand to her mouth to suppress a chuckle. My father and Dave laughed openly. While they couldn't see the windows, it was clear where my conversation with Smegma led. Looking around at the walls, and the plaques of Ores that decorated them under the glowing moss, I added, "That doesn't mean we can't make our own, though."

The others followed my gaze and gave appreciative looks. For about a split second, I thought there was hope…

"You and what smelter? What hammer and anvil? You flaming Felhound turd!" Smegma asked, his voice as derisive as ever. "Sure, you can buy one that runs on Crystals, but where are you going to get the molds or the husking wood for handles and other materials needed?"

Instead of being insulted by Smegma's tone, everyone nodded along. He was mostly right—however, his disagreement to my plan actually helped me refine it. "We don't need to make anything too fancy, though. What about a club with a sharp edge or some spikes?"

Smegma gave me a look and then motioned to my father's Pickaxe, which was grounded beside him. I nodded and returned to refining my plan. Using the Pickaxes as weapons was something at least, but since we weren't going up against a slow-moving Rock Golem, I could see a few problems with it.

Still, is a club better?

"Either way, let's Mine these Crystals," I said as I pointed to the carpet of Crystals that covered the ground. Thanks to the sparse algae moss, this cave system was different from the other ones we'd Mined in other Dungeons. With the Algae, the Crystals rarely grew on the wall and were concentrated most heavily on the ground. I huffed out a breath as I realized just how different Dave's first experience of Mining was from my own. Everyone looked at me, thanks to the noise of amusement.

I held up a hand to wave away any concern as I explained, "I was just thinking Dave sure is lucky to have such a wonderful first experience with Mining…"

"Gallows humor, *really*?" Dave asked but joined the others in the very muted snuffing laughter.

Smegma just shook his head as he said, "May I offer a suggestion?"

Everyone stopped and turned to look at the Demon.

"You three should Mine here. Brodie and I should scout the cavern and look for other ways out."

My eyes found my father's, sure he would protest. His face certainly looked like he was about to. However, his blotchy flush soon morphed to entirely red as his jaw clenched. To my utter shock, he nodded.

What in the husk?

Willa put a hand on his shoulder, probably understanding what just went through his head more than I did. First, she had known him a very long time, but second, and more importantly, she was also a parent. I could only imagine what it would feel like to let your child take a risk like Smegma suggested. *Wait—do I even want to do as he suggested?*

Smegma floated up beside me and simply stared. "If your father already agreed, then it's clearly the best husking plan, dumb-dumb!"

I inhaled sharply at the increase in volume, thanks to Smegma's proximity. I took one more look at my father, Dave and Willa, gulped and said, "I'll be careful—we'll be back soon?"

I wasn't sure why I made the last part a question but saw Smegma shake his head and likely roll his black eyes—the actual eye movement was nearly impossible to discern.

Smegma began floating away and making noises humans reserved for pets. "Come on, boy." He even added in some tongue clicks. "Let's go. This way."

This time I definitely rolled my eyes. *What a husking asshole!*

Soon we were away from the group, and I realized I didn't have a Lightstone thanks to the darkness that made me squint my eyes.

"Shoot, I should go back for a Lightstone," I said.

"No, let your eyes adjust to the low levels of light. You don't want to have a lit beacon with how much we'll be moving," Smegma said before I could even spin. "I think the White Goblins aren't very active Monsters, or they likely would have found you lot multiple times already thanks to those husking things."

"How did they capture the Hunter, or all the Hunters, then?" I asked, trying to understand the Demon's logic.

"Total conjecture, but most likely those idiots attacked them or fell into a trap on the way to attack them. They were certainly cocky enough to think that F-Rank humanoid Monsters were easy prey."

Something felt like it was stuck in my throat, and I swallowed heavily. If the Hunters attacked them with all those weapons and didn't win—we would have close to a zero percent chance with our Pickaxes. The conversation raised a late flag. "Wait, then leaving them alone like that to Mine is dangerous. We should go back!"

"They're over a mile from the White Goblin village and tucked away in an alcove. The only safer place is back up the tunnel we came down with Jarred."

Even with the assurance, I was frozen in place, not able to move forward and unable to return.

"Remember when you lectured me about trust? Have you ever explored a Portal before?"

The paralysis broke enough for me to shake my head.

"I've not only been in Portals, but led expeditions to clear them, research them, and strip mine them. So, why don't you trust me, and I'll see you all out of here. Even Jarred…"

His voice was more sincere than I'd ever heard it. I wasn't sure if it was because of that, or the internal voice that was screaming at me to take this opportunity to live as a Hunter, but I managed one step. Each one became easier after that—and soon we were hugging the wall and exploring.

Mentally, I cataloged any Ores that I could see—the ones with red plaques. I still wanted to make some weapons if I could refine that plan a bit further. Smegma, on the other hand, kept moving at a measured pace, oftentimes vanishing for half a minute before I saw his form again in front of me.

I kept toggling *Heat Sense* on and off on my eyes, but didn't see anything.

[Where do you keep going?] I asked in a mental whisper, unsure if we'd gotten closer to the Goblin village in the few minutes we'd been walking.

"Ranging afield," he said in a normal tone. "I've made myself imperceptible again, also stop whispering in your head that's just weird!" I must have broadcasted my lack of understanding in the term, 'ranging afield' because he explained, "It means I'm scouting around you in a hundred-yard semi-circle."

Well, that certainly made more sense. After ten more of the thirty-second disappearances, Smegma returned and said, "I've found something, but it's strange."

[Strange how?] I once again mentally whispered my question—this time trying to piss the Demon off. He gave me a look that told me he noticed but ignored it.

"Well, at first, I thought it was a second Goblin village, but the creatures I found were using Crystals, wood, algae moss, and mud to create dwellings. What I found is a Grotto that seems to be abandoned and the dwellings are dug right into the stone."

[Okay…] I answered, trying to convey my lack of understanding.

"Just follow me, and I'll take a closer look."

CHAPTER 7: CHAPTER 59

Friday, April 26th, 2069

It was strange to scout an area by literally crouching near a precipice and just waiting. But that was pretty much my entire contribution. I tried to find ways to occupy myself and continued to flip *Heat Sense* on and off . Nothing really changed no matter what body part I used it on. This deep underground, my immediate area was almost devoid of heat.

Since the moss was glowing, I had expected it to give off a great deal of heat, but that wasn't the case. It did glow with some residual warmth, especially when compared to the surrounding rock, but that was it. The other interesting point was that I was far enough away from both the White Goblins and my group to not 'feel' either when placing *Heat Sense* on my body.

I also couldn't see them—I'd checked.

One thing did stand out due to *Heat Sense* though, and that was the Grotto I was waiting atop. It was darker to my vision, and colder to my senses, than any other place within range. Studying it with my Skill, I realized that there was a shift in the rock formation, or perhaps material was a better descriptor. Running my hands forward allowed me to feel where the rock had been cut. It was subtle, but the texture change was too straight to be natural.

The rock didn't look different to my eyes, either—appearing to be the same grayish-black stone in the low levels of light. However, the material used was clearly different, and I was guessing Smegma would return to tell me that this place had been excavated and then *built*. For what purpose, I couldn't even guess—but the Grotto was clearly dug into the stone. Then, either the same stone had been shaped or another similar stone had been used to build the place.

Smegma floated toward me, seeming like a shadow that exited the center of the crater. I followed his outlined, dark form as he seemed to glide over on a non-existent wind. Everything about the Demon seemed extra terrifying and creepy down here in the cavern. Right up until he spoke.

"Well, numb-nuts, it's totally abandoned and was some sort of facility. It has more of those yellow Crystals in the caves, and they are clearly being used for light. I couldn't find anything usable, but there is also a fountain, which should mean a reservoir with water."

[So, it's a good place to make camp?] I asked.

"I'd say yes, but we should probably scout it fully. I couldn't go as deep or as far into the carved or constructed caves as I'd like because of the tether."

[Okay, well, let's check it out,] I said but was surprised when Smegma just stared at me.

"Yeah, one other *small* problem with that. I didn't find a way down for those afflicted with gravity."

I scratched at my head but slowly started circling the crater-Grotto as Smegma 'ranged afield.' It actually took nearly an hour, according to my watch, before Smegma said he'd found a way down. However, when I arrived, I realized that his 'way down' didn't mean he'd found stairs.

[I'm supposed to climb down *that?*] I asked, staring at a huge column that made it even clearer that this place was built or carved from the stone. The wear also made it clear that it had been done a very long time ago. The column's face was pockmarked with porous holes that looked like something termites might have done to wood.

Regardless of why the erosion pattern looked the way it did, it undoubtedly looked unsafe—ready to crumble, collapse or shatter.

Smegma looked at me, and then the column, before nodding. "I guess it isn't the best option. Let's keep looking."

An hour later, it turned out that it or another column on the opposite side, nearer to where I'd started circling the massive crater, were the only two options.

[Wait a second,] I said, a thought coming to me. [You're a Merchant, right? You'd be a pretty bad one if you didn't have supplies and things, right? How much for some rope or climbing gear? Or were you not going to offer me anything and make me just Bare Grillz my way down to the bottom?]

"The husk? How are my skills as a Merchant being called into question and not your stupid team's lack of preparedness?" Smegma said, his voice affronted. "Of course, a Skill as great and wonderful as *Demonic Vault* doesn't sell climbing supplies! No self-respecting Demon would have that gear in their husking Rings of Holding! Well, maybe a Flesh Demon would, and I think we've established you're as stupid as them. Maybe this 'Bare' person is actually a Flesh Demon if he's as naked as his name suggests, which would explain so much if the worst of my race got to Earth first."

My eyebrows rose as I took in his spiel. I could tell he was covering for something, and I thought I knew what it was. [So, you've realized that stocking climbing gear would have been helpful?]

"Yeah," Smegma said under his breath. "Pretty big oversight, I think."

[Agreed. Now, how wide is this cavern?] I asked, trying to distract myself as I inched toward the second column. I told myself it looked safer than the last one, but if I was honest, I couldn't really remember.

"Well, this hole is easily two of your Earth miles in diameter—"

[It's got to be bigger than that,] I countered. It wouldn't take me two hours to walk two miles. Then I remembered the math terms and realized that he hadn't said circumference. [Never mind,] I quietly corrected, also realizing how cautious I'd been while walking due to the Crystals and uneven rocks.

Not to mention the times I'd waited for Smegma to return before continuing. Again, I was trying to distract myself, and when I realized that I couldn't anymore, I gulped down saliva to wet my throat.

It took me several steadying breaths before I reached out a shaking hand that managed to latch onto a handhold on the column. I gave it a few experimental tugs while sitting on the edge of the drop. It held my implied weight…

What was this column meant to hold up? I wondered, but knew I wasn't going to get an answer.

"Get on with it," Smegma said, his tone conveying that he knew I was stalling, and he had read my surface thoughts.

Slowly, I lowered my first foot down until it, too, found a place that I deemed could hold my weight, with some testing flexes of my feet. This was the moment of truth. I looked back at the ledge and then down into the pitch darkness below. I could just push myself back up and keep looking for another way down...

"Oh my god. Just husking start climbing down. It's not even a hundred feet to the bottom."

Smegma's words made it worse. A hundred feet was like ten stories, wasn't it? *Mental Fortitude* kicked in and logically explained that Smegma had a point. This was the hardest part, and if I didn't focus on the fact that I couldn't see the bottom...

"Easy to say for someone who can *fly*," I grumbled. "Or—someone who's completely incorporeal." I was nervous enough I forgot to use my mental voice.

I pushed off and found a second foothold, followed by another grip for my other hand. Then it became simple as I slowly felt around with a foot, then hand, repeatedly. Often reusing my previous footrests for handholds. I had one minor scare as my foot kicked a stone loose and I heard it fall, bouncing and echoing in a strange way. It was so odd that it took me a moment to realize I had kicked the stone with my toe and it had fallen inward—not out.

That meant the sound I heard was the stone falling down a hollow center?

Had the column eroded that much? What kind of erosion or corrosion happened from the inside-out?

My heart started hammering in my chest, but thankfully, I could see the bottom at that point and stressfully rushed down the remaining twenty feet to it. Once I was back on flat rock, and had caught my breath, I looked around and found caves that shone with the same metallic yellow light I'd seen coming from the mural. It wasn't bright, which was likely why I hadn't seen it from above, but now that I was on the same ground level, it was apparent.

Smegma moved ahead of me, turning his form back into a shadow backlit by the entrance. I followed and realized mid-step that I was walking on perfectly flat stone tiles. There were no Crystals growing here, and while the tiles may have had some erosion from time, it was hard to discern with the low levels of light. That puzzling difference vanished between one step and the next, when I entered through a doorway.

Calling it a cave at this point was wrong. It was rectangular and only missing a door to make it a habitation. Sure, it was wider than most doorways humans would build, but it was also clearly decorated with scrollwork carved into the edges. What the carvings were meant to depict was difficult to discern, but I would call it vines or maybe coiled rope?

The room inside was likewise squared off, with flat, level walls and perfectly ninety-degree corners. If there had been furniture, it was either long since pillaged, decayed, or destroyed. Instead, it was just a large, empty room of dark gray stone with three metallic yellow light fixtures in the ceiling.

There were two doorways leading out of the room that looked identical to the one I'd entered through. Smegma was already moving toward the one that led deeper, seeming to ignore the one on the right. I followed, but did glance into the right doorway. Another room identical to the one I was walking through greeted me.

I toggled *Heat Sense* and found no heat sources in the room at all. The light fixtures were the same black as everything else, making me realize that they were even more efficient than the glowing plants outside.

Smegma stopped in the next room's center. As soon as I cleared the doorway, he asked, "The stairs down? Or deeper in?"

[Which one couldn't you scout before?] I asked.

"Both, but I think I was looking more in that direction," Smegma responded quickly, pointing vaguely to our right. "It seemed like these square rooms repeated over and over again, no matter which way I went, but what would they need all the separation for?"

[Maybe the separation isn't really meant to keep areas separate. Maybe the walls are load bearing,] I suggested.

"Possible, but they could have just used columns, I'd think," Smegma said as he tapped his teeth with a talon. After a moment, he pointed deeper and I walked around the stairs that were dead center in the room. They had a half wall that surrounded them on three sides, and a quick glance down didn't reveal more than what was likely an identical room below.

We were another ten rooms deeper into the structure before we finally lost the option to continue straight ahead. Smegma was standing still in the room's center, asking which way to go simply with his body language. This room was the first one I'd seen with a left door, though, and I pointed to it. He smiled and nodded before we continued.

There wasn't another room, which was both welcoming and surprising as we passed through the doorway. Instead, there was a hallway that was the exact same width and height of the carved rectangle doorway we had passed through. The carvings continued onto these walls, and I was finally able to discern that it was meant to be coiling snakes. I shivered despite myself—hoping we weren't about to enter some sort of snake-filled chamber or spawning ground.

I toggled on *Heat Sense* but found nothing new, both with vision and my— wait, above us there were faint traces of heat… They felt far away, though, and familiar.

Due to the wall carving and the distraction of discovering a source of heat, I didn't realize that the floor was graded until I looked back down and discovered we were climbing. I also didn't notice the bend up ahead until Smegma was already rounding it. It made a perfect one-hundred-and-eighty-degree turn in a slow semi-circle. Smegma stopped on the other side and stared up a steep flight of stairs that seemed to climb for an unreasonable amount of time.

Probably about a hundred feet, give or take.

Spaced evenly up the staircase and in the tunnel were more metallic yellow Crystals. I sighed when I realized just how many we'd passed in this place— they clearly couldn't be that valuable if there were so many, right? I debated dumping the ones that were 'useless' out from my Necklace of Holding but decided against it for now. I could hope that they'd at least be valuable to those that collected curiosities.

"And right now, it's like you need to make room for all your other amazing finds!" Smegma added derisively to my thoughts with a chuckle.

"I'm guessing this will lead to the surface?" I asked the Demon while sighing and raising a brow in response to his comment.

Smegma stopped chuckling, shrugged and then flew up the stairs. I followed, and sure enough, I found myself stepping out of a stalagmite back onto the surface a few minutes of climbing later. This time when I toggled on *Heat Sense*, I discovered why the sources of heat I'd detected earlier had felt so familiar. We were probably a few hundred yards away from the group.

[Well, at least we found a place to rest and an easier way into the Grotto,] I said as I motioned in the direction of my father, Willa, and Dave.

Smegma looked at a nearby stalagmite and a few others close to it, seeming to frown. It had become harder to see again now that the lighting levels were so low—wait. I spun and realized that the stalagmites appeared solid and weren't releasing any of the light from the metallic yellow Crystals that had been so abundant and bright moments ago.

"I scouted these earlier and didn't think anything of it. How do you think it's doing that?" Smegma asked, and I could tell it was rhetorical because he was already tapping his teeth.

Instead of answering, I walked up and placed a hand on the stalagmite I'd just exited. It passed right through the 'stone' veneer, and I followed my own hand back into the stairwell. I came back out a moment later to find Smegma still tapping his teeth as he hovered around the rock formation.

I doubted he was going to want to stop his study anytime soon, so I said, [I'll go get the others? They might be close enough.]

He didn't even wave a hand in acknowledgement of my words. I shook my head but walked off. Before I reached the group, he popped into the space beside me. His twitch made me sure he hadn't been expecting the tether to reign him in. I kept walking without bothering to apologize. He could study it after the group was inside and safe.

* * *

The sale of the Mined Crystals brought me above one hundred and fifty-five thousand mC. It made my breath come easier, realizing we were closer to having enough crystals to purchase two days of Mana Apples. It also made me feel better when I realized that we'd done about thirty thousand mC in trade in about three hours. Some rough math made me confident we could manage to keep ourselves fed for a few days if we worked eight-hour shifts.

We set up 'camp' in the last room before the hallway that led to the staircase and stalagmites—figuring that we could Mine near the stalagmites tomorrow and have an easy retreat if White Goblins did venture out this far from their village.

"Let's scout deeper," Smegma pointedly said, as he phased through the floor not fifteen minutes after the group settled in. I gave him a look, feeling like he was a bit too demanding with his request. "It's literally just four floors of this, but I think there's more stuff under the outdoor courtyard."

"Outdoor courtyard?" Willa asked before I could do the same.

"That's how Brodie got down here," Smegma explained. "He climbed down a hollow column into an open courtyard."

My head tilted at the explanation. Without a real light source, I just thought I'd climbed down onto a deeper cavern floor and then entered a cave. Yet, I'd quickly realized they weren't caves, thanks to the perfectly square rooms and doorways. I should have made the connection to the 'courtyard,' or whatever that floor was, myself.

Dave started to stand up, looking excited. Everyone watched him trying to understand what was going on. It took him a moment to notice his actions were being scrutinized. He started but then sheepishly asked, "Well, can't we all go?"

Smegma put his arms up with his hands out to his side and shrugged in response. That made me replay his earlier words. He hadn't implied that only he and I should go. I just needed to be in attendance so he could move further. Still, everyone looked tired—even the way Dave had gotten to his feet with an exhausted sigh, and knuckling the small of his back, had made me wince in sympathy for him.

"Can it wait till tomorrow?" I asked.

"No," Smegma said simply. At my and everyone else's worried looks, he pointed to the two other doors leading off from the room. "There might be little to no chance of something attacking you from those directions, but when you're in a Portal overnight, you don't take that chance!"

I could only speak for myself, but at that moment, Smegma did sound like an experienced Hunter. He was someone who had spent nights in a Portal before. I stood up and heard Willa and my dad moving as well. Once we were all standing, Smegma began to lead the way through doorways to a room with a staircase.

As he moved, he pointed one of his three talons at Dave. Somewhat mockingly, he said, "A bit of a walk will help the newbie—I'm betting twinkletoes here won't be able to move tomorrow if he just falls asleep right now."

That made us all spin to look at Dave, who was in fact walking gingerly enough that 'twinkletoes' turned out to be an accurate description and not just sheer, Demonic taunting. No one laughed, but despite my best attempt, I did smile.

"Hey!" Dave complained, seeing my amusement. The crack in his voice made the group, minus Smegma, burst into laughter. If anything, Smegma drawing attention to his ginger movements exacerbated it, making it even more noticeable.

Now Dave seemed like an old man needing a walker.

CHAPTER 8: CHAPTER 60

Friday, April 26th, 2069

"What da hell be that?" Willa exclaimed, staring at a carved rock pedestal with two hollow rock tubes that hung above it. I was staring at the same thing, and if she hadn't asked, I would've. In fact, a quick scan showed that everyone was studying the four-foot-high, recessed pedestal, as well as the two hollow descending rock tubes.

My scan of the area brought my eyes across the walls and the patterned holes that adorned it. I pointed them out and asked, "And those holes?"

My father was already studying them. He ran a finger inside of one and examined it. "This is rust," he said, showing the brown residue he'd uncovered to everyone. I squinted my eyes, trying to picture what would have been 'hanging' from metal, or perhaps supported by stakes into a wall…

"It's a smithy," Smegma said simply, which shattered many of my misleading thoughts and organized the room and its features into a neat, understandable layout. "The crucible would have gone there." Smegma pointed out the tubes and even motioned to a foot pedal or some type of pumping lever I hadn't noticed. It was made of the same rock as the pedestal and still hung at the top of a long rectangular hole, possibly ready to be worked. Smegma continued, "Then, either finished ingots were placed on shelves—or this room also had an anvil and forge, and those were pegs for finished equipment."

Smegma was already on his way out of this room and moving to another, as if his answer completely solved the 'mystery.' As far as I was concerned, it hadn't, but seeing what the other rooms held would probably paint a more complete picture, so I jumped to follow.

The next room was somewhat the same, but not. Smegma volunteered the function of this room as he pointed to the four-foot-tall stone boxes, which were filled with soil and weeds. The boxes rose from the floor, and there was an overabundance of the 'Crystal' lights in here.

"A grow house for Herbs. The Pill Cauldron likely went here, along with Stills and other Alchemical Apparatuses." Smegma pointed out what could have been a kitchen island in a modern home, but made more sense as a long lab table, with his description.

We moved through room after room—some of which were identical to the ones we'd seen already, and others that weren't.

"A walk-in freezer—a Tannery—probably a Bakery or a specialized Smithy—Livestock Pens," Smegma said toward one particularly worn down and overlarge room. Again, once he made the pronouncement, the circular pens carved into the floor made a great deal more sense. This room did seem to be on the lowest level and only had one large archway leading off it. We had entered through the typical rectangular, carved doorway, so the archway gave me pause.

As we tentatively moved through it, we didn't get a warning from Smegma. So, we continued with a bit more confidence. In the next 'room,' we found an actual cavern and the rocky shore of a lake. Not just a small cave lake like the pond near the White Goblin village—but a massive body of blue water that I couldn't see the other side of, despite the multitude of metallic-yellow-Crystal sconces and hanging lights above me.

A splash sounded from somewhere out in the water, causing me and the other three humans to jump.

"Fishery," Smegma said. "That and a fresh water source. I think it's safe to conclude that this was a town or village of the people that once lived on this world."

"What happened to them?" my dad asked.

Smegma stayed silent, and since he was the only one who had a hope of answering that question, the rest of us held our breath.

After a time, Smegma looked away from the water and shook his head sadly. "They failed to Ascend. We can hope they found their way to another planet that succeeded, since there aren't any bones or remains here."

"Do you think we can Fish here?" Dave asked, seeming to combat the oppressively heavy mood with optimism.

I was about to chuckle and dismiss his question before I realized that the Shop might actually have a rod and bait. Smegma sent me a window right away.

Miscellaneous Professions Gear

Fisherman's Rod & Knife (1)
Low F-Rank
Durability: Unlimited
Damage: 0-1

This Fishing Rod comes with the ability to create Mana Bait from the user's Pool. It also contains a self-repair Enchantment that will strengthen it over time. It will also funnel excess Mana from catches to Brodie Flacarada's *Overdraft* Skill.

Cost: 10,000 mC

"There is a 'Fishing Rod.' Do you think we can convince Jarred to come back with that?" I asked excitedly. Because of the order of my words, I saw Willa and my father's faces grow excited and then fall at the reminder of Jarred's religious stubbornness.

"In time, maybe," my dad whispered. "Still, he'll definitely eat some fish if we bring it to him."

I nodded and immediately purchased the Fisherman's Rod. It wasn't like I wasn't going to get one in this situation, anyway. I was just hoping we could have an additional set of hands for Mining or Fishing. Plus, we'd be much safer in one group until help arrived.

As soon as I clicked the purchase button, Smegma asked, "Are you sure you want to purchase the Fisherman's Rod and Knife?"

"Uhhh, why he be goin' suddenly robotic?" Willa asked.

"He has to confirm my selections when I make them," I answered and turned back to Smegma. "Yes, I'm sure."

"You must answer the question immediately. Are you sure you want to purchase the Fisherman—"

"Is he being compelled to ask that?" my dad interrupted, and I could see that Smegma was getting upset.

"Yeah, he's really annoying about it," I responded.

"I guess you don't want to catch food, then?" Smegma interjected heatedly. Everyone seemed to get the hint and let Smegma finish this time. "Are you sure you want to purchase the Fisherman's Rod and Knife?"

I hesitated for just a moment, thinking about pissing him off further—but also thinking better of it. We needed food and I was wasting time. "Yes, I'm sure."

A blue light formed and congealed until it was roughly the shape and length of a long parcel tube—then the Rod dropped out of it, and I caught it. A clatter on the ground told me I'd missed something. I followed the noise and found a fileting Knife that had a decaying handle and rusted tang. The blade itself looked so dull it was practically square. I placed it in my Necklace before studying the Rod.

To call the Rod lackluster would have been an understatement. Then again, it was similar to calling the original Miner's Picks less than perfect. The blank was made out of a piece of wood that looked like petrified driftwood. The guides might have been metal at one point, but currently looked one step away from rusting through. The reel seat and reel were rattling from its short drop into my hand. On top of all that, the wound fishing line was so frayed it could have passed for thin yarn.

I wasn't sure how catching fish would give the thing Mana for repairs, but I hoped it wouldn't fall apart before it did. "So, all you have to do is connect your Mana Pool to it and it should—"

The flinches from all three in my group made my eyes widen, even as I jerked back from them. I scanned the immediate area, expecting a Monster to be exiting the lake. When I found nothing, my mind made the obvious connection. They hadn't ever willingly used their Mana Pools …

"Come on, you two have been bitten by Mana Leeches," I complained, pointing out both my father and Willa. "It's the same damn thing."

"You might be right," my dad responded, even as his mouth twisted into a sour expression. His face paled right alongside it. "Still, I hate those things too—" My dad shivered noticeably, and he began brushing imaginary insects off his arms.

"If I must, I can be tryin'," Willa said but she, too, wore a look that showed how reluctant she was.

Dave stepped forward. "You'll have to show me how," he volunteered with clenched, determined fists. After a moment of silence in which I smiled at him, he looked back to the last room and asked, "Should we move our camp down here?"

"Nope," Smegma answered quickly. "No telling what's in the water. Alright. We're going to have to create a system. We'll need to do this in groups. Two Miners and two people Fishing for now. The problem is that I can't reach the surface from here if Brodie is Fishing, or I can't come down here if he's Mining above, so if any Goblins show up…"

"What about scouting the rest of the cavern?" I asked, pointing out the fact that we hadn't finished checking out the massive space.

"Let's put any more exploration on hold for now," Smegma said. "You've got things you can do to ensure your survival in the short to medium term while we wait and hope that the Mirage Guild digs you out in a few days. In that time, we shouldn't have to venture too far from this 'town' or the lake." Smegma tapped a talon on a tooth as he stared through the cavern ceiling. My sense of direction was pretty bad, but it felt like he was looking in the direction of the White Goblin village.

* * *

"Think about a straw," I coached as I studied my own Fishing Rod, which now had a 'Mana worm' wriggling on the end.

"A straw from where?" Dave asked, sounding frustrated.

"From your Mana Pool to the Fishing Rod."

"Great explanation," Dave said sarcastically. I looked at him as a frown came over my face. This was very reminiscent of Smegma teaching me. Just this time, *I* was the bad teacher.

"Can you try to picture a Mental Universe inside yourself?" I asked.

"Yeah, because I think I have a solar system that just sits in my thorax," Dave responded, clearly aggravated with his lack of success.

Sighing, I scratched at my neck. Dave's sarcasm was infuriating, and I could admit that this was going to be harder than I thought it should be. Internally, I avoided thinking about apologizing to Smegma.

"Still heard you," Smegma crowed, even as he floated to Dave. "How about a garden? Or maybe a bank?"

"What in the hell are you on about Smeg?" Dave asked just as scornfully. "You want me to picture a bank?"

"Yeah, do you also keep your money in something like that, virgin-boy?" Smegma responded derisively.

"Sure," Dave answered, sounding unsure. "And I told you I'm not—"

"Sure, sure, you and the three fingered woman, have got it on many times." Smegma seemed to realize that we had five fingers to his three after he said it. Only then did I realize he'd told Dave that sex with Pamella Handerson didn't count. I laughed even as Smegma explained, "Picture that bank and its security for your money. Or maybe one of those cash-dispensing machines. Can you see it?"

"No," Dave answered stubbornly, now pouting.

"Hmm, your friend is actually dumber than you," Smegma said to me but stayed hovering in front of a now blushing Dave.

"Husk off! Give a better explanation!"

"Okay, you need to feel for your Skill inside your Soul. It should be sitting metaphysically atop your heart. Feel the steady rhythm of your heart. Are you thinking about each beat it makes? Is your subconscious mind controlling it?—Is your Soul? Dive into that question, let yourself relax. Think about your breathing—"

"What the hell?" Dave exclaimed, clearly not happy with this method either.

"As I said, Brodie. Kid's a dud."

"Wait, is my Mental Universe my *Soul*?" I asked.

"A depiction of a part of it, yes."

"How come you never told me that?"

"How come you never asked?" Smegma retorted. "Anyway, Brodie, you should get started if there's any hope for you to catch a fish before bed. I'll work with the slow one."

"I'm not slow, you both just suck at teaching!"

For the next hour, I cast my line, and Dave grew increasingly frustrated. There were many times I was happy to be facing away from my friend and also to not be his teacher. I was glad to be facing away because I could hide my smile and chuckles in coughs—and to not be the teacher because I doubted I'd be smiling if I was the one explaining things.

An hour later, I hadn't gotten a single bite and was forced to interrupt Smegma. "Am I doing something wrong?"

"I don't know. Do I look like a husking Fisherman?" Smegma said angrily, clearly doling out some of his frustration with Dave to me.

My dad walked through the doorway and said, "Let's get some sleep. You two can try again tomorrow if we're still stuck down here."

* * *

Saturday, April 27th, 2069

"You should have caught a damn fish by now," Smegma complained as we descended through the levels of the underground city.

I had spent forty thousand Mana Coins on two additional Mana Apples just moments ago. From there, my father and Willa went up the staircase to the stalagmites, while Dave and I began walking down.

"Ahh, but I didn't have a Fisherman to teach me how to use the Rod," I responded, biting into my Apple and heading down the stairs. "Too bad, that. Maybe I could have kept saving for one of them fancy Skills you keep showing me."

Smegma growled as he hovered in front of me, flapping his large wings in irritation. I would have kept poking fun if the taste of the Apple didn't cause my entire body to freeze up. It was like I had just bitten into a sweet blueberry with the crunchiness of an Asian pear. My mouth salivated and I was forced to quickly swallow or risk drooling on the carved stone steps.

Mana Apple Regeneration

Your Mana Pool is now regenerating 1% faster for 10 days. Your Mana Capacity is also increased by 1% for 10 days.

The distraction of the pop-up red window made me forget to swallow a second time, and I unfortunately made a rather gross sucking noise when I realized a split second too late and almost drooled all down my Miner's gear. Smegma spun around on me with a wide, vengeful grin.

Right up until Dave made an even louder noise and exclaimed through a spray of flying spittle, "Holy shit! This thing is like a giant Sour Garden apple!"

"I'm literally with two Sloth Demons. Uncouth pieces of trash," Smegma commented while shaking his head.

"Usually, we call disgusting people 'skid marks,'" Dave answered. "At least on this planet. You know, 'cause they leave unwiped butt stains in their underwear."

Smegma's eyes widened, and he made a gagging sound that had to have been staged. How could he be 'nauseous' if he didn't eat? Or did he pull things like the popcorn out of thin air after we all went to bed? We walked and bantered the whole way back to the lake. Dave took the brunt of the punishment since Smegma still seemed to vividly recall the attempt at teaching from last night.

That was highlighted further when the first thing Smegma said upon arriving on the rocky shore was, "Sit down and shut the husk up. You're going to try figuring out your own way to touch on your Mana, since you seem to have an answer for everything—"

"How am I supposed—"

"I said sit," Smegma growled. "Shut that damn mouth. Try thinking instead of husking talking. Internalize your bullshit for a while. Your Mana Pool is at the center of your being. Different people create different mental representations of their imagined understanding of that place. Figure yours out, Mr. Know-it-all."

Dave looked at me and I tried not to smirk, but his face morphing to a mask of betrayal meant I'd failed. Smegma gave Dave a look until he eventually obeyed by sitting down.

"Cross your legs or whatever will help you keep your bad gaseous attitude to yourself."

The look on Disaster Dave's face told me he wanted to retort, but if there was one person who could probably beat my friend in a war of words, it was Smegma. Not because he was more intelligent but because he cared less about hurting someone's feelings. Dave either felt that as well or truly wanted to learn to gain some control of his Mana Pool.

Smegma moved to the edge of the lake and then pointed to me. "Dumb-dumb, show me how you've been Fishing."

I did so, first baiting the line and then casting it out as far into the water as I could. Smegma raised both hands once I was done, as if to say 'get going.' That action made me blink. I slowly started reeling the fishing line in, adding an occasional jerk on the Rod to simulate the way the 'Mana worm' might move.

"Are you an imbecile?" Smegma asked after a moment.

"I'm starting to feel like one, yes," I said pointedly. I tried to picture what I was doing and find the obvious flaw. There wasn't one I could see. My eyebrows drew down a moment after, what was I doing wrong? This is how you Fished, right?

"Keep supplying the Rod with Mana, you moron."

My narrowed eyes and angry eyebrows instantly morphed into shocked understanding. Of course! That made a ton of sense…

I did so and two things happened almost instantly. The fishing line 'vanished,' and ripples of a pale blue light pulsed in the distance, creating a steady 'beat.' My hand inched toward the reel, and Smegma's hand instantly passed through it. Clearly, the action had been intended to be a slap and it startled me enough to freeze.

"Looks like bobber Fishi—"

"I told you to sit quietly and reflect!" Smegma interrupted Dave. Still, my friend had said enough to make me realize why Smegma had slapped my hand away. Since the lake water was as still as a sheet of glass, I hadn't seen it at first, but now—the pulsing light really did look like a bobber floating on a wavy lake.

Suddenly the light changed, and I felt a slight tug on the Fishing Pole. Thanks to the poor quality of the Rod, the tug made me think it would snap in half, but it held. Then the fish on the other end must have realized it was hooked because the small tug became fierce.

Beyond fierce, actually. I slid on my butt for a few inches before I dug my heels into a crevasse in the stone shore. Even then, the fighting fish managed to lever me up to almost standing before I flexed my legs and heaved back. The driftwood Rod bent precariously, but I could tell that the fish was also yanked back like a toddler whose father had stopped him from walking into traffic.

I held my breath, praying that the line and Rod would hold. To my surprise, as the fish pulled, I could actually see the pulses of blue Mana feeding back down the invisible line into the reel, and then into the rod. Before my eyes, the wood gained an iota of color, morphing from white to off-white.

With increasing confidence, I began to spin the reel, pairing it with slackening my flexing legs and arms. I started to truly fight back against the fish as I reeled it in.

Between one flexing tug and the next, I felt the strain on my muscles increase. I was even forced to take a step forward to maintain my balance as the fish pulled hard enough to overbalance me. Using all my Strength, I heaved back on the Rod, but found that the fish or creature on the other end of the line and I were at a minimum equal in Strength.

To my shock, the pulsing Mana on the Rod continued, but the repair seemed to have stopped. Cracks began to form up the Rod, and I felt my hammering heart attempt to freeze in my chest. This thing cost ten thousand mC!

"Time your pulls with the pulses, you Flesh Demon!" Smegma shouted.

I blinked but then managed to pull in time with the tail end of one of the pulses of Mana. The fish jerked in my direction, seeming to be pulled with ease. I hurriedly reeled in the slack of the invisible line and waited. The next pulse, I managed to react faster, and again the fish was jerked toward shore. I pulled in the slack and continued.

After another five minutes of fighting, I discovered I had already burned through half of my fifty points of Mana. I couldn't continue for more than another five minutes or this epic battle could not only turn in the fish's favor but also break my rod.

A splash of something exiting the water made my head jerk in a direction slightly to my left. There I found water in the shape of a fish—no, not a fish— something that looked *shark-sized* exiting the lake. Still, when the water fell away, I couldn't find the body of a shark, fish or otherwise.

I thought I could make out some red, brown, and pink accents hanging in the air before the water splashed again. This time, in the pattern of something submerging. A pulse followed the splash and I heaved. That splash was now only about fifteen feet away.

I was winning.

Another minute or so, and I could see those same accents struggling in the shallow water near shore. Instead of reeling the line in at this point, on the next pulse I backpedaled and heaved the massive creature out of the water and onto the wet rock. I stared at the space a massive fish-creature should have been. I frowned at it, not liking the look of what I was seeing.

I could see the internal organs of a creature but not the creature itself. I toggled on my *Heat Sense* and did find a massive fish-like shape, at least the size of a small car, flopping around on the rock. I blinked off my Skill to find Smegma floating closer, seemingly excited.

"A Mirror Fish! That's really good eating! If you kill it while it's on the line, the Rod should get more Mana."

I blinked at the Demon, and then looked around, realizing I had nothing to use to kill it, let alone filet it. That's when I remembered the dull and rusting filet Knife. With a thought, I pulled it from my Necklace and stabbed the massive fish through its very visible brain. The dull knife skittered across a layer of skin and flesh that I couldn't see. Pulling back, I lined the point up and punched forward toward the brain. It felt strange to hit the skin of the Mirror Fish while only being able to see the brain inches further than where my knife impacted. Leaning into my Strength Stat, my bicep flexed as I grunted, shoving the blade through the feeling of skin, cartilage, and other tissues until I watched it crash into the fish's brain. Its frantic flopping and snapping at the air suddenly ceased as the entire fish went limp.

"Do you know how to filet it?" I asked Smegma, and he shook his head.

Dave growled from behind me, causing us both to turn and look at him. He loudly stood up, each action slow and deliberate, highlighting that he was still in pain from Mining. When he got to me, he attempted to snatch the knife from me but was so slow, I had to fight a laugh from escaping at his expense. Smegma seemed like he was ready to burst as he either held back his own laughter, or his urge to shout Dave back to his place for meditation.

Dave studied the see-through fish.

After a moment, he handed back the knife, with a wince, and moved to slowly sit back down, grumbling, "I know how to filet normal fish. Making me get up for that thing?! What the husk even *is* that?"

His complaints, mixed with his movements, made him seem like an old man, and I continued to fight back my laughter. I realized, thanks to his complaints and 'swift' turn around, that fileting a mostly invisible fish might make things quite difficult.

Smegma saw the problem too because he said, "It will become visible as its Mana drains."

Five minutes later, I was staring at a fish that easily was the size of my mother's rusty two-seater.

Dave stood beside me, transferring his gaze between it, the fileting Knife and me. "First, how in the husk did you pull *that* out of the water?"

He didn't wait for a response before he held up the somewhat repaired Knife and continued, "And how the hell am I supposed to filet an eight-foot fish with a six-inch knife?"

Smegma, thankfully, answered the second question, "If you knew how to tie the Knife to your *Mana,* it would get longer to suit your needs. *Dimwitted student.*"

"And *how* can Brodie pull a fish that husking size out of a lake?" Dave asked, ignoring the Demon's chastisement.

"I guess I should probably tell you about my Strength Stats growth," I said sheepishly.

Dave's eyes grew wide and he pointed the semi-dull knife at me menacingly. "You probably *should* tell me, and anything else you might not have thought was important!"

I chuckled, which caused Dave to lower the knife and join me in laughing. After a moment, he motioned at the fish, "At least we might only need one of these things a day!"

"Yeah, but how are we going to cook it?" I asked.

Dave hiked a finger over his shoulder. "There are some forges back there, right? Now, about this Stat growth! I'm guessing it's growing like crazy?"

I started explaining how the same way I unlocked it, was how it grew, and even pulled up my Stat screen. To my disappointment, my Strength was still at ten points.

"Wait, you pulled out *that*," Dave said, pointing at the large four-hundred-pound fish, "with *ten* points in Strength?"

I shrugged, breathing on my knuckles and rubbing them on my chest. "Well, that shouldn't be surprising. Aren't I ten times stronger—?"

"The shit! That's not how that works," Dave and Smegma said at the same exact time. They both looked at each other. Nodding, Dave gestured magnanimously to Smegma.

Smegma turned back toward me, frowning. "Who told you that Stats are straight multiplicative?"

My mouth worked like a fish out of water, which I put a stop to thanks to the *dead fish* in front of me. Smegma had never suggested that they were or weren't multiplicative. In fact, I had no idea where I'd gotten that idea. Clearly,

I'd just assumed something, and Smegma either hadn't heard my internal thoughts on the matter or had never bothered to correct me.

Dave smiled, seeming to relish in knowing something that I had assumed *incorrectly*. "You actually thought Gamonji was tens of thousands of times stronger than a normal human?"

I glared. Mostly because I *had* thought that.

"Dude, did you never watch the Monster Hunters of Our Generation documentary?" Dave looked at me sadly. "They actually experimented with Hunters and Stats before discovering it's straight logarithmic until Breakthroughs. It's a"—Dave saw my falling face and interpreted my mood—"Forget about it. Let's just talk about your cool Stat, Bro. Tell me all about it."

"Wait. Hey! Don't change the subject!" I glared, indignant. "You watch *one* movie, or *clips* from it, that I haven't seen, and suddenly you're acting like an expert? Do you even know what logarithmic means?" I glared at Dave, hoping my poor insult would somehow phase him. It didn't. I transferred my glare to Smegma. "And *you* told me you didn't know how Stats worked when I asked!"

"It's husking obvious you aren't ten times stronger, though," Smegma answered matter-of-factly. "Yes, you fought against a four-hundred-pound fish, but only because of your Mana and the Fishing Rod's Enchantments…"

Dave put a comforting hand on my shoulder but accidentally leaned a great deal of his weight on me, most likely due to his body's soreness. "Shhh. It's okay, man. We're all friends here, and it's our job to elevate the lowest members of our group to our intellectual average. You know, so they don't get left behind. Don't think about it too much. Tell your ol' buddy here all about when you grew your sweet, new Stat and why you think it's stuck at ten."

I gave Dave a playful elbow to the stomach, and he groaned like I had just hit him with everything I had. He did stop leaning on me, which let me fold my arms and glare at the two idiots in front of me. The silence stretched out for an uncomfortably long time before I unfolded my arms and gave up.

"So, the first time I ever really noticed that I might be *ten times* stronger than *normal* weak and pathetic humans, like Dave over here, was when this big-ass Golem formed in the room we were Mining in…" I saw Dave, still somewhat doubled over, roll his eyes, even as Smegma snickered.

CHAPTER 9: CHAPTER 61

Saturday, April 27th, 2069

"Wait—you pulled these out of that lake?" my dad asked skeptically. I sighed and told the story I'd shared with Dave, again.

After the first Fish, Dave had directed me on how to filet a fish, while Smegma coached me on how to use my Mana Pool to create a lengthened blue ephemeral blade. While the Mana did 'lengthen' the fileting Knife, it did nothing to sharpen the edge or keep it sharpened. I thought back to the description of the item and remembered that it had a 'one' next to the item name, similar to our Pickaxes. I hoped that meant that the Rod and Knife could level, and more importantly, that leveling meant this damned thing might actually gain a usable edge. As it was right now, I felt like a caveman trying to invent fire.

Smegma seemed confused by that, but didn't speculate on why the Mana couldn't sharpen or Strengthen the blade. Either way, that first had taken almost an hour to gut, skin and parcel out.

After that, I had discovered just how lucky I had been on the first catch. Dave had been right that we likely only needed to catch a single a day, but having a few as backup—and maybe even a full one to give to Jarred—would be helpful. Not to mention the effects that catching more would have on the Rod and Knife, since they were a package deal. However, multiple times in a row, the Mirror Fish out in the lake, or possibly some other creature, had made away with the bait— meaning it had eaten my Mana.

The first time it happened, I almost vomited, reminded of the unwanted Mana Connection by Morgan. However, the sensations were different. Whatever took the 'bait' seemed to suck the Mana down the conduit I'd connected to the rod. Feeling aptly like a pop drink being drawn up a straw, which was still my visual aid for directing Mana. If I realized it was happening fast enough, I could either cut off the Mana or give the Rod a yank to attempt to snag the creature doing the sucking.

The problem was that instead of snagging a catch, more often than not I just lost about ten points of Mana, and since I didn't want to try another epic fight against a four-hundred-plus-pound without a full Mana Pool, this forced me to wait for my Mana to recharge. Thankfully, the Mana Apple was reducing my downtime.

Still, I'd only managed to catch four of the Mirror Fish and taken the time to filet three of them. A single one, I'd dragged back.

"Why not you just put dat in your Necklace of Holdin'?" Willa asked.

"The space inside is just five by five by five feet. It might have fit, if folded right, or on the angle, but look—" I pulled out a piece of frozen steak. "The

Necklace seems to freeze things inside. I don't think we want to try to clean a frozen Fish of that size."

I stared at the smallest of the four Mirror Fish I'd caught. It was probably six or seven feet long and not quite as round in the belly as the others. It hadn't been easy to drag the thing to the nearest room with a 'forge.' Actually, my heart was still beating fast from that, as well as my jog up to the cavern to collect the Mined Crystals and the two doing the Mining.

Now, we had the recessed portion of the smithy filled with Crystals and were ready to start cooking—after I answered some shocked questions from Willa and my dad, of course.

"So, you be havin' Stats like dem Hunters?" Willa asked, her voice a mix of skepticism and excitement. I simply motioned to the car-sized sea Monster that had become visible, and she whooped loudly, losing the skepticism.

My dad licked his lips, looking nervous, but eventually nodded to Smegma, of all people, and asked, "Can we eat these?"

Smegma nodded. "They taste fantastic, and if prepared properly, can even give a boost to Endurance recover—oh wait, I forgot you don't have that. They can be eaten, yes!"

"Okay, let's figure out how to cook them," I said, motioning at the pit, the Crystals inside, and then the large pile of thawing, skinned and portioned sections of the tuna-like steaks. I should probably put a huge amount of those back into my Necklace. I'd only emptied them to make sure I had room for the Crystals. However, looking at the pile of steaks, I had room for both.

Not to mention I planned to sell the Crystals we didn't use.

This was the real reason I wanted everyone here. I had no idea how to get started in burning Crystals. Unfortunately, from the lost looks of Willa and my dad, they didn't either.

"Well, obviously we have to light the Crystals," my dad offered.

Since we'd just had a similar conversation, I looked at the hunched and elderly looking Dave, obviously tender from the abuses an entire day of Mining had put on his body. Dave managed a smirk and answered the same way he had when I'd said that. "Perfect. Give me your lighter."

My dad and Willa looked at each other. Then they looked back to me, Dave, and then Smegma. "Don't tell me that none of us have fire?"

"Bunch of husking noobs! Who enters a Portal without an Adventuring Kit?"

"Oh, so that should mean you must have one for sale, like that rope I asked about earlier, *right?*" I said to the Demon, not in the mood to put up with his shit. He stared at me and raised both three-fingered hands to give me a shrug. "So, we have food, Crystals to burn, but no way to light it?"

"Maybe da forge be havin' an auto light like dem barbeques?" Willa suggested.

"Right, cause that would still be work—" my dad started to answer but stopped when Smegma began floating around the device. In moments, everyone had joined him, studying the gray-black stone in close detail.

It took an entire minute before I realized something was wrong. It took me another minute to find Smegma no longer hovering around the space, and instead watching us all like the idiots we were. I stood up and pointed at him. "You're a dick."

"Well, it was a stupid suggestion," Smegma retorted, which got everyone to stop looking and stare at him. "Anyone have anything of *value* to try?"

I could tell by the looks Smegma was getting that people were torn between liking his joke and attempting to punch him in the face. I knew the feeling well. Still, Dave, now supporting his hunched frame on the pedestal, was the one who attempted to move toward Smegma.

Unfortunately, the pedal for stoking the fire was between him and the Demon, and he wasn't exactly graceful at the moment. His foot caught on the pedal's underside, and he instantly tripped, collapsing over it. His knee landed on the pedal, which caused it to depress. Along with the falling pedal came the sound of a mechanical gear cranking, even as air rushed out of the lower of the two hanging hollow tubes.

To everyone's surprise—but none more so than Smegma—at the bottom of the pedal, a second, far louder clank sounded, and a blue spark became visible in the center of the recess. The spark merged with the blue of the Mana Crystals, and the ones in the center started to change color, going from blue to an orangey-brown.

The wave of heat made it clear that Dave had just lit the Mana Crystals. If that weren't enough, his cry of pain and groaning agony from the floor confirmed he'd hit the pedal, and that he needed help. By the time I helped him back to his feet, the entire recess was alight and radiating heat.

Dave looked at the Mana Crystals, the pedal, and then sneered at Smegma. "A dumb idea, was it?" he said scathingly.

"It *was* a dumb idea—the fact that the mechanical device still worked is actually beyond impressive," Smegma answered, but I could tell by his lack of volume and derisiveness that he was embarrassed. He further muttered, "They must have Enchanted it…"

He flipped me the husking bird when he heard my surface thoughts, confirming his embarrassment. Then he instantly sobered the excited room. "So, who has the cookware?"

He started laughing a moment later as everyone's heads fell. This time, though, he did send me a red Shop Window, even as he muttered, "Husking morons."

Miscellaneous Professions Gear

Huge Frying Pan (1)
Low F-Rank
Durability: Unlimited
Damage: 0-1

This Huge Frying Pan has a self-repair and maintenance Enchantment along with some other inactive options, which will

activate upon leveling up. It will also Funnel excess Mana from fire and food to Brodie Flacarada's Overdraft Skill.

Cost: 30,000 mC

I sighed, even as I confirmed the purchase with the Demon. That brought my total to about eighty thousand Mana Coins, with perhaps five to ten thousand in Crystals to sell after cooking the steaks. That number, of course, depended on how many Crystals we would need to burn to cook all of this.

This time, what fell out of the blue light from the Shop purchase was large enough that I dodged out of the way. A dark black, crusty Frying Pan, four feet across, bounced loudly off the floor, creating a dent in itself and not the tile. I stared at the disgusting-looking cooking instrument.

I looked around the room and saw everyone else staring at it as well.

It was my dad who spoke up first. "He's supposed to cook *food* in that lump of carbon. You actually expect us to eat something cooked in that?"

Smegma scoffed. "Sure, it looks like it's rusted and crusty but just think of it as seasoning."

"That's not seasoning," Dave said pointedly.

"My mother would be smackin' me with a sandal if I be cookin' in dat!" Willa exclaimed.

"Brodie, put it atop the Crystals," Smegma directed as he sighed helplessly. With narrowed eyes, I lifted the thing and placed it as directed. It didn't cover the entire recess but easily occluded the burning Crystals in the center.

"Now place some of the Fish inside," Smegma directed.

Willa, Dave and my father twitched toward a space between me and the cuts of Fish. I hadn't moved, so the gesture was pointless.

Smegma gave me a withering look. "You can either leave it there and keep feeding Crystals into the fire to have it slowly repaired. Or you can cook some of the easily caught Fish and have it repaired faster."

"Easy?" I responded. "That took me all morning!"

Smegma just stared at me. "Right, and one Fish could feed you all for multiple days. You kept Fishing to repair the Rod and have *some* Fish as backup. You've husking got four! Stop being a miser and get some Fish steaks."

Everyone seemed chastised after Smegma's rebuke, and no one moved to stop me as I picked up multiple pieces of the portioned Fish.

As soon as the meat hit the Pan, I felt my mouth start to water. The sound of the searing Fish was accompanied by a smell that was nearly impossible for me to describe. It was like I'd walked into an expensive restaurant that specialized in old-world dishes.

Specialized was too mild a word. That had *perfected* old-world dishes. There was a rich aroma that reminded me of seafood—maybe farmed lobster? Or crab? Then there were overtones of beef steaks I had only had the pleasure of seeing from afar.

Dave wiped at his mouth with a sleeve, even as I felt my own saliva threaten to spill out. My father and Willa stared dumbly at the Pan, seeming torn between snatching the meat out to eat now, and simultaneously disgusted by the fact that a Pan that crusty could produce these wonderful aromas.

"You should flip them in the next thirty seconds or so," Smegma directed. I looked around and realized I had no spatula or tongs. So, I pulled the fileting Knife out of my Necklace of Holding and used it to stab and then manipulate the Fish steaks onto their other sides.

The smell and noise of cooking intensified. Again, with Smegma's direction, I managed to pull the Fish off the grill at the appropriate time. Unfortunately, the 'seasoning' of the Frying Pan had come off with the first batch of Fish. Which made me choose to just drop these pieces onto the cave floor.

"What are you doing?" Smegma asked.

"I'm not letting anyone eat rusty, carbon-covered Fish," I answered, pointing out what was obvious to me.

"You husking morons and your hang ups from before the System. Sure, it might not taste as good, but it won't kill you," Smegma retorted.

"You just told me to stop being a miser," I retorted while pointing to the huge pile of uncooked Fish steaks. "Are you going to keep acting like an old man whose views change with the wind?"

Smegma made a face but did look between the pile of portioned Fish and the ones on the floor. "Fine, whatever, but at least throw them into the lake after, like you did with the carcasses."

After ten rounds of Fish steaks in the Frying Pan, it was finally cleared of the rust and most of the carbonized deposits. While it didn't look *exquisite*, it also didn't look like a Health Department's worst nightmare.

"Dave, can you toss these *disgusting* Pan-crusted Fish steaks into the Lake? They're garbage—"

"They are not—" Smegma began as Dave moved to do as instructed.

"Yeah, look at all this disgusting charring. Ughh, only a Demon with no taste buds would eat this shit," Dave said, causing the group to chuckle even as the smell of the Fish caused them to continue to salivate.

"Husking waste, of both Crystals and Mirror Fish," Smegma complained.

"Oh, you know what? Since Smegma thinks they're valuable, I'll just sell them to the *Demonic Vault* Shop," I said pointedly, bending down to touch one of them. Nothing happened, which is what I'd expected. I'd tried selling an uncooked one before and had managed it. So, clearly, this 'cooked' version was inferior.

"Totally worthless, really," Smegma said with an uncomfortable cough. I shook my head, and Dave chuckled as he began taking out the *unappetizing* steaks in stacks toward the Lake.

At this point, we had about half of the original pile of steaks, if I counted the whole Fish still on the floor. We also ran into an issue...

The problem was where I could put the 'good' cooked meat. After some quick thinking, and one... *small* mistake, I managed to get the remaining pieces into the greenhouse and on the lab table.

It turned out that putting freshly cooked food into my Necklace of Holding flash-froze it, or close enough, because even that short walk to the lab table had them coming out with the same consistency as frozen ice bricks. This surprised me since the Pickaxe didn't freeze in there.

[Enchantments, and the non-living component, are keeping it from changing, but if you want to put that shitty gear you're wearing inside—] Smegma mentally sent.

I heard a mental chuckle and realized that the gear wouldn't be worth much until it thawed if it went inside. That was if it came out the same as it went in, after freezing solid.

So, while the Necklace of Holding might be a good idea for storing the cooked fish-steaks for Jarred, or the raw for cooking later—it wasn't a great plan if we were thinking of eating any now. Instead, I managed to balance the thick steaks on the Knife's side and rush them into the adjacent chamber.

I could tell at this point that the others were torn between going to that room to stuff their faces and sticking around to continue smelling the cooking Fish. Seeing everyone's reaction brought my own craving for food to mind, so I asked Smegma, "If the Mana Apples satiated all our hunger, why am I starving right now?"

"They can satiate your need for nutrients, but not your 'hunger.' The Apples are magical in nature and derive their nutrition not through calories or true minerals. Think of it like that show Brown's Anatomy. It's essentially a magical IV. It'll keep you alive, but it's not exactly food. Similarly, when your body needs something, Mana creates it in your bloodstream, but only if your body is already looking for it. So, your empty stomachs are still going to scream at you to fill them."

"So, if we be eatin' more, we ain't goin' to be suddenly gettin' fat 'cause the Apple be doublin' our caloric intake?" Willa asked.

Smegma shook his head, and just like that, she was through the doorway to the lab table at a near sprint. My father followed suit. I growled jealously as I looked at the Frying Pan and the Fish. If I went to eat now, it would waste some of the Mana Crystals currently burning. Dave ended up being the last to join the others because of his final trip to the lake, but he didn't take long to follow after them once he'd returned and heard the cooked steaks were in the other room.

Dutifully, I grabbed more steaks and put it into the Pan, planning to keep one of this batch here for myself. At least Smegma—

I looked around and found that the Demon was gone too. Mentally, I shouted, [Get your ass back in here. You can't eat food anyway.]

Smegma didn't return and so I angrily added, [I need your direction so I don't husking burn them.]

Mentally, I got back, [Three minutes a side. These three are really going to town!]

I accidentally ruined one of the currently cooking Mirror Fish steaks, stabbing it a little too viciously.

CHAPTER 10: CHAPTER 62

Saturday, April 27th, 2069

Endurance Pool—error.

Endurance Pool does not exist, unable to apply buff to [Locked] Regeneration.

Staring at the *Demonic Vault's* red screen, I tried to focus on it, but my mind was currently occupied with categorizing the incredible flavors playing over my tongue. The smell of the cooking Mirror Fish didn't do the taste juices–*I mean justice.*

Normally, the texture would have caused me pause since it literally didn't require chewing. Instead, the tenderness of the Fish could be pressed with my tongue and practically melt. Melt because eating the Fish this way released so much 'juice' or 'blood' or 'husking fantastic flavor' that my mind felt confused. How could it feel like a mouthful of the juices came from a tiny forkful?

I didn't have the ability to compare the tastes to anything I had ever eaten. I'd only experienced this palate-shattering moment once before. One time, relatively early in my budding attempts to become a Mana Bank to the Stars, I'd attended a meet and greet with some 'up and comers.' It took place at a restaurant I could never even hope to make a reservation at, let alone eat an entrée from. The price for an hour-long time slot was a thousand dollars, at least for people like me. The few canapes I had managed to snag from the server trays while trying to stand out from the crowd had been the best food I'd ever tried.

Those canapes were canned Spaamm when compared to unseasoned Mirror Fish.

[*Not* unseasoned,] Smegma mentally argued, clearly picking up on my surface thoughts. [I told you. The Pan is plenty seasoned.]

I rolled my eyes, still thinking about how delicious the Fish was. Part of me wondered what a trained chef could do with meat of this quality. I only managed to stop my thoughts from focusing on the flavors when I'd finished eating my current steak, and even then, I hungrily eyed the other cooked pieces.

How many of them could I fit in my belly without dying?

"You need to cook the rest and take some to Jarred," Smegma interrupted, having returned from the other room unnoticed.

He startled me out of my hyper-focus and I checked the doorway, wondering where everyone was.

"They're eating that entire batch of Fish steaks. My guess is that they are going to pass out right afterward."

"Pass out?" I asked, not understanding how food could cause people to fall asleep.

"Take a moment and let the food settle in your stomach. You'll understand."

As instructed, I took a moment and placed a few more fish into the Huge Frying Pan. Only after the first flip did I feel what Smegma was talking about. It was like someone had placed a refreshingly warm and heavy lead weight in my stomach. Part of me wanted to sit down and relax into the sensation. I closed my eyes as a contented smile rose onto my face.

"Dumb-dumb!" Smegma shouted from right beside me, startling me enough that my eyes flew open.

I realized I was halfway to easing myself to the floor.

"You need to take that Fish out of the Pan in forty-seven seconds. So, no sleeping!"

Sweat broke out on my forehead as I managed to straighten my legs and stop myself from focusing on the comforting sensations coming from my abdomen. I only managed to stay standing thanks to my hands bracing me on the side of the stone pedestal. As I fought my own body, I asked, "What in the hell is going on?"

"The Mirror Fish is one of the most nutrient-dense foods that Crendalar ever found and studied—especially in the F to D-Ranks. A single filet can provide a creature with enough macronutrients to force your body to send almost all available blood to work on digestion. It has Protein, Ecklam, Fats, Maordana, Sucrites, Peptilsaurides, and Carbohydrates. Basically, your stomach is working overtime to break down hundreds of milligrams of each of those."

"Was that English?" I asked, and seeing Smegma's confused face, I explained, "I've only ever heard of Proteins, Fats, and Carbohydrates. What in the hell were those other things?"

"I'm actually not surprised your backward-ass race doesn't know about Ecklam, Maordana, Sucrites and Peptilsaurides. They are nutrients that supposedly came with the System and Monsters. We couldn't figure out exactly how they originated but assumed it had to do with Stamina, Mana and Force Pools, and the effect of those insubstantial powers on plants and bodies. Either way, they are known to help replenish your Pools a bit faster, but mostly to increase your Awakened Potential…"

"So, Portal foods have an effect on Awakening?" I asked, shocked that Smegma might have just settled a debate Earth had been having for years. Even my family and I had discussed it over dinner.

"Yes, no, maybe?" Smegma said, oscillating his hand. "What we know for certain is that eating Monsters helps acclimatize children to Mana, Force and Stamina. Since you don't have those—" Smegma shrugged. "Regardless, Mirror Fish is one of the densest foods in those nutrients that you can find in the D-Ranks and lower."

"Husk!" I swore, even as I started to win that internal war against soporific sleep with my own body. Knowing why I felt an intense desire to fall asleep went a long way to helping me in that struggle. Maybe even *Mental Fortitude* played a part, as my brain began overriding my stomach's desire to nap. I pulled the currently cooking Fish from the Pan and studied the cooking instrument.

It already looked markedly improved. The dent from it falling to the floor was no longer visible, and while there were still a few dark black patches of 'crust' in the Pan, a great deal of the bottom shone like it was seasoned cast iron.

I looked at the pile of food—no, the insanely valuable gold mine of food we'd stumbled upon. While Smegma couldn't guarantee that it increased our Awakened Potential—his people had still valued this Fish as the *best* ingredient up to D-Rank. I smiled. Maybe I could get out of here with a huge stack of the stuff…

I assumed that the race that had lived in the Complex had intentionally stocked the Fish here, since it was right beside their home.

Before starting the next batch, I did check in on the other three. I found each one in a different 'comfortable' position, but all of them were napping.

How could I be sure?

Dave had Mirror Fish oil smeared across his chin and cheeks, his back against the lab table, and was snoring softly. Willa was somehow planted face first into the table, her front and face resting in remnants of the food, and while she wasn't snoring, her tongue was lolling out—like she'd passed out in the process of licking juices from the surface. My father was snoring the loudest by far but was also the 'cleanest' of the three. He didn't have any Fish oil on him, and also hadn't fallen asleep in what I would deem an uncomfortable position. No, he had climbed into one of the grow beds and had passed out atop the weeds and soil.

To further distract myself, I returned my attention to the notice that *Demonic Vault* had sent me as I returned to cooking the remaining steaks. "Smegma, *Demonic Vault* tried to notify me of a buff to Endurance Pool but created an Error. Did you see it?"

"I did," Smegma answered. "From the wording, there is a resource Pool that may be similar to Endurance but not the same. I can't even guess what the System has done to change it, though." Smegma finished with an open-palmed shrug.

"Can you explain how your Endurance Pool could be used?" I asked, curious as to how it differed from Mana and what this [Locked] Pool might be capable of.

"Finish cooking and fileting that last Fish. We can talk on the way to get Jarred."

* * *

As soon as we entered the cave halls that led to the first caverns, toward the cave-in, I repeated my question eagerly.

"Okay, okay!" Smegma answered like an annoyed parent. "Endurance had a huge number of uses. It could instantly supercharge the user physically, making the individual twice as strong, fast or accurate. Over time those increases accumulated and became more permanent. It could be pushed into a weapon, increasing the things' durability, damage and destructiveness when released. Some experts could use it to power Skills in place of Mana, but only if those Skills were physical in nature. Like a Bow Skill or Sword Skill.

"We ran some studies on those Demons and discovered that not only was it more efficient to use Endurance, it also jumped the Skills' level by a letter tier or more. Endurance was a strange Pool, in that it was always on a value of a hundred points and didn't grow—but higher ranked individuals with more points in it could do more with a single point of their Pool than a newbie could do with all one hundred. If that makes sense?"

"So, it was a power that could be concentrated?" I clarified.

"Yes and no," Smegma said. "That was our first hypothesis, but we dismissed it eventually. It was more like it could Evolve and rank up. Like it was a Skill and had grades. It was also tied to the physical world—unlike Mana, which we determined was tied to the soul."

"What about the last Pool you mentioned, what was it again? Force?"

"Look at you listening and remembering stuff!" Smegma said condescendingly. "Force was something intangible. Like Mana, it could be considered a power that came from the soul but was affected by what we hypothesized was the intentions of the Mind. Force was a power that existed all around us but could be manipulated by the Pool we had.

"How it could be manipulated was drastically different for each person. That part I've already told you. In addition to that, my research team couldn't figure out where this Pool resided, nor could we truly confirm it was affected by intentions of the Mind. The only conclusion we reached was that it had to be felt and intrinsically understood by the wielder. Our best guess was that it was like 'muscle memory.'"

At the end of Smegma's explanation, we were nearing the final chambers before the 'entrance.' With a sigh at the lack of 'new, usable' information, I stopped walking. Turning to Smegma, I asked, "Can you make yourself invisible for this next part?"

I felt bad asking, right up until he answered, "Way ahead of you, Brodie."

I'll admit, it took me a few extra seconds to get my feet to take another step toward where I knew Jarred would be. I'd known the man my entire life, but I wasn't exactly a fan of his decision to return to the entrance because of Smegma's appearance. Sure, the Demon was terrifying, annoying and verbally abusive, but—

I realized I didn't have a true reason for why I trusted the Imp turned human-sized Demon. All I could say was that, through all of his actions, he'd proven to me that he was at the very least here to help me. The fact that Jarred, firstly, didn't trust me enough to take my word on that, and secondly, didn't give an intelligent creature the chance to prove itself, didn't speak well for him.

Still, he was my Uncle, and from what I'd recently learned, had gone through a lot—was *still* going through a lot...

I walked through two more caverns before I found Jarred. The first thing I noticed was the stack of rocks that had clearly been moved away from the entrance. The next thing I made note of was where Jarred was. He'd climbed the cave-in and was attempting to roll some of the bigger chunks of stone off the pile. The man looked alien due to the gray stone dust clinging to his gleaming, sweat-covered skin.

It was like someone had painted him gray and peppered his hair and clothes with a textured paint. He noticed me entering the room and stopped pushing at a stone easily the size of himself. Between large intakes and exhalations of air, he managed to ask, "No Demon with you today?"

"He can never go farther than a hundred yards from me," I answered and then continued before Jarred could react negatively. "We discovered a safe place to sleep, and it has a *freshwater* lake with Fish. I came to get you to come back with me."

Jarred shook his head sadly. "While you're all down there sleeping and hiding, I'm clearing this cave in. If I had more people—" he said as he placed both feet on the stone and heaved with an accompanying weightlifter's grunt. "We could probably be out of here—"

What he was saying got drowned out when the stone seemed to jump free. The accompanying rockslide easily covered up his words but didn't manage to override a human shriek that rose in the center of the cacophony.

Before the stone and dust settled, my heart was already racing, and I was moving. Smegma clearly had gotten the jump on me because he shouted, "Over here!"

With the newly kicked up dust, it took me a few moments to locate the winged shadow, but when I did, I sprinted to his side. I saw a leg with worn Miner boots and ripped cargo pants sticking out of a pile of fist-sized stones. It wasn't moving.

I began clearing the stone by hand but quickly realized that it was deep, and Jarred's body was buried vertically. I'd seen documentaries where Hunters got stuck in avalanches and mudslides during missions. One thing they always harped on was not to pull the person out by a limb.

You just couldn't know the state of the person's body. So to yank with superhuman power on a broken limb or a pinned body part—could cause worse injuries. *Still, it's either pull on the leg or risk letting him suffocate.* Smegma gave me a nod, confirming his agreement.

I had exposed Jarred's pelvis a bit and chose to pull him free from there instead of the leg. It took another couple of seconds of clearing to get a grip, but thankfully, he easily came free with one Strength-assisted heave.

Where he'd been glistening before, he was now caked in stone dust and chips, looking more like a Golem than a human. I carried him away from the still-shifting stones and gingerly placed him down, only to discover he wasn't breathing.

My mind screamed at me to start CPR, but *Mental Fortitude* came to my aid and reminded me to clear his airway. Opening his mouth, I found it full of stones and dust. I ran my finger around inside of it and even pulled a great deal out from his nostrils. Only when I had his mouth and nose relatively clear did I start CPR.

It had been a very long time since I'd learned the technique in high school, which made me start off tentative and slow. Still, parts of the teacher's instructions came back to me as I worked. Move to the beat of the popular song 'Staying Alive.' Check. I hadn't checked for a pulse before starting. There wasn't one. Plug nose and give rescue breaths. Only two. Check.

Reassess. Still not breathing. Pulse. None. Chest compressions. Rescue breaths.

Check for—

A cloud of wet stone dust rocketed into my ear as Jarred coughed out a cloud of the stuff. I flinched but immediately celebrated as well. Smegma had watched the interaction quietly but now sent over a red screen.

Miscellaneous Potions

Weak Healing Concoction
Low F-Rank
Durability: 1 Use
Heals: 30 Health Points

This mix of herbs, fruits and liquids will stimulate the body of the imbiber to heal itself at an increased rate. Warning: This increase in healing factors will cannibalize the body if insufficient nutrients are not available.

Cost: 100,000 mC

I frowned at the screen, knowing my current total of Mana Coins was under a hundred thousand.. I sold the Mana Crystals in my Necklace of Holding. Still not seeing enough of a balance, I looked to Smegma helplessly. I could hear the wheeze and rattle from Jarred that likely made Smegma send this over.

"Sell the Fish!" Smegma suggested. I nodded hurriedly and watched as the total for Mana Coins climbed to ninety-nine thousand. I was about to start swearing when I saw Jarred's Mining Pick leaning against a nearby wall.

"Can I sell that back?" I asked.

Smegma grimaced but nodded. I rushed over and sold it, realizing why Smegma was grimacing. I only got twenty-five hundred mC for it. Despite the fact that it was purchased at ten thousand and had repaired itself significantly.

"Are you certain you wish to buy Weak Healing Concoction?" Smegma intoned.

"Yes!" I shouted as I rushed back to Jarred. His breathing was becoming shallow and fast. The bottle fell from the Mana Cloud, and I was twisting off its lid and pouring before the sloshing pinkish water had even settled.

Jarred sputtered, and I began to massage his throat and Adam's apple. Thankfully, he swallowed, once, twice and a third time, emptying the bottle. I didn't know how much 'thirty points' of Health would help, but it wasn't like I could have gotten anything more.

I held my breath, listening and hoping for a change in Jarred's struggling breaths. For a terrifying moment, it got worse. Then he coughed and coughed again. Gray sludge began to foam out of his mouth. I leaped forward and turned him onto his side, even as I continually cleared his mouth and nose, which also ejected bloody gray stone dust.

Finally, when I thought my heart was going to burst, Jarred stopped coughing, spitting, and took in a deep breath—before sighing and starting to breathe normally. Or at least, much more normally than he had before. I sat back on my heels for just a moment before deciding I would carry him back to the group.

He could yell at me later, when and if he woke up.

Smegma floated beside me silently as I slung Jarred up into a princess carry and began walking. Whether it was due to the adrenaline of what had just happened, or my Strength Stat, it felt like my Uncle weighed nothing.

"How come the Fish gave me so few mC?" I asked, too mentally exhausted from the excitement and terrifying fear from just moments before for it to come out as more than a whisper.

"You did nothing to increase the meat's value, even though it was all cooked. If a real chef got a hold of the Fish, and had proper ingredients, they could probably have made each steak worth ten times what *Demonic Vault* paid you. But, honestly, the Fish might have been worth more raw since you couldn't even season it with salt."

That caused me to blink, and after a moment, nod in confirmation. I probably should just be happy I had nearly eight hundred pounds of Fish *to sell*. Otherwise, uncle Jarred would probably be dead.

Everyone was still napping when I returned, so I first took Jarred down to the Lake and attempted to wash off the crusting stone dust as best I could. The stuff looked like concrete that was setting. Once he looked a bit more human, and had less of a chance of inhaling more caked-on stones from around his mouth and nose, I returned to the greenhouse and laid him down atop one of the planter boxes and its weeds.

Then, and only then, did I collapse onto my butt, sliding my back down the planter box. Smegma stared at me worriedly before he came to join me.

"That was impressive—" he began but then froze as a red screen popped into existence.

Class Awarding Feat Achieved!

Class Available:
Common Rank: Healer

You have used your knowledge of the human body, potions and hard work to save someone's life. You can now select the Healer Class.

Healers are granted two Skills:
Minor Heal (1) - F-Rank
Weak Cleanse (1) - F-Rank

No Stats are unlocked or increased by the Healer Class.

CHAPTER 11: CHAPTER 63

Saturday, April 27th, 2069

I blinked at the screen and then spun on Smegma. "*Healing* Skills are some of the rarest ones humans ever get!"

Smegma stared at the screen like it had just insulted his mother, or whoever he cared about with the same level a human loved theirs. The look he wore was so hateful it caused me to scan the screen again. And then after another glance at Smegma, where I saw his teeth bared, another perusal.

"What?" I finally asked.

"*Common* Healer?! This is Felhound Shit!" Smegma growled. Blinking, I read the Class title again. Eventually, I gave him a look that conveyed my continued confusion. "Common, Brodie, husking common. Look, the very fact that it mentions Stats tells you that there are Classes that not only unlock other Stats but *raise* them!"

"Okay," I said slowly, letting the 'y' draw out. "Still, you were the one who said that the terms and conditions said I could change Classes. Maybe I can even Evolve it?"

Smegma scoffed and looked away, conveying that he was still disgusted by the choice. However, I got the distinct impression he might have forgotten about the *Class* sub-Skill letting him change selections later.

I shook off the tangent and hurried to accept the Class, recalling that Jarred could likely use some *Minor Healing*. When I clicked accept, I felt something begin stirring inside of me—no—in my Mental Universe. It took me steadying my breathing to be able to enter that space, but when I did, what I found was the ring around the Saturn-like planet spinning at an ever-increasing pace.

As it rotated faster, the color of the gold planet beneath began to go from a striated gold to yellow, and finally—emerald with flecks of yellow. The ring itself began to change as well. I watched, fascinated as I tried to distinguish what I was seeing. Had the ring become thicker?

It was impossible to understand what had happened to the ring until the rotation—no until the *orbit* of the two verdant *moons* slowed enough that the afterimages resolved and removed the illusion of rings. Where the *Classes* sub-Skill was an emerald planet orbiting the 'sun' of *Demonic Vault*, these two verdant 'moons' orbited the planet.

The planet's emerald color faded from rich to luscious grass and then to a plain green as the moons continued to drop in speed. Finally, the planet became a tan or beige that was distinctly unimpressive when compared to its earlier bright emerald.

Staring at the moons and the planet immediately brought an issue to mind. *I want to use Minor Heal on Jarred—but which one of the two is it, and which one is Cleanse?*

Smegma must have been watching as well, and heard my commentary, because he coughed pointedly. Then, in his snootiest voice, he said, "I've been meaning to talk to you about this, but you never had multiple Skills that needed Mana. Finally, you've grown enough to create your Mana Nervous System…"

Exiting my Mental Universe, I found the Demon with his arms crossed and his wings spread wide. He even went as far as to look over the bridge of his nose at me. I licked my teeth and rolled my eyes.

"I'm guessing that the 'Mana Nervous System' has something to do with supplying Mana to Skills in a more efficient way than *your* stupid 'Straw' method…" I said dryly, making sure to highlight who had taught me the flawed method in the first place.

"You wouldn't have been ready to create a Mana Nervous System if you didn't at least understand the concept of creating conduits to Skills," Smegma said confidently. However, his nose dropped and he uncrossed his arms, so I counted his attitude change as a minor victory.

"Okay, oh-glorious-one, what is a Mana Nervous System and how do I create one?" I asked when Smegma had stopped speaking, and the silence became unbearable.

"Well, I've seen that you humans have a grasp of your Central Nervous Systems and Peripheral Nervous Systems—so, for simplicity's sake, you can think of it like that. But instead of starting with a series of 'nerves' in place and shearing off connections to make them more efficient, you must grow the Mana Nervous System and form pathways that you intrinsically understand. Then, when you want to send Mana to *Demonic Vault*, for example, it's kind of like picking up that piece of Fish." He made a gesture with his own three-fingered hand and it passed through a small morsel of cooked Fish that Dave apparently hadn't finished eating.

My head bobbed in acknowledgment, understanding the concept, but waiting for Smegma to describe how I would 'grow' a Mana Nervous System. He, of course, didn't elaborate, which forced me to verbally encourage him. "And how do I grow one?"

"Thought you'd never ask," Smegma said smugly.

I clenched my jaw, knowing he could read my surface thoughts, which should have removed the need for me to ask.

"Simply start at your Mana Pool, then envision a conduit—similar to the 'straw' but permanent and protected. You humans understand the sheaths that surround nerves, right?"

I personally didn't understand them, but high school gym class had talked about them briefly. Myelinated? No Michelin? Whatever. It was a sheath that helped not only protect the nerves but also increase signal speed. I nodded and watched as Smegma smirked at my internal dialogue.

Husker!

Still, my last thought made me ask, "So, can I send Mana faster if I create conduits that are insulated?"

Smegma gave me some odd-looking finger-guns in confirmation. I raised an eyebrow and stared at the strange, sexual-looking gesture. Chuckling, I asked, "What the hell is that?"

"Don't you need to hurry so you can heal Jarred?" Smegma retorted as the red decals on his face noticeably darkened.

I would have relished the moment more, but he was right. I fell into myself and moved toward my Mana Pool. Beginning with the Straw I was familiar with seemed like the most appropriate starting point, so I envisioned it.

"Make it smaller," Smegma coached. "Part of the reason you can't make permanent connections is that a large Straw construct currently takes up most of your capacity. Since you have a Mental Universe, try thinking of a pathway, like a star chart."

If I could have blinked in surprise, I would have. That was actually helpful. Using the sun of *Demonic Vault* and the black hole of my Mana Pool for reference, I envisioned a spaceship. Humans hadn't really advanced the concept of space travel since the early two thousands, but that didn't stop TV and movies from creating fictional renderings for me to base a ship on.

I chose the most advanced vessel I could think of—the Starship Energize. Sure, there were some newer movies that tried to one up it, but the Energize was a classic. Now, to add an ability to create Space Tunnels, or Warp-gates, or something that could create a protected space-corridor to travel down at light-speed.

The Energize gained a ring rotating around it, perpendicular to the crew-cabin disc that was also rotating to create gravity. I smiled and launched the spaceship on its mission to explore where no man had gone before.

"Amateur," Smegma scoffed.

"What the hell are you talking about, you giant flying rat?" I glared. "My ship is husking awesome."

"Pffft," the Demon snorted. "The Warp Cores' are obsolete. It's old tech. *Horizontal* gravimetric field displacement manifolds? *So* 'twenty-second' century. Move aside, casual. Let me show you how it's done."

Incredibly, Smegma husking *appeared* inside the Starship Energize. Mentally, I followed him as he moved through the engineering bay, shaking his head and muttering to himself.

He pointed at the matter/antimatter reaction assembly housing the deuterium and antideuterium that reacted inside the dilithium crystal matrix. "You see, in 2269, the Federation came across a revolutionary breakthrough. You need to add a vertical segment to the dilithium crystal converter right *here*." He pointed at a spot bisecting the location of the crystal matrix.

"That'll never work," I argued, pointing at the problem. "The nozzles on the antimatter injectors won't generate the necessary quantum-laminar flow with a setup like that. It'll introduce too much instability on a very precise system. Are you trying to blow up my ship?"

Smegma's eyes widened in shock. "You're still using *physical* injector nozzles? What are you, nine? Everyone knows they went to magnetic injectors before the turn of the century when they converted to magnetic containment. The magnetic antimatter containment also guides and directs the antimatter through the matter integrator to the injector coils. It then precisely compresses and streams it into a quantum spindle that enters the intermix chamber here. The deuterium, stored in the ship or attracted by the Arva Collectors from highly charged particles during space travel, is then funneled in a similar stream from the opposite deuterium injector over there. The resulting energy plasma molecules enter the lattice matrix of the crystallized dilithium chamber, reacting inside and releasing a tuned energy stream in the form of electro-plasma. The plasma gets carried by the magnetic plasma conduits throughout the power transfer system."

I nodded, warming up to the topic. "Right, that all seems to make sense, but that doesn't explain how you're supposed to get the electro-plasma to the warp nacelles. The magnetic field has a little something called *polarity*, numb nuts. It's not going to flow on a horizontal axis with this setup."

Smegma's eyes were manic. "Exactly! That was the breakthrough! Sure, the vertical conduits travel into the dilithium crystal converter, but the resulting warp plasma energy is directed to the nacelles through horizontal conduits leading out from—"

"The rear of the core..." I whispered, awed.

"Yes!" Smegma nearly howled with glee. "It changed *everything*, allowing for speeds of up to warp factor twelve on the old scale with just the *prototype*. In fact, the scaling for warp speed had to be revised because of this breakthrough, to account for the logarithmic increases in light speed with the new Cores."

Quickly, I began making the changes with Smegma giving pointers on precise proportions and modeling.

Wiping my metaphysical brow, I stood back and took in the wondrous changes to the Warp Core. Resting my hands on the engineering console, I whispered, "Incredible."

Placing my palm on the biometric scanner, I began the boot sequence that initiated the gravimetric field displacement matrix.

A gentle hum rumbled through the deck as a cool blue light lit the engineering deck like a gentle, dawning sun.

I smiled, turning toward Smegma, whose broad grin was somehow less terrifying with the small oil-black tear that traced its way down his Demonic face. He looked over at me, and I raised my hand up for a high-five. Grinning, he swept his three-fingered hand forward. As it passed completely through my arm, we both seemed to realize at the same time what had just happened over the last... minutes.

"Ahem," Smegma coughed, loudly. "Alright, show's over, jackass. Go figure out your new stupid Skills, I gotta take a dump." He glared over his shoulder at me in parting, gesturing at the entire ship and the Warp Core in particular. "Also, don't think I don't remember you making fun of me for all this. Not a Star Trip fan, my ass."

He disappeared through the walls of the ship as I awkwardly rubbed the back of my head, pretending I'd never offered the high-five in the first place. I wasn't about to tell him that I was simply extrapolating most of the Star Trip stuff from clips on MeTube. He'd probably never leave the TV or tablet again if he knew *those* existed.

Wait, did he say he needed to shit?

I rolled my eyes. What a lame excuse… Still, after he'd left, I turned back toward my new Warp Core with a proud, fatherly grin.

Sadly, despite the remodel, I discovered the vessel couldn't reach a speed higher than what felt like a snail crawling across a counter. I frowned at it, even as I tried to encourage it to use Warp, or a Stardrive.

"Stop!" Smegma shouted, suddenly reappearing and startling me, and not only stopping my attempts to speed up the ship, but also freezing it in place. "Look behind it, you moron! If it's a snail, think of what it's leaving behind…"

My heart racing, I did as instructed. Behind the spaceship was a blue tube—or if I wanted to continue the snail analogy—a slime trail. I swallowed to wet my dry mouth and throat as I realized what I had almost done. The ship wasn't going slow because it *couldn't* go faster—it was building this stable corridor for future expediency!

"You're basically building a wormhole. Let it take its time," Smegma added, his voice now calm and consoling. I nodded sheepishly and chose to watch as it began to map out a 'star route.'

The first indication that something was odd was when, instead of moving directly to the tan moons surrounding the *Classes* Sub-skill, it tracked toward *Demonic Vault*. While I needed that connection eventually—I didn't exactly have an immediate need for it.

"Remember when you tried to connect *Demonic Vault* to the *Classes'* planet?" Smegma explained, clearly feeling and hearing my distressed thoughts. "If your intentions are to form a connection to your new Skills, then what's happening is the most efficient way. Those are sub-Skills of a sub-Skill—maybe?"

Sure enough, fifteen minutes later, the ship reached the Sun of *Demonic Vault*, created something like a waypoint or perhaps a synapse, and continued toward the tan *Classes'* planet. This trip was much shorter, and within five minutes, another synapse was made. The connection from there to the first moon was the work of a minute at most. Then the ship vanished, startling me. Until I saw it begin tracing its way from the waypoint on the *Classes'* planet to the other moon.

It was exactly like a synapse! The ship had just used the Warp Gate back to the *Classes'* planet! I felt myself squee mentally.

Once everything connected, I felt something change, even as the ship vanished again. What had changed didn't become apparent until I opened my eyes in the greenhouse.

Minor Heal
(1)
Skill Type: Healing
Skill Rank: Low F-Rank (Evolvable)

Minor Heal can only be used on others the Skill User is touching and heals the individual's Health Pool at a rate of one Health per one Mana expended.

—

Cleanse

(1)
Skill Type: Healing
Skill Rank: Low F-Rank

Cleanse can only be used on others and removes contaminants, poisons, venoms and diseases from the individual. Limited to Common or Uncommon maladies.

Costs 10 Mana per use.

Seeing screens for my Skills, I immediately wanted to jump back into my Mental Universe and try to connect more. Surely *Mental Fortitude*, *Heat Sense*, *Recovery*, *Dragon Heart* and—wait, *Demonic Vault* was already connected.

"Correct," Smegma began. "Not only will you not get description windows for *Demonic Vault*, you won't get any for Passive Skills or Skills that haven't manifested…"

"But *Demonic Vault* has manifested as a planet, kind of, hasn't it?"

"It has, and I'm not sure why you don't have a description for it, but honestly it isn't a traditional Skill… Plus, I'm totally guessing. Maybe you can only see these two because they are *Class* Skills?"

I tilted my head a bit, acknowledging that point, even as I stood up and moved to Jarred. "So, if I want to add more Healing?"

"Just intend to do so and allow your Mana to find the right path," Smegma said encouragingly.

I laid my hand on Jarred and felt my Mana flow into the man almost immediately. Something happened to the Mana long before it even began to run through my body, causing it to feel different. Perhaps the green glow was a hint?

"It is," Smegma answered the unspoken question. "Your Mana is being converted to Health. This is why the Common Healer is so sad. First, you have to touch the individual, but more so, you use one Mana to heal one Health Point. That's extremely inefficient."

The feeling of the Skill activating was too amazing to get bogged down in whatever mire Smegma was on about. I was *Healing* Jarred, simply by husking touching him! I could *Heal people*. Just the thought of that was invigorating. If that wasn't awesome enough, add to it the pay of a Healer back on Earth, and I could be set for life—

"Don't you dare!" Smegma interjected. "If you're going to be satisfied with being a husking Healer and not get any better, I'm going to—"

He cut off as he realized he couldn't really do anything to me. I shook my head and chuckled at his deductions. "Smegma, I still want to become a Hunter, but having the ability to make money this easily is something to celebrate. Essentially, I could fund all my lawyer fees, business plans and more with just this!"

"Okay, but you can be so much more!"

"And I wi—" My response was frozen as something changed. The pull on my Mana Pool and the green energy stopped. I checked in on my Mental

Universe and found at least twenty-five blue orbs circling the black hole. So, I wasn't out of Mana…

"He's at full Health," Smegma explained.

Oh! For a moment, I considered sitting back down but then thought better of it. Instead, I moved one by one to my sleeping group members, starting with Dave.

In the end, Dave took the most Mana to heal—after Jarred—consuming five Mana in total, where my father and Willa both only needed two each.

"Perhaps when they all wake up, they'll be feeling 'well rested.'" I joked to Smegma. I could tell he didn't understand the reference, but he did seem to at least infer something because he pointed to Dave.

"At least the newbie will be able to set aside his wheelchair."

CHAPTER 12: CHAPTER 64

Saturday, April 27th, 2069

"White Goblins incoming!" Smegma shouted as he phased through the ceiling. I stared at him for a long moment before what he said registered, and then I shot to my feet.

The others were still passed out from the lunch of Fish, and admittedly, I was on my way to joining them before Smegma had sped back into the room. My *Mental Fortitude* Skill stopped me from taking off in a random direction, thankfully, but just barely. Instead, my panicked gaze moved from one sleeping body to another, desperately trying to think of a way to save them.

"Calm down," Smegma chuckled. "I meant they're at the lip of the cavern, studying the place. It will be a little while before they make it down here. They seem scared of the place."

My eyes transferred to the Demon with a hateful squint. "You said—"

"I know, my bad. But they *are* coming! I'm not sure why they're here now, but my guess is it has something to do with your earlier Cooking, or maybe your Mana usage?"

I looked to the room with the smithy that I had used to Cook. Could it have caused smoke? No, we'd burned Crystals, which produced no emissions we knew of on Earth—well, no emission other than heat…

I toggled on my *Heat Sense* and instantly saw the change. The stones in the room, which had been as cold or possibly colder than the surrounding cave, now radiated with the tiniest traces of heat. Most of that was concentrated in the smithy room, but I could tell that not only had some of that heat spread to the walls, but a glance up showed me a rather phallic shape that was still holding some residual heat.

"One of the columns is an exhaust!" I exclaimed, and then motioned to the walls and next room. "Whoever designed this place likely piped the hot air through the walls, and eventually out into the cavern above through that stack."

"So, the White Goblins came to investigate because of the heat?" Smegma asked rhetorically and then zipped back through the ceiling. A moment later, he popped back into the space beside me. "That explains why they are standing on the ridge, scanning the stones! Plus, I saw a few from closer in the village, and they had milky-white eyes! They probably can't see anything but heat signatures.

"Can you see them up on the ridge? It's probably a couple hundred yards that way." Smegma pointed to clarify his question.

I shook my head, and Smegma nodded while cupping his chin between two of his fingers. Only a few seconds passed like that before Smegma concluded,

"If you can see the stacks, and their vision works like yours, then once they get down to the courtyard, you're all screwed."

"What can we do? Going up the stairs and out the Stalagmite is only going to bring us closer."

"When you look at the lake, what do you see?" Smegma asked.

"Black, with some heat signatures where there are fish," I answered and then instantly saw the solution he was thinking of. "If we are in that room, and they know the place, they will probably not see anything amiss!"

Even as Smegma confirmed my conclusion, I was rushing from sleeper to sleeper and waking them up with mild shakes that morphed to violent ones in the cases of Dave and Jarred. My dad and Willa opened their eyes almost instantly, and just in case, I gave them the universal 'stay quiet' sign with a finger to my lips.

I did the same for Jarred, but Dave either didn't see it in time or wasn't as used to being in a Portal because when he awoke, he shouted, "What the husk?! Oh, I need to be quiet…" at least he turned his shout into a whisper toward the end. In an even lower whisper, he asked, "What's going on?"

Since he was the last I woke up, I gave them all a whispered explanation. No one spoke after learning of the White Goblins, and I added, "Prioritize speed over quiet. I don't know when they'll get to the courtyard. We need to get to the lake fast. Got it?"

Everyone nodded and we took off. Thankfully, we went through the room with the Huge Frying Pan, which I quickly put in my Necklace of Holding. I hoped they wouldn't make it all the way down here, but with the heat concentration—they might be motivated to give it their best shot.

We were only two rooms from the lake, so we arrived in less than half a minute. My dad pointed to the water, "Do we need to get in?"

I looked to Smegma, who was tapping a talon to fang. He oscillated a hand a moment later before pointing along one wall that had a ridge above the water. "You saw the Fish you pulled out of this thing. They'd eat you alive if you went in and they found you. Plus, there's no telling what else might be in this lake. Let's avoid going in unless it's a last resort. For now, try to head that way as far as you can. Hopefully it leads out of sight around a corner somewhere."

I moved to follow but Smegma held up a hand in front of me. Sure, I could have phased through it, but he was acting as the leader, and other than the accidental scare on announcing the White Goblins, I thought he was doing a fantastic job. Sure enough, what he said next, I also agreed with.

"You stay here so I can scout. If the Goblins come this way, then we'll head down and join up with the group." Smegma only waited for me to nod before he zoomed away into the facility. Once again, I was left standing with nothing to do as the Demon moved around.

Spinning, I watched as the others followed his direction, surprised to find Jarred leading the way. I would have expected him to reject the order, or at least argue, but a near-death experience would have affected *my* priorities. So, maybe it did his?

Or maybe I was going to hear all the complaints after the current crisis…

To call the progress of the group along the ridge slow moving would be doing a disservice to inch-worms. Due to the extremely low light of the chamber, each person was forced to feel for handholds, even though oftentimes they used the same ones as the previous individual. I realized I was watching them through *Heat Vision* at some point, which further explained just how dark it likely was for them as they moved further from the lights near the shore. I didn't exactly have it easy either, since the only things that stood out in my thermal vision were the people in my group. However, their hands left heat imprints on the rungs that caused them to stand out, which made the pathway look easy to follow from my vantage.

When Jarred turned a corner and became far harder to see with my *Heat Vision*, I smiled. I could still feel his heat source if I toggled the Skill to senses other than my eyes, but I could also feel Fish. Not to mention seeing the creatures in the lake. It took a count of two hundred before the rest joined Jarred on the other side of the bend, but I did get a thumbs up from my father, who was the last one around the corner.

I hoped that meant there was a better space to stand over there since the heat outlines seemed to spread out more. I squinted, trying to see if they were still latched to the walls—

"They're following the heat from the smithy," Smegma said as he popped into the space beside me. I jumped but thankfully managed to not cry out. Heart hammering, I nodded and motioned to the pathway the group had taken.

Smegma oscillated his hands again. "It'll take them at least five minutes to get down here. I think they came down the chimneys, like you first did. Right now, they're moving through the facility to the staircases."

Nodding, I sent Smegma off again. Now alone, with my heart hammering its warnings, I will admit I continually inched toward the ridge and the others. Once I caught myself doing it, I managed to stop but could feel my legs twitching in a desire to continue. Thankfully, *Mental Fortitude* quashed what little fear I had and allowed me to trust in Smegma to give me fair warning.

That fair warning came a minute or so later as he popped up and pointed to the ridge. "Time to go. They clearly have a better heat sense or vision than you. They're eerily accurate in their pathing."

I didn't wait for more and sprinted to the ledge I'd watched the others use. Thankfully, I was faster than the group, not because of the heat traces, since they'd vanished. Why I was faster, I could only guess. Either because I'd watched them or because of my Strength Stat. Regardless, in less than three minutes, I was around the corner.

It turned out that the others weren't gripping a wall anymore. Instead, there was a rocky shelf high above the water level. The shelf was probably only eight feet deep and maybe ten feet long, but it definitely would make hiding here more comfortable. Still, everyone in the group was faced away from me, looking out over the water.

I followed their gazes and didn't see anything but a vast expanse of relative darkness with a large concentration of glowing moss in the distance. I looked at the group and turned off *Heat Vision*, thinking it might be too dark for them to have noticed my arrival. Everyone stood so still they could have been statues.

Wait, why could I see so well without *Heat Vision*—

86

Just like the bend in the wall, the lake continued to the left of the original fishery cavern. Like everyone else had seemed to, I froze, staring at the massive accumulation of green moss above the water. The group freezing wasn't only because of the bright illumination.

It was the shape the brightly glowing moss formed.

My heart, which had been hammering, decided that it could beat even faster—but somehow my face and hands got colder despite the increased blood flow.

There, in the distance, was a *huge* coiled creature. It was so large that, at first, the distance became hard to gauge, right up until I scanned from the ledges' edge across the water to the creature. It was likely five hundred meters away but was so massive that the scale of the thing made it seem as if it could have been right atop us.

The ledge was deathly silent as everyone continued to stare at the coiled Snake. It turned out that the earlier artist had depicted the creature very well in the mural we'd destroyed. Smegma popped into the air, hovering out over the water, and opened his mouth.

My arms waved frantically to stop him from speaking, and I was actually fast enough to interrupt him. His eyes narrowed and he looked at me but then took in everyone else's pale-faced stares as well.

Slowly he spun, until the Snake's light first illuminated his face, and then washed over his spinning torso and legs. I saw the moment he realized it was a Snake because his jaw dropped open.

The moment stretched for untold seconds, all of the group standing stock still and staring. Taking in the terrifying beast.

I couldn't speak for the others, but I was cataloging things on its body and near it. First, the scales were a deep green or black on top, and white on its belly—at least, if my color palette wasn't too skewed by the moss. Second, each scale was easily as large as an ATV and likely just as thick as the Necrograph.

The next discovery I made gave me an 'ah-ha' moment, but not in a good way. The Snake was resting atop the water, but it wasn't on an island as I'd initially thought. No, it was atop a heap of fishbones and—wait, was that a humanoid skull?

Another one! Okay, so now I had some idea why this lake was so well stocked by the previous inhabitants, and probably why the Goblins had been so hesitant to come down here in the first place. The Snake's head wasn't visible, which either meant it was on the far side from us, or it was coiled in on itself.

My brain finally relaxed my tense muscles when it realized that the moss growing on the Snake meant it hadn't moved in a very long time. I, of course, re-tensed my muscles when I realized that could also mean it was due to move at any moment.

Smegma thankfully snapped all of us out of our stupor as he whispered, "The Goblins are on the shore."

I silently shook myself and inched back to the rounded edge of the ridge. I peeked around the corner and found five humanoid figures staring out into the water. At first, I thought they were twitching their heads forward and back. Until

I realized they were sniffing the air repeatedly. I took a testing sniff myself and found that I could still smell a hint of the cooked Mirror Fish.

It had either clung to my clothing or wafted this way—but it definitely wasn't as strong as it would be in the smithy chamber. The White Goblins, from this distance, looked small, but having seen my father and the others turn this corner with *Heat Sense*—I knew that wasn't the case.

Each one was easily as tall as Jarred, our shortest member, but they were far wider than anyone I'd seen before—looking more like gorillas than humans.

They continued to sniff the air but now added grunts at each other in between. Then a conversation occurred with a great deal of grunts and gestures before they eventually turned back around and walked through the archway to the pens.

I leaned back from the edge of the ridge and began to sigh in relief. Until I remembered the far larger threat of the Snake—and nearly choked as I tried to simultaneously stop my sigh and exhale quietly. It caused me to swallow a lump of saliva, and I coughed extremely loudly.

I looked up to find many eyes staring at me in horror. I only had eyes for the moss-covered Snake, which thankfully wasn't moving. We waited on the ledge for our best estimate of thirty minutes, allowing Smegma to scout back into the facility—before we eventually concluded that we had to move back to know more.

And get away from the hibernating terror Snake.

CHAPTER 13: CHAPTER 65

Saturday, April 27th, 2069

"Now I think I know why the Goblins are scared of this place!" Smegma stated when the group made it back to the greenhouse. "That thing was at least on a World Destroyer level, if not Universal Power…"

"What does that mean?" Jarred asked, sounding irritated to be talking to the Demon. Still, the fact that he was even trying made me hopeful for him remaining with us and not trying to return to the higher caverns.

"Because of the Skills the System provides, it's quite common to use the ranks of F, E, D, C, B, A and S. Then you get into double and triple S, before the System rates Skills as Ex, which is technically undefined or what Demons referred to as Extraordinary.

"SSS-Classed Demons could destroy armies of other lower Skill users by themselves—as long as they didn't have anything above S-Ranks with them. So, the ranks above them had to be distinguished in other ways. Just calling them Ex wasn't helpful for determining the threat of a given being. So instead, creature's with destructive powers above SSS were given new categories. National, Continental, World, and Universal Power. The fact—"

"Wait!" my dad cut in. "You switched from talking about Demons to 'creatures.' What does that mean?"

Smegma looked at my father for a long time and then ran his gaze over everyone. I stared at him with a dawning realization. He had said *creatures* because the Demons didn't have any powerhouses that would rank above SSS. It turns out I was close.

"After thousands of years, the highest ranked Demon on Crendalar was a Continental-Ranked powerhouse, or at least we think…" Smegma scrunched up his face and bared a few fangs before admitting, "It was never proven. We know for sure we had multiple National Powerhouses, but the single person who could have potentially been on the level of a Continental Powerhouse died in the Seven Deadly Realms along with his entire army before it could be confirmed."

"Hold on," my dad said, holding up two hands and staring sickly at the floor. "You're telling me that humans will have to face creatures like *that* one day?"

"I don't know. My guess is that creature is either on the verge of Ascension or already past it. The fact that it's here, though, does suggest that the inhabitants of this world faced it at some point, but I'm assuming it wasn't a World or Universal Power then. Regardless, it was strong enough when the locals found it that they couldn't defeat it—that's why they stocked this pool with Mirror Fish and worshiped the thing. Most likely they couldn't kill it, so they kept it satiated and 'contained.'"

"So, how come somethin' that strong be *here* in da F-Rank Dungeon?—shit—Portal." Willa asked, her voice higher than usual.

Smegma shrugged but gestured up through the ceiling. "We're probably as much as a mile below the surface. I'm just guessing, but this Lake is likely both inside and outside the Portal's time bubble. That or you stupid humans misread the rank of this Portal."

"What did the Mirage Guild face on the surface again? Goblins?" Dave asked.

I shook my head. "Lizardkin, I think."

"So, how come there are White Goblins down here too, then? Is it normal for two types of Monsters to be in Portals?" Dave followed up.

"Extremely common. You'll notice that usually, the System creates or brings in creatures suited for the environment. So Lizardkin, which thrive in water, likely didn't fit the ecology of this massive cavern. So instead, White Goblins that use *Heat Vision* or *Sense* are down here. We're probably lucky that they were likely occupied with the Hunters from Mirage when we went to refill our bottles."

"I still don't be understandin'," Willa interjected, making motions with her hands. She seemed to be trying to think of a way to ask a question but was stuck somewhere in the process. "Goblins and Lizardkin be F-Rank, right?"

Smegma nodded, but did add, "They can be considered E-Rank due to the intelligence they possess but don't always use."

"Okay. So, why would the System be puttin' F or E-Rank beside a World-Killer-thing?"

Smegma nodded. "The *System* didn't put the Snake here, that part I'm certain of. At least, it didn't put it here as a part of the Portal. The two are likely completely unconnected. On Crendalar, the creatures from inside the Deadly Realms didn't exit them after we failed. So, I'm unsure if this thing was local wildlife or something that came after failure. So, I wouldn't worry about it being the Boss that needs to be killed to close the Portal or anything like that. Is that what you're asking?"

Willa shook her head but ended with a shrug. "Not really, maybe, kind of. I just ain't be understandin' why the *System* wouldn't be removin' somethin' so powerful from a low-rankin' Portal, ya know? Like you be makin' this System out to be all-knowin', no?"

Smegma just slowly put his hands out in the 'I don't know' gesture before saying, "If you or any other human discovers the 'why' behind the System, let me know. Me and my research team spent a couple centuries trying to understand a miniscule portion of it and only came away with a singular breakthrough. However, I am sure that things beneath the surface are often overlooked by the Time Bubble. Remember the Sandworm?"

"So, what do we do now?" I asked, changing the subject away from the death of a B-Ranked Hunter. I gestured toward the lake, trying ineffectually to convey just how close we were to it and the creature it contained.

"Knowing that the White Goblins see thermally makes this the only place we can stay," Smegma said quietly. "I wouldn't worry about the Snake for now. It's been asleep for a long time, and even if it wakes up, it probably can't fit into this facility. The cooking of fish and Mining up above is the real problem with the information we now have…"

"Would it even *need* to fit down here?" I asked. "I'm guessing that the whole 'World Destroyer' classification isn't for show."

"Well"—Smegma shrugged awkwardly—"I was trying to be nice about it, but yeah. The truth is that if it wakes up, you guys won't have to worry about it because your survival is no longer something you get to control. So… Best to just not worry about it and focus on what you *can* control. Which brings us back to Fishing, Mining, and Goblin's sensory organs. We're not going to be able to Mine or cook for some time."

"How so?" Dave asked from where he'd moved to lean against the lab table with his arms crossed. I tilted my head, not understanding how he hadn't put the simple calculation together.

The others also eyed Dave askance. The boy gave a smile I knew too well, telling me that I was thinking too narrowly. We couldn't Cook, surely—since that was what had brought the Goblins here. So, was he thinking that the Mining was somehow still a safe option?

"Granted the Mining might have to be minimal," Dave began, causing my line of thinking to stutter. "But the Fishing and Cooking shouldn't be a problem," Dave continued, confusing me and everyone else greatly.

He pointed meaningfully back toward the Lake. "It's pretty simple. This facility transfers heat into the walls and those courtyard smoke stacks, right?"

I nodded, and even caught Smegma's head bobbing, along with the rest of the groups'.

"Then it's simple. We don't Cook in the facility."

Either I was dense or that wasn't enough of an explana—wait, the lake doesn't sit in the same stone as the facility!

"Oh!" I said at the same time my father and Smegma exclaimed something similar. Jarred looked a little lost but seemed to be slowly putting the pieces together. Willa, on the other hand, was looking from face to face, lost and irritated by the looks of understanding she could discern.

"What?" she blurted after no one volunteered the conclusion Dave had reached.

"We Cook in the lake cave and Mine only the Crystals we need to Cook," Dave concluded with a broad grin.

"Wait, you want us to cook food near that huge husking World Snake?" I asked, feeling my mind whirl. Sure, the noise and us Fishing hadn't woken it up yet, but I had to assume there was a reason Mirror Fish were in the lake and their skeletons were so abundant under the thing. They probably were like a bag of favorite chips to the husking thing!

"And how be that da plan ain' goin' ta bring the Goblins back?" Willa shouted.

"The stone is different in there, making it less likely to conduct heat into the facility like the smithy—the smithy's exhaust had been used as a method for heating the facility, ending on the smoke stack above," Jarred answered quietly. After a moment, he looked at me, "Even if there's a chance of waking up that creature, what other choice do we have? We can't cook here, right? So instead, we move as a group from now on? Mine what we need before moving down here and surviving on Fish?"

After a moment to think, I agreed with the logic and smiled. I knew Jarred enough to know that he wouldn't be admitting he was wrong, and that this was the best 'apology' or 'acknowledgment' I was going to get. In response to his question, I nodded.

Jarred surprised me by scratching at the back of his neck and mumbling, "Speaking of the Fish—is it what healed me as well?"

His stomach growled loudly, letting me know how hungry he was. Most likely the Potion had consumed a great deal of his nutrients to get that process started.

Thankfully, I'd left a small mound of Crystals and ten fish steaks out of my Necklace of Holding when I went to get Jarred. The Crystals could last us a few days if we used them wisely.

"Partially, yeah," I answered. A few of the others moved their bodies around, seeming to just realize that they too felt better. Dave in particular tilted his head, and took a few testing jumps to feel the difference.

"I thought it was the adrenaline," he said. Then his eyebrows drew down, telling me he was questioning the foods ability to remove his pain and fatigue. I gave him a sign we'd worked on in first year. It wasn't a sign I was particularly proud of, because it was most used to indicate to the other person that we wanted to talk about a specific person when no one else was around. Most commonly we'd used it with Manbat—Dave's first roommate.

Still, I splayed my fingers wide and massaged my thigh, hoping Dave would get the message. He looked at me and ran his tongue inside of his mouth. Should I have just told everyone about my Healing Skills? Certainly.

[Don't want your dad to start bringing up a career change?] Smegma mentally commented. Clearly reading my internal debate from my surface thoughts.

[That and my current criminal case...] I responded and left the others to discuss how much better they felt. I doubted I'd keep the secret for long but I wanted to run it by Dave first. Have a false argument with my friend before having the same one with my dad.

Jarred seemed to suddenly remember what I said, as he turned to regard me and asked, "You said partially. What's the other part?"

"I purchased and gave you a Healing Potion from Smegma," I answered, motioning at the Demon. I watched as Jarred's eyes widened and then frantically moved to Smegma and then back to me. It was tough to discern what he was thinking, but in the end he nodded, and his stomach growled again.

So, with an overly dramatic gesture, I 'ushered' the group back toward the lake cavern. I figured it was likely late enough by this point that it was time for a meal and a catatonic Mirror-Fish sleep. Most likely they all needed it since my *Minor Heal* likely consumed nutrients.

I was carrying a lit Mana Crystal inside the Frying Pan, courtesy of the mechanical lighting apparatus on the smithy, when Jarred surprised everyone by venturing directly into the shallow waters of the lake. He was certainly the dustiest of everyone, thanks to the second cave-in that he was literally a part of—so his desire to rinse off wasn't that surprising.

Still, his nonchalance at entering the lake that was filled with car-sized Fish, was a little terrifying to watch. He didn't go deeper than his shins, and I held my breath hoping these things couldn't get him there. By the time I couldn't hold my breath anymore, he was still fine.

His desire to clean himself, safely, made me, and by extension the rest of the group acutely aware of our own rather untidy and dusty appearances. Everyone took a turn, except Willa—at least until the food was finished, and the others took their steaks out of the chamber—then I assumed she stayed behind to also clean herself up.

The Fish was just as tasty the second time and had the same soporific effect. This time, since I consumed an entire piece, I hardly had time to think about my trial on Monday before my heavy eyelids refused to open again, and I drifted off to sleep amongst the weeds.

CHAPTER 14: CHAPTER 66

Sunday, April 28th, 2069

With a tug and some furious rotations on the reel, I pulled a particularly large Mirror Fish into the shallow waters. Being pulled from the water increased the effective weight of the Fish almost instantly, but simultaneously removed its ability to fight back. Using my legs and arms, I backed up until the creature was fully ashore. Then I summoned the filet Knife from storage with a smile—

"No!" Smegma hissed from behind me, causing me to jump and spin with the Knife held in front of me defensively. Dave was getting pretty close to supplying the Rod with his Mana Pool, actually managing to get a worm on the line with each attempt, but failing to continue supplying the resource—thus making continued practice necessary.

Smegma had been coaching him using a flower and water metaphor before his terrifying hiss. Now, Dave was staring at empty space with open-mouthed astonishment. My eyes scanned the area, desperately searching for the Demon. Eventually I let them linger on Dave, and he began to sputter, "I didn't do anything, I swear—umm—suddenly there was some sort of white fog, and it looked like it consumed him. He's gone."

White fog?

I blinked as I recalled another time he had vanished, and white fog had been involved. Hadn't that been when the System exchanged out the old Enchant, then directed the stored Mana to the *Mining* Skill?

What about me almost dying and the Shunting? Surely, that wasn't going to happen again! I dove into my Mental Universe and found white fog coalescing into a small sphere in the same orbit as the ever-enlarging Mining moon turned small planet.

My relief only lasted a moment before I grimaced and recalled that Smegma claimed *he* also almost died the last time. Hadn't he talked about a puzzle made of razor blades or something? Still, there wasn't much I could do to help him, other than hope he made it through and formed a new Skill planet—if the Miner's Pick gave me *Mining*, then was this going to be *Fishing*?

"I think he'll be back—he kind of vanishes unexpectedly all the time," I said, without revealing the entire truth. Thinking better of it, I told Dave a bit more. "He's creating another Skill, I think. Probably for Fishing."

"Are you husking kidding me?" Dave shouted as he stood up far too quickly. His shout made me immediately shush him and look over my shoulder in the direction of the world-ending Snake. Even Smegma had managed to control his volume as he vanished.

Dave's face stopped reddening, and he motioned over his shoulder back toward the animal pen. I nodded but first returned to kill the Mirror Fish while it was still on the line.

Once we were through the pens and into the smithy, Dave hissed, "You're getting *another* Skill, even after the Class and the two Skills I came with?!"

I'd told Dave all about the Class and the two Healing Skills, while also letting him in on the dilemma that came with them. Dave's first response had been that I should tell my father anyway, but when I pointed out that may turn into an argument about careers, he'd asked to think on it.

This response didn't seem like an answer to that conundrum, and so I shrugged, and answered the first part. Pointing at the Fishing Rod he was still holding with my own, far-more-repaired version, I explained my thoughts, "Probably. There's an Enchant on these that funnels excess Mana to my *Overflow* Skill. It's what created the *Mining* Skill, while almost killing me…" I shivered remembering the message about Shunting. Shaking off the goosebumps, I continued, "And now, maybe *Fishing*—" I stopped as I thought of something. "I wonder if I'll get a *Cooking* Skill from using the Frying—"

"Focus, moron!" Dave exclaimed while simultaneously using his Rod as a switch to swat my behind. I jumped and looked at him with a confused frown.

"What?"

"I don't know! I just don't think it's husking fair that you are suddenly going to have *eight* Skills!"

"You do realize we're trapped in a Portal, right?"

Dave grimaced but nodded in confirmation. Then looking at the ground, he mumbled, "I think you kind of have to tell everyone about the Healer Class, Bro."

"I know," I answered, having felt that inevitability coming when I first omitted the truth. "Can we run through some fake arguments my father might make?"

There in the animal pens Dave and I ran through every argument we could think of. Until I felt slightly more confident telling the group.

Once we were finished I gathered my nerves and we kept going. Once we were back in the greenhouse, we found ourselves face to face with Jarred, Willa and my father. My courage fled, and I decided I'd wait for the right moment.

They'd spent the morning pulling weeds and churning soil so we could move it around for pillows. What I hadn't expected was to find Willa and Jarred now weaving the long, green, grass-stem-like weeds into 'blankets.'

Dave the *friend* that he was pushed the issue by stating, "It's totally unfair, man!"

I glared at him and got an encouraging smile in return. His statement brought the three others to a stop and drew all their attention. To ease the omitted information I started with what was going on right now. I gave the best explanation I could, without divulging the risk to Smegma. I wasn't sure how they would react to the news of that, considering that, in my opinion, he was what was keeping us alive down here.

I finished by revealing my lie. "Plus, it wasn't the Fish that healed you guys. I kind of got another couple of Skills from getting a Healer Class."

Jarred and Willa jerked back in surprise but then smiled broadly. They looked like they were on the verge of celebrating, but I only had eyes for my father. He was regarding me seriously. Jarred and Willa took a moment to follow my gaze but when they did, I saw their smiles dry up.

After an agonizing moment of silence, my father asked, "You didn't tell us immediately because you thought I'd force you to become a Healer at a hosptial?"

My swallow was more audible than I expected. My eyes slowly drifted off my father's face, and I nodded, sheepish that I hadn't told him right away.

"Shouldn't you keep Fishing?" my father said, a few moments after my nod. Since I hadn't been looking at him, I hadn't seen what had transpired. My head jerked up to meet his eyes now. He was smiling paternally. "My guess is, even if you were going to try your hand at being a Healer, you'd want to join a Hunting team?"

I shook my head, and then caught myself, before nodding. Clearly, he knew me well. I didn't need to appease his and my mother's desire for me to take some sort of safe desk job. They knew my dream now…

"Alright, get back to Fishing, and then we'll go up to Mine," my father said, ending the moment of levity and awkwardness. To my surprise, Willa came and clapped me on the back—seeming to decide that congratulations or something was in order. It felt more like congratulations for something more to me. Like recognition of becoming an adult in hers and clearly my fathers eyes. Jarred smiled and nodded at me in time with Willa's gesture.

A wave of warmth ran over my shoulders and up to my neck.

Smiling, I hiked a thumb over my shoulder, pointing back toward the lake. "I caught a Fish and left it on shore for now. That's what triggered Smegma's disappearance and the *new* Skill. So, we should probably have a small piece of what is cooked and thawed, finish setting up this room for a long stay, and then go Mine some Crystals."

"You sure we should attempt that without Smegma being able to scout for us?" my dad asked. He was right, of course.

"Good point," I answered. "Let's just set up down here until he's back, then. Hey, who knows, maybe Mirage will dig us out soon."

Jarred coughed politely, which turned all of us in his direction. "While I was in the chamber nearest the collapse, I didn't hear any indication that they had started trying to clear it."

Just like that my moment of exhilaration ended. I licked my teeth and forced my breathing to remain calm even as my heart hammered in my chest. If they weren't digging from the other side, just how long would we be down here? Likely until they cleared the Portal—

My mind, ever the 'fortress,' logically took me out of that depressing spiral of negative thoughts by running some calculations that indicated a rather positive outcome on the chances of our survival.

One Fish could easily feed our little group for multiple days; an increase in time spent down here wasn't going to get us killed. All we had to do was avoid the White Goblins and wait…

My mind also *helpfully* decided to tell me about the flaw in its own calm, calculative logic. What if this was a Permanent Portal or the Boss to close it was down here with us? If it was the former, then they never had to dig out the entrance. They could just keep fighting respawning Lizardmen, farming the Portal for Monster Cores, and earning a steady income. If it was the latter, then the Guild would have to clear away the cave-in to take out the Boss and close the Portal.

"Don't worry, they'll dig us out eventually," my dad said. "For the yellow Crystals, if nothing else…"

I didn't really agree, but after I was sure I had control over my facial features, I nodded to my father. "You're right. I'll go clean and portion out that Fish I just caught. You guys keep working on this room till Smegma returns."

I figured I could always return to Fishing and building a stockpile while we waited. To Dave, I said, "Let's head back to the lake, then."

Before leaving to head back to the lake, I looked to the others in turn, receiving a nod from each of them. Dave put a hand on my shoulder as we left, offering his 'apology' for his part in the awkwardness. I smiled at him to let him know what he did was very helpful.

"Thanks," I whispered, as we moved through the doorway.

"You've got good parents, Bro," Dave whispered, back. Reminding me of the strangeness that was his family. His family I knew next to nothing about. I considered bringing it up, but a glance at Dave made me rethink that. His smile was gone, and his features were set into a depressing sneer, which was highlighted by the yellow lights above.

I was still considering how to bring it up tactfully when I felt a strange sensation of heat well up from near my heart. I stopped, midway through the animal pens.

"That was *so* much better!" Smegma announced as he popped into space beside me. It startled me for a moment, but his voice was distinctive enough that I smiled just as quickly. Having him back took a huge weight off my shoulders.

"Better?" I asked as I exhaled a breath, along with a great deal of my earlier stress.

"Yeah, first, the puzzle pieces were smaller and less numerous. Second, they came in one at a time, and rather slowly. So, while they were still razor sharp, it was Imp-play to complete that Skill Planet."

"I've gotta ask, how is an Enchantment that seems to be able to create Skills of equal value to one that can create Crystals?" I asked, trying to figure out why the System banned and destroyed the first one—only to give me this one.

"Skill limits, kid," Smegma reminded me. "Eventually, you'll probably fill yourself up with nothing but useless Gathering Skills…"

I froze at his response, unsure if I believed that. Sure, I believed that the System would have limits to the amount of Skills one person could have—but ever since *Demonic Vault* had called *Overdraft* and *Classes* sub-Skills, it just felt like limits couldn't be the entire story.

Or at least it didn't seem to explain the disparity I was seeing.

My internal thoughts did seem to force the Demon to pause. As usual, he assumed his thinking pose, but this one seemed off. He looked confused. No, not exactly. He looked… worried?

"What's wrong?" I asked.

"Hmm?" Smegma startled slightly. "Well, your thoughts highlighted something to me. You see, the System doesn't make mistakes, so I just gave a rather straightforward and simplistic answer. *Maybe* I was even a little glib." He gave me an apologetic smile but didn't bother actually apologizing.

"Okay?" I prompted, confused about where Smegma was going. "But thinking about sub-Skills and the ability to continually create Skills got you thinking?"

"Yeah…" Smegma said thoughtfully. "When I said the System doesn't make mistakes, what I mean is not that it can't, but just that it *doesn't*. It's not in its nature. You might think of the System as a very advanced program from one of your 'computer-things,' though that's a terrible analogy that doesn't even begin to do the phenomena that is the System justice whatsoever. Still, thinking about it as a computer with programmed responses might help understand a vital aspect of the System's nature. The System is *justice*. It is *fair*—but has an executioner's blade's justness and is just as unforgiving. You can't reason with it, or befriend it, or bribe it. The System is precisely, unwaveringly, unequivocally, and impossibly *impartial*. It is a core aspect of its principles."

"Alright. So, it's like binary code. Its response to a situation takes in all the available data and spits out a response," Dave interjected. "So, what's the big deal?"

"The 'big deal,'" Smegma scoffed as he looked to Dave condescendingly, "is that what the System has done here with this Enchantment is definitely *not* an Equivalent Exchange. That's what the idiot over there said, along with his thoughts that clued me in on the disparity."

"You say that like it is explaining the problem and not just reiterating what I already tried to point out," I answered, somewhat annoyed at the recap and Smegma calling me stupid again.

"But it *does* explain it! The term 'Equivalent Exchange' is an explanation my research team created to help us understand a fundamental law of the System. Like for like. Impartiality." Smegma began hovering back and forth as if he was pacing. "When you activated the Enchantment on the Pickaxe, the System intervened. Which is no small matter.

"Not ever.

"It put you on *Trial*, Brodie. System Trials are…" The Demon shuddered. "They're *rare*. Nearly unheard of, except as vague legends and threats to children to get them to go to sleep. They are the universal boogeyman, if we're speaking in Earth terms. What's more was that you were found innocent. That… doesn't happen. If you're in a position to be tried by the System, that scary son of a bitch makes Mr. Varnish look like a toddler playing with a gavel. If the System is 'taking you to court,' so to speak—it already has all the evidence it needs, don't you see? Yet somehow, you were found innocent. Which means that the System either made a mistake—or something about that Miner's Pick made it take action."

A chill ran down my spine as Smegma's words finally sunk in. I'd assumed with something as large as the System and Earth, that these sorts of trials and bugs in the code were pretty common. However, with something that had perfected itself over thousands, millions, or even billions of years. Just how many more errors could it have?

That thought alone made me question Smegma's continued assertions that the System never made mistakes. The System sounded like it made constant changes to itself, or at least to how it functioned on different worlds. That was, in essence, an attempt to better itself. To fix things within its own 'code' to help users, right?

Rather than argue, I decided to focus on Smegma's concerns since I was smack in the middle of them.

"So…" I swallowed. "What does that have to do with these new Skills?"

"Equivalent Exchange," Smegma whispered. "The System *took* something from you, Brodie… Tell me. Do you know how much an F-Ranked *Mining* Skill costs in my Shop?"

I blinked at the sudden change in subject. "Uhh. Maybe? I'm pretty sure we looked at a lot of Skills a while back."

The Demon nodded. "Two-hundred and fifty thousand Mana coins for an F-Ranked *Mining* Skill. Now, do you remember how much Mana was in your Pick when the System broke the Enchantment?"

Dave looked at me, his eyes widening as if he understood where Smegma was going. I hated that he was somehow ahead of me already—even though I was the one being impacted by it all.

I thought back to the prompt from *Demonic Vault* when I purchased the Pick all that time ago. "A thousand? I'm pretty sure it was a round number like that, and one hundred seems like too little and ten-thousand, well… that's a *lot*."

"Exactly." Smegma smiled grimly. "But we've already talked about the fact that the System didn't Exchange the Enchantment on the Pickaxe for your *Mining* Skill, Brodie."

"Right," I said, almost forgetting the distinction. It hadn't *given* me the Skill. Not exactly. What it had done was put an Enchantment that funneled Mana from the Miner's Pick, and now the Fishing Rod, into my *Overdraft* Skill…

"Not just into your *Overdraft* Skill, but in a specific way. Right now, you just have the *Overdraft* Skill targeting you in general," Smegma clarified, clearly picking up on my surface thoughts. "You could theoretically target *Demonic Vault*, *Mining*, *Fishing* or maybe even any one of your Skills to help them level."

"Right, I remember you wanting me to target you at first. So, the System made the new Enchantment do what? Create and continually level a new Skill and only that Skill… Not just funnel the Mana into an existing one that I chose?" I asked.

"Every single Profession item in my Shop now has that same Enchantment. Each of the Skills associated with them would cost you at a minimum two-hundred and fifty thousand Mana Coins to purchase, and the System created and replicated that Enchantment on each item. Then, if you're right in the thought that these Gathering Skills are classified as sub-Skills of my Skill, or maybe some weird sub-sub-Skill since it's technically *Overdraft* that's creating the Skill—then that would mean what I said earlier doesn't even apply. That the System isn't penalizing you by adding a somewhat shitty Skill that takes up cap space. Not only that, the Enchantment is so efficient that it can create that very Skill with less than a thousand Mana absorbed from the Profession item."

"Wait, what?" I said, shocked. Dave was nodding along, making me even more confused as my friend seemed to be following the conversation better than I was.

"I told you. The Exchange was the Enchantment, not the Skill." Smegma shook his head as if he, too, were in disbelief. "The Skill formed because it had met the requisite threshold of Mana." The Demon looked at me. "Which was not even the total inside the Pickaxe, no wait—the Pickaxes—at the time... Remember you had three full ones."

"*Shunting...*" I breathed. This finally made Dave's face scrunch up in confusion, which I will grudgingly admit made me happy.

"Wait, back up," Dave interjected. "What's *Shunting?*"

I explained my near-death experience and the messages from the System after the trial. Dave nodded along like I'd somehow given him a puzzle piece he was missing.

"So, you're saying that it took the Mana from the Pickaxe that was meant to create a Crystal, used some of it to create the *Mining* Skill, and then had to Shunt off a great deal more to stop you from literally exploding."

I nodded and Dave smiled. I narrowed my eyes. That didn't seem like the type of thing he should be smiling about.

He explained a moment later, "I'm just happy the Skills didn't come entirely free!"

My eyes rolled and I punched Dave in the arm before I started to turn back to Smegma.

Dave stopped me, though. "I do think I see where you two idiots have confused things though."

Smegma and I both turned to stare incredulously at Dave. Smegma pointed at Dave menacingly as he growled, "Okay! Now you have our attention. Time to back those words up, imbecile."

"Let's say that each of the Pick took in a thousand Mana. So, three thousand total, right?" Dave began, waiting for Smegma and me to nod before continuing. "So, three thousand Mana would be what—an E-Rank Crystal?"

I looked to Smegma, who nodded but also made it clear with a hand motion that it wasn't that simple. Dave shrugged away the need for Smegma to elaborate and continued, "So, it was collecting Mana Spillage from F-Rank Crystals and creating something greater, right?"

"Husk," Smegma whispered, sounding like he was seeing something that Dave was saying, where I definitely wasn't.

"Stop talking to each other and tell me what the husk is going on!" I complained.

"Well, there's only really one possibility here, Brodie," Dave explained. "It was collecting Mana, as we think of it, into Points. Then, it was creating something greater than it took in, to some extent. So then, what would happen if you were Mining in an S-Rank Mine?"

"It would be filled with each swing," I answered. "Still not getting what you're saying, though."

"This part is totally hypothetical. But what if those 'thousand points' was a progress bar? Or it grew with the Pick? What if it popped out Crystals based on the Pick's Rank and not the Crystals you were Mining? Could you fill it with F-Rank Crystals and get S-Rank?"

"Holy hells," I whispered, going silent like Smegma had.

"If that was a progress bar," Smegma began, "then it starts to make some sense. The Picks didn't just have three thousand Mana; they had the potential to essentially Create more from less. The System called it a Creation Enchant, didn't it? And the Funnel Enchant was Growth Grade. I was going to say even three thousand Mana shouldn't be enough for a Skill, Brodie. It shouldn't be enough to pop you like a balloon either. So, either the System gave you something of more value than it took, *or* it gave you a highly efficient Funnel Enchant to replace something that would have grown and become astronomically powerful."

"See, I told you I thought I had the answer," Dave bragged but then immediately sobered. "Still, I can't begin to imagine how something that can endlessly create Skills would be worth the Creation Enchantment, even with everything I just said. It just raises its value to make the Exchange closer to equivalent."

Smegma was quiet for a long time, his eyes unfocused. Finally, he spoke. "I'm missing memories, Brodie."

"Yeah, you mentioned something about that. You get new memories when *Demonic Vault* Upgrades, or updates, or something like that."

"Updates. Yeah," Smegma confirmed.

"And you think, what? You might have memories that would make sense of what is going on here?" I asked.

"That's exactly what I think." The Demon nodded. "And we need to find that answer as soon as we possibly can."

"What do you mean? How? I'm doing everything I can, and if you've forgotten, we're kind of stuck in a Portal. Maybe even on some desolate planet somewhere out in the multiverse. What more do you want me to do?"

"I'm not sure, but I do have some ideas. I just need to flesh them out a bit and figure out the best way forward, for everyone."

"Okay," I huffed, slightly exasperated. "Well, you just tell me when you get it all figured out, alright? Now, what should we do in the meantime?"

I changed the subject, not wanting to dwell on the weight of everything Smegma had just revealed.

"We had just decided to wait to Mine till you return, but I never expected you to be this fast," I explained. "Should we go back to the earlier plan from this morning?"

Smegma nodded. "I still can't be sure, but something feels off about how fast those Goblins left. Let's keep Fishing for now, I want to see if they come back with reinforcements."

"We'll keep to the same strategy as earlier?" Dave asked. Smegma nodded, and Dave turned around to head back to the greenhouse. "I'll let the others know the plan. They'll be happy to know our scout is back."

Smegma floated after Dave, "I'll join you—maybe we can keep discussing hypotheses of what's going on without being held back by a dumb-dumb."

"I'm right here!" I growled but began walking away toward the Lake, knowing there wasn't much I could do to stop the two jackasses without making it worse.

* * *

"It's not so bad," Dave said from beside me as he channeled Mana to the Rod. I smiled, having already caught two more Fish this morning before my Mana Pool of fifty ran dry. My new Skill must be helping, since I couldn't manage a single Fish with fifty just a few hours before.

What I'd caught was an excessive amount of meat, and I'd stored it all in the Necklace along with the rest—making the Holding space over half full. The bones and guts, I tossed back into the lake, just like I had the previous day with the four I'd managed to catch. I'd debated about using it for bait, but Smegma assured me that was a bad idea.

According to him, I was only managing to pull the Fish ashore thanks to the Mana Pulses of the Rod, and the Enchantments that my steady supply of Mana activated. Maybe to a less degree my new Skill now as well. All those and to a far lesser degree my Strength, as well.

Now, I watched Dave closely as he prepared to cast his first line into the water. I just couldn't be sure what would happen to someone without a Strength Stat of ten. I was still embarrassed about thinking I was ten times stronger than I had been, but no one could actually give me a decent answer on how much of a difference the Stat made. Sure, I was strong but just how much stronger was tough to measure. I hadn't gone to the gym or tried lifting anything since I'd gotten it—which I was regretting at the moment.

However, I figured if I was right beside Dave, I would be able to assist in dragging the Fish onto shore if there was even a hint of him being overpowered. According to Dave's Awakening Assessment, admittedly a better and more expensive version of the standardized one I'd received, it showed that he had thirty points of Mana, which meant he may be able to pull in one Fish based on my experience.

It may be a close thing though…

Almost as soon as the Mana worm hit the water and pulsed, the line tightened, indicating a bite. Dave tugged once and snagged the Fish, making my eyebrows raise. It often took me four or five bites before I snagged a Fish on the line. Dave managed to reel in a few feet of line before the Mirror Fish reacted. Then, just like I expected, the Fish tugged back. Hard. I wrapped my arms around Dave's stomach, ready to save him—and discovered that Dave's weight barely shifted forward. Sure, his arms and legs tensed, and sweat broke out on his face and forehead as he resisted, but it was also clear that his weight and braced feet would be enough to resist the tug.

I stayed poised and ready to help with my arms still clasped around his stomach, though, just in case I was missing something. Dave, having seen me

102

struggle and knowing of my Strength, didn't complain. *Instead, he focused on executing the technique I had discovered.*

[What was *discovered?* I literally had to feed you the method, like a mama bird and her disgusting featherless chick, you ingrate!] Smegma chastised me internally, from the other room—where he was supposed to be checking on the others.

I pointedly ignored Smegma. Pulse, pull and reel.

I began to relax on the second successful pull and subsequent counter-pull that didn't move my friend. It wasn't until the fifteenth that I felt a change. The line pulsed, and Dave moved to pull back on the Rod, but instead, seemed to go limp in my loosened grip.

"You okay?" I asked. I craned my neck forward to look at my friend and found him pale and drenched in sweat. His eyes were half closed, his breathing shallow and fast. "Dave?!"

He gave me a weak grin before grunting, "I'm out of Mana and exhausted."

"Oh," I managed to say before shaking myself into action and repeating, "Oh!"

In a somewhat jerky and awkward motion, I snatched the Fishing Pole and pulled back on both it and Dave, even as I channeled my small remaining amount of Mana into the Rod through my new fledgling Mana Nervous System method. Dave, thankfully, cranked the reel, which stopped me from having to try to awkwardly grab the handle over his hand.

I only noticed then just how much more line he had drawn in. No wonder he ran out of Mana sooner than me.

Disappointedly, I also ran out of Mana before we could get the Fish to breach the surface, and I was forced to use the filleting Knife to cut the line. I wasn't sure it would be sharp enough at first, but without the Mana, the yarn-like line thankfully broke without much effort. I toggled on my *Heat Sense* and watched as the large fish took off from the shallows to move far deeper into the lake and out of my range.

"That wasn't bad," I said as I let go of Dave. I then joined him in a boneless collapse onto my butt.

Dave gasped in lungfuls of air before he turned to address me. "I'm just glad that shitty Demon—"

"Isn't here to see your budding bromance taking its next step?" a shrill voice asked. "That hug sure was long and tight!"

"God dammit!" Dave finished as Smegma floated from the wall that held the ledge we'd traversed yesterday.

"The other group is finished prepping the room, and I still haven't seen a sign of more White Goblins. So, if you two are finished getting *closer,* I think it's time to try Mining."

"I know you're just jealous that you can't touch anyone or anything. Is little Smegma feeling lonely?" I retorted between gasps for air.

"Yeah, 'cause I'm just dying for a reach around like that!" Smegma countered annoyingly fast.

"Woah." I held up my hands in surrender. "You quickly jumped on the gay-train there. I'm not judging. I'll still love you like a brother—it's just that I was talking about some attention from a Dominatrix Demoness or something."

Smegma glared around, but Dave snorted. "Let me guess, you watched for a while and were thinking of things to say," Dave interjected before Smegma could respond. His words were also forced out between lungfuls of air. "It's kind of sad the best you could come up with was a homo joke. Do better!"

"Shut up. You two Greeds only ever retort with penis jokes."

"That's 'cause we *have* penises," I pointed out.

"So, that means you have to always bring them up?" Smegma questioned. I truly hadn't expected a response in that direction from my own childish jab.

"Bring it *up?*" I asked, pretending to be shy. "Well, you might not remember this, but sometimes when you wake up, it's just like that. It's a normal biological function for us *men.*"

Even Dave rolled his eyes at my rather lame comeback.

"See what I mean?!" Smegma practically shouted. "It's just phalluses and *manliness* with you humans."

I nearly felt bad for the Demon. Nearly. However, being the magnanimous and upright specimen that I was, I graciously accepted my *'victory'* and stopped poking the bear. Admittedly, I was pretty sure Smegma gave as good as he got in that two on one.

Smegma noticed that Dave and I seemed finished with the witty retorts and waited for us to recover with a scowl that showed far too many fangs. It might've also been why we stood up earlier than we probably should have to follow him back to the others.

* * *

"Go back!" Smegma shouted as soon as he popped into space beside me. "They're waiting in rooms two floors above you."

"Shit," I said as the others swore as well. I toggled back on my *Heat Sense* and saw a few outlines rushing toward the stairs above us. "Hurry!" I shouted, adding urgency to Smegma's warning.

It wasn't needed, but I figured it couldn't hurt.

The group spun on the top step and returned the way we'd come at a dead sprint. We'd been climbing with caution, thanks entirely to Smegma's 'gut-feeling' that something wasn't right.

Even with being cautious, we might still be caught! I thought, even as my semi-weakened legs pounded down the steps to the lower levels.

"Don't panic," Smegma coached, likely responding to my thoughts but directing the words to everyone—I hoped. "They're big and bulky, so not exactly fast. As long as you get to the lake before them, and around that corner, you should be okay."

As I spun at the bottom of the current flight and moved to take the next stairs that were stacked under it, I heard a guttural growl followed by a terrifying howl. I glanced up and met eyes with a pair of milky-white orbs set in the scarred and blackened face of a White Goblin.

I would have frozen in place if my father didn't bump into my back and shove me. The jolt got me moving again, even as my brain calculated how close behind us they were.

And Smegma had said that they weren't *fast?*

CHAPTER 15: CHAPTER 67

Sunday, April 28th, 2069

Sprinting in Mining boots that were practically falling apart wasn't comfortable nor quiet. Each footfall from everyone in the group sounded like Mining Picks hitting stone, and my own steps carried a distinctive metallic noise on the left foot.

My brain told me it was my imagination since my heartbeat sounded like a drum to my own ears as well. I'm sure it was only sounding a marching cadence because of the grunts and guttural cries that seemed to be right on our heels.

The worst part was that my body and mind were also fighting a war. With my Strength Stat, I could push off the ground harder and likely outdistance the others, making it to the ridge and around the corner to the safe spot sooner. But with my *Recovery* Skill and unlocked Stat, I had the greatest chance of survival if they caught up to us.

My father was still the issue. In that I was literally shoving him with each of my own 'sprinting' steps to keep him in front of me. I considered shouting at him to move or stop fighting me but felt that could make him 'dig his heels in' both literally and figuratively.

The lighting changed and I knew we'd entered the animal pens chamber. I could even see the backs of Jarred and Willa running through the archway to the fishery chamber and the lake it contained. My dad also noticed the change and attempted once again to get behind me. Admittedly, with adrenaline coursing through my body and the anxiety of the gorilla-like vicious-carnivrous humanoids closing in from behind—I probably shoved him a little harder than I should have.

Why do I think that?

Well, it looked like he jumped, flew over two edges of the depressed circular pens, and landed just before the archway.

I saw him catch himself and start to turn to look back at me, so I shouted, "Husking *move*! I'll toss you again if you don't get on that husking ridge!"

Excessive? Probably, but I was already at war with my own desire to go faster and maintain my current 'heroic' spot in the back. Thankfully, Smegma flew up beside my father, and while I didn't hear what was said, I did see Gary's legs unlock as he resumed his sprint.

My 'shove' had placed him ahead of Dave, and my father did wait at the ridge for him to go first, but thankfully he was right behind him.

The guttural cries and grunts grew louder and gained more reverberations. I knew that meant they'd entered the larger animal pens' cavern and clenched my fist on the handhold as my desire to move faster screamed at me loudly enough that it almost overrode *Mental Fortitude*.

I was only four feet from the start of the ridge but couldn't go any faster because of everyone else. Each of the four individuals in front of me moved at what felt like glacial speed to me as they desperately searched for handholds and failed numerous times before discovering one.

I couldn't see it happening, but I could hear the heavy breathing and scrabbling hands repeating themselves over and over again. I managed two more small shuffles of my feet before I truly heard the grunts for the first time.

When the White Goblins had been on shore 'conversing,' they had been quietly grunting in comparison to whatever this was. It sounded like a mix between a Warhog, a Manticore and a Frenzied Gorilla—with a dash of something neanderthal too. Like a guttural celebration of catching sight of prey. My eyes found the milky-white orbs of the scarred Goblin I'd seen at the top of the stairs, and I watched, horrified, as gobs of saliva dripped out of its mouth before splashing down its already slicked legs and onto the lake stones beneath.

For an instant, I thought time had frozen as I stared at the beast, its arms rippling with bulging, overexcited muscles. The comparison of its physique to that of apes grew more apt as those arms twitched spasmodically, seeming to want to beat its chest but being just humanoid enough to stop the urge.

The moment shattered as the next White Goblin entered the room. The scarred one flexed its knees and pushed off the stone—hard—sprinting at me with such ferocity that I flinched even though he was twenty yards away. Thankfully, the group had inched farther out onto the ridge, and I was able to shuffle another two to four meters out as the Goblin advanced. Surely, it would have to slow down to—

It leaped when it was ten yards away, and my foot slipped as my leg spasmodically attempted to jump up, forward, sideways, or any way that wasn't in the path of the flying husking *freak*.

I couldn't breathe. My fingers cracked the rocks I was holding as my grip tightened. My heart even stopped hammering as my wide, twitching eyes watched the ascension of at least three hundred pounds of Goblin. His leap was impressive, easily carrying him five feet above the stone and propelling him forward with even more speed than he had when charging.

However, five feet of rise, with ten *yards* of distance, just wasn't enough. My brain cataloged all this in the background, informing me of the discrepancy, but in something of a muted whisper that couldn't drown out my screams of overwhelming terror.

It wasn't until the milky-white eyes I was staring into fell below the height of my own and widened comically that I managed to gasp a lungful of air and listen to that logical voice. The White Goblin continued to lose to gravity right until it hit the wall under the ridge below me. It sounded both like what I expected a three-hundred-pound, muscled freak hitting a wall *would* sound like, and like nothing I'd ever heard.

The entire cavern ledge I was standing on shook as a resounding *thud* hammered noisily through the air and stone I was desperately holding onto. The part I hadn't been expecting was the frantic scrabbling, grunting, and shrieking that accompanied it. I could no longer see the beast and had to imagine he was attempting to find hand and footholds to climb up to me.

I moved further down the ridge before I leaned back and peered over the edge. Sure enough, the creature was jumping up and down from the floor fifteen feet below the ridge, trying to get to us. Relief flooded my limbs, causing them to almost feel weak compared to the adrenaline-induced hypertension from split seconds before.

It didn't last long, as I heard Dave shriek. My arms tensed again, and I spun my head around to try to find my friend. I couldn't see him but knew he wouldn't make that kind of sound without a reason. A reverberation through my hands, accompanied by the sound of rock hitting rock, clued me in on the projectiles.

I spun back around toward the shore and found a group of twenty White Goblins winding up to throw stone-tipped spears. I also saw ten of them in various stages of retracting arms from a throw or standing empty-handed—like they'd already thrown.

My eyes found the airborne weapons just a moment before one almost skewered me. I managed to heave on my right arm and pull myself a foot in that direction, which was only enough for the spear to collide with my lower left back and pierce right through. Thankfully, the wall was also stone, so it didn't pin me in place like it might have with wood. But when stone hit stone, it caused vibrations—and while I hadn't felt pain when the spear had entered my back, driven through my muscles, organs and out my front—I felt it now.

The shaft of the weapon vibrated violently, sending ripples of cascading agony screaming through my body to my brain. I managed to turn a shriek of pain that might have been similar to Dave's into a roar of challenge as my body attempted to seize up, and I fought it. I would not fall off here. I knew what awaited below.

Either the Fish or the Goblins…

I won't fall! I repeated that mantra as I clamped my teeth shut and clenched my jaw. More spears thudded against the wall, and two other screams from my group echoed over the cavern as I rhythmically planted one foot to the right and shuffled.

My grip, only maintained by my increased Strength, had no feeling— each handhold was created by chipping away loose waterworn rock with my bare hands until my fingers dug in to a solid piece, rather than finding anything existing. I was numb, and so when my lead arm swung toward the wall and didn't hit anything, I didn't fully notice or comprehend what it meant. I started to shuffle and my foot found empty air. I was going to fall—my brain was certain of it. My body, while stronger than it had ever been before, couldn't recover from this—

My momentum changed and I was heaved around the corner by strong hands tugging at my arm that had just missed the non-existent wall. I swung for just a moment out above the water and even heard a few splashes as multiple spears missed the wall and me, before sinking into the deep.

Then I realized that it could also have been the spear that was still protruding from my back…

My father swung me, allowing me to dip below the stone ledge before heaving me up like a kettlebell. My weight was not distributed like a kettlebell, however, and so my dad was forced to release his grip on my arm or risk overbalancing and tipping into the water. I became airborne for just a moment, unsure if I was out above the lake or above the stone ledge.

My earlier odd question was answered as my injured back collided with hard stone, snapping off the shaft of the spear. Like the vibrations from the tip hitting stone, the agony redoubled, even as I was dimly aware of rolling twice before I lost momentum. My body continued to scream its distress through nerve endings that were likely severed from a semi-sharpened rock-spear.

"Your *Recovery* is already working to heal your kidney. Dave needs you, *now!*" Smegma insistently whispered. "Do *not* close your eyes. Stand up."

I heard him. Certainly. And I wanted to do as he said, but even the thought of moving sent renewed cold, glass slivers screaming out from my wound. *Is the spearhead still in there?*

"It isn't. Now stand up! Dave doesn't have a *Recovery* Skill!"

I managed to plant my hands beneath my shoulders. The urgency in Smegma's voice moved me in a way I wouldn't have thought possible even milliseconds before.

Smegma continued to coax me, making sounds of encouragement or berating my laziness anytime I even hinted at pausing or collapsing.

My mind fought my agony-riddled body and might have lost. Luckily, one of the two had a high Ranked Skill assisting it. Sure, I crawled the last bit of the way to my friend, but husk anyone who says I didn't make it there as fast as I humanly could.

My numb hands didn't register the sensation of wetness that they rested in toward the end of my trek. My eyes were mechanically focused on the ground, but my next ponderous crawling 'step' ending with a sickening splash finally broke through my pain-fogged brain. Glancing up, I took in the strange gleam of greenish-black liquid and traced it back to Dave's leg.

A spear protruded from it. Dave was facedown and unmoving. How my friend had made it around the corner, I couldn't say—but the need for Smegma's coaxing ended with that sight. Dave was dying, and I was kneeling in his blood.

"Pull out the spear," Smegma ordered, getting my father's attention. "Use it to keep any Goblins from getting around that corner. Brodie—"

I froze, my hand already halfway to Dave's leg.

"That's right. Heal him."

My eyes cataloged a fountain of blood that followed the spear, a fountain I thought was only reserved for theatrics in movies. The sight made me twitch, even as I jerked toward the sucking noise and leg wound that caused it. Shaking from fear and exhaustion, my hand hit Dave's hamstring as I began pumping my Mana into *Minor Heal.*

I was immensely thankful for my MNS at that moment. I doubted my old straw method could have functioned in the stressful environment. My hand glowed green, adding its own soft light to the abundance coming off the moss-covered Snake I knew was there.

"Pull a cooked Mirror Fish out of your storage," Smegma ordered, and it took me a moment to realize he was talking to me. He actually repeated himself before the connection sparked. As soon as I pulled out a steak, Smegma continued talking to someone else. "Thaw it with your hands. Then flip Dave over and feed it to him.

"In fact, pull out all the cooked fish you have. It needs to thaw," the Demon said calmly, seeming to change his mind.

I managed to obey but felt my eyelids flutter, then close.

"No!" Smegma shouted. "Someone smack him!"

Something lightly hit my cheek, and I attempted to lean on it.

"Not lightly, Willa! Hit him hard. Wake him the husk up!"

An electric crack sounded from inside my ear, from my jaw—from my scalp? The electricity permeated each pore of my skin individually and jolted me awake. Smegma's black eyes stared into my own. "Do *not* fall asleep. Each drop of husking Mana you regain goes into Dave! Willa, keep smacking him if he even husking blinks."

At some point, Jarred flipped Dave over and fed him—already chewed fish? Thankfully, the need for Willa to keep smacking me let up as my own wound passed some sort of threshold, allowing my body to feel exhausted but not catatonic. I saw why the fish was already chewed as Jarred spit a mouthful into a hand and then transferred it to Dave's mouth.

He then massaged his Adam's apple, like I had for my uncle in the cavern to get the potion down his throat. Dave's throat moved and I managed a weak smile in celebration. He was alive—

My own stomach shuddered violently and then growled insistently.

"You need to eat something too," Smegma said. "That Passive Skill might not use Mana, but it sure uses your body's existing biological systems, which need fuel. Grab some fish and let it thaw in your mouth."

I picked up a cold fish steak and broke off a semi-softened corner before I heard a splash that drew my attention. At the corner stood my father with the bloodied spear from Dave's leg. I could see him leaning back from a thrust—and tilted my head before Smegma's face filled my vision.

"Eat, moron. Dave needs your continued Healing. Your father will keep knocking the White Goblins into the lake!"

A voice echoed out from our corner of the ridge and shelf. The same corner we all hid around.

"I'm not sure how much longer I can keep knocking these bastards into the lake!" my father shouted.

"You husking will do what must be done. We don't let our Sect-mates die if we still draw breath," Smegma growled.

CHAPTER 16: CHAPTER 68

Monday, April 29th, 2069

"**B**rodie, you need to wake up and take a turn," Smegma somehow not only shouted in the physical world but also inside my dream. I couldn't even recall what the dream had been about, but I did know I had been about to either die or narrowly escape—and the final image was of a scar-faced White Goblin…

My eyes opened but felt heavy, unable to fully break the crust from the sands of sleep. My vision started to resolve into green-highlighter-like.

I inhaled deeply and the first thing my nose registered was a different smell—the caverns we were Mining smelled of damp and swamp the deeper we were, at least until we entered the facility, where the air seemed to be dusty and stale. The lake chamber in comparison was cleaner still, smelling exactly like my memories of a rocky beach.

Now there was a cloying smell. It was a combination of sweet and rot that instantly caused my gorge to rise. It also caused me to both cough and contract my core, sitting me up.

"What the husk is that smell?" I groaned and adjusted my breathing to my mouth only.

"They're cooking on shore," Smegma answered, even as his winged, human-sized black form seemed to resolve itself out of the green highlighter.

"Cooking what?"

"It's better that you don't think about it," Smegma answered quietly. This usually would have been a perfect time for him to either call me stupid or show off his superiority in some way. The fact that he hadn't, and his serious tone, told me to drop it—but I had a few niggling suspicions in the back of my head that I pointedly ignored.

My vision finally adjusted to the green light, and I found Dave asleep beside me on the shelf. I couldn't remember how long I had stayed by his side Healing, but I reached a hand over and tried to use *Minor Heal* again. Only a single point of Mana went through before his body rejected further efforts.

I had determined earlier that this meant he was fully healed, so I breathed a sigh of relief as his chest rose and fell. His face wasn't greener than it should have been, that was just the lighting. He wasn't breathing heavily, that was just my overactive brain.

Beside Dave, I found my father curled in a fetal position, shivering. His breathing was shallow and quick. I stood up and moved to his side, sending *Minor Heal* into him through his exposed tricep. He took five points of Mana.

The next person in line was Willa—she needed four points. Finally, Jarred, the last one still awake, was found at the corner with the spear. He wasn't using the weapon, instead leaning around the edge in ten-second intervals, even as he sweat profusely. I could tell he was scared, amped up, and tired. *Surely, Smegma was warning my uncle of an impending attack by the Goblins on shore...*

I turned to the Demon and he nodded to me, confirming my unspoken thought. I hadn't even been awake since the initial assault and seemed to have understood the situation better than Jarred—tensions must have been high after I passed out...

[Can you fill me in on what went on—after I relieve Jarred?] Smegma nodded again, and I reached out a hand to Heal Jarred. As soon as my fingers touched his elbow, the man jumped and screamed bloody murder. I pulled back and ducked as the spear was swung like a staff in my direction. Thankfully, it missed.

"Husk!" Jarred said breathily. "It's you, Brodie. Don't sneak up on me like that!"

"He's been awake for a few minutes, moving around Healing the others. How could you have missed him, you imbecile?" Smegma insulted. "It's your turn to sleep, Jarred. Brodie, heal him. Then, Jarred, you eat some food and sleep. Brodie will take over as sentinel."

Jarred looked like he wanted to be upset and showed his distaste of Smegma by not even glancing in the Demon's direction. Still, the primary emotion that played over his face was relief. I decided to not scold Smegma, instead reaching out one hand for the spear and another to once again attempt to touch Jarred's forearm.

As soon as I made contact, I sent eight points of Mana into *Minor Heal* and saw even more relief and exhaustion wash over my Uncle. He, of course, didn't release the spear, gripping the weapon like it was a handhold that was preventing him from falling off a cliff. Feeling this resistance, and not wanting to overpower him, I coaxed, "Give me the spear, uncle Jarred."

The man looked at me in confusion, and then at his own hand, before he managed to send the signals to the limb to release the shaft. He managed a sheepish grin after that, and a pat on my shoulder, before he slunk by me toward the others.

Smegma followed him, "Eat some of the fish, you blithering monkey! Don't go right to sleep!"

Jarred was literally in the process of lying down and only just managed to stop himself, stumble to the very diminished pile of cooked Mirror Fish, and suck back a steak without chewing before he collapsed right beside it. Smegma looked at the man with distaste but hovered back to me a moment later.

"I'm invisible to them now, so this will work better than with the others," Smegma said before hovering out and around the corner. He faced me, but at an angle that was clearly intended to keep an eye on the Goblins on shore as well. "So, there were fifty of the creatures on shore after your narrow escape and desperate Healing of Dave. They tried multiple times to climb the wall, walk the ridge and even hit you through the solid rock walls with thrown spears, even though you're all around the corner and out of sight.

"That's why they're all weaponless. I can say with certainty that they won't try to come to the edge, or the water route again, either."

[What?] I interjected, glancing at the placid lake below.

"Imbecile, wake up!" Smegma scolded. "Do you think the huge Mirror Fish just eat each other?" My eyes widened when they made the connection, and I shivered at the thought of facing the car-sized creatures in the lake. "Now, there are probably only ten on shore, and the others left in a huge group. I assume they are heading back to their own village because one or two did return with the cook-pot and food. They also brought more spears, but..."

Smegma chuckled and motioned at the water. I knew that we were in a dire situation, but his amusement was infectious—causing me to both realize what had happened and smirk at the stupidity of the White Goblins.

Did that make them any less terrifying?

Maybe a tiny bit, but stupid creatures driven by primal instinct that could tear me apart with their bare hands were hard to find unthreatening. Still, it gave me a bit of hope in an otherwise dark and depressing situation.

[So, do we try to escape?] I asked, looking at the ledge and the continued ridge we could traverse deeper.

Smegma tapped a talon on a fang but shook his head. "I scouted out as far as I could in all directions. While I did come up with an option for later, I think it should be a last resort. First, I didn't find another shelf like this one for a hundred yards, which means you might find yourself trapped out there on the ledge without a place to stop and rest safely. Second, if you don't hit the Time Bubble, which I would *hope* you would—then that means you've exited the Portal Grounds. Then, you and the group would have to survive on a dying world without any hope of rescue..."

Instinctually, I hugged the spear as I shivered. That sounded like a nightmare. I recapped what Smegma had already said, realizing that getting off the shelf wasn't really an option.

Obviously, going back the way we came to shore meant facing the White Goblins. While we had a single spear and Miner's Picks, and they had no weapons, at this exact moment, a direct conflict was sure to end badly. Even if a single one of the group died-which I figured would already be a miracle—that still meant a loss of a close friend or family member.

None of us were Hunters, though, so even a single one of us surviving seemed unlikely when I truly thought it through. So, fighting was out...

Swimming. I shivered, not even wanting to consider trying to survive in the water with the Mirror Fish that only I could see with *Heat Sense*—nope. Swimming was out.

Going deeper, the thought I'd initially proposed, seemed to be the best option, and admittedly, my brain subconsciously knew that without me having to dive into the why—but Smegma, who had thought it through longer and further than me, seemed to believe that we could get trapped out on a dwindling ledge with White Goblins behind us, occupying our current shelf.

I was inclined to trust that. He had also brought up an even more terrifying possibility. Just like swimming, I didn't even want to consider the possibility where we did escape but ended up outside the Time Bubble.

"Husk!" I whispered.

Smegma sighed, having likely listened to my entire inner thought process. "The good news is that you still have the ability to Fish. You have some Crystals and a defensible position. You can easily survive up here for a few weeks."

My muscles tensed. A few weeks! Living on this ledge, catching Fish and being ever watchful of the White Goblins? Unbidden, I checked the cooked Fish pile—four pieces, and we only needed one per day. Next, I checked the Necklace of Holding and found enough Crystals to likely cook up three more Mirror Fish, maybe five if I overfilled the Frying Pan, using the edges of the cooking instrument as well.

One Fish could probably feed the entire group for one week, and that's where Smegma got his numbers. Three to five weeks of food. Water below us.

Okay, surely the Mirage Guild or another Guild would come down here by then, right?

The distinct lack of an answer to that very pointed hope made me stare just as sharply at Smegma. [What?]

Smegma was looking at the shore, a talon tapping a fang. When he didn't answer, I leaned out around the edge. The Goblins who had left were returning, carrying more wood and metal. I stared at the stacks they were making, even as the ten who were around the fire and cook-pot stood to begin unstacking the piles being made. What the hell?

A scar-faced White Goblin carrying a massive circular, metal-wrapped and tipped log clued me in on what was happening.

Smegma also 'helped.' "They brought a ballista…"

I re-ran all the options in my head again. Swimming away, no. Fighting, no. Still leaning around the edge, my head spun, and my eyes tracked the ridge leading deeper into the lake cavern toward the farther ledge. We shouldn't take the risk, but we may have to.

Smegma was continuing to 'think,' which made me stop my disaster-planning and once again ask, [What?]

"While a ballista is strong—and probably can break through this stone— I'm not sure how well they will be able to aim that thing, and if they have enough bolts to truly break out the entire ledge."

I translated. 'We should wait and see?'

The ballista was assembled in relatively short order. I was partially surprised that the creatures who had thrown away their spears in haste could assemble something so complicated. Not to mention where they had gotten the thing—

"The System has likely given them some understanding. This could be the result of a Skill, even. That or there is a highly intelligent—husk!"

Ten White Goblins entered through the archway holding two more ballista bolts on their shoulders. However, these bolts held a throne atop them, and in the throne sat a tiny White Goblin, with two AR15s in his hands and more human weapons sitting beside him in the copious space his small frame didn't occupy on the throne.

The scarred Goblin returned and lifted the leader from the throne, placing him down on the ground as the ten others lowered the carriage. *Did those morons carry the leader here like that the whole husking way? Were they complete idiots?*

114

"It might be why it took them so long," Smegma answered. "And at least it makes me slightly less worried—"

Smegma was cut off as the four-foot-tall leader of the White Goblins began firing both AR15s in the general direction of the ledges' corner. Thankfully, his aim was beyond poor, which gave me time to duck back into hiding.

The report of the weapons woke up everyone instantly, but while they were all sitting up and looked extra green in the face due to obvious paling—they were all looking away from me.

The green light moved strangely on their faces, almost seeming to create wave patterns that shouldn't—

I scanned the water and found ripples that grew into large waves in the otherwise still water. I followed those waves back to the epicenter and found two serpentine yellow eyes with pupils shrinking as they focused on something to my right.

Since I was facing the creature, and on the very edge of the step, the massive Snake could only be staring at the White Goblins.

I could barely breathe as the creature slowly uncoiled to the sound of repeated gunfire. A strange, hollow *thump* rang out, followed by a ting of metal on stone, before there was a quick splash down into the lake—and a hammer-blow to my eardrums.

I reeled away from the sound, which luckily was to my left, and further onto the ledge, even as water, stone chips and a concussion wave slammed into my right side.

Had that been a husking grenade launcher?

Smegma's mouth moved animatedly in my vision, but I couldn't hear anything but ringing. Seeing my wide-eyed look of confusion, he pointed to the ledge off the shelf that led deeper into the lake cavern. Accompanying the gesture, Smegma screamed, [It's time to go!] mentally into my mind.

I didn't disagree with Smegma, but I was transfixed by a sight so cold— so chilling—it froze me in place, *Mental Fortitude* or not. Behind the Demon, the Snake finished uncoiling and dipped its head into the water. Seeing the creature move and watching the moss fall off its scales to reveal gleaming, thickly-impenetrable, perfect black 'armor' shook me to my core.

As more of the creature entered the water, more moss fell off and sank into the depths, taking the majority of light we had with it. Another grenade exploded as the shelf grew darker. Then another. I stared at what little moss was left on the ever-diminishing body of the Snake, slipping into the dark waters.

Some moss had fallen onto the island of bones, making me hope that the cavern wouldn't become completely dark. But as the Snake moved, the island shifted and started to break up. The few pieces that I counted on for sustained light fell into the water, along with fishbones.

I'm not sure how long I, and the group, watched the Snake slither off his perch. It couldn't have been too long, based on the grenades continuing to explode behind us, but just as the tip of the tail descended beneath the now turbulent waters and the final pieces of moss sank away in dimming green patches—the Goblins began to scream.

CHAPTER 17: CHAPTER 69

Monday, April 29th, 2069 or Thereabouts

It took my eyes quite a while to recognize that there were still low levels of light in the large lake cavern. The shore was illuminated by the metallic yellow fixtures after all, and a few tiny pieces of moss clung to what little remained of the island of bones. Still, by the time my eyes adjusted, and I found the courage to peek around the corner—the screaming had stopped.

More terrifying, the shore was devoid of all White Goblins—bodies, weapons, campfire, everything! Eerily, there was no sign of the massive Snake's body either. Unless you counted the shape of the cavern now. I wasn't entirely positive, but the shoreline looked distinctly larger—taller, deeper and wider. Almost like a Snake's mouth had bitten out a piece of the stone the way I might take a bite out of a cake.

I heard it then. Or I guess what I 'heard' was an utter lack of sounds. Till that moment, I could hear the increased tempo of everyone's breathing, shuffling feet, the scratch of Mining gear rubbing itself over outdoor clothing. The creak of work boots. Or just under the breath, fearful prayers to any God that would listen.

All of that was gone. All that remained was the steady lapping of waves in what should have been a still lake. My mind picked up on the disparity in that wave pattern. There were waves hitting the walls under our little ledge, but there were also waves crashing against another surface very nearly atop of those walls.

My head turned slowly, hoping I wouldn't find what I expected.

The metallic yellow light from the shore bounced back to me, and my body convulsed. Close enough to me that I could touch it, I found an amber-tinted glass-lens of an eye with a vertical, slivered pupil.

My brain froze, making it hard to look away for two reasons. First, the pupil of the eye was larger than I was tall, and wider. The eye itself was at least five to ten times bigger than me stacked atop myself. Second, and the far more pressing reason—if an eye of the Snake was that close to me—so was the massive World Destroying creature.

"Etu dea vas?" the non-existent wind in the chamber seemed to hiss at me.

"Elan evan cos, tua don," Smegma responded, making me realize that someone had actually said something—it was just in a language I didn't know.

The Snake's pupil, eye, and body pulled back and away for a moment, making me realize I had been staring into the 'smallest' eye in the center of the things *forehead*. I could still see two other eyes on each side of its head like a normal snake as well. That entire head—easily as large as four of the ATVs—tilted, seeming to regard the hovering Smegma.

116

Then all of its eyes closed and its entire body vibrated, causing the wavy water to ripple, then undulate, creating highs and lows that crashed against each other so quickly and furiously that I involuntarily stepped backward before discovering I was already pressed into the wall.

Was it preparing some sort of attack?

"Bow, you morons! Even among the highest echelons of S-Rankers, this thing would be considered a Monarch," Smegma whispered angrily. I managed to peel my eyes off the creature and looked around the shelf. All of the group was likewise pressed up against the wall, in some cases still attempting to back up further into it.

Smegma's words hadn't registered with everyone—so he quickly sped toward each person in turn. Ending with me. "Bow your husking head or become an appetizer for this thing!"

The nearness and urgency of his words made me fall to my knees in a full-on yoga Child's Pose. As I descended, I took in the others and found each one in different bows. My father was bent fully at the waist to almost ninety degrees with his hands held above his head.

Jarred was holding a necklace and only bowing his head, while his legs and body shook with uncontrolled fear. Willa had gone so far as to lay face down on the floor, not even in a semblance of a bow—maybe she had passed out and face-planted?

Dave had chosen a similar position to myself, but was leaned far more forward. I didn't dare look up to see what Smegma was doing after he'd given us all 'instructions.' I just stayed bent and staring at a small watermark on the rock ledge.

"Isss thisss the language they ssspeak," that same whispered, windy hiss said. My body twitched at the familiar voice suddenly speaking words I could understand. I wasn't sure if that made this situation better or worse?

"Yes, Great One," Smegma's voice answered, a strange deferential reverence in the tone that I'd never heard from him before.

"Good. Are thessse the creaturesss going through the Trialsss of Assscendancsse?"

"Yes, one of them, Great One."

"Then perhapsss one of them can be of ussse to me. Which one of them isss your massster, little fly?"

"This one, Great Being," Smegma said, and I felt my heart attempt to stop beating as it clenched hard enough to cause my chest to bloom in physical pain. Thankfully, after a very short pause, Smegma continued in a deferent whisper, "However, this entire group is related. If you kill any of them—none will help you willingly."

"Do not presssume, little fly. If thisss bunch will not help me, then they all die, and I make the sssame offer to the sssurfacsse dwellersss. The sssurfacsse dwellersss that abandoned thessse sssimiansss here."

"Forgive me," Smegma bowed. "I only meant to inform the Great One of the most ideal lever for coercing these primitives. I have spent some time with them and have learned that they possess a baffling level of concern for the wellbeing of relations. I understand that the Great One was the deity of those who once called this place home, and that the Great Being is well aware of ideal applications of power—that often destruction or the threat of such are not always the best methods of motivation over his subjects."

"Indeed?" The Snake seemed pleased. "Well sssaid. Yesss, it hasss been sssome time, but I do remember quite well my role and oversssseeing my domain."

I was somewhat put out by Smegma's words, but understood that he was trying to keep us alive. Did he have to sound like he believed what he was saying so much, though? Also, how did the Snake know that the Mirage Guild had abandoned us in the cave? I didn't know and probably shouldn't care. Either way, I still felt a gong of confirmation ring through my chest at the pronouncement. Like I could somehow tell it knew what it said was the truth.

The situation, or perhaps my *Mental Fortitude*, allowed me to assess the situation. First, we were going to be abandoned down here by the Mirage Guild forever—which, in the current situation, didn't mean much, but it put the entire last two days into a new perspective. *We've been dead down here since that cave-in.*

It had just been a question of *how* we were going to die. Somehow, that freed my terrified mind from the grips of whatever power held it in place. I lifted my head just enough to see the Snake regarding the respectfully bowed Smegma.

Coughing to unclench my throat, I got the thing's attention and instantly felt my already dry mouth fill with sand. I swallowed, once, twice, and a third time before I managed to croak, "The Demon is right. We would be nothing more than grains of sand in your stomach, Great One. Please allow my group to cook you Mirror Fish, while me and my Summon perform whatever task you desire."

"Cooked Mirror Fisssh?" the Snake said. It then closed its eyes and stuck out a forked tongue that was easily the width of all five of us humans laid side-to-side. Even the length of the slithering tongue seemed absurd as it crossed a good distance back to the shore. "Isss that what I sssmell? I have not tasssted cooked Mirror Fisssh in many eonsss. Not sssincsse the Naga fled."

Smegma twitched, and I felt something from our connection. Thanks to my clarity of mind, I finally felt it. Just out of my conscious awareness, there was a ball of feelings coming from the *Demonic Vault* Skill's Sun in my Mental Universe. Smegma was… hopeful?

"Then, Great One—allow this one to Fish from shore—" Smegma motioned at Dave, the only other one in the group who had attempted to learn to touch his Mana Pool. "Allow one of the others to Cook atop the forge—and as my Summoner suggests, we will complete whatever task you desire. But, as I spoke before, I believe that you will find that the best service will be gained by keeping everyone alive. From my study of these people, I believe that the threat of harm to any of the others will serve as excellent motivation for any of them to work faithfully and hard toward any desires you have."

The Snake's eyes remained closed for seconds, then stretched to minutes—and longer. No one spoke, even though I felt the need to ask multiple questions—I held them tight.

Surely, the Snake hadn't fallen back asleep?

"Very well. *You*"—The creature looked directly at me and then panned over the group—"will catch and cook for me one hundred fisssh," the Snake hissed contentedly.

My face paled. I had maybe four in my Necklace of Holding—and Dave could maybe catch one before waiting for his Mana to recharge.

"My apologies, Great One," Smegma said. "None of these simple simians have the Mana Pool to catch that many Fish. If you wish to give us a few days—"

"No. You will have twenty-four hoursss," the Snake hissed over the Demon's words. "But, I will let you ussse the Naga'sss baublesss…"

In a motion too quick to follow, the Snake vanished. I jerked back onto my heels as the massive head of the Snake was suddenly missing. I heard the water of the lake sloshing violently, and then simultaneously heard the sound of clattering glass, stones and metal from around the corner and back on shore.

Then, all in a blink, the Snake's head was back. What in the hell had just happened?

"You two will alssso need what isss assshore. You may move there." When no one instantly stood up, the Snake barked in a sharp hiss, "*Now!*"

I jumped to my feet and began scrambling around the corner. I discovered that the ledge back to shore was not the same as it had been when I climbed out here. Thankfully, it wasn't narrower, and instead was deeper, but sloped in the exact shape of a Snake's bite.

This forced me to do something of a bear crawl, or forward-leaning-push-up shuffle, along the edge back toward the now-deeper shore. Only when I arrived did I scan the shore and discover that there was a pile of shining spheres, orbs, and metallic items.

Slowly, I moved toward the pile—hoping it was what the Snake had called 'baubles' that we could use. I definitely didn't want to try and take something that wasn't granted us by the massive creature.

"Yesss, thossse," the Snake hissed disdainfully, seeming to respond to my slow, shuffling steps. "The Coresss encasssed in metal are Mana Batteriesss. The other Coresss you will need to take with you to the Goblin village."

I looked at the Monster Cores, the ones on display quite different from the ones I'd seen in the Malls. The colors, specifically. There were just too many greens, yellows, and blues…

"Sorry, Great One. Why would we need to take these Monster Cores to the White Goblin village?" Smegma asked, even as I made the connections to what 'Cores' the creature was talking about. He was *giving* us Monster Cores? From the pile in front of me, it wasn't just a few. There were hundreds—if not a thousand—unadorned Monster Cores in the pile.

"You musssst close the Portal, ssstupid fly," the Snake said. "You. Fisssher Boy. Take that blue bauble with the purple metal. It wasss one of the Naga'sss favoritesss."

Dave had moved as far as to stand shoulder to shoulder with me, so I felt him jump beside me at the Snake's words.

I scanned the pile with my friend, trying to find the item that Dave was intended to use. Thankfully, while there was quite a bit of purple, it wasn't an overly abundant color in the pile, so we found it after a few seconds that felt like minutes. I breathed a sigh as I pointed it out to the already moving Dave. He'd jumped forward, his reaching hand already tracking the same orb I'd found.

Once he picked it up, he spun and looked at me with wide, confused eyes. I started to sputter at his unspoken question. I didn't know how to use the thing either. Thankfully, Smegma either read my thoughts or Dave's paling, terrified face. "Use the same trick you used with the Rod. Simply grow a connection from the Orb to your Pool, and then from your Pool to the Rod."

I pulled a Rod out of my Necklace of Holding and hurriedly handed it to my friend.

Willa shuffled her feet behind me, and at my glance, held up a shaky hand, clearly wanting me to give her something. I pulled out the other Rod and passed it over.

As her shaking hand and fingers closed around the Rod, I whispered, "Get Dave to help you feel it out."

My father and Jarred moved forward as well, and I realized that one would need to cook for the Snake while the other likely cleaned and gutted the fish that Dave *hopefully* caught. "Okay. Uncle Jarred, you filet the fish." I handed him the better repaired fileting Knife. "Dad, you come with me, and we'll get the Frying Pan heating up."

"Oh, Great One," Smegma said deferentially. "Do you have any Mana Crystals we can use to cook?"

The Snake scoffed and vanished again. Then, out of the water shot a great deal of F-Rank Mana Crystals. Probably a couple thousand. The group ducked and covered as the Crystals flew over their heads, bounced off the walls and then clattered to the shore all around them.

I got struck by at least four dozen, but thankfully they weren't traveling fast. I heard a few of the Crystals crack, but as I raised my head, I discovered that the vast majority hadn't. I moved around the shore, collecting as many of the Crystals as my Necklace of Holding could contain.

Once it was full, my father and I moved to the furnace room. As soon as we exited the pens, my father grabbed my arm hard. "Don't do this, Son. Surely we can es—"

"No, you heard Smegma and saw that thing. Not to mention that it knows what's happening on the surface. It can likely hear this conversation even now. We do what it asks, and we do it to the best of our ability. Or we all die."

"Why does it need *us* though?" my dad whispered, even as his grip slackened on my shoulder. I turned, dislodging his hand, and moved to the furnace indent in the smithy room.

I first dumped some Crystals into the depression, and then placed the Frying Pan atop them. The rest of the Crystals became a pile beside the raised apparatus. The cooked and uncooked Mirror Fish steaks, as well as the yellow Crystals, I dropped on a nearby floor—clearing out everything in my inventory other than the Mining Picks.

Then I stepped down hard on the foot pedal and instantly rushed to my dad with the second fileting Knife in hand. "In case you need to help Jarred clean more fish. Three minutes a side, when cooking. I'll finish whatever task I must to get us all out of here. I'm going back—don't do anything stupid!"

His arms closed around me and pulled me into a hug. I was forced to cradle the fileting Knife between us so I didn't stab myself or him. The hug grew tighter and tighter, but eventually I pushed back, dislodging my father. "I need to go back. Or risk everyone."

Seeing unshed tears in my father's eyes, I spun and rushed out of the smithy and back toward the lake shore. Smegma was looking at me, as I ran through the archway and back onto shore.

"Good thing you talked him out of that," the Snake hissed. "I wasss about to eat one or two of thessse onesss if you two attempted to leave."

I swallowed—so, the Snake could hear or somehow sense what was going on, even outside of its immediate vicinity. While that didn't confirm it knew what was happening on the Portal's surface, it sure seemed to point that way.

"We are just scared, Great One," I answered softly with a bow. "But we will all do our best to do as you ask." I looked meaningfully at Willa, Jarred, and Dave's back. I guess my pointed reminder wasn't needed as my friend was already fighting against a hooked Mirror Fish on the line.

"Umm—" I stuttered for a moment after making that realization. Then caught myself and spat out, "What exactly should we do at the Goblin Village, Great One?"

"Clossse the Portal, idiot."

"Great One?" Smegma questioned. "These here are simple Crafters and Laborers. They cannot defeat a Boss."

"The Bosssss of thisss Cave Sssysssstem is already in my ssstomach. Justicsse hasss been sssserved upon that pathetic 'king,' who woke me from my sssslumber. You will need to dissspatch some Worker Goblinsss, but no Bossss. No, thisss Portal is clossssed by Ssskill Ritual."

"Skill what?" I said before I could think better of it. Then I started as my brain whirred to life and added, "Great One," deferentially.

"Ssskill Ritual—Endowment. Whatever you wisssh to call it. Placsse nine of the Coresss upon the Bossss'sss Altar."

"May I ask why you need our help to do that, Great One?" Smegma asked, sounding as confused as I felt. "You've clearly got enough undigested Cores here…"

"Undigesssted?" the Snake hissed a rhetorical question to itself and then slithered its tongue out. "We do not consssume thisss energy. No matter the age. Thisss energy isss under the purview of the Sssysssstem. It isss not meant for usss."

I blinked as the Snake's tongue slithered in and out of its mouth a few more times. "We Asscend if we complete a Sssysssstem-given tasssk or if the Planet we were born upon Asscendsss. Only the Sssysssstemsss' Chossssen can ussse itsss direct energy."

"So, these Cores are like Skill Cards?" Smegma asked, seeming to interpret something in the Snake's words that I couldn't have even hoped to comprehend.

"Ahh yesss, the Cardsss. That bringsss back memoriesss from an era long passst. For the Naga, it was Papyrusss. These Coresss are the sssame energy, yesss."

"So, we just have to place them on an Altar and the Dungeon will close, Great One?" Smegma asked.

"Yesss, and the actor of the accomplisssshment will be granted a Ssskill."

CHAPTER 18: CHAPTER 70

Monday, April 29th, 2069

I'll admit I didn't know what to say in response to that bombshell. Was the massive Snake saying that there was an Altar inside the White Goblin village that just *granted* Skills in exchange for Monster Cores? Surely, I'd heard wrong…

"An Altar that exchanges Monster Cores for Skills, Great One?" Smegma asked. "So, these Cores have taken the place of Card Shards?"

"No, and yesss," the Snake answered. "The Sssysssstem removed the Cardsss due to functionality issssuesss. Sssincsse I never usssed them, I don't know the particularsss, but sssurely you'd have sssome guesssesss."

"Problems with the Card System, Great One?" Smegma answered and then began tapping a talon to fang. "Well, people hoarded the Cards in attempts to get Sets and sell them for more. Others complained about the lack of chances to find the Skill they needed to complete existing Sets. The variability on what got created, even from 'high rank—'"

"You missstake my commentsss for caring," the Snake cut in. "I jussst want my fisssh and you to clossse the Portal. If I Asssscend now, I would need to begin by breaking the Sssysssstem Time Bubble, which would impossse sssanctionsss and make my Asssscensssion Trial more difficult. Take the Coresss and go. Or ssshould I partake of the… appetizssersss."

Everyone shivered. Except Smegma, who only smiled and bowed. "I can see that I was quite right that the Great One would be adept at motivating his subjects."

Husking teacher's pet.

I saw Smegma give me the middle of his three fingers behind his back as I jumped forward toward the pile of Cores and began summoning them hurriedly into my Necklace of Holding. Smegma had floated just as quickly behind me. I could see the Demon twitching and blinking as I stuffed more and more of the pile into my Necklace.

I was in such a hurry that I didn't even realize why Smegma was reacting until I got to the center of the pile. The Cores were growing in clarity and size. Even more strangely, many of the Cores were iridescent, containing no color but hints of every color as the light refracted through the perfectly clear, circular Cores.

My hand began to shiver as it approached the largest Core in the pile, easily the size of my entire head and chest. Clenching my teeth, I summoned it into my Necklace and kept going.

Soon, there were only the Cores with metal attached remaining. What I assumed were Mana Batteries. I reached out and summoned the largest of those into my Necklace, hoping I could use it to fuel Skills or items like Dave was for Fishing.

"You will give back what you don't ussse," the Snake said as it slowly began to curl in on itself. My quick glance at it made me shiver again. While the action and its half-lidded reptilian eyes gave the impression of laziness, I recalled just how quickly it moved—when it wanted to.

I nodded, unsure how I could return the 'excess' if I closed the Portal, but willing to do whatever the thing wanted if it kept everyone alive. With a shaky bow, I stuttered, "We'll head out, then, Great One."

"The timer already ssstarted," the Snake said offhandedly.

I couldn't rush from the lakeside faster unless I broke into a jog or sprint. I didn't want to do that in case it would look like I was running away, so I held myself to the speediest walk I could manage.

Passing through the animal pens, I found my father walking back to the lake with a stack of Mirror Fish Steaks balanced on a large stone. I wasn't sure where he'd found the brick or chipped piece of wall, but I was happy he wasn't burning his hands to get the food to the Snake.

My walk froze as I saw him. He stopped as well. We stared at each other for a stretching minute before his jaw visibly clenched. I swallowed hard against the lump in my chest, my hands and jaw clenching as well.

"We don't have time for this," Smegma stated. "Get moving. We don't know what's left in the Village."

My father's eyes and my own were locked on each other. As if we had planned it, we both nodded in near unison, which unfroze our legs. My father walked by me toward the lake, and I resumed my speed-walk to the stairs.

As soon as I was through the smithy, I turned the walk into a jog and then a sprint. My lungs screamed at me, even as I used my increased Strength to climb the stairs two and even three steps at a time—thanks to my hands also pulling on the stone railings.

"Slow down, getting there tired isn't going to help—" Smegma shouted after me, but I didn't listen. I just continued to sprint. I needed to be doing something, and the screaming from my lungs at least made it feel like I was trying my best.

My mind told me the same thing as Smegma, but I ignored it too. Sure, I knew they were both being sensible, but sometimes action is needed. Sometimes, talk and planning can wait. My lungs and muscles continued to scream at me, and I continued to run.

Stamina Increased by 1.
Stamina Stat Unlocked.

—

Stats
Strength: 10
Locked.
Stamina: 2
Locked.

Locked.
Locked.
Locked.

The red screen jumped into being in front of me. I blinked at the color and white words on it—trying to understand why Smegma had sent me a Shop item. Right up until I realized that my lungs and muscles had stopped screaming at me. Then, between one blink and the next surprised one, I read the message.

"What the husk?" I exclaimed out of surprise. "Simply sprinting and fighting my own body unlocked Stamina?"

"No, you moron!" Smegma said from beside me. "Look at your Mental Universe."

I realized I'd stopped all forward progress in my shock and resumed a light jog, even as I attempted to fall into that Soul Space Smegma wanted me to. I failed and was forced to wait, despite my desire not to. I guess running while navigating hallways I wasn't fully familiar with wasn't a mindless task like Sharding.

Once I stopped and my heart rate grew slightly calmer, I was able to enter my Mental Universe. What I discovered was a *Fishing* Skill that was easily the same size as the *Mining* Skill had been at level ten. Just like the *Mining* Skill, moons were beginning to form around the planet, even as wisps of blue smoke entered a space where I presumed another moon would eventually form.

"It's from Dave's Fishing?" I asked as I opened my eyes and kept moving.

"And Willa," Smegma added. "No way a single Enchant fed *Overflow* enough in that amount of time. If she's truly never used her Pool before this, and picked it up that fast, that woman might be a prodigy…"

"Really? She would have had to cast her line right after we left?" I said, glancing over a shoulder as I jogged up another set of stairs toward the illusory stalagmite.

"Well, the *Fishing* Skill was probably already level ten before they started. Still, Stamina as a Stat and not a Resource Pool? You humans are *weird*."

Shrugging, I started sprinting again, making it to the courtyard level, and then through the side caverns before climbing toward the stalagmite. Smegma remained silent, clearly examining his own earlier thoughts. I did recall the Demon claiming that Stamina was a Resource Pool like Mana, but while it was interesting—I wasn't interested in it—at least, not at a time like this.

What I *was* interested in was just how long I had been sprinting and climbing stairs at what I would call my top speed. I had never been considered athletic in high school—even our gym class's cross country never saw me finishing even a short race in the top half.

Now, all I had to do was reduce my pace for a minute or two and I could resume my full-on sprint again. Thanks to my new-found ability to maintain a fast jog, I was quickly able to exit the stalagmite and begin jogging through the large cavern lit by green moss.

Eventually, Smegma's silence had stretched too long—if only because I could use his reassurance that I was jogging in the right direction. "Smegma, am I going the right way?"

"Huh? Oh, yeah. Try using your *Heat Sense*, dumb-dumb."

I felt like slapping my forehead. Right, *Heat Sense*. I toggled it onto a body part and instantly felt the heat sources of the Goblin's Village a little to my left. Adjusting course, I slowed my jog to a walk and waited until Smegma glided even with me.

Then I watched as he floated right by me, Demon-Bat wings flapping as he cradled one elbow and tapped talon to tooth.

"Smegma!" I hissed. "Kind of need to start planning the infiltration now!"

"Oh, sure, *now* let's start planning. Earlier you just wanted to husking run!" Smegma sneered at me, but after running his tongue over fanged teeth, he shrugged. "I think it's pretty simple. I scout it out. You sneak in—kill anything that gets in the way."

"I think you *overestimate* my ability to kill things!" I hissed and then, hearing my own words echo back to me from a nearby wall, switched to thinking my words at the Demon. [What do you want me to do? Pickaxe the things to death?]

"I don't see why not?" Smegma said, tilting his head in a gesture that looked like genuine confusion.

[What the husk? I've never killed a Monster before, moron!"]

"What about the Mana Leeches and the Golem?" Smegma asked.

[You know that's drastically different!] By this point, any forward progress toward the heat signatures had stopped as I mentally screamed at my Demon Summon.

"Why, because you could kill those insects with a swat of your hand and had a group of helpers on the Golem?" Smegma asked. At my stupefied look of confirmation, Smegma continued, saying something I didn't expect, "With your current Strength Stat, you should be at the very top of F-Rank. If you slap a non-warrior Goblin, I'm guessing you'll break its neck."

For the briefest of moments, I was taken aback, feeling a swelling of something in my chest. Was it pride? Confidence? The rising sensation turned to nausea as I realized what bothered me about the Demon's statement. [Wait! Am I fighting women and children?]

"Holy husk! They're *Monsters*, you batty, Selfless, stupid idiot. They are created by the System and will die when the Portal closes, and they're exposed to the things the Bubble is keeping back." Smegma paused and studied my face, which I could tell was paling by the word. Then in a much softer tone, he added, "It isn't like I'm telling you to slaughter all of them. Just ones that are between you and the husking Altar."

When I didn't immediately start moving again, Smegma sighed.

"It's them or your family, *Mana Battery!*"

I flinched back at the derogatory term for what I had dreamed of being. Then my face began to heat up as blood returned, and my jaw clenched.

Hadn't I told Evelyn I wanted to be something more?

If I was going to be a Hunter, wasn't it my job to close Portals—to kill Monsters? I nodded to myself and was about to take a step forward, breaking my momentary paralysis.

But the Demon's words made a connection I had clearly realized but not fully bridged. I had a Mana Battery that was filled with an abundance of Mana. I also had a Skill that absorbed Mana and gave me Mana Coins. *I could probably suck this thing dry and finally buy a Weapon, or if the thing held enough Mana, maybe even a Combat Skill.*

I pulled the Mana Battery out of my Necklace of Holding and saw Smegma float closer to it, clearly having listened in on my realization. We both stared at it, prompting me to ask, "How do you know how much Mana these things have?"

"Connecting it to your Mana Pool should give you an idea," Smegma answered in a whisper.

That lent itself to the question of how I 'connected' something like a Mana Battery to my core, but Smegma gave me a look that told me just how stupid I was being. Just in case, I asked, "Opposite of a Fishing Rod, I'm guessing."

"Wow, it has a brain," Smegma said with a slow clap.

It wasn't difficult to connect the Mana Battery. As soon as it made contact with my Pool, I could see in my Mental Universe just how abundant and huge the Constellation of Mana Stars were on the other side. Hundreds of thousands at a minimum—maybe even millions of yellow stars spun around each other in a distant orbit so tight that it almost looked like a Sun more massive than *Demonic Vault*.

Smiling, I sent my fifty Mana to the Sun through my Mana Nervous System, and then mentally commanded the Mana in the Battery to feed *Demonic Vault* as well. It vibrated and started moving down my straw-conduit to my Pool, where my Mana Nervous System immediately funneled it onward to the Vault.

The slow siphon started to increase in speed as the two connections were made, and like a water tower feeding a culvert, the Mana rushed into my Pool and then onward—right up until the Sun that was *Demonic Vault* pulsed—hiccuped, and then increased ten folds in its luminosity.

"Ouch," Smegma said. "Husking ow! Stop, shit—*stop!*"

My eyes flew open as I tried and failed to cut the connection I had made between the Mana Battery and my Pool. Smegma had cracks forming on his body. Cracks that looked like a planet's magma core trying to erupt through his skin.

Husk—husk-husk! I internally swore as I tried and failed to cut the connection three more times. It was hard to return to my Mental Universe in my current panicked state, but I had to thank whatever God had orchestrated *Mental Fortitude* falling into my hands. With its help, I managed to force a connection to the Soul Space and then cut the Soul Synapse connection off by blocking a way gate.

I felt the Mana Battery in my clenched hand 'liquify' before 'vanishing,' allowing my hand to snap closed into a fist—surrounding, sand?

I opened my eyes and found the 'Mana Battery,' or the coarse, glass-like sand that was left of it, falling to the ground to make two piles. That... couldn't be good...

[Wasn't I supposed to return that—I mean, the Snake did say to return anything I hadn't *used*. So, this counted, right? *Right?* Smegma?]

When I didn't get a concerned or even a flippant response, I checked on the Demon and found the cracks slowly closing as he stared down at himself. He looked like a vain bodybuilder right after they finished a session at the gym. However, instead of checking his pump and vascularity in a mirror, *he* was trying to make sure the cracks that covered him were vanishing without leaving a trace.

To me, it looked like they were. He heard my thoughts and looked at me. His voice was a bit high-pitched again, like he was still that same Imp I'd first 'summoned.'

He ordered, "Never do that again!" His squeaky voice ruined the tone he was trying to go for.

"What just happened?" I asked, not feeling the need to answer or tell him I wouldn't. That shit had scared me just as much as it had him.

"Remember the yellow Mana Crystals and the incompatible Mana," Smegma answered. I nodded and he made a gesture that connected the sand on the floor to himself. "Incompatible…"

"Shit," I answered eloquently.

"Yeah. Shit is right. Let's hope the Snake didn't see—" The cavern rumbled—which I presumed could only be from one source. Smegma swallowed visibly and then said, "Let's get going to the Village and close this Portal."

I still wasn't totally on board with killing noncombatants, but Smegma had never said that the Monsters in camp were actually women and children. *He called them workers and warriors.*

"Exactly," Smegma encouraged my thought process. "The ones in camp cook, gather, and clean. I didn't want to tell you this, but that stew pot on the lake shore—it had *human* meat in it. That's what the workers cook!"

My stomach gurgled a nauseating warning; I now knew what had happened to the Hunters. Like my mind wanted to torture me, with perfect clarity, I pictured the White Goblins around their cook pot and recalled the smell.

Surely, it hadn't been appetizing at all, right? *I remember thinking it smelled putrid, or was that—*

Mental Fortitude seemed to realize that clarity in the current situation was causing distress and shut that shit down. It was fast enough that I managed not to eject the contents of my stomach—instead, I used the new information and theft of the dead Mirage Hunters' weapons as fuel to flatten my momentary empathy.

All these Monsters deserved to die.

CHAPTER 19: CHAPTER 71

Monday, April 29th, 2069

There were at least a few hundred White Goblins still moving about in the village. I personally could only 'see' about fifteen with my *Heat Vision*, but could feel at least ten times that number of heat sources when I flipped *Heat Sense* onto a body part.

The second, far more distracting 'sense' this close to the village was the smell. Down in the lake cave, the smell of the cook pot had been like something I'd at least associate with cooking. Even though I was still desperately trying to convince myself that the odors of said pot had been nauseating—well, admittedly, the smells coming off the village were going a long way to help that internal unsure dialogue.

The village was foul. It smelled like the body odor of a man who had showered in rancid spiced meats and fecal matter. It was the only way to explain how the malodorous fumes permeated my nostrils and burned my nose hairs; even when I was consciously breathing through my mouth. I fought my urge to gag as the imaginary 'taste' of the air assaulted my tongue.

[If they see with Heat Vision, won't they be able to see me up here, too?] I mentally asked Smegma when he returned from a quick scouting mission.

He'd decided that the safest route would be to follow the small stream down from the lake. And so far, we hadn't run into any Goblins, so he might be right…

They sure didn't seem to wash themselves regularly. I gagged again as I accidentally inhaled a tiny portion of air through my nose. Dammit!

"Would you be able to tell the difference between you and a White Goblin, using *Heat Vision?*" Smegma asked, his word choice sounding condescending, but his tone serious.

[I mean, from here, no. But from closer, I think I would be able to.]

"We'll deal with that, if and when we get to it," Smegma suggested. "Let's not attribute too much intelligence to the Monsters until they show it to us, okay?"

I thought back to the smaller, likely-smarter-than-average Goblin 'King' firing the weapons indiscriminately at a cave wall—and what it had brought him and the warriors. The short confirming nod came pretty easy after that. If that was their brightest bulb, then perhaps sneaking in would be simple.

With Smegma leading the way, we advanced another hundred yards before I crouched behind a rock that probably only hid about a quarter of my body. Still, with both me and the enemy using *Heat Vision*, that wasn't important— or so Smegma had explained rather disdainfully.

The pattern continued, and the smell continued to intensify. I'd pulled up my faceguard at some point, but even it was being completely overwhelmed. As we moved forward again, I discovered why the smell was increasing.

We skirted around a rather large, semi-warm rock—wait—only a few places were warm, like it was a mound of elongated pebbles. Or—shit! My steps stopped as I took in the massive pile of Goblin crap. It was easily three times my height and wider at its base than even the Snake's head.

Then I realized where this huge pile of feces was and wanted to vomit immediately. The poop pile was creating a literal dam in the small stream. I flipped off *Heat Vision* and saw that it wasn't a dam, since a small pathway in the base of the fecal monolith had been eroded—so the water could continue, through the dung and onto the village.

[Are they husking stupid?] I asked, staring at the city-destroying biohazard. This simple act, if perpetrated on Earth, would likely wipe out an entire population of a village or city a hundred times larger than—

"You humans and your hang-ups. Water cannot be contaminated. The System will remove all contaminants if the water is pulled from a proper source. Of course, if the water is in a tank, or container, it can be poisoned. But from a lake, stream, river or even marsh—it can't hurt you!"

[But the taste, then!] I argued, feeling my earlier meal of Mirror Fish climb its way up my throat before I managed to swallow the lump down again. It left a sickly acidic taste behind, which I tried to focus on over the smell.

"Maybe they like it?" Smegma suggested but crinkled his own nose in disgust at the thought. I knew the Demon couldn't smell the putrid, violating smell, so his show of distaste came simply from imagining that taste.

Mirror Fish attempted to 'breach' my stomach through my throat a second time.

[Let's go,] I managed mentally, even as I swallowed the larger lump of my last meal. It felt like it clawed its way physically back down my throat.

Smegma led the way, and we made it far enough past the poop pile for me to at least stop worrying about vomiting—I hoped.

All the movement did mean more reddish-orange outlines of Goblins became visible in my *Heat Vision*. I could see fifty now, moving about in what I assumed were rock huts. Why did I make that assumption?

Toggling off *Heat Vision* showed me one such 'hut.' It was something between an inukshuk and an igloo, with stacked stones that looked like they had been chipped out of walls in whatever shape the Goblins could manage. Those stones were stacked in precarious circles, climbing to about six feet before they tapered inward, forming a very rough dome.

How they stayed standing was why I thought of inukshuks. The stone 'artwork' somehow stuck together and seemed to defy gravity. Supposedly, the sculptures used water as a 'mortar' to give the stones a bit more stick. These rock stacks also had no mortar, which led me to believe that they were created—

"By the System, moron," Smegma interrupted my study of the architecture. "Can we keep moving now that you're done comparing System-created scenery to artwork?"

[I wasn't comparing it—]

"Just be glad the System didn't have them use the shit pile back there as mud!" Smegma interjected again, and I swallowed the bile that tried to rise at the thought. I also flipped him the husking bird! That was a dick move when he couldn't smell the lingering odiferous toilet stank.

I followed Smegma, skirting between the houses, which had Goblins inside. We made it past about ten of the structures, and I was just congratulating myself on my ability to sneak silently when I kicked a rock, bouncing it off a 'hut' and into the brownish-white water of the stream. I summoned my Mining Pick into my hands and clenched the handle tight.

Nothing happened. No grunting shouts or guttural cries of alarm sounded. I looked around me and saw four White Goblin heat outlines in stone huts, all within ten yards. What in the hell?

Smegma of course was nearby and saw the entire 'mishap' and my reaction to it. "Did you think you were being extra sneaky? You sound like a baby Giant taking his first steps, idiot! Just listen to your own breathing for a second."

I did so and instantly felt my face flush with embarrassment. Surely I hadn't sounded like a smithy's bellows the entire time?

"You did—the creatures in the huts are just decoration. Free Monster Cores if Hunters want them, but if you go in there, they will fight, so don't delude yourself about your own combat abilities. Getting injured would be a bad thing." Smegma's black eyes regarded me seriously, telling me that this wasn't meant as an insult. Was it… coaching?

"Up ahead there are four warriors guarding the largest hut. Inside, there is a three-legged chair and a stone dais. I assume that's where the Altar is. Sneaking won't get us inside. It's time to fight—do you understand?"

My hands re-clenched around the haft of the Mining Pick, having slackened after my realization that I wasn't about to be assaulted by a village-worth of Goblins. I took a deep breath, gave a small nod, but simultaneously said, [I can't win against four.]

"I know that, and despite what I just said, that doesn't mean you can't surprise them. They are guards, and they are stationed in front of the two entrances to the stone hut. The hut itself is large enough that they can't physically see each other. If you look right about here, you should see the first pair." Smegma hovered slightly to his right and then pointed to empty air beside him.

Sure enough, I could see two humanoid outlines of heat standing about four feet apart. Behind them, I could just vaguely see two smaller shapes standing in a similar pattern behind the first two. The fact that they were on the very edge of my *Heat Vision* spoke to just how large the leader's hut was.

Knowing my targets gave me a single wave of terror that wriggled and morphed as my *Mental Fortitude* began planning in its wake. Surely, I could charge at the White Goblin pair and dispatch one of the two—then it would just be a one on one, which I might win…

The Goblins had spears, and I had a Mining Pick—wait—why had I pulled the Pick out and not the spear stolen from the Goblin at the lake? I could only blame it on fear. I swapped the 'weapons' and got a nod of confirmation from Smegma.

Now, if I charged—

Smegma interrupted my planning with a strategy of his own that nearly matched mine. "Rush the nearest of the two and attempt to pierce it with your spear. Then release the weapon and pull out your Pick. Do not try to retrieve the spear for the next fight. It is built horribly, and the head is too rough to pull back out of a foe. Stab and release—understand? Grab one of *their* spears if you need to."

I nodded, even as my wide-eyes took in the misshapen head of the spear. How come I hadn't noticed that? My calm and logical brain pointed out my inexperience in combat, as if I wasn't already acutely aware of it. Then again, I guess I had kind of asked the question.

Smegma continued, interrupting my internal thought spiral. "After the first one is injured—don't count on killing it. If you do, great. If not, it still should be out of the fight. On the second one, remember your advantage. You have a high rank *Recovery* Skill, the Strength of a Peak F-Grade combatant, and the Stamina of a low-to-mid F. Use them. Swing as hard as you can, and just avoid taking a fatal blow. Let your *Recovery* and Stamina tank the injuries—okay?"

I gave him another nod but found Smegma's look of earnest coaching shift to confusion and then incredulity. Finally, the Demon added, "No time like the husking present, Brodie."

Oh. Oh! I managed to think to myself as I nodded a third time.

I had a plan—now it was time to act. I took a deep breath and loaded my knees, flexing my quads and calves. I needed four more deep breaths before I pushed off the ground as hard as I could and charged at the two heat outlines.

The issue with *Heat Vision* had always been depth perception. So, when I was sure that I could see them without *Heat Vision*, I deactivated the Skill and slightly adjusted my aim, realizing I had been about to attack the one that was slightly farther from me, which would have left me more exposed to the one on the right.

My brain whirred in front of my actions, telling me that attacking the one on the right from my right gave me the cover of the target's body, which might buy me a fraction of a second for the Mining Pick switch.

Between one slapping, sprinting footfall and the next, both Goblins turned, white eyes training on me. In unison, they lifted their spear shafts off the ground and began to level them in my direction. They were too late. I only had two steps remaining if I continued my current run.

I didn't.

I lunged forward, pushing off my back leg and driving the stone spearhead at the center mass of the right-most Goblin. Unfortunately, my hasty plan to attack from the right wasn't possible thanks to my commitment to the attack and the way the right Goblin stepped back while the left Goblin stepped forward. But other than those initial reactive steps, neither of them really managed much more. They did get their spear tips to drop to about seventy degrees, but then my own weapon slammed home.

I thought I was ready for the blow, having attacked a Stone Golem before. However, what had amounted to a baseball bat swing with a Pick against a stone was nothing like a spear thrust to flesh. Even if the spearhead I was using was rather dull.

There was a split second of resistance, where my hands and arms were forced to flex, before I felt the spear continue past the thing's skin and into a new fleshy medium, with just slightly more resistance than the air.

I instantly released the haft and summoned my Mining Pick, shifting my weight right and away from the left Goblin guard. My peripherals registered something odd flying out of the Goblin and rushing into the hut, but I ignored the strange little light because whatever it was moved away and through the hut door with speed.

I'd have time for that after dispatching guard number two.

"Don't retreat, just swing!" Smegma shouted, causing my lean to the right to falter for a moment. The spear was coming down, though. Every fiber of my being wanted to jump back, but I managed to arrest my momentum with a side-step.

Thanks to my momentum and attempt to jump, I also loaded that leg. With all the strength I had, I pushed back against my own weight and simultaneously swung my Pick, bladed side first, at the Goblin.

The spear was aimed and the Goblin was lunging. The point coming straight at my heart. Still, I was in side-profile to the blow. My heart wasn't easily accessible from that angle. I crunched my lower back and abdomen away from the spearhead, which pulled in my chest a few inches.

The stone point of the spear hit the meat of my left deltoid, then my pectoral, leaving behind it a searing, tearing agony—right until the dullness of the stone edge was forced away from my body by the resistance of my skin.

It was then that my Mining Pick collided with the hip of the leading leg of the White Goblin. My aim was either never good to begin with or my attempt to dodge its blow had thrown it off course. I prepared myself to pull back and exchange another round of strikes—when the blade of the Pick sank through the meat, crunched past the hip bone, and traveled past more meat before finally stopping at the other side of its hip.

It lifted the Goblin off the ground, leaving me semi-supporting the bulk of the creature on the end of my Pick. It didn't last long as my momentum died and my arm muscles bore the entire load. Still, I discovered that if I truly wanted to, I could probably lower the creature softly to the stone floor.

However, that was something I didn't want. In fact, I wanted my damn weapon back. There were three other—

"*Two* others. Trade the Pick for the spear it just dropped. The next two are rushing through the hut—now!" Smegma commanded.

It felt like it took me too long to do as instructed, but my clenched hands let go of my pick. I scanned the ground and found the spear a few feet to my left and in front of me—where my chest and deltoid had deflected it.

Two steps later, I had the spear and found myself staring at two white, ghostly outlines growing in size as they charged me, spears leveled in front of them. It looked the way I imagined I had during my first surprise strike.

But now I was facing two of them, and they were forewarned—

"Stop!" Smegma shouted. "Did you see what happened to the hips of the second guard? It's dying right now because you are several times stronger than it. Don't panic. Move to the right, behind the wall—force them to round the corner."

I jerked in surprise at the Demon's volume but managed to follow the instructions despite my body still attempting to freeze in abject fear. Growling, I forced my legs to listen and took five quick shuffles to my right to get behind the sloppily stacked stones of the hut.

Only then did I manage a single inhalation—I saw a spearhead pass through the opening, and there was no more time to collect myself. I pulled back the haft of my spear and loaded my right leg, which was staggered behind my left in a boxer's stance—meaning my chest was facing the stone, where my front would be most protected.

At the first sign of white skin, I was thrusting the spear forward again like I was a seasoned veteran. The spearhead sank directly into the abdomen of the closest Goblin before it could even get a second step out the door. Of course, that left me without a weapon, unless I pulled this thrust—

"No!" Smegma shouted. "Better to fight barehanded than try to retrieve the spear. Push harder and try to overbalance the one behind. Then release and start stomping or punching."

I followed Smegma's instructions and shuffled my back leg to my front and heaved. My Strength sent the stabbed Goblin into the air, and its body collided with the second guard. I wasn't sure what Smegma had actually intended with this tactic, but I knew now that I was hoping that the second Goblin would somehow be trapped under the first.

The remaining Goblin was sent sprawling to my left, falling to its knees before catching itself, while the body of the first was sent spinning across the stone floor. I released the spear, as instructed, and attempted to organize my feet so I could kick at the kneeling creature.

"No! Punch! Dammit!"

Smegma's instructions this time didn't help; in fact they might have made it worse as I tried and failed to follow them. I was just preparing a kick and tried to turn it into a punch, but I ended up just falling atop the White Goblin guard.

I didn't even land on the back of the Monster. Instead, I'd given it enough time to drop its spear and spin. I felt one of its hands close around my forearm as another attempted to reach for my throat.

My awkward fall, and the fulcrum of its hand on my wrist, made that second grasping mitt punch me in the chest, reminding me about my chest and shoulder wound. With only one free hand and the imminent risk of strangulation, I latched onto the thing's forearm, which felt like a human leg under my fingers.

Something crunched, and for a moment I held my breath, expecting pain, but only felt something press into my chest. I heard Smegma scoff, clearly displeased with something. Still, in theory, I was in what Hunter Mixed Martial Arts called 'mount,' wasn't I? My head was close to the White Goblin's chest and my legs were wrapped around its hips and legs, trying to control the creature. Still, I doubted that the White Goblin was about to pull guard.

As we struggled against each other, I realized why Smegma hadn't wanted me to grab the second wrist. We were now both awkwardly pushing and pulling each other's arms as we tried to gain an advantage—and I couldn't release the arm I held to throw a punch because that would free his clawed hand to gouge at me. But if I had initially thrown a punch, I may have ended the fight right there.

Knees from below attempted to hammer at me, but I managed to keep the wrap of my own legs around the thighs of the Goblin, which only highlighted his superior height and weight. I was now stretched out atop the creature. Thanks to my Strength Stat, I was safe from being attacked, but I was also incapable of attacking.

"You've got to cede control of the legs or the arm. Choose and strike. Otherwise, you'll be stuck like this until one of you tires out," Smegma assessed after several long moments of grunting from the Goblin and myself.

Even with my Stamina Stat unlocked, I was breathing heavily trying to control this beast. Smegma was right; I needed to release control of something. I took a deep, stuttering breath through my mouth, attempting not to smell the disgusting flesh of the creature my face was nearly pressed into. Then I decided on legs.

If I was fast enough, I could release my hold there, jump up and drive my knees into the creature's abdomen. I figured it would find it hard to retaliate with two knees in its stomach. Once I thought I was ready, I followed through with the plan.

It worked even better in reality. Thanks in large part to the Goblin's knees rising up in an attempt to buck the hold that no longer existed. Those knees propelled me into the air, straining and stretching my arms straight. Smiling, I heaved with both of my arms, pulling myself down while my knees slammed together and became a wedge shape.

My aim was slightly off, and one knee hit the solar plexus while the other crashed into the sternum. I felt a jolt of force traveling up my knees, thighs and back. Pain followed, telling me I had likely broken a bone or the skin or both—but I also descended almost a foot farther than the initial point of impact.

My knees had caved in the White Goblin's chest and crushed its heart.

When I attempted to stand up, I discovered that the pain, at least in part, was from where the Goblin's broken ribs had badly gouged my knees and legs.

Extricating my own limbs required me to pull out those bone fragments from my own legs—which finally caused the vomit that had been threatening since entering the village to spill from my mouth.

"Well, that certainly wasn't *good*—" Smegma stated. "Still, you're alive and they're dead—so, congratulations?"

His tone managed to get me to look at him. He wore a smirk that I didn't like. He was basically saying I'd gotten lucky—even though I knew he was right, I growled, "Get husked!"

CHAPTER 20: CHAPTER 72

Monday, April 29th, 2069

Fascinated, I watched as the wound in my chest and shoulder appeared to literally knit itself closed. It had not been bleeding when I felt the intense itch there. Still, I *had* bled—and profusely enough to stain most of my undershirt a ruddy red.

Now, though, I watched as my wound seemed to come alive, small tendrils of what I assumed must be blood reaching across and bridging the gap. Once there were too many to count, they contracted, pulling taut and forcing the wound to close by millimeters. This started deep in the gash. The area 'closed' and then grew red and healthy looking even as more tendrils sprang up from the next spot—this one closer to the surface of the wound.

It repeated itself, and I began to count. The wound had indeed been deep enough that I could see ribs—and if I estimated, a few minutes of fighting occurred after the spear had cut me—so it was going to take about five minutes to heal two wounds that were at least an inch deep and several long.

"Are you done staring at yourself?" Smegma asked.

I lost track of my count and slowly turned my head to glare at the Demon. I countered, [I distinctly remember someone admiring themselves as the magma cracks closed!]

"What? It isn't like I was in the center of a Goblin village, where I just killed four Guards. You nitwit. Time and place. I'm *absolutely sure* that those four were all of them…"

His condescension made me wince. I stood up and moved toward the center of the stone hut, where I could see a pillar. The hut itself was far darker than the cave outside—lit by mesh sacks filled with Mana Crystals that hung from the ceiling. Since they were likely F-Rank Crystals, they were a terrible source of light.

That was probably why it took me getting to the *support* pillar to realize it wasn't the Altar I was looking for. Not to mention that strange light orb that fled the first two Goblin Guards. Was it an alarm or something?

"Yes. It was an *Alarm* Skill. Do you see how silly the System is—imagine giving an *Alarm* Skill to creature's with the ability to see through walls…"

My brows drew down when Smegma pointed that out. *So wait…the System made a mistake?*

"Well, probably not a mistake. It only notified the other *two* Guards. Normally, it might have brought all the fighters in the village down on your head. However, the rest might be in that Snake's belly. Now, let's find the *Altar*, moron," Smegma said, sounding like he knew it wasn't the support pillar all along. I felt he only 'knew' because he'd gotten there before I did and had time to check it out. I shook my head and spun in a half circle, assessing the room. It was sparsely furnished.

There was a stack of rags, or dust, or something, along one curving wall, which I assumed was a bed. There was the tiny 'throne,' which was decorated to look ostentatious but failed miserably. Lastly, there was a small stack of stones that reached my knees.

Shrugging, I went to the stack of stones, only to find a wider, recessed stone attempting to be a washbasin on the top. My nose scrunched at the smell of the water inside, and the color. Good thing the leader kept himself 'clean.'

Now on the other side of the central pillar, I scanned again and found a few stacks of dried herbs hanging from the walls but nothing else. I raised both of my hands helplessly and finally responded to Smegma, "Okay, *genius*. Where is this Altar, then?"

"Right, ask the guy who can't even interact with the world…"

"Oh, come on, you stupid husker. That's a horrible excuse and you know it. You can literally fly through walls."

"Whatever, maybe it's not in here," Smegma responded. "I'll go scout around; you watch yourself heal or something."

Smegma promptly flew off, and I got the distinct impression that he was either embarrassed or as frustrated with the lack of an 'Altar' as I was. Despite the derogatory nature of his words, I did go back to watching the skin of my wounds slowly knit itself back together. It was interesting but didn't last long.

Just in case, I took another scan of the room. Nothing new. *Figured*, but you never know. I guess I could collect the White Goblin Cores and probably take down the Mana Crystal mesh bags. I looked from one to the other before deciding to start with the mesh bags. First, I needed something to cut the rope.

Each Goblin had a spear, and my Pick was also still on the ground. I moved from body to body and found two stone daggers in the waistbands of two of the Goblins. Not that a dagger would help me cut down the mesh bags. They were too high for me to reach, but I did figure they might help me cut open the Monsters for the Cores later.

Yet, the first thing was to get those Crystals down, for a mobile light source, if nothing else. *I knew I should have asked my father for his Lightstone before leaving the lake. Stupid Smegma…*

[You wanted to be a walking beacon? Moron,] Smegma mentally sent from wherever he was.

For just a moment I closed my eyes and centered myself, fighting my desire to retort to the Demon. Once calm, I used the spear and sawed at the rope that was somehow wedged between two rocks in the ceiling. The bag and rope jumped and skipped, moving about, spinning and being generally uncooperative with my attempt.

My arms began to tire by the time I heard a snick and watched the fraying rope part. It didn't drop the bag, though, since it was essentially many ropes woven together and then braided into the supporting one at the top. Instead, the bag fell open, and the Crystals spilled out. I jumped back to avoid them falling on me but still felt one collide with my chest. It made an odd sound, followed by the somewhat heart-wrenching noise of something breaking. Remembering what

136

that was, and finally understanding what that crunch earlier had been—I closed my eyes before slowly looking down.

I found the expensive three-sixty-degree camera I had forgotten I was wearing, with its lens and protective case broken. I ran a hand through my hair and clenched my teeth in frustration. While I knew my donations on CashMe could cover the repairs—it was still a needless expense.

I put the camera in my Necklace, where it should have been at least a day ago since it only had a forty-eight hour battery anyway. Then I asked Smegma a rather important question that I probably should have thought of much earlier. [Is recording in Dungeons really a good idea with you floating about?]

[You think a piece of mechanical equipment is sensitive enough to pick up frequencies and images from another dimension?] Smegma mentally asked.

[Well, you're making yourself visible, aren't you?] I asked, confused as to what he was getting at.

[I mean, maybe it can? I don't know how sophisticated these 'cameras' and 'computers' are.] Smegma floated back through a wall of the hut, startling me.

Once I recovered, Smegma pointed at my eyes. "However, after some of our research into the System—Mana, Force and Stamina or Martial Power revealed that living creatures are hypersensitive to things that are created by those forces. Like they have an extraordinary sense that is somehow tuned to them—"

"Oh, we call that our sixth sense," I interjected.

"That's not really the right word for it, though. You definitely have a sense for Mana already, which would likely be your sixth sense, no? This is something beyond just Mana. While other planes of existence have Mana, they aren't created by it. If that makes sense? It's a bit too complicated to explain to an idiot like you," Smegma responded, still hovering just inside the wall with a devious smirk.

I gave him a playful finger in response, only making his smile grow.

"In any case, that video is much more likely to be showing the whole group going insane and talking to a figment of their imagination. So, I wouldn't worry much about it. Especially with Geneva and Kristen being in on the secret. They'll cut anything too odd out—even if that thing can capture different planes."

"Yeah, I guess. There's just been a lot going on in here, with the…" I gestured vaguely in the direction of the Grotto and lake.

"Naga Complex?" Smegma offered, clearly reading my confusion.

"Naga Complex is as good a term as any, I suppose. But you know what I mean—the huge husking Snake—and my 'stealing' of Crystals. Not to mention me picking up Skills like others pick up quarters, or massive Frying Pans and Fishing Poles appearing out of thin air. I guess I just don't like having video evidence that could be used against me in the trial," I responded, trying once more to get my point across.

"Then don't give the camera to them?" Smegma asked, sounding unsure what my hang up was.

"I can't do that. We need footage for reels and promotions of our company."

"Tell them to delete any footage that is suspicious? Better yet, *you* can delete whatever footage you want before you even give it to them," Smegma tried again. I went silent and his smile returned with a vengeance. "That was a simple solution—moron. Now, can we get back to searching for the husking Altar?"

My silence must have been an answer because Smegma flew back through the wall. After that, I shook my head and sheepishly continued my search. I did find a very worn small backpack that was clearly one of the Mirage Hunters'. A quick mental prod told me it was a small Bag of Holding too.

That will be helpful later, I thought, and returned to looking.

With the Bag of Holding, I moved around to collect the scattered Crystals. I really didn't love that Smegma, who wasn't even from our world, came up with a simple solution to the camera before I did. Still, the fact that I hadn't worried about it till now likely meant I trusted Geneva and Kristen quite a bit. Maybe they were already deleting stuff like that...

It was then that I noticed the grooved tiles of the floor, and just as I went to dismiss them and return to examining my trust of Sparkle Legion—my brain questioned the rather stupid Goblins' ability to tile anything, making me perform a double-take. Then, and only then, did I realize that the 'tiles' were carvings in the cave floor.

Following one of the grooves with a Crystal held inches above it, I discovered a half-sphere depression. The depression was far too perfect for it to have been carved by the stone tools of the Goblins.

[I think I found the Altar,] I mentally sent to Smegma as I pulled out a Monster Core and held it above the half sphere. This Core would be too small— but it was definitely the right shape...

Did that mean I needed the bigger Cores? Or that the depression was just made big to support any Core?

Either way, if this Altar would award a Skill—

"Wait, the Altar was the whole floor—*building*?" Smegma asked angrily as he floated back into the room. I jerked back and spun to see why he had added 'building.' Sure enough, Smegma was studying a wall.

It looked like dark stone to me, so I brought a Crystal over for a closer look. He was right. There were carvings on the walls of poorly cut stones as well. Smegma looked at me, and I looked back to him. We both shrugged in near unison.

"Okay, so—let's go through the Snake's pile of Cores," Smegma said out loud. Then he made some strange hand gestures that were not something I could interpret.

I realized with a start what was going on. The Snake could probably hear us. [I have no idea what you're trying to say with those hand gestures. You can use mental communications...]

Smegma looked at me like I was a puppy that had just peed on the floor. Then after a world-weary sigh, said, "Dump out all the Cores, we'll *go through them*."

Licking my teeth at another tone shift, which again I didn't understand, I reluctantly emptied out the Necklace of Holding. It had taken me a while to get them all in there—and I didn't really want to do it again. Smegma hovered over to the pile and made a gesture from a small, salt-block-like sphere with almost no illumination, and then very pointedly motioned at a huge, nearly perfect specimen with a fierce inner light.

Oh! I slapped my forehead and nodded to the Demon. I had been thinking the same thing before he arrived—just from a different angle. Surely, higher Ranked Cores would mean a higher Ranked Skill…

We sorted through them and were left with some decisions to make. There were probably twenty-five huge spheres that would perfectly fit into the depression. Each one of these spheres was double the size of a basketball and quite clear.

[So, we just pick the biggest ones?] I asked, even as I looked to the next largest pile. Some of these crystals seemed to be brighter and free from almost all imperfections.

Smegma shook his head and pointed to one of the Crystals I had just been looking at. I pulled it out and moved to one of the largest ones that looked just as clear. Smegma shook his head emphatically. Then he tapped talon to tooth, looked down and away toward where the Snake might be in this huge cavern, and shrugged.

[Why don't you just make it so only I can see you?] I asked. Smegma rolled his eyes and pointed down before mouthing, 'Universal Power.' [I'll take that to mean he might still be able to hear you?]

[Even though I doubt it, he might even be able to intercept mental communications,] Smegma mentally sent while nodding, but he eventually shrugged before clearly deciding that he might be being a bit overly paranoid. Sighing, he pointed out some Crystals in different piles. "My thought is that we should try to pick similar colors of Cores. Usually, that's what we did with Card Shards. It increased the chances of getting a powerful Skill—well, it never could really be proven since it could have been luck…"

[Okay? So, we want the clearest Cores with similar coloring?] I was still confused by the coloring of the Cores on display. Sure, there was almost every color of the rainbow, including those iridescent cores that had all colors of the rainbow, but there were just too many—greens, blues, yellows and purples. It didn't look like the Monster Cores I was used to seeing, but I shrugged that off for now.

Smegma nodded and we sorted the Cores once again. This time by color. No two were 'identical' in color, but there were several that were blue in varying shades, or green, yellow, purple, and so on.

A pattern did begin to emerge, and by the time we were finished, I was looking down at only two iridescent Cores. Nine orange, twenty purple, a hundred plus blues, several hundred yellow, and uncountable greens. The second pattern was that the colors with fewer of them all seemed to be of better quality.

Then we had other grouped piles of colors that all only contained one Core. Pink, black, brown, white and so on. These colors gave me a strange feeling even holding them—but varied in clarity and size. I raised both palms to indicate my confusion.

Smegma, who couldn't help in my physical categorizing, had been studying the groups while tapping a tooth for a while now. At my gesture, he glanced in the direction of the Snake. It was a presence that defied walls and cavernous passageways, and clearly, he was still worried about it taking some sort of offense and leveling the entire Mine to kill us all.

After another sigh, he shrugged and answered, "My guess is that these piles are something like Card Rarity. So, Godly, Legendary, Epic, Rare, Uncommon, and Common." He pointed at the iridescent, orange, purple, blue, yellow and green in turn. After a moment, he pointed around us and back toward the Lake before adding, "They must not be the same types of Cores that are found on Earth." He pointed to the assortment of colors that had no pairings. "Then these may be Unique?" Then he shrugged to further indicate his uncertainty. "Maybe not Unique, though. At least, not in the way you're thinking of. Perhaps they'd be considered Unique on Earth. Perhaps, back during this civilization's heyday, this was just how things worked. Obsolete might be a better term. They could be something like ingredients. So, that brown one would add an Earth Element to a Skill—or something?"

My hand scratched my temple as I looked at the collection from that perspective. The Cores on Earth were said to all contain an Element already. However, here, if Smegma was right, these Cores were sorted by rarity and the Element came from outside? So, if I combined one of the Unique stones with Godly Cores—I should get a—

My brain instantly put a stop to the rabbit hole I felt myself exploring. Smegma, who had likely heard my tangent and subsequent halt, shrugged at me. "There's no telling. Just give it a try?"

[Okay—so Godly and Legendary first?] I asked, pointing at the two small piles. Smegma shrugged, and I got to work moving about the hut. Each depression had long been marked by one of the Mana Crystals, and so it didn't take me long to locate and place nine Cores.

Low Rank Skill Altar Activated.

Cores Offered.
Ex: Eborisk Dragon Core
Ex: Faneral Dragon Core
S+: Drake Portal Core
S+: Morenquai Core
S: Ego Portal Core
S: Halo Portal Core
S-: Treant Core
S-: Ultralisk Core
S-: Lich Core

Would you like to add an Elemental Core?
<Yes> | No

Proceed with Skill Acquisition?
Yes | <No>

I stared at the blue screen, clearly shocked that the screen was so similar to the *Demonic Vault* ones but also shocked at the Cores currently slotted—and the fact that it told me what they were.

"So—"

Smegma cut me off with a vigorous waving of his arms in front of my face. Then he floated in front of me and shook his head to join the clear hand signal to stop.

[Sorry, I was just thinking we can probably do this differently. First, I'm guessing you were right, and those are Elemental Cores.] I was pointing at the Cores that were all varying colors. Then I motioned back to the rest of the abundant Cores that were clearly color coded. [I'm thinking we should try to get Cores that have a theme in terms of what Monster types they came from?]

Smegma's eyes widened as he began to nod to himself at my suggestion. I could tell that he was about to go off into researcher mode, and so I just shook my head and began by swapping the two remaining orange Cores in.

They both weren't Draconic—but one of the ones I removed was. I placed a Mana Crystal there to mark it as correct—and then began swapping in purple Cores. Only one of the twenty purple Cores were 'Draconic'—being an A+: Wyvern Portal Core.

I looked to the blues, now a little worried that my earlier 'brilliant' idea might not be the right choice.

[No, keep going. I think the Cores are glowing brighter,] Smegma mentally sent, clearly deciding that our mental communications weren't being overheard, at least.

Smegma motioned at the two red Cores, and I narrowed my eyes, trying to see what the Demon meant. They looked the same to me. Still, it wouldn't hurt to keep going—I supposed.

The blue Cores took a while, but by the end, I had all but one of the indentations filled with Draconic, or at least, what I thought were Draconic cores. Kind of like the Wyvern, which I believed was Draconic—but may not be.

It also was clear that the iridescent Cores were growing brighter. The problem was that I was now moving onto the yellow Cores—which seemed like a waste. Surely, the larger, rarer Cores would be better at this point. Smegma shook his head and pointed to the two iridescent Godly Cores.

[The increased brightness is telling us something. Keep going.]

The last spot was filled, and the Godly Cores did once again visibly brighten a few lumens. While that was a triumph, it also made me reassess the Wyvern Core again. It hadn't made the red Core brighten noticeably like this D+: Dragonkin Core had.

Husk!

I started shifting it, and a few other Cores, in and out until the rainbow light was bathing the entire hut in its extremely bright halo. I looked longingly at the big, expensive Cores—then shrugged and clicked the 'Yes' to adding an Element. I moved to the pile of Cores that didn't fit with the rarity color scheme and picked up the one I'd been eyeing from the start.

I practically leaped back in shock when the first one I slotted in was Space. The color of the Core was black with white dots floating in it—and I had honestly been drawn to it because of its similarities to my Mental Universe—but it actually being a Space Element Core threw me.

[Okay, I hear your internal dreams of power, but it still might not be the best choice. Slot them all!] Smegma stated.

My nose crinkled as my mouth fell into a frown. Sure, the Demon was right, but *Space*—

"Dumb-dumb," Smegma interrupted my thoughts, and I sighed before doing as instructed.

CHAPTER 21: CHAPTER 73

Monday, April 29th, 2069

River, Dust, Magnetism, Heat, Heavy, Growth, Bubbles, Fairy, Pink—wait, what? I put back the pink Core and blinked at the description on screen. It actually read Pink. [What the hell is Elemental about Pink?]

Smegma's face soured and he shook his head as if to shake off cobwebs. Then, after swallowing what looked like vomit, the Demon said, "If that is something similar to our Card System on Crendalar—then it's probably an accent Element. People collected Skill Cards to match colors of the back together. Then to everyone's surprise, they merged and created color Elements. They were totally useless too. They just allowed the users to throw pink Fireballs or turn their Stamina Aura pink—that sort of thing."

The Demon shuddered again and even brushed taloned fingers over his arms to brush something off.

[Okay,] was all I could manage to think. Sure, that sounded utterly frivolous but to have such a strong reaction—

"If your world was ending—no—*did* end, and you had people who were essentially trading potential to win a popularity contest, how would you react?"

That made me duck my head in recognition of his point. I wasn't fully on board with disgust at people who chose this path—but I could definitely see myself being frustrated, especially after the fact. What if some Demon could have saved Crendalar and instead frivolously wasted Skill opportunities on something like 'Pink'...

Still, if it made those same people happy—wasn't that kind of the whole point of life? I shook my head, dispelling a bit of the empathetic distaste that clearly was coming from Smegma's feelings on the matter. Finally, I admitted to myself that I agreed with both decisions. Intelligent creatures could choose for themselves, and Smegma was allowed to feel a certain way about what those decisions *might* have led to.

I returned to changing the Elemental Cores, still just daydreaming on what the combination of Draconic Portal and Monster Cores might give me with the Space Element. I did find a few others that sparked my imagination as well, though.

Time, Metal, Magma, and Inevitability. Two of which I thought I could at least imagine Skills with—two of which I found difficult. Space was the same, though. What would Space, Time or Inevitability do in a Skill?

By the time I finished slotting all the Elemental Cores, those three were set aside. I looked to Smegma, who had been watching and reading over my shoulder. [Any suggestions?]

"I think you're right to go with one of these three. I personally think Time might be best but…" Smegma faded off, looking at Space and Inevitability. After a time, he shrugged. "I'll admit that Time would only be great if you could go forward or backward—see the future or something along those lines. Often Time Elemental Cards were things like Haste or Slow, though. So, maybe Space or Inevitability has a better chance to be something truly powerful?"

[I mean Time Dragon, Space Dragon or Inevitability Dragon all sound plenty powerful,] I mentally commented but found my eyes drawn once again to the black orb with white dots contained within. [Still, I think I kind of understand Space—maybe? No, that's probably not the reason why I'm drawn to it. It's like it resonates with my Mental Universe.]

"Brodie, there is always something to be said for instincts—and as long as you weren't drawn to something like Pink—I'm not going to fight what your *Soul* is telling you."

With Smegma's confirmation, I collected the remaining cores back into my Necklace and activated the Altar.

Low Rank Skill Altar Activated.

Cores Offered.
Ex: Eborisk Dragon Core
Ex: Faneral Dragon Core
S+: Drake Portal Core
A+: Drako-Lich Core
B+: Dragonkin Core
C-: Komodo Portal Core
D+: Quasi-Croc Core
D-: Kobold Portal Core
E+: Wyrm Leech Core

Elemental Core:
Space

Proceed with Skill Acquisition?
<Yes> | No

I took one more look at the other two Elemental Cores, then inhaled deeply—and held my breath.

Then pressed 'Yes.'

The Altar screen vanished, and I blinked in confusion as nothing seemed to happen.

Just as I exhaled, the black of the Space Core did something. I assumed it was the first to react to my confirmation. Or maybe it was the first thing I noticed because it was right in front of me, in the slot that opened up on the central pillar.

I became more sure it had reacted before the other Cores, because the color inside expanded out. Once it reached the circle of Cores in the floor, it simply washed over them, and they looked the same as they had before. The two largest iridescent Cores were the only notable exception. Since they were not only glowing brighter but also lifting up into the air.

When the Space Core 'swallowed' the entire interior of the hut, the two Godly Cores jumped into action—rushing toward me. I flinched and jumped backward, terrified that the cannonball-like orbs would simply carry on through me. They of course weren't even targeting me. They moved to a spot where the support pillar of the leader's hut had been—before the Space Orb took over.

Then they began circling each other. My eyes were fixed to them, but in my peripheral, I noticed the other Cores had lifted out of their recesses and slowly formed an orbit around the two large Sun-like Cores in the center. I also noticed that the orbits were ranked, having the highest Ranked Cores nearest the center.

Those closest to the two red Cores moved through the oval circle faster than the green Cores farthest out from the pillar.

A new blue screen appeared in front of me and Smegma.

Low Rank Skill Altar

First time use bonus. Skill Altar Rank increased to Mid Rank.

Cores inserted far exceed maximum Skill Altar Rank.

Are you sure you wish to continue?
<Yes> | No

I turned my head to stare at Smegma, unsure if I should push 'Yes.' He motioned at all the Cores and then pointed emphatically down in the general direction of the lake and massive Snake.

[Good point. Anything I don't use will just go back to it…] then I realized what I'd mentally sent and held my breath. If the Snake could hear me, now would be the time it would react.

My exhalation was beyond relieved, and I took a moment to catch my breath before I clicked 'Yes,' and the screen changed.

Mid Rank Skill Altar

Outdated Cores, being modified for Ascender File 17,411,129
Due to Cores Value exceeding Skill Value, a High Growth Rated Skill is being selected.

Scanning intended recipient…

Two Skill Synergies Available…
Demonic—Rejected
Draconic—Chosen

Optimizing Skill Selection...

Skill Selected
Imparting...

I spun to Smegma, my eyes wide. [Is this like the Card Sets you—]

Smegma wasn't there… I scanned around myself, looking up and down. Nothing remained of my Demon Companion, and I highly doubted he'd floated into the floor at such an important time. The fact that there wasn't white smoke likely meant he wasn't involved in the Skill formation—so why had he vanished?

Maybe he was putting together the Skill the System was imparting? But I doubted it. Perhaps whatever gave him form couldn't maintain him and take the pressure of a forming Skill? I looked around the Altar Room and realized that all the Cores were increasing their orbiting speeds—while also collapsing toward the two Godly Cores.

Did that mean the System hadn't imparted the Skill yet?

I closed my eyes and checked on my Mental Universe. Immediately, I discovered what was happening. A new planet was forming around the *Demonic Vault's* Sun. I assumed it was Cooking, since it was the only other option for where *Overdraft* could be receiving Mana from.

There was an instant I felt torn between watching that Skill form or the System Altar outside—and then I opened my eyes. System Skill versus a Gathering one, and all that…

The 'planets' spun ever closer to the central two, which were now circling each other so fast, it looked like a single, larger donut. Still, if I squinted, I could see the small space in its center, and it was shrinking fast.

As if I was watching a Galaxy collapse into a Black Hole—the timing where the two rainbow Suns touched was perfectly in sync with when all the outer orbits reached them. The Space Mosaic grew brighter as all the white, 'distant' stars pulsed.

And then the entire tapestry of Space and collapsing Black Hole sunk into me at a rate I couldn't describe. I expected pain, heat, or maybe even a terrible cold—but instead only felt a small prickle of what could have been electric shock.

I was about to close my eyes and see what had happened inside my Mental Universe when a screen popped up.

Releasing [Locked] Dragon Body.

Available and necessary energies vastly exceed safety thresholds for chosen Vessel. Balancing required...

Vessel destruction imminent upon release of [Locked] Dragon Body. Assessing Options...

Upgrading [Locked] to Balance [Locked] Dragon Body...

Error!

**Upgrading [Locked] to Balance Hatchling's Body
Error!**

Upgrading [Locked]…

The small shock of current inside of me grew, making it feel like I had accidentally forgotten to turn off a breaker then touched both sides of an outlet. It didn't stop there, growing worse with each millisecond—forcing my diaphragm to freeze.

My heart followed shortly after, and finally, every muscle in my body. I had never experienced pain like this in my life. There was a component of physical pain as my entire body convulsed and flexed so hard that I thought I might actually break my own bones—but no, that wasn't the sensation that threatened to consume my sanity.

It was like something was both digging around in my brain, body, and… was it my Mental Universe? An agony so deep inside of me that it had no source to pinpoint. No remedy that could ease it. No consciousness to shed in order to escape from it.

Simply put, it felt like something was ripping me apart over and over again—but simultaneously putting me back together just so it could keep creating Brodie confetti.

The worst part—since the pain wasn't actually inside my body, or mind, I didn't pass out. Instead, my brain tried to analyze the sensation and give me comforting, logical solutions. Like simply ignoring what was happening. Surely, the System wasn't going to kill me. It even consoled me with the equivalent of a 'there, there.'

I swore at it—and was actually surprised when that seemed to help. So, I just kept going.

I hoped *Mental Fortitude* would be able to keep me sane after this.

My mind broke.

CHAPTER 22: CHAPTER 74

Monday, April 29th, 2069

It was strange to both be conscious, but in so much pain that I was pretty sure I was hallucinating. I couldn't really be watching the Big Bang—right?

Or maybe I was in my Mental Universe?

The first thing I'd seen had been a Black Hole—hadn't it? Or had I seen that outside after the Skill Creation? Maybe…

Regardless, one specific area—this Black Hole inside my imagination—had been bombarded by asteroid after asteroid. The first two had been huge, multicolored things that smashed into each other like two Evolved Moose fighting for territory. Unlike the Moose, this display led to mutual destruction and so much heat I could feel it.

No, wait—had I felt it or imagined it?

Whatever. Then more asteroids had flown in, bombarding the mass of undulating magma—like bad referees attempting to break up a fight. The first few had hit and seemed to almost cause the superheated, melded asteroids to separate. Then the two, now one—turned on the newcomer and swallowed it. Were they alive?

After the third strike, that phenomenon went away, and instead the newer asteroids sank into the orangey-red substance like it was a pond, and they were pebbles thrown by children.

Now I thought it was after the sixth asteroid, or was this one a comet? Either way, another change occurred. This comet didn't even make it to the surface to sink into the mass. Instead, the massive blob of magma sent out an attack in the form of waves of heat, vaporizing the newest comet.

Surely, it didn't consciously send out an attack? That would make it alive, and me—crazier than I already appeared to be…

I tried to shake my head and failed. Three more comets flew in, vaporizing before they made 'land.' Only when the last one disintegrated did the clouds of the other four turn gray, and then black.

Lightning arced between the clouds, even striking down at the orange, liquid surface of the planet. I didn't realize until the first drop of rain fell just how much pain each asteroid, or comet, had caused me. I think I was at my threshold for recognizing more sensations.

Sure, I had seen something like a force wave expel outward after each impact. Well, those had started with that Black Hole, I think? That did explain how the impact waves could be darker than the blackness of space. Wait—that made no sense?

Whatever. The point I was trying to make—did I have a point?

Husk!

The rain seemed to bring the first new sensation I'd felt in millions of… years? Months? Days? Hours? Minutes! Surely it had only been minutes. The sensation of rain touching the superheated surface without evaporating above it— was like aloe vera on a terrible sunburn.

No, it was far better than even that. It was a drop of water hitting my tongue in the middle of a desert. Had I even been in a desert before? No, no, I hadn't.

My brain reeled at that truth—shattering some of my fugue along with it. I was truly in my Mental Universe, and I had watched as a Skill was created. I had even seen those darker waves of force vibrate through the space.

What I hadn't been able to notice was the other Skills' planets they had passed by, or the edges of that Universe when they had struck. I could tell that the limits to my Mental Universe had grown. The nothingness of 'space' Smegma claimed was my Soul was getting bigger—more expansive.

My awareness narrowed back in on the newest Skill's planet as the rain turned from a drizzle to light rain, moderate, and then heavy—before becoming something akin to a tropical storm that raged over the entire planet.

To my distress, the planet, easily four to five times larger than the 'Sun' of *Demonic Vault*, was shrinking. Sure, a bit of shrinkage probably should be expected—I guess. Maybe it had just gotten out of the pool. I'd be a hypocrite to throw stones. Yet, this was like watching a beach ball deflate, turning itself into a bowling ball, and continuing to collapse.

I shouldn't complain since the more it shrank, the better I felt—but with the *Mining* Skill 'planet' growing and getting stronger, this did feel like I was losing something. I couldn't help but wonder what Skill the System had granted.

It had said something about *Draconic Chosen*—so maybe something like—
The planet vanished.

"Are you husking kidding me?" I exclaimed as my eyes flew open.

My body was still in full contraction—making me feel bound—but I could also feel *Recovery* going to work, attempting to unclench muscles and repair whatever damage my involuntary spasms had left behind.

I didn't stay in the hut for long and dove back into my Mental Universe. Surely, I had imagined the planet vanishing. No, it was still gone. I searched the new expanse of my 'Soul,' looking for a sign of the tiny Skill Planet—and found nothing.

There was my Mana Pool, Mining, Fishing, *Demonic Vault*, and the still forming Cooking—but no new planet for the System-granted Skill. Even the moons surrounding Fishing and Mining—well, the large moon, singular, around Mining—were there.

The System notices had said something about me being unable to handle the chosen Skill, hadn't it?

So, what? It just took it away to save my life? I thought the System was supposed to be fair?

That's what Smegma had claimed at least—but I supposed he knew of the System from however many eons ago. What was the saying? Power corrupts— or something. Oh, that was it!

Power always corrupts, and absolute power corrupts absolutely…

I shivered and exited my Mental Universe, not wanting to think about just how much power this System wielded. I was left staring at the mesh bags of hanging Mana Crystals as my body slowly unclenched itself.

"Well, that couldn't have taken too long—since Smegma is still forming the *Cooking* Skill," I said to myself, assessing my situation to pass the time. "Good thing those other Goblins are staying in their stone huts," I added, realizing the extremely compromised position I was in.

Dungeon Cleared.
Rewards Granted.
Portal will close in twenty-four hours. Finish looting or risk losing spoils upon closure. Any human inside the Portal Grounds when it closes will be transported back to Earth.

"Yeah, some reward!" I complained, my voice attempting to rise to an indignant volume but managing to crack before becoming a froggy croak. I continued in a much more subdued rasp, "Take away *my* Skill—"

Something punched me in the stomach. My body reacted, heart rate increasing even as the sensation forced me into a painful, unwanted sit-up. Thankfully, there wasn't a Goblin standing over me with a spear. Instead, there was a moderately sized garden fountain sitting atop me.

"Oh, you've got to be husking kidding me!" I said as I looked at the thing. Where had it even come from?

Low-Level Skill Altar Awarded.
To use, simply insert nine Monster or Portal Cores and place palm on impression.
0/10 Uses.
First world clear of Low-Level Skill Awarding Portal Detected.
Doubling uses of Altar from 10 to 20.
Congratulations.

I blinked at the messages. This fountain was a portable, condensed version of the Altar? *Recovery* must have done a fair bit of work since I was now sitting up without feeling like a groundhog or some type of other burrowing rodent had made a home inside my abdomen. Hesitantly, I reached out my hands to the fountain-looking Altar and removed it from atop me. Placing it beside me, I noticed a few very glaring differences between it and the hut-sized Altar I was recovering inside of.

Helped by the Cores that still surrounded me, I first noticed the size of depressions the Altar had for Cores. They might be able to take the green or blue Monster and Portal Core, but they weren't ever going to be able to fit one of the remaining orange ones. Not that these were typical Cores I'd find on Earth—but the thought still held.

I waffled on my next discovery, recalling that the accenting Element slot only opened up after I placed all nine outer Cores. Still, not only did this altar not have a spot for it—even if it did, the smaller Elemental Core wouldn't fit.

Maybe a big enough space would somehow reveal itself if I placed nine Cores? Or maybe this Altar was truly designed for human usage.

That made a lot more sense since it was very hard to imagine a spot for a tenth core. The entire center was taken up by carved lines and an indentation clearly meant for a human palm.

Struggling, I got to my knees and attempted to climb to my feet to experiment, but I was forced to stay on all fours when my legs wobbled beneath me. Determined to get at least one Skill from all this, I began crawling to the blue Cores. I sent the closest nine in the pile into my Necklace and returned to the smaller Altar.

About halfway back, I realized that I was still in a larger Altar, and could try again for a better Skill, but I was still curious about this 'System reward.' I slotted the nine blue Cores and found I was absolutely correct on the size. Nothing bigger was going to fit the nine indentations.

I waited and nothing happened. My staring at the fountain Altar showed me the obvious reason why. The palm imprint!

I placed my palm down, and a similar screen to the one I'd gotten for activating the larger Altar in the room I was occupying appeared before me.

Low Rank Skill Altar Activated.
9 Cores Offered.

Average Rank: E+

Proceed with Skill Acquisition?
Yes | <No>

The floor I knelt on rumbled like it was accentuating a big moment in my life. I frowned at it. Was that another cave-in—

"No, you imbecile," Smegma said, startling me.

Thankfully, I was currently on all fours, so other than a slight jump, I didn't react much.

"That would be the Snake warning you not to do what you're trying to do."

"Oh, that Husking Greed—" the ground rumbled far more menacingly. "Selfless, I meant to say that beautiful, Selfless…" I tried to correct my earlier frustrated insult and knew I failed miserably—but the ground didn't rumble again.

"Collect all of his Cores and let's head back!" Smegma stated but was giving me a look that clearly demanded a bit of an explanation over what had happened since he vanished.

Jaw clenched, I mentally relayed what had happened and how the System had stolen my new Skill. I pointed to the small Altar in the end and mentally screamed, [It thinks this somehow makes up for it!]

"Ahh, I don't think that's it. First, if you looked around, you would have noticed all of the depressions in the hut are gone. So, you couldn't use the larger Skill Altar again. I think this Smaller Altar is actually just a condensed version of the big one. Remember, it was only supposed to be a Low Rank…"

[Still, the Skill is gone!]

"Even if that is true—first, it took it away to save your life. Second, it upgraded your Soul—which I have never even heard of, *and* it gave you a method to give even more Skills to yourself *or others*. So, I think you're focusing on all the wrong things."

My mind unhelpfully agreed with Smegma. I cursed under my breath as I moved about the room, collecting the Snake's Cores. I also took the spears and cut out the guard's Cores before moving to the mesh sacks and collecting the F-Ranked Crystals. The Bag of Holding turned out to be smaller inside than even my Necklace. So by the end my Necklace of Holding was looking pretty full, but I managed to squeeze everything in only because I'd dumped everything else back in the smithy.

I took one more look around the room when I was finished and discovered that there was a Core in the space that the Space Elemental Core had resided in. It glowed a dull white, highlighting it in the now dark hut.

I moved back and snatched the Core, and then picked up the small Bag of Holding, a bit moodily. Despite my *Mental Fortitude* Skill and Smegma continually telling me to get over it—my heart wasn't ready to let go. I thought for just a moment I was going to get some sort of cool Skill. Something that would make me a Hunter right now. It was a thought I'd been desperately clinging onto as I underwent that trial by pain…

Whatever!

Using Smegma's scouting, we made our slow way back out of the Goblin village. It was very slow going at first because I was still trying to be sneaky. Then when I remembered my *Heat Sense* and turned it on, I became fully distracted by another discovery. There were no heat signatures in the stone huts anymore.

Where had the White Goblins gone?

We never discovered the answer, even as we passed the massive shit pile and the huge cavern back to the Naga Compound.

CHAPTER 23: CHAPTER 75

Monday, April 29th, 2069

"You managed it?" my father asked as soon as he saw me walk through the doorway into the smithy-turned-kitchen. The heat in the room was sweltering—both dry and stifling.

My father didn't wait for an answer and wrapped me in a very sweaty hug. The warmth and wetness contrasted each other, making the sensation both uncomfortable and comforting.

I got over the wetness and tried to lean into the hug, happy to have made it back—but he was gone again before I even managed to squeeze him back. I watched him hurriedly flip fish in the Huge Frying Pan, and then saw the stack of more Mirror Fish steaks building on the floor beside the pedestal contraption.

Smegma must have taken in everything going on faster because he asked, "What's the count up to?"

"Caught or cooked?" my dad asked.

I scratched my head. Realizing that at least five fish worth of Fish steaks were piled on the floor. It would appear that with two people catching Fish, and only one Cooking—we had created a bottleneck. Smegma must have responded because my dad finished answering the original question, "Fourteen caught and five cooked."

My brain attempted to calculate the time passed since I'd left and failed. An hour, certainly—two was possible, but no more than three, surely. Still, with that math, we would not have caught that many Fish—let alone cooked them.

"We need another Frying Pan," Smegma said. I instantly nodded but motioned at the pedestal that wouldn't be able to hold another of the things. Smegma got my meaning. "There're a few other smithy rooms. We'll get Jarred to work in one of them. Still, you can purchase smaller Cooking pans to fill up the space around the large ones..."

"With what Mana Coins?" I asked, opening my screen to confirm what I already knew. I was running very low.

"All those Crystals you found in the leader's hut—and the ones given by the Snake for this very task..."

A strange guttural growl sounded, and the room shook. My dad blinked at the doorway to the animal pens, and his eyes went wide as he brushed a forearm over his face to remove some sweat. I, of course, couldn't see sweat on his forehead, the heat from the Frying Pan evaporating it faster than it could appear.

"That's the second or maybe third time that Snake has done that!" my dad said, his voice nervous. "I can't cook any faster!"

"I don't think it was in regard to your Cooking," Smegma said and pointed through the doorway. "I think it wants to talk to Brodie and me."

"What for?" my dad asked anxiously. "You did what it asked, right?"

"We did," I answered placatingly while moving to hand my dad a full water bottle and taking his empty one. Maybe it had been more than three hours already?

He took the bottle, and a big swig, before speaking, "Can you take that rock we're using as a serving plate back with you?"

He was clearly in rough shape, seeing how fast he was jumping from concern to concern and being unable to hold two thoughts in his head for long. Was it only dehydration or also nutrition? Perhaps it was simply raw stress. Potential death by Snake belly was enough to stress anyone out.

The answer didn't really matter. He couldn't continue like this. Not for long at least. My worried stare and thoughts got through to Smegma and he came to my side. "The only way you can help him is getting more Cooking instruments. Maybe enough Coins to purchase a Mana Apple too since it will magically give him nutrients as he needs them."

With his words, he attempted to usher me through the door that led to the pens and lake behind it. My feet felt stuck to the floor, but I lifted the piece of rock with stacked cooked fish on it and hurriedly trudged out.

When the consequences were death, how could I not? Once we were in the pens, Smegma whispered, "The trick is going to be finding a way to complete the task and keep everyone alive. I'm thinking, rotating shifts. Standing near the heat should only be done in short shifts. See how cool it is as we get away?"

Since I had just shivered from the temperature change, I did know what he was talking about. I felt it as soon as I exited the smithy. The problem was that my father couldn't use his Mana Pool and so couldn't Fish…

Another problem stared me in the face when I got to the lakeshore. Each individual looked haggard. It was a different type of exhaustion than my father's, but no one looked good. Dave and Willa were soaking wet and shivering, which admittedly lent itself to confirming the importance of position switching. Jarred was covered in Mirror Fish guts, because he too couldn't use his Mana, and was needing to reach his entire arm inside the Mirror Fish to cut them up. Just the way everyone was moving spoke of true exhaustion.

Then there was the Snake, towering over them all. It was just on the edge of the light given off by the yellow metallic Crystals in the ceiling.

Originally, I thought I had the harder task. But I could tell now that wasn't even close to the case…

"Ssso, you've sssuccsseeded," the Snake growled menacingly. "Now not only have you destroyed a Mana Battery but you'd like to use more of my Cryssstalsss and Coresss." The jaw clicked loudly, echoing over the water, off the walls, and then back in an eerie punctuation. "Thisss wasss not in the bargain!"

The Snake, which had been just visible on the edge of the light, suddenly snapped its jaws above me, casting a shadow over the entire group. Everyone shivered as it echoed around the much smaller space, including me.

It was a stark reminder that this massive creature could eat us before we could even blink. I assumed it was also contributing to the exhaustion on everyone's faces. That threat was hanging over them, and it wasn't exactly energizing or husking subtle.

154

"We simply wish to accomplish the task you've set before us, oh Great One," Smegma said deferentially. "It was also in *using* the Mana Battery that it broke, Great One. These things commonly break, I'm told. Still, with the right tools, and a schedule, we'll have the hundred fish cooked for you in the time allotted."

Desperately, I tried to school my face and not give away Smegma's plausible lie for the Mana Battery. In the end, I just looked at the floor in hopes that the Snake wouldn't notice.

The Snake pulled back, and the shadow receded—seeming to allude to a stay of execution. As it slowly returned to its spot deeper in the lake, it hissed, "I get nothing by granting thisss requessst."

"Except for the cooked Mirror Fish, Great One."

I realized that all the cooked Fish on my slate carrying board were gone, only at Smegma's words. How had it taken them?

Jarred motioned for me to put the plate down near him, and I did so as Smegma and the Snake continued to talk.

"I've already had sssome cooked fisssh. Perhapsss I am already sssated."

"Surely not, Great One. Someone as magnificent as you would need thousands of Fish to truly be sated."

"Are you offering me thousandsss of fisssh?"

"Your magnanimity in the previous request of a hundred is the best we can do in such a short period of time. We each are only mere mortals, whose weakness only serves to highlight your strength, Great One."

As soon as I had dropped the platter nearby, Jarred began stacking more fish steaks atop it. I noticed he, too, had an empty water bottle. I was happy Smegma was talking since I didn't think I could remain deferential to the tyrant of a Snake. Not with my family and friends suffering like this.

Taking the bottle, I hurried to the water, passing by the shivering Willa and Dave. They, thankfully, had full water bottles, but their lips were a dark color in the shadows of the light—likely blue.

[Smegma, we need to be able to get my dad out of that room, and these two into it. That and breaks!] I mentally sent the Demon.

"Asss I've sssaid you ssstill will not meet my gracssiousss quota."

"It is true that, at the previous pace, it is obvious that we would be found wanting. However, as you clearly would be aware from your history commanding an entire civilization, organization can achieve what mere intentions cannot. We can fulfill your desires now that everyone is here. As long as you give us the chance to rotate workers, eat, sleep and hydrate as needed."

"Sssurely thessse fragile apesss can work for twenty-four hoursss?"

"Perhaps if their entire civilization weren't so backward, that would be true. In fact, this moron," the Demon gestured to me in clear disgust, "possessed only a Mana Pool, and no capacity to use it, until I came along. Most of his ignorant race are similar. They have no understanding of the truth, nor of how to leverage Portals into strength. Thus, as you noticed, theirs are the most fragile of species. They have only the single Skill. Though..." Smegma paused meaningfully, as though he'd just come up with a clever solution. "We could change that, Great One," Smegma suggested, and I felt my heart skip a beat. Was he suggesting what I thought he was?

"They are truly that pathssetic?" the Snake asked, turning its eyes to each of the group in turn. I saw Jarred visibly shiver even though his back was to the creature. "I will grant you the Goblin Coresss and allow you to do asss you asssk. But if you fail—you and that child will be coming withsss me—willingly!"

I had begun to nod my head, not caring what we had to agree to if we could grant everyone one or two Skills. Of course, that's when the System got involved.

System Contract

[Redacted], the Great Snake of Nagsind, has offered a deal.
Catch and cook 100 fish in the next 19 hours, forty-two minutes and twelve seconds.
Succeed, and keep your life and the lives of Willa, Gary, Dave, and Jarred. As per System norms, you and the group will be transferred from the Portal upon its closing.

Fail, and you will be entered into a <u>Slave Contract</u> under [Redacted], the Great Snake of Nagsind, and you will not exit the Portal upon its closing. The Great Snake of Nagsind can do with Willa, Gary, Dave and Jarred as it sees fit.

Sign?
<Yes> | No

The 'Slave Contract' was even a sort of mentally clickable link with a terrifyingly long document in a legalese that I couldn't hope to translate. Even with the System's involvement, I didn't have a choice. I was about to hit 'Yes' when Smegma hurriedly shouted, "If we are going to become the Great One's slaves, then I would like the time limit to be until the Portal closes."

"Asss you wisssh, my future slave!"

A line on the contract flickered and changed.

Catch and cook 100 Fish before the Portal Closes in 22 hours, fifty-eight minutes and thirty-three seconds.

"And our Fish we've already fed you count, Great One?" I asked, realizing that it was a negotiation only because Smegma had interjected.

"Of courssse. You are at five and a quarter Mirror Fisssh, my sssoon-to-be pet! Now, empty out that tiny Ssspace Pocket, and give me what isss mine," the Great Snake of Nagsind crooned before snapping its jaws.

I did so and blinked. Even before the Cores landed upon the stony lakeshore, they were gone. It was eerily similar to when I placed things into my

156

Necklace of Holding. Did the Snake have a similar item? Wait—was that what had happened to the Fish?

A tinkling clatter from nearby made me scan the shore and find a new and truly massive pile of Mana Crystals. A glass clank from in front of me drew my attention back. One blue Core and many green ones were piled in front of me, right where I'd dumped my Necklace.

How could the Snake tell these Cores from each other without the help of the system Altar? Smegma gave me a warning look, telling me not to ask, or maybe that he'd explain later, once—or rather, *if* we made it out of here.

"Jarred, go get my father," I said as I made a rough count of the White Goblin Cores. Fifty-eight. That included the blue Core and the larger white one that I'd taken from the Altar space that the Space Core had previously occupied. I realized that it was likely the Portal Core.

I could give out six Skills…

Or two Skills to two people and one to the others. It would probably be for the best if I excluded myself from this round because I already had Skills and Stats that would help me get through the next twenty-two hours. Looking at the haunted eyes of Willa and Dave, I knew they needed something. I just hoped what they'd get from the Altar would help.

[Get everyone one Skill, then give an additional to the people who might need it the most?] I suggested. Smegma nodded slightly but kept his half-bow to the Snake going.

Still, with his agreement to my plan, it was time to give out some Skills!

"Dave and Willa, come here," I ordered, realizing that time was very much a commodity we didn't have. Plus, the Skill bestowal could knock them out, like it had me…

CHAPTER 24: CHAPTER 76

Monday, April 29th, 2069

My feet danced beneath me as I stared at all four members of my group passed out on the floor. It had been a bit of a struggle to convince them to use the Altar in the first place—but it had become especially difficult to convince the rest after Dave, who had been first to go, had passed out. Now everyone was lying on the ground, and I could practically feel the Snake gloating behind me.

"Husk, husk, husk!" I cursed under my breath, even as I picked up another Mana Crystal and sold the Mana inside. I was well past the amount needed for Frying Pans, and had at least a hundred Spent Crystals to check the group's acquired Skills when they woke up. Still, it was like I could hear the timer, and while I could run off to the smithy and start Cooking—I also needed to be here when they awoke.

"Who shot that potato gun?" Dave said as he sat up clutching his chest, his hand over his heart.

I didn't bother answering his nonsensical question. Instead, I shoved a Spent Crystal against his chest. "Fill it with your Mana for five minutes. We need to know what Skill you got."

Dave blinked and then gained his traditional goofy smile when he remembered he'd just been granted a second Skill—a beyond rare re-Awakening. His hands closed possessively around the Crystal, and it almost instantly started to glow blue.

Close to the five-minute mark, my breathing stopped as I waited in anticipation. The Crystal started to shrink as two Cards formed. I smiled a bit then, despite the seriousness of the situation. Dave's hands were clenched so hard on the shrinking Crystal that I was surprised it didn't crack. He really wanted those forming Cards, and *now*.

His forefinger and thumb clamped down audibly on the Cards, and he spun them to face himself. I only got a look at the blue-backed one before he was looking at the front of the other. It had a rim of white, and I moved closer to read the description.

Cut
(1)
Skill Type: Active Energy Manipulation
Skill Rank: Low F-Rank (Evolvable)

Use your Mana to turn a single strike into many or to manipulate the strike through your Mana and intentions. This skill is limited by the wielder's imagination and Mana.

20 Mana Per Use

—

**Mana Reservoir
(12)
Skill Type: Resource Pool
Skill Rank: Mid E-Rank (Evolvable)**

A Mana Reservoir, if used responsibly and carefully, can deepen over time. One of the fastest growing but most fragile forms of a Mana Pool, prone to breaking if the user isn't careful.

25 / 42 Mana

Dave, who had been practically bouncing up and down, sobered immediately after he flipped to the second card. I could see why and was about to say something comforting when Smegma cut in.

"Oh, poor you, there's a chance your Mana Pool could break but also grow with you. Stop focusing on the 'fragile' line, and take a look at the *deepen* and *fastest growing* ones, you nitwit."

Dave twitched. Then he narrowed his eyes at Smegma before transferring them back to the *Mana Reservoir* card. For one more instant, I considered consoling my friend. But Dave's face had broken into a small, satisfied smile, so I clicked my teeth together.

"Husk! You're right! And with *Cut* too!" Dave began excitedly.

I shivered as a chill swept over the lake shore. The vibrations on the water gave away the source, and all three of us looked up to the Snake.

"I don't sssee any fisssh," the Snake hissed angrily.

Two things happened then, thanks to the Snake's outburst. First, the rest of the group woke up, shooting to sitting positions. Second, I realized something and narrowed my eyes.

The Great Snake had been content to sit there and wait, but something about the *Cut* Skill upset him—it might remove the need for Jarred's position. Dave, with the help of the Mana Battery, could catch fish and gut them with one swing of the fileting Knife.

Well, maybe…

"O' Great One," Smegma said placatingly. "Now that everyone is awake, we will get started soon."

"Tick tock," the Snake hissed, but I could still hear its displeasure. Clearly, it wanted me as a slave. I crossed my fingers and hoped the others' Skills would be just as good.

I handed Willa a Spent Mana Crystal and then hesitantly gave one to Jarred and my father. "We need to figure out what Skills you got. Then we'll decide who gets another Skill if what you have isn't the best. This thing can identify any of your Skills that are ranked C and below. Just push your Mana into the Crystal for five minutes."

Willa blinked and then nodded in understanding. She, like Dave, would likely have no trouble with this. Jarred and my father, on the other hand, just stared back at me helplessly. "Smegma, can you try to coach them?"

"Why do you always stick me with the idiots?" Smegma complained, even as he floated over. "Okay, so try picturing a small lake inside yourselves..."

I tuned him out and moved behind Willa as her Crystal glowed blue. Dave was on her other shoulder, a few minutes behind me. Likely taking the time to further study his own Skill cards. Two cards fell into her hands, one the familiar blue of Mana. She, unlike Dave, flipped that one first.

Mana Funnel
(13)
Skill Type: Resource Pool
Skill Rank: Mid E-Rank

Mana Funnel grows slowly but simultaneously reduces the Mana Cost of Skills when powered by personalized Mana.

9/30 Mana
—

Shatter
(1)
Skill Type: Active Energy Manipulation
Skill Rank: Low F-Rank

Create devastation with a single blow. Only works against armored targets, Ores and walls. Shatter will create cracks as the user intends, destroying armor, walls or deposits. Against Armored targets the blow can carry to the flesh beneath.

15 Mana Per Use

I blinked at the Skill and then at Willa. She was staring at the Card. Feeling my gaze she turned to me with her mouth hanging open. Eventually, she managed to close her mouth and wet her lips enough to exclaim, "I be knowin' eight top-tier Specialists that be usin' somethin' like this!"

"Of course your stupid race would get something to make Sharding easier," Smegma muttered grumpily.

[Dude, sense the mood!] I scolded him, glad that Willa didn't seem to have heard him. [You know, we really gotta talk about you climbing up the ass end of assumptions.] I added.

"The ass end of—" Smegma said, tasting the saying. "I like that one."

I rolled my eyes, finding his approval of the saying fitting. Then I heard it—a low Snake chuckle. I had been happy for Willa, but so was the Great Snake of Nagsynd. So, this Skill wasn't going to help us in our current situation? I glanced at Jarred and my father. Smegma's choice to come over and his pompous reaction to Willa's Skill told me most of the story. This might take them a while. So, I pointed to the Altar. "Go get another Skill."

"Wait—what?" Willa exclaimed. "I can't take another—"

"You can and you will," I ordered with a more emphatic point.

Dave looked at me, clearly torn between jealousy and understanding. In the end, he nodded and looked at Smegma, and the Demon's less than impressed face, before beginning to move to help coach Jarred and my dad. I shook my head then ordered, "Go warm up by cooking some Fish for now."

We needed to start making headway on the Snake's Fish. I followed him to the smithy, glad that Smegma didn't have to be beside me for the purchase of more cookware to work.

He mentally still got a few bitter remarks in, though.

[Are you sure you want to purchase the Small Frying Pan? It can go extremely well with your small brains.]

[Yes, asshat. I would like—]

[Sorry, you added extra and must just say 'yes' or 'no.' Let's try—]

[You added extra, you stupid, steaming pile of—]

[Are you sure you want to purchase the Small Frying Pan? It won't make sausages look any bigger.]

[Yes,] I responded, even as my teeth clenched.

[Oops, that's on me. I can't add anything either. Are you sure you want to purchase the Small Frying Pan?]

[Yes,] I responded, holding my breath. When the blue cloud of Mana started to form, I popped. [I husking can't stand you. There is a giant Snake ready to eat my friends and enslave me, and you're being a husking jackass!]

[All this tension, are you sure—]

[Purchase another five, and no funny business!] I interrupted, realizing that Smegma was incapable of feeling the gravity of the current situation.

Blessedly, he chose to stick to the 'script,' and soon enough, the entire indentation on the top of the pedestal was filled with Mana Crystals and topped with very disgusting-looking pans.

Dave worked the foot pedal and started the fire again as I navigated the rooms and found a second smithy. I loaded it up with Crystals from my Necklace and then cookware from the Shop, mirroring the first room. Smegma once again stuck to asking the scripted question and allowing me to respond with a simple, 'yes.' Maybe my scolding had been taken to heart, but I doubted it. I didn't start this one yet, but I did realize that we hadn't tested the mechanism in this room.

I shook my head. I didn't want to start the fire only to have no one working here, right?

What was I thinking? The Snake had provided a pile of thousands of Mana Crystals. Running a necessary test with a few of them wasn't the huge loss I was making it out to be. I worked the foot pedal and groaned when it didn't budge, even as I ramped up the pressure, using all ten points of my Strength.

Husk!

I moved everything to a farther smithy, and this time tried the mechanism first. It depressed, and so I loaded it up and tried again. I was forced to wait impatiently until I felt some heat rising from the space.

With a massive sigh of relief, I rushed back to the lake, passing by Dave. I could tell he was trying out *Cut* since a great deal of the Fish steaks were portioned differently than my last check. I left him to it, figuring the better of a grasp he had on it, the faster gutting would be later.

In the lake cavern, my father was staring at two cards in Jarred's hands while still holding his Spent Mana Crystal between his own. I rushed over as I asked, "What did he get?"

Smegma didn't answer despite the fact that he was clearly reading the two Cards. I slid to a stop and hurriedly read for myself.

Mana Pool
(3)
Skill Type: Resource Pool
Skill Rank: Low D-Rank (Evolvable)

A pool that can hold Mana. The uses that the user puts the Mana to will determine the path of Evolution. Cannot grow in size before it evolves.

55/65 Mana
—

Puncture
(1)
Skill Type: Active Energy Manipulation
Skill Rank: Low E-Rank

Use Mana to drive blows far deeper into targets than the user can with strength alone.

25 Mana Per Use

I frowned at the Pool, which was larger and higher ranked than my own, and then at *Puncture*. Wasn't that another *Mining* Skill? I looked over to Willa, who was holding her head and chest. She was in front of the Altar, and the pile of Cores had shrunk. So, she'd likely gotten a third Skill.

Thankfully she hadn't passed out, but I figured there was a reason she hadn't moved yet. That and her shallow breathing meant she needed some time. Still, *Puncture* wasn't going to help us with the hundred fish.

Sighing, I pointed to the Altar. "Go get another Skill."

Jarred blinked at me before looking at my father. "Shouldn't we wait—"

"No, this idiot can't touch his Mana yet, and you can. Go!" Smegma ordered more firmly than I had. "Now, *you*," he returned his attention to my dad. "Let's try the garden analogy…"

It was another stressful fifteen minutes before Willa was ready to check her third Skill. My father still hadn't figured out the trick to using his Mana and was well into a talk on electrical conduits.

Heat
(1)
Skill Type: Active Energy Conversion
Skill Rank: Low F-Rank (Evolvable)

Convert Mana to heat in an area or on a specified target. The amount of Mana used determines how fast the temperature will rise. The higher the temperature desired, the more Mana used.

1 Mana for 10 degrees Celsius

While this was still likely a good Skill for Mining, it would also help her if she continued to Fish. I smiled and pointed to the shore and one of the two Rods. "Go Fish and use that Skill to keep yourself and whoever is with you warm."

"How do I use a Skill though?" she asked. I blinked, realizing that Dave had quite literally figured that part out on his own. I would make sure to compliment him if we made it out of here.

Still, I did have the answer to this—thanks to *Minor Heal* and *Cleanse*. Before anything else, I smacked my forehead and offered to Heal Willa. She smiled and reached out a hand. It took nearly thirty points of my Mana to get her Healed, which surprised me, but also put into perspective how much the others would likely need it.

"Just a sec," I said and moved to the lake's edge to collect one of the two remaining Mana Batteries. Then, moving to each in turn, I *Healed* Jarred, who was just finishing getting ready for another Skill, and my dad. I looked through the pens and nodded, "Smegma, can you coach Willa on how to use her Skills? I'm going to go *Heal* Dave."

I rushed off, *Healed* Dave, and was back just after Jarred got his next Skill—if his being passed out on the floor was any indication. I rushed to his side and sent in twenty points of Mana converted to *Minor Heal*.

To my disappointment, he didn't wake up. I guess that was a good thing, though, because that would have meant my own stupidity from earlier when everyone was passed out had cost us time.

Willa was already Fishing, and a glance at Smegma got me a nod. She'd picked up the Soul Synapses that quickly? Was she truly a genius?

My father was still trying desperately to find his own Mana Pool and infuse it into the Spent Mana Crystal. There was nothing more I could do for administration. It was time for me to help with the task. I decided it would be best to help Cook first and rushed out of the chamber with the refilled platter Jarred had stocked what felt like an hour ago.

Dave nodded to me as I passed. He was just picking up his own stone platter to carry it back to the group. "Make sure everyone gets a small piece of that. We need to stay hydrated and fed!"

"Roger," he gasped, sounding slightly constipated. The sound of exertion made me spin, and I saw him struggling to lift the platter. Only then did I realize how heavy the thing was in my hands. Still, Dave did get it off the floor, if slowly.

I couldn't micromanage everything, or we were doomed to fail.

CHAPTER 25: CHAPTER 77

Tuesday, April 30th, 2069

Dexterity Increased by 1.
Dexterity Stat Unlocked.

Stats
Strength: 10
Locked.
Stamina: 7
Locked.
Locked.
Dexterity: 2
Locked.

The screen jerked me out of my routine, startling me enough that I missed the Mana Pulse and felt the reel let out a great deal. Thankfully, I managed to get the next one back on time and continued reeling.

I left the Stat Screen open, though. Was every Gathering Skill able to increase a Stat? Smegma gave me a look when I turned to regard him. I could tell he was not wanting me to ask anything about it aloud.

It had been many hours since we'd restarted working toward a hundred Fish. Thankfully, or perhaps unfortunately, my father had only taken another hour to figure out how to touch his Mana Pool. The unfortunate part was that he too received a Skill I already knew.

Mining
(1)
Skill Type: Gathering
Skill Rank: Low D-Rank (Evolvable)

As you Mine, you slowly improve your understanding of Minerals, Ores, and Crystals. As this Skill grows, this individual will notice improvements to all actions related to Mining.
—
Mana Bowl
(15)
Skill Type: Resource Pool
Skill Rank: Low E-Rank

A bowl that can hold Mana. The amount in the bowl can grow, but the Skill isn't evolvable.

10/15 Mana

That meant he wasn't able to truly improve his speed at either Cooking or Fishing. Still, the fact that he could now Fish was helpful for rotating people out of the sweltering smithies. I briefly considered having him simply use his *Mining* Skill above to quickly unlock his Strength Stat, but I dismissed the idea after remembering how many shifts it had taken me to do the same. That Strength might help him reel in Fish better or faster, but I'd be enslaved to a Snake demigod long before he'd likely manage to unlock it. Also, his Mining Skill was already a higher rank than even mine, so who knew how it would work, especially without my *Overdraft* Skill.

Jarred's second Skill was proving to be far more valuable, even though it too was meant for Mining.

Miner's Strength
(1)
Skill Type: Passive Body Enhancement
Skill Rank: Low F-Rank (Evolvable)

Strength Stat unlocked. Strength doubled when used in Caves or Mining specifically.

Strength: 2

And yet, even with Jarred now easily carrying back and forth cooked or fileted Fish—we still weren't going to make it. Sure, we would be close, and were improving by the minute, but we were just too far behind.

"What's the count at?" I asked Smegma.

"Fifty-ssseven," the Snake hissed happily. "Withss only eight hoursss remaining."

I scanned to my right and found Willa pulling another Mirror Fish out of the water. I pulled mine, and Dave looked like he would only be a few more minutes for his. That would make it close to seventy caught, I supposed.

Smegma nodded at me, confirming my running count. While Cooking was no longer the bottleneck it had been, we were still thirteen caught behind. The way I figured it, we could catch one hundred before setting up another smithy to Cook.

But to do it all in eight hours?

I cast back out my line and noticed some changes to the motion. I'd discovered a few hours back that I could cast my line farther and deeper than anyone else, including Jarred, the only other one with a Strength Stat. Now, though, I could feel that the slightest twist of my wrist or pressure of my finger could direct the throw.

It seemed obvious that this was a result of my Dexterity and rising *Fishing* Skill. That and my increasing Stamina made me wonder. Could I start going faster?

Surely rising Stats had made all the famous Hunters I'd heard of stronger. Well, I guess that wasn't true. I wasn't even sure all of them had unlocked Stats. But the ones who did were stronger than those who didn't.

The line bobbed and I heaved, trying to use every ounce of my Strength. I simultaneously reeled, finding that the action was easier than before. In less than ten seconds, I had a Fish on the shore.

Sure, I was breathing hard, but I didn't feel like I couldn't do it again. Cast, wait, and heave. My life became simple commands inside my own brain. Or was that Smegma saying it?

"Count?" I asked sometime later, approximately ten Fish after losing my running tally.

"Ninety-six with two more on the lines!" Smegma crowed. "Cast!" He ordered, confirming that the commands were indeed coming from him.

The lake rippled as I heard two unfamiliar twangs from beside me. They sounded like someone had strummed an out-of-tune guitar. My Mana Worm and line hit something before splashing into the lake.

"Isssn't that too bad. I ssscared away all the fisssh," the massive Snake hissed. I blinked as my line and the water directly in front of it pulsed. No Fish latched onto it, and for very obvious reasons.

"You cheater," Dave shouted, pointing an accusatory finger at the Snake.

The Snake's three eyes widened comically, and its tongue slithered out of its mouth mockingly. A rhythmic hiss sounded, and I looked around as the strange noise bounced off the walls and atop the water. Was the thing laughing?

"There wasss nothing in the contract that sssaid I couldn't prevent you from catching the fisssh," the Snake mocked. "You ssshould have read it more carefully."

Blinking, I looked at Smegma. Not because I blamed the Demon, but because for the briefest instant, it looked like he'd smiled. My eyes didn't find what my peripherals thought they'd seen. Smegma looked introspective, if I had to classify his hung head.

The three of us who were on a *Fishing* shift stared at the Snake and the Demon, waiting for something more. But it didn't come. Eventually, I got fed up. I wasn't ready to give up—

"We're at ninety-six caught, let's go get them all Cooked up," I ordered, simultaneously standing and moving to Willa and Dave to collect the Fishing Rods. When I reached Dave, I said, "Can you filet the most recent catches?"

Willa, when I reached her, had tears in her eyes. She opened her mouth to say something, once, twice, and even a third time. Failing with each attempt. I put a steadying hand on her shoulder and said, "We'll figure something out. Let's go help cook and carry."

Part of my forming plan to figure something out included Mana Coins and the Demonic Shop. So, I moved to the Mana Crystal pile and sold a great deal before putting the others in my Necklace of Holding.

Smegma hadn't moved from his spot since I'd gotten up. He still hovered where the rock met the water—the Snake behind him in my view. It looked almost like the Snake was smiling at the Demon's misfortune. My teeth clenched hard enough to creak.

Dave, who had grown more proficient with *Cut* over the last half a day, hurriedly gutted and portioned Mirror Fish. Willa took the Fish steaks and stacked them on a rock plate, and I moved to help.

My father was surprised to see the heaping rock plate as I carried it in, followed by Willa carrying her own. I continued through his smithy to Jarred's, but Willa began slowly lowering her far-less-full platter down.

Jarred was in the process of picking up a cooked platter on my arrival. "I'll get these started," I said, indicating the uncooked Fish with my head. "Dave will have some more fileted to carry back."

I wanted to say more, but the words caught in my chest. Everyone had been counting on me—

Between one step and the next, Smegma popped into space beside me, still in his introspective contemplations. My previous thought and his look of defeat merged together, washing over my *Mental Fortitude's* insistence that his reaction was natural.

"Are you going to mope about or try to come up with solutions?!" I shouted. Smegma started at the sudden shout, and Jarred flinched. My Uncle, with his stack of cooked Fish on a large stone, stopped and began turning back around. I hurriedly shook my head and motioned with a hand for him to keep going.

I hadn't meant to shout. But having the Demon giving up, accepting Slavery, not to mention the *probable* death of my group, wasn't acceptable either. Surely together we could come up with something.

"What?" Smegma said quietly before seeing my face. I could feel my jaw clenching, and I didn't think the sweltering furnace was the sole reason for my face burning with heat. Then he narrowed his eyes, looked back to the lake, and then spun on me. His voice rose to match mine. "I warned you about reading through the details of terms and conditions. Sure, this is different, but I'm not the only one who failed to see the Snake's husking loophole!"

"What's done is done," I shouted back. "We've got three hundred thousand Mana Coins—surely your stupid Sect has some Mirror Fish!"

"Right, because I suggested buying Mana Apples when there were other food options…" Smegma said, the sarcasm was so thick—I could taste it. I wanted to shout back but knew he was right.

Angrily, I began slamming Fish down into the much-improved cookware while muttering curses at Smegma, the Snake, and just about anyone. It went a long way to venting my current mood, which eventually let my brain start thinking.

"What if all five of us Fish off five different spots around the lake and shelf?" I asked.

"Sure, 'cause that Snake isn't able to spread out and take up the entirety of the place," Smegma said, shooting down my first idea. The anger resurfaced and I began muttering again, but thankfully it also vented far faster.

"Okay, what about entering the lake and fighting them?"

"Brodie, you barely defeated White Goblins and are thinking about taking on a Fish in its Elemental advantage?"

"What? We're supposed to just roll over and let our friends be at the mercy of that *thing*, then?" I argued. In that moment, I meant it too. I truly meant that it would be better to fight a Mirror Fish and lose my life than do nothing and become a slave that had let the others die. I just couldn't see the cheating Snake choosing any other option for my family and friends.

Smegma's face morphed into something I couldn't read. The only thing I could get from it was that the Demon was conflicted. His mouth formed a half-sneer and his jaw clenched—while his eyes looked at me like I was a lost kitten.

My fists clenched around one of the uncooked Fish steaks, turning it into a paste between my fingers. I threw it into one of the smaller Pans, making it splat as it landed. Did the Demon think I wouldn't wade out into those waters because of the risk?

Husk him and husk the stupid Naggy Snake!

* * *

"How much time do we have left?" My father asked, his voice resigned.

"Should be just over an hour," Smegma answered, sounding just as fatalistic. I glared at the Demon, but Cooking the rest of the Fish had given me time to calm down enough that I didn't start screaming again.

"I still think I need to go into the lake and catch them as they attack me," I growled.

"Nope," Dave said, startling me. I transferred my glare to him.

"What do you suggest, then? I'm the only one that can husking see them!"

"Would seeing an Evolved Shark coming change anything?" Jarred asked.

"Sharks are classified as C to B grade threats. Mirror Fish can't be higher than E to D!"

"You're forgetting that facing an E-Grade threat in the water immediately jumps its rank by one or two!"

No, I wasn't forgetting that. Smegma had already explained it to me multiple times. "I still haven't heard any other options!"

"You should try the plan you had originally," Smegma suggested. "Buy two more rods and cast as far away from each other as you can. We only need to get lucky and catch four Fish!"

Everyone nodded, agreeing with that plan, and I partially wanted to shake each and every one of them. Smegma had rejected that plan before I came up with the other. So, we were abandoning something that I thought had a better chance of success to go with a long shot?

Smegma looked at me and then put a nail in the coffin. "Since it looks like Brodie still plans to jump in to save the day, I suggest Jarred stays right beside him on the shore. The rest of you, take the ledges."

The Demon was reading my thoughts again, and of course he had chosen the best option to stay beside me—the only other group member with a Strength Stat. I pointed at Smegma, "You're an asshole!"

"I thought we established I don't have one of those!" Smegma countered. Somehow his comment almost made me laugh and allowed the tension to escape my body. I knew that if we didn't catch anything after thirty minutes or so, I would still jump into the lake, Jarred be damned, but I supposed giving my first plan a chance wouldn't hurt.

Before heading back into the chamber I put the Frying Pans from one smithy into my Necklace, but left the other stocked with Crystals and Pans; ready to cook *when* we caught those four husking Fish.

Going back to the lake was far harder than it should have been. We weren't burdened with full platters of Fish to bring, and thus didn't have any physical reason to drag our feet. But everyone's eyes were still locked on the ground, as they dragged worn Miner's boots over the stone. Since I was the last to enter the lake cavern, it even looked comical, when I did look up. Four Miners carrying their *chosen* weapons of Fishing Rods, with a monstrous, half illuminated and mostly submerged World-Ending Snake in the background.

What was this, a husking anime?

The Snake watched us lazily as we spread out, its tongue flicking in and out of its mouth. The farther we moved from each other, the more it seemed to realize the intention of our plan. Eventually it laughed, sounding like a boiling kettle.

"Thisss isss foolisssh. Perhapsss if you sssurrender, I'll let the othersss live and return home!"

I blinked and was about to shout my agreement to the offer when Smegma flew in front of me. "Don't husking agree, you moron. Listen to the wording. Have you learned nothing? *Perhaps* doesn't mean he will!"

The boiling kettle laugh returned and ended with a click of the Snake's jaws. "I'm only misssssing four fisssh. And look at thisss. One, two, three, four sssimiansss to take their place!"

The hissing laughter intensified, and my jaw popped in my ears as I clenched my teeth together. This asshat really wanted to provoke us before killing my friends and enslaving me?

My mind whirred as I desperately tried to think of a solution. I still had two hundred and sixty thousand mC. Could I purchase a weapon to help in the water? Maybe there'd be a Demonic wetsuit. Did Demons swim?

"We don't. Well, we can. We just hate it. Now shut up and stick to the plan," Smegma said.

"Time left?" I growled.

Smegma ran his tongue over fangs and said, "Fifty-five minutes."

"I'll give you till thirty. But if we don't catch any Fish by then, I'm diving in. Better dead than a slave!"

Jarred grew tense beside me, and Smegma sighed before pointing out to the lake. "Get to casting, then."

Ten minutes later, I was positive the plan wasn't going to work. Why?

Well, we'd hooked at least four Fish, to cheers and whoops of the person whose line had pulsed, only for the Fish and half the Mana Line to vanish…

Clearly, the Snake wasn't going to let us reel in four Fish.

I threw my Rod into my Necklace and got into a sprinter's stance.

"Sit on him!" Smegma ordered Jarred. Then there were arms wrapped around my waist.

I grabbed both wrists and pried my uncle's grip open, stepping out of it. I let him go with a warning look and spun to re-attempt my jog into the lake. Jarred's arms wrapped around me again. This time tighter.

I growled as I moved to repeat my earlier action of prying them apart. Something hit me from the side, overbalancing me since I hadn't expected it. Still, my Strength and Dexterity stopped me from going down. Until two more collisions occurred and I was flattened under all four of my companions.

"You can't just give up!" I growled from the bottom of the scrum-like pile. "Let me go. I still have time to catch enough by hand."

"Stop fighting, you imbecile!" Smegma said with his usual haughty annoyance that I hadn't heard in a long while. It was so out of place that I did, in fact, stop fighting the others and raised my head to look at the Demon.

He wore a fang-revealing smile. This husking Greed betrayed me?

He was so desperate to survive that he was going to sacrifice everyone else?!

CHAPTER 26: CHAPTER 78

Tuesday, April 30th, 2069

"What the husk, Smegma?" I shouted. I angled my head to glare at the rest of the group. "Why are you all helping him and the Snake?"

I felt most of the hands holding me down slacken slightly, but the weight of three men and a woman was still a bit too much for me to struggle out from. Not specifically because of a lack of Strength, but the weight was shifting and spread unevenly.

That didn't stop me from trying, though, and eventually the group redoubled their holds when I started to squeeze free.

"Stop, Brodie," my dad pleaded. "Even *if* we die here, isn't it better that someone lives?"

"But we could all live if Smegma hadn't betrayed us!" I shouted and glared at the Demon. Smegma's face confused me. Was he… hurt? The others looked at him too, and I could feel their confusion at the situation.

"Remember that talk about trust?" Smegma whispered, his voice definitely conveying pain. Those words made my heart pang in my chest, like a reverberating string of a guitar. My emotions and the situation told me he was betraying my desires, and I had thought it was because he'd rather not die himself. However, my brain was telling me something else entirely.

I shouldn't have jumped to conclusions. I should have trusted him. Why I should have done those things were total guesses, but I could recall the Demon's small smile when the Snake put its foot on the proverbial scale of this task.

My breath stuttered in as I fought back against my assumptions—trying to calm my body and feelings of betrayal that seemed to be far stronger and resistant to my attempts than they should be. Finally, I did manage to get enough control to say, "What do you mean, Smegma? Aren't you stopping me so we— no, *you* can live?"

Smegma blinked, even as he gained an introspective look. Then he chuckled. "Well, yes, there is part of that in this decision, I suppose. But if you had just kept trying to Fish, we could have bent this stupid Snake over Felhound Style!"

The air around the lake had always been cold, but after Smegma's words, it became arctic. Three eyes shone in the darkness of the deeper water, and they carried nothing but malice. The entire lake reverberated like a tuning fork as a loud, threatening bellow sounded out.

"It'sss time for you all to die," the Great Snake of Nagsynd hissed. Then it struck. I'd never been able to see it move before, but this time, it must have deliberately struck in slow motion so I—no, so we could see our demise coming.

A gong sounded out, canceling out the bellow, but I was too busy pissing myself to notice. A few other warm spots appeared on my body as my group, currently atop me—also lost control of their bowels.

I didn't even blame them.

"What isss thisss?" the Snake exclaimed, sounding like it had food in its Snake mouth.

Its exclamation startled me enough to make a realization. I could see the 'strike' because it wasn't moving closer. Three more gongs, at a much-reduced volume, sounded out when the massive serpent pulled back and pushed forward to try and close. But it was like it was being stopped by a wall of air.

Each time that 'wall' stopped it, a gong sounded. The first one must have been the loudest because he had been striking at full speed.

"This is what you get for giving out a task, signing a contract, and trying to cheat!" Smegma crowed. The Demon didn't even bother looking over his shoulder at the Snake, instead regarding the group—no, regarding *me* with a smug 'I told you so' smile.

I grimaced, realizing that the Demon and I weren't finished with the 'trust talk,' but he was going to put it on simmer while he dealt with this. Still, I nodded to convey something of an apology. Obviously, it was easy to say I should have trusted Smegma, given the current situation…

But it was infinitely harder in the moment to do so when I had thought he was ruining the chance of my friends and family surviving to save his Summoner. It felt like a flimsy excuse even as I thought it. Smegma's smile grew, and I knew he was listening to my thoughts. Still, why in the hell hadn't he just mentally told me any of this?

['Cause you're a piss-poor actor. Remember when I lied about the Mana Battery, and you couldn't even look up? You would've given it away. Then the Snake could have come up with a different way to tilt the *scales*.]

[Did you really just pun?]

[Sure did. Most importantly though, and in all seriousness, we never figured out if it can husking hear us!]

I met Smegma's eyes and let a small, acknowledging smile come onto my face. He was right—my acting skills weren't even up to SwiftGrammer standards.

"So, *Great* Slithered," Smegma said as he turned around. "You thought you could cheat a System-signed contract and get away with it?"

"There isss nothsing in the contract that forbidsss my intervention!" the Snake complained as it sounded the air-wall gong again in frustration. "I cheated nothsing!"

"Ahh, you must come from a time before the System adopted Implied Terms," Smegma continued to gloat, likely being intentionally vague. A low, menacing bellow sounded again, but this time Smegma laughed. "There is nothing you can do, you stupid overlarge limp-noodle. In fact, when the Portal closes, I think you might gain a bit more of the System's scrutiny than you wanted."

"What? Sssurely you jessst. The Sssysssstem caresss little about the weak!"

"What System do you speak of? How long have you been on this planet preparing for Ascension, Stupid-Snake?"

"What doesss that have to do withsss anythsing? The ssstronger I am, the better chance I'll have to defeat the invadersss and Assscend! How isss that ssstupid?"

Smegma tilted his head, blinked, and then looked back at me with wide eyes. No, he wasn't looking at *me*, I realized. He was looking at us, as a whole. Why became evident in a moment when he stated, "You are going to be an opponent for the Seven Deadly Trials!"

"Of courssse," the Snake said while tilting his head. "Wait—are you not aware of thisss?"

Smegma began tapping a talon to tooth, clearly contemplating what this meant. Before he could get too engrossed in a scientific hypothesis, I shouted, "What is the System doing, and why do you think the Snake is husked?"

"Husssked?" the Snake asked, clearly unfamiliar with the term. "I've ssshed recssently, though?"

Thankfully my interruption startled Smegma enough that he stopped making his 'thinking' face and pointed at the wall. "The System has deemed there has been a breach in the contract. The Snake gave us a task and signed a contract but then intentionally, and *personally,* attempted to prevent us from fulfilling its request. It's something like your world's insider trading. Or maybe more similar to Game Fixing?"

The wet spots on my clothing suddenly became gross and uncomfortable as I shook the others off me. They didn't struggle, and so I was able to push myself up, and then slowly stand, as I considered the Demon's implication. The System had deemed the Snake to have cheated and fixed the results so it could get what it wanted.

"So, we're going to live?" Dave asked, his voice barely a whisper.

Smegma huffed out a breath in clear amusement. "Yes, dumb—"

The cheering of the group cut him off. It took me a second, but then I joined them. We hugged, no one even commented on feeling uncomfortable from the stains in their crotch regions.

They were going to live—and I wasn't going to be a slave!

The merriment cut off rather abruptly as the Snake shouted, "You will exsplain what you meant about the Sssysssstem!"

Smegma gave the Snake a look he usually reserved for me when he thought I was being particularly dense. "I have no obligation to tell you anything, *reptile!*"

"A trade, then?" the Snake offered after it bellowed again in frustrated anger. "I will tell you what I know about the Assscensssion Trialsss, if you tell me about what you meant about the Sssysssstem!"

"You first—I'm not about to trust someone who just cheated."

To my surprise—and everyone else's, if the gasps from beside me were telling—the Snake nodded its head. "Asss you wisssh. Two Dragonsss came out of the Portal on Nagsssin. They claimed to be children of the one who Assscended when ssshe defeated the Naga Contendersss."

"So, they too faced a Dragon?" Smegma whispered.

"Yesss, sssuposssedly it isss very common to find Dragonsss in the Trialsss. They told me why on their deathbedsss."

174

The Snake paused for a moment, tried the air wall one more time, creating another gong, and then coiled itself up with a sigh. "The Minor Beastsss of thisss planet will join me when I challenge a contending racsse. The reassson that the challenge is usssually Dragonsss isss rathser sssimple. Only the Leading Monster of the Portalsss getsss to Assscend. So, the ssshe-dragon in thisss cassse sssent her children here, to conquer Nagsssin and Assscend asss well!"

"But you defeated them?!" Smegma replied, seeming to connect dots I was still having trouble even identifying.

"Yesss. My victory sssurprisssed the two Dragon children. They ssseeemed to exsspect an easssy time killing the creaturesss of Nagsssin."

"That's why the massive Wyrm Worms we fought on Crendalar are now on our planet!"

"Possssibly?" the Snake responded. "I cannot sssay. Ssstill, all that isss left on Nagsssin now isss my offsssspring and food. It isss why I am ready to challenge the Trialsss. To sssstart my legacssy!"

"Can someone be explainin' that in English?" Willa asked, looking at each of the others but finally settling on Smegma.

"Simply put, I think the Snake is saying that the Trials are essentially pitting a race ready to Ascend against a Monster ready to Ascend. Furthermore, the Dragons have created a sort of inheritance or bloodline, where they defeat a race and send their children to the defeated planet to prepare to Ascend themselves?" Smegma turned the last part into a question, which the Snake nodded in affirmation to.

"So, we have to face Dragons in the trials? Or something like—that?" Dave asked, seeming to try to think of a way to describe the Snake but eventually failing and just motioning at it nervously.

"Only now, talking to you, do I realizsse that thisss knowledge is not widely known. Dissscusssing it makesss me happy. I made the right decssisssion. Now the Sssysssstem."

"That's rather simple but also complicated," Smegma said with a wince. "I've been through each planet since my own—"

"You've been on every planet and failed to Assscend?" the Snake asked with clear mocking in its tone.

Smegma's head fell but he did say, "Yes, all five."

"Five?" the Snake asked derisively. "The Sssysssstem has at least a hundred competitorsss at any given moment. Maybe thoussssandsss!"

Smegma's head shot up, and he canted his head back and away from the Snake. His body language seemed to reject the claim.

The Snake began laughing. "Maybe you are not the bessst perssson to be lecturing me on the Sssysssstem."

The Demon's arms crossed, and then he chuckled himself. "Maybe not, but you still don't seem to be aware that the System updates, learns, and changes."

"Of coursssse I know that!" the Snake hissed.

"Then, how did you not know about Implied Terms?" Smegma asked, seeming genuinely curious.

"If it isss not written down, it isss not enforcssible!" the Snake countered.

"So, did your System have verbal contracts, then?"

"Verbal contractsss? No, what are they?"

"Your first request for the hundred Fish and letting us live would have constituted a verbal contract—or what was sometimes called a Quest. Essentially, you asked for something, and we were trying to fulfill your request. So, until the end of said Quest, you couldn't have harmed us or hindered us."

"This is not sssomething that exissstsss, sssurely. It would be usssed to—" the Snake's head snapped up. "That isss why you made the offer in the firssst placsse!"

"Correct." Smegma glanced back at me, his eyes twinkling with amused superiority. I couldn't help but think that cockiness was going to get us in trouble one day.

"Sssmart!" the Snake complimented. "Exsplain more of thessse changesss to the Sssysssstem—I'll ssstop you if I know it already."

There wasn't much time left, but Smegma used it to fulfill his part of the verbal contract with the Snake, explaining all the changes he knew of since the System had been on Crendalar Five.

Most of those changes the Snake was aware of, but it seemed to have a rather obvious blind spot. Things that would be considered parts of the System that changed due to societies. Things that made contracts, negotiations and deals on a planet or between races safer.

When the timer for the Portal closing finished counting down, the entire cavern and lake shore, usually illuminated in the metallic yellow of the Crystals, went gray.

I scanned my group and found them all frozen in place. Smegma hovered over to me with a smug smile, and the Snake hissed angrily at a large screen that had appeared in front of it.

Then a screen popped up in front of me.

CHAPTER 27: CHAPTER 79

Tuesday, April 30th, 2069

Contract Reparations

{[Redacted] the Great Snake of Nagsind}, hereby referred to as [Nagina], has offered a Contract that threatened death.

Under System laws of protection 2005.3-1, [Nagina] has prevented the successful completion of the terms 12 times and attempted to take the lives of the [Brodie's Party] 23 times.

This results in 35 breaks of the contract's implied terms.

Reparations are set!
1 accepted item of Low Quality for each Breach.
1 accepted item of Mid Quality for every 5 Breaches.
1 accepted item of High Quality for every 10 Breaches.

Failure to meet [Brodie's Party's] terms will result in System Sanctions on [Nagina].

Negotiations have begun between representatives of both parties.

"I've given you and your ssstupid group far more than thirty-five low-ranked itemsss. End thisss farcsse."

"Ahhh, but that was to help the group with the completion of your Task," Smegma answered, his voice filled with condescension. "You truly wanted to have cooked Fish, *Nagina.*"

"Do not call me by that name!" Nagina exclaimed. "That name is only allowed to be ssspoken by my children!" Something was clearly restraining Nagina because the heat in *her* words was greater than anything I'd heard to date. I'm positive she would have paired it with an attempt on my life.

"Thisss isss ssstupid!" she complained a moment later, her body seeming to tremble with unchecked rage. "The boy ssstill isss holding hundredsss, if not thoussssandsss, of Crysssstalsss of mine. Take them all; I have more important thingsss to do!"

"That's not how this works, Nagina," Smegma said. "Can you prove ownership of those Crystals?"

"He usssed nine high-ranked Coresss—thossse I can prove ownersssship of!"

"Again, stupid-Snake, they were given in good faith to complete your Task. Had you not given them, you'd have been in Breach of Contract for initiating an impossible Quest, and we'd be right back here in the same position. If you continue to negotiate in bad faith, we'll be forced to let the System *Sanction* you. I think you and I both know how well that would go for your Ascension."

I realized I had become nothing more than a spectator to this 'trial,' and I was quite alright with that. There were the obvious reasons, like Smegma knowing more about the System. But there was another reason I knew I could never be the leader in this situation. Each time the idiot-Demon insulted the massively powerful Snake, I shivered, flinched or twitched.

If I was honest, I would have just taken the Crystals and fled. *What if the powerful Snake came back to exact revenge?* Smegma gave me a look, clearly reading my thoughts as the Snake trembled and snapped its jaws in the background. I could tell that its rage was reaching a crescendo as spit, or perhaps globs of venom, flew from its jaws.

[Maybe ease off with the provocations?] I suggested to the Demon. To my surprise, he nodded in agreement, even as his face grew worried.

[Yeah, maybe you're right. It's kinda equal parts fun and terrifying, but it's not really getting us anywhere.]

I guess he hadn't really expected this large of a reaction. It was like watching a full-grown man throw a tantrum like a child. One where he slammed his fists and legs into the floor—where he clearly had lost control and couldn't even form a single thought in his head.

[It's like she's a child,] I finally concluded.

Smegma blinked several times but then nodded. "Great Nagina, we do not wish to see you under Sanctions. We wish to send you off to Ascend. Surely you have many items you've collected over your long life. Items you care little for but may help us? You've seen how the System has responded to your acts of bad faith. Imagine its response if you were to, instead, act in good faith and provide something that would be legitimately beneficial."

Thankfully, Nagina's snapping jaws and vibrating body slowed and then stilled. She turned all three massive, yellow eyes on us, narrowed them, but somehow seemed to shrug? Then, what could only be described as a mountain of items fell into space exactly between her and me.

I stared as the mountain settled. What was all of this? The fact that I could see Plate Armor, Bows, Swords, Spears and other assorted Hunter gear in the pile made my heart catch. Still, it was the larger pieces of gear that made me blink. I guess I had found where the items that used to be found in the Naga Complex had gone.

There were even beds, each of which was large for a human but equivalent to a toothpick to the Great Snake. There were flasks, beakers, graduated cylinders, and other equipment I thought could be used for Alchemy. Was that the Smithy and Forge equipment? Were those living Plants? Animal skeletons? Oh, shit!

Two skeletons in the pile stood out far more than the rest. Firstly because they were easily the size of eight or nine T-rexes, but the size wasn't what made me stare. It was the shape and predatory implications the thing carried. They were so much more than 'dinosaurs,' so much more than 'predators.'

Even Dragon Skeletons were majestic, terrifying and *proud?*

I shivered and looked behind the pile at the Snake, and then Smegma spoke into my mind. [She killed two of those and kept their husking skeletons!]

Smegma visibly swallowed, seeming to realize just who or perhaps *what* he had just sent into apoplectic rage. I swallowed too, and immediately prayed to any God listening that this thing didn't hold grudges.

The glare from three yellow, hate-filled eyes that I met over the top of the treasure mountain told me that only one 'god' was listening, and it apparently did, in fact, hold grudges.

[Husking Greed Demon,] I swore. The target was Smegma but also the situation. Why had we ended up in a collapsed Mine with a damn Universe Snake, or whatever the Demon called the thing.

"We'll choose items from this pile and be on our way, Great Nagina," Smegma said, his voice back to meek.

"I told you not to call me that!" Nagina responded, each word snapping out, accompanied by her clicking jaw.

"But, Great Nagina, you said that only your children were allowed to speak your hallowed name. After all the time we've spent together, I feel like you've become like a mother to me, so please—allow me this small favor." The Demon bowed low with a flourish that would make a court jester blush.

The next hiss rattled the walls of the cavern as rocks and stalactites fell from the ceiling overhead. One enormous sample of which smashed into the ground inches from me.

[Are you out of your mind? Knock it off and stop using that husking name!] I complained as I repressed a shiver.

Even Smegma shivered and went silent for a long moment. Not even moving toward the pile. Thankfully, *Mental Fortitude* wasn't affected by the Snake and pointed something out. We had an opportunity to nab three potentially very useful objects of the Snake's, depending on how well we chose. Objects that would not only help immediately with Mining Contracts, but for a very long time afterward.

"O'," I muttered and then coughed as it came out slightly squeaky, "Great One, could we also choose things like the Mana Batteries you lent us for the Task?"

The Snake blinked then narrowed its eyes. "Why did you have me pull out thisss ssstuff if you already had itemsss you wissshed for!"

That drew my 'courage' up short. Was I about to piss the Snake off further if I answered, since I destroyed its Mana Battery I'd kind of forgotten about it?

"We only have *two* Mana Batteries, Great One," Smegma answered, following my lead and returning to the moniker the Snake had accepted in the past. "To fully clear this debt, we'd need to pick five—" Smegma froze as something popped up in front of us.

Contract Reparations

[Nagina] has attempted to kill [Brodie] 7 more times during negotiations.

42 Breaches Occurred

[Was the System listening?] I asked mentally, shocked at the response and timing of the notification.

"Sorry, it seems to clear this debt, we must choose *twenty-two* more reparation items, or two more high-quality and two low-quality ones." Smegma's voice had shifted once again, this time sounding like a salesman trying to do the Snake a favor.

"We still only wish to help you avoid the System's notice," Smegma added, acting every ounce the slimy car-salesman.

"Cssertainly," the Snake hissed, its voice confused. It was then I realized that, in some ways, it truly was a child. A child with unimaginable power, but mentally, just that. A child. Surely we could turn this around.

[Let's pick one more Mana Battery, another high-grade item, and we should probably accept the Crystals as the remaining payment?] I sent to Smegma. [Call it an act of goodwill, a toast to its bright future or something.]

Smegma looked at me and rolled his eyes. Then motioned me forward to look at the pile with him. I did so, even as Smegma said, "We will choose another Mana Battery, a high-grade item from this pile, and then to show our goodwill, we will accept the Mana Crystals already provided by the Great One—to zero her Karmic Debt."

Nagina's eyes narrowed again but then widened happily. Her head bobbed up and down in agreement. I heaved out a sigh of relief, earning her attention and suspicion for a moment. I coughed and said, "I'm just relieved that we could help you, Great One."

Mental Fortitude pulsed. Well, not really, because I didn't know where that Skill resided. Still, something in my mind shuddered and then expanded. My eyes narrowed slowly to slits as I looked into the eyes of the Snake. Gone was the strange feeling I'd had a moment before. Like fog in the sun, the notion of child-like innocence evaporated. [Oh, husk. It's using a Skill on me!]

Smegma spun on me, his black eyes so round it was almost comical. His mouth slowly fell open as he gave the smallest of nods. We were being played, but if I was honest—my first thought wasn't that we should retaliate. It was that we should pretend to let Nagina 'win.'

"Surely, you have other items to offer as well—Nagina," Smegma stated, even as a smirk broke out onto his face.

[Mother-husker!] I swore.

Nagina's eyes fully returned to baleful hate as she began to vibrate and spit globs of poison or venom ineffectually again. This time not in some sort of act, but in true anger at being discovered. Unfortunately, the window for negotiations already had three items confirmed and accepted. One S-Rank Mana Battery and two A-Ranked ones.

Where had the third Mana Battery come from? I looked down to my hand and discovered I had picked one up in whatever fugue state the Snake had placed me under. I truly had been under some type of mind control—but *Mental Fortitude* had helped me through it!

Maybe Smegma too. Was he somewhat of an extension of me?

I shook that off and stared as the scene changed again. The reason it was *unfortunate* that I'd accepted the two unbroken Mana Batteries and accidentally picked up another was because the mountainous pile had grown to at least double its previous size, occluding Nagina from my sight. If it wasn't for the Snake's mind control, I was nearly one hundred percent sure we could have found three S-Rank Mana Batteries in there—if nothing else. With the pile of new treasure, I heard more than saw the Snake stopping its temper tantrum.

And yet, despite the choices on clear display, there was only one thing my eyes focused on. The *why* was hard to explain, but every time I looked at the things that drew my eyes—because there were more than one—I couldn't look away.

They were clearly scales, and by some power of immense deductive reasoning… I could tell they were Dragon Scales. Two, in particular, exuded an allure that I couldn't resist. In fact, I didn't even remember walking over to the larger black one. Or reaching out to run my hand over it.

"We'll take this," I said before I'd fully thought the decision through.

"Hold on—" Smegma began to complain, but the menacing, bellowing growl and subsequent hiss drew the Demon up short.

"You dare choossse the Heart Ssscale of [Static]," I could tell the Snake clearly didn't speak the strange static noise. But what it had actually said was entirely indiscernible. I tried to think back on it and found a sharp, stabbing migraine whenever I tried to recall the specific word the Snake had used. As soon as I stopped looking for the word, it went away.

"Pick your two othser low-ranked itemsss, Contendersss. I'll be ssseeing you." The hissed threat practically shut down my brain. I'd husked up. Bad! Exactly what I had wanted to avoid, I had just done.

"Ahh, but stupid Nagina, did you forget that you tried to kill us—look at that—ten more times?" Smegma interjected, and I slowly turned horror-stricken eyes on him.

Okay, blaming myself might have been premature…

All three of the Snake's eyes narrowed, and I could feel the baleful hate radiating from the creature. Seeing the Snake in this state made me shiver, even as I internally raged against the damn Demon. [Smegma, what the actual husk!]

"Well, then, *Great One,*" Smegma said, his tone back to overly pleasant. "We'll simply take the other scale and two more of the smaller black scales," Smegma said in my place. I heard him and my brain attempted a reboot. Had he just claimed the second Heart Scale? I glanced down at it and then at the Scales that surrounded the two large, shield-like Scales my hands were unconsciously caressing. I started and pulled back my hands as if burned. The smaller ones held an allure to me as well but were simply overshadowed by the two 'Heart Scales.'

With this almost over, I looked behind me recalling the Frying Pans, and Crystals I'd left behind in the Naga Compound. Then I looked at the grayscale abandoned Fishing Rods. *It's going to suck to leave those—*

[They'll get placed in your Necklace, if you have room, since the System intervened. In the future I wouldn't count on that though...] Smegma mentally sent without looking at me.

"Agreeeeed," the Snake said, its mouth barely moving as it drew out the word. Just the utterance felt like a razor peeling back my skin. "Now, let usss end thisss Sssysssstem farcsse! Just know, Brodie Flacarada, *Grubsssack* called Smegma, I've heard all your communicationsss! Me or my children will find you!"

The grayscale to the world vanished, as did the two Heart Scales, and two of the smaller ones. In fact, the entire mountain of treasure was missing. Still, I was only concerned with the—

Nagina struck!

Well, she vanished, and I thought I saw just a hint of her open-mouthed strike before everything around me changed. We were back in the public park we'd entered the Portal from on Earth.

I scanned around myself, seeing my group doing the same, even as I realized the park wasn't the same as it had been when we'd set out... How many days ago had that been? How long had we been down there?

I didn't get a chance to voice those questions since my brain was cataloging the most pressing change to the public park—the armed 'soldiers' pointing every manner of gun at my group. Then, of course, there were the hastily erected concrete barriers that were just in front of the temporary fencing that had been there on our entrance.

The scene of weapons trained on me was terrifying, certainly, but my body found it distinctly hard to find the mundane action as terrifying as Nagina had been. I slowly raised my hands over my head and saw the rest of my group follow my lead. Smegma didn't, and I just hoped he had turned himself invisible before any of these guys saw him.

'Cause if a floating winged Demon exiting a closed Portal wasn't a reason to start shooting, I didn't know what was—

CHAPTER 28: CHAPTER 80

Tuesday, April 30th, 2069

"Down! On the ground!" a commanding voice shouted. I may not have been the first to lie flat, but I certainly followed that instruction as quickly as I could. A glance up told me that everyone else had as well.

"What Guild are they from?" someone asked, the voice somewhat overridden by weapons being lowered or holstered again.

"No clue," someone answered, sounding shocked. "I can't believe another Guild was threatened enough to send a strike-force in to try and close our Permanent Portal!"

"What kind of strike-force gets caught and lays down obediently? Also, if they closed it, doesn't that mean it wasn't Permanent?" another voice asked as boots approached in measured steps. I also heard velcro tear multiple times.

"The smart ones," a grizzled voice chuckled. "Mission's accomplished, ain't it? Whoever sent 'em will buy 'em back and give 'em a nice bonus to boot." I heard the grizzled voice pause to spit, then continue, "Still could've been a Permanent Portal if it was some sorta hidden Boss, right?"

"That's *total* bullsh—"

"Stay down, and don't resist!" the commanding voice ordered from nearly atop me, drowning out the rest of the voices. I tried scanning my eyes toward the voice, but found ten identically dressed individuals with masks pulled up over their faces.

"Hands behind your back," a female voice said firmly from beside me, and I blinked for just a moment, trying to make sense of why someone would give that order. I got a poke from a gun muzzle in response. "I said *hands behind your back, you husking Greed!*"

The second time she said it, I didn't need to think twice and followed her orders. Instead of the expected cuffs, I felt something being slid over both of my hands and then heard the repetitive clicks of zip-ties locking down. The woman wasn't friendly with her pressure, and I could instantly feel the plastic digging into my wrists.

"Get them up and to the command tent!" the first voice spoke again. From the startled groans from my group, I could tell that my jailor took a moment longer to register the order. When she did, she yanked on the zip-ties, which were painfully digging into my wrists. The pull caused my shoulders to reach the edges of their range of motion, sending a searing pain down my arms.

In no way did her pressure help me get to my feet, and I cursed under my breath as the pain of the plastic digging into my wrists intensified and was joined by the two wrenched shoulders. Despite her best attempts to unbalance me,

I fought to my feet. In fact, I was surprised by how well I'd managed the feat while my balance was completely off. I was kind of proud of myself—I hadn't even been working out.

"It's the Dexterity, idiot. I'd move your butt. That girl looks like she's not messing around. Good thing I'm not really here—those restraints look terribly uncomfortable."

I tried and failed to raise my middle finger through whatever had been slid over my hands, but I knew Smegma would read the intent in my mind. It was the thought that counted, after all.

Then I was shoved from behind and almost returned to the ground. Thankfully, my new Dexterity, high Strength, or maybe even Stamina stopped me from tripping. Of course, the vindictive woman wasn't done there, and as I started moving in the direction I'd just been shoved—she used her weapon to cross-check me in a new one.

I growled, starting to get fed up with the treatment, but knew better than to antagonize her. Not with what I had heard from my father and uncle Jarred about low-ranked Guilds. Not with what I had just been through, where they'd wanted to leave us to die. Surely this would all get settled once they realized we were just the Mining team they'd *brought* inside…

Thankfully, once I was on my new trajectory, I could see the backs of Dave, Willa, Jarred and my father in front of me. Everyone was being taken to the same place, which hopefully was a good thing. Several additional shoves came from the angry woman at my back, but now that I was expecting them, I used my Strength to endure it.

We exited through the temporary concrete blockades and fencing before the people in front of me turned and moved toward a large red tent. I started to turn, and the woman who was progressively shoving me harder tried to give me another shove, using a bit of a running start.

I planted my next step hard and braced, fed up with the bullshit. When the woman hit me with her shoulder, I didn't budge. Unfortunately for her, however, she had jumped into the shoulder check. I heard the air in her lungs expel violently, followed by a loud crack and a noise I would usually have referred to as a gut punch.

It's kind of a grunt, but more than that. The sound when someone's lungs freeze and they instantly feel sick to their stomachs.

The following shriek of pain made me jump, and I looked down to see that her shoulder was quite clearly no longer in its socket. My eyes widened for a moment, then I blinked rapidly down at her, not believing what I was seeing. Very suddenly, I became a target in the shooting range again.

"Hands up now, you piece of shit!" someone yelled.

"Get down on the husking ground!" another shouted.

Two more said something I couldn't hear over the others' shouts and the woman's continued wailing. I winced as I started to lower myself to my knees, simultaneously trying to make it clear I couldn't put my zip-tied hands above my head.

184

Any moment now, I was going to get shot, all because I got annoyed at a little bit of pushing. Thankfully, the man with the commanding voice shouted, "What is going on here? Lower your damn weapons. He's cuffed and compliant."

"Echo, sir, he just dislocated Greta's shoulder!" one of the men answered as he lowered his semi-automatic rifle. He then used a freed hand from the muzzle to motion at the still-shrieking woman on the ground.

The leader looked at me, Greta, and then shook his head. "No, soldier," Echo-Five said. "Greta decided to shoulder check him and he stood his ground. Someone get her to the medics." He then pointed at me with a finger. "You, anymore stunts like that and I'll shoot you myself. Got it?"

I nodded, already chastising myself for the situation. Smegma, who had been oddly silent, chose that moment to guffaw, which startled me slightly. Thankfully, my jump-scare happened from my knees and didn't look like I was about to attack anyone.

"This is husking hilarious. How has no one realized you're the Mining team?" Smegma asked as we started moving toward the tent again. I could see the rest of the group's eyes on me. Most of them were concerned, except for my father, who just looked upset.

[Mining teams don't close Portals.] I shrugged.

[What? Of course they do. Mining teams close Portals all the time.]

I locked eyes with the Demon for a brief moment. [Human ones don't.]

We entered the tent behind Echo-Five and a few of the guards who'd escorted us. Another five filed in behind us, and two untied the flaps and let them close. Echo pointed to the floor in front of a desk with neat piles of papers upon it and said, "Kneel!"

When no one moved to obey the Mirage Guild leader, we were physically manhandled to the spot indicated and then made to kneel. I couldn't speak for the others, but I hadn't been sure what Echo's words had meant.

Each guard that made us kneel took a single step away but stayed threateningly at our backs. Echo's commanding voice changed then. Becoming low and matter of fact, he said, "The one who tells me how you got into our *Permanent* Portal, closed it, and what Guild sent you, lives. The others will have had a tragic accident before getting out."

"You're making a huge mistake," my father said. "We're—"

"I don't care how powerful the Guild behind you is. I don't care what Skills you have. Here, in this tent, I am judge, jury and executioner if I want to be. Now, answer the husking question or I will give you an example of just how serious I am!"

"Please, just be listenin' to him," Willa cried. "We ain't be from a Guild—we be yer Miners!"

The Guard behind Willa had stepped forward with his gun raised, and Echo-Five looked furious at not being obeyed, but even as the man looked to his Guild Leader for approval to hit Willa with his gun, Echo-Five raised a hand.

"You're *what*?"

My father swallowed visibly in my peripherals but took back the lead from Willa. "We're the Miners you hired. We got stuck in the caverns when they collapsed."

"You're the *Miners*?" Echo-Five asked and then motioned for the Guard behind Willa to step back as he moved to his desk. "I do recall negotiating with you. What was it—ahh—Gary, correct?"

My father nodded eagerly, probably happy to see the Guard behind Willa no longer training the butt of a weapon on the back of her head. "So, you survived for four days and *nights* inside a Portal Mine? How did you do it?"

"There was a *small* lake down in the caves. Plus, the moss on the walls turned out to be edible."

"Your dad's not a bad liar—" Smegma interjected.

"Let's come back to that," Echo-Five said skeptically.

"Well, shit, I think this guy might have some sort of *Truth Detection*," Smegma corrected his earlier assertion.

Echo-Five reverted to the same quietly threatening voice and asked, "So, you have nothing to do with the Portal closing?"

My father blinked at Echo-Five and then looked around himself, seeming confused. "I thought you killed the Boss?"

Everyone else in the group managed to look confused—likely because they were also hearing this lie for the first time. I blinked first at my dad and then at Echo-Five behind the desk.

In some ways, the tactic of the Mirage Guild was now being used against them, and from the man's grinding teeth, I could tell he wasn't happy about it. I also assumed that even if he had a *Truth Detection* Skill, the second thing my father said was nothing but the truth.

Still, Mirage had clearly brought us in here to have us turn against each other—which admittedly would have been a good plan, but only if we were a strike-team from another Guild. Now, though, the Guild leader himself recalled we were Miners and my father had laid out the general lie for everyone to stick to if he wanted to ask anyone else.

"You know, he could still just kill all of you," Smegma said. "Search your bodies for clues afterward."

I coughed politely before it got to that. "We recovered the storage devices of your Guild members who died down in the caverns. Here…"

I indicated a knapsack that Dave had been carrying but was now in a pile with the rest of our remaining gear. That Bag was currently filled with a few of the mural's metallic yellow Crystals and as many F-Rank Crystals it could hold.

Echo-Five narrowed his eyes at me but motioned for a Guard to bring him the bag. In short order, he'd upended its contents onto the floor. He didn't seem impressed with the F-Rank Mana Crystals but did lean down to pick up something I couldn't see.

Since I was expecting to see him get back to his feet with a shining yellow Crystal, I was surprised when he was holding a Shard of brightest blue verging on purple. Even as a Shard, the clarity of the Crystal was leagues beyond anything I'd seen personally. If I was going off of movies and TV, it was S-Grade—

"A C-Rank Crystal Shard?" Echo-Five asked and began digging through the pile. He soon found the rest of the Shards and two of the full-sized mural Crystals I'd placed there. Only they weren't the mural Crystals. "These were inside this Portal?"

"Where did those come from?" Smegma asked, his voice as confused as I felt.

Everyone was looking at me since I'd prepared the Bag in the Portal when we still thought we'd catch enough Fish. I coughed and told the truth since there were likely a few Mirage members who knew about the mural anyway. "Umm—those weren't like that when I checked the Bag earlier—they were yellow and metallic looking."

"Those are from the mural we Mined?" my dad asked, genuinely surprised.

"Too bad the guards didn't get to put more in the Bag!" I complained openly, trying to use his own trick from earlier to tell the group the lie. I was careful not to say anything that wasn't true. The guards could indeed have put more in the Bag...

Echo-Five handed the Bag back to the guard and motioned at the pile of F-Rank Crystals. He then said, "Clean this up," before placing the Shards and two full C-Rank Mana Crystals on his desk.

"This all checks out, but how come you're so strong if you're just a Miner?" Echo-Five asked.

Knowing that the man might have a *Truth Detection*, I took a split second to assess if the truth would give away anything. I decided it was safe and answered, "I have a *Mining* Skill that unlocked *Strength*."

"Hmm," Echo-Five made a noise of dismissal. He then scanned around the room before pointing at a different guard. One that wasn't currently putting F-Rank Crystals back into a bag. "Go get Geoff, he was the one leading the Mining team."

The silence that descended upon the room after the order was stifling. I began to sweat, thinking of all the ways this could go wrong.

[What do you think is going to happen?] I asked Smegma and discovered the Demon was missing. Surreptitiously, I scanned the room and didn't find him anywhere. Where the hell did he go at a time like this?

The wait and silence became even more concerning, especially without Smegma to bounce ideas off. Not to mention just how pale and worried each member of our group looked. It would seem that Echo-Five's earlier threats were *very* effective.

Finally, a familiar man came into the room, his hair standing up like he'd just been pulled out of bed. Still, he saluted smartly and said, "Geoffrey Fir, reporting as ordered, Guild Leader."

"At ease, soldier," Echo-Five said, clearly attempting to run his Guild like a military. Still, something felt off about the comment. Maybe it was because I was used to it in movies, or maybe Echo-Five wasn't entirely comfortable with the structure. I couldn't tell, but it definitely felt forced on both sides of the coin.

Simply put, it felt like neither man had actually served in the military.

"Are these the Miners you escorted into the caves?" Echo-Five asked with a hand pointed in our direction.

Geoff scanned us and then nodded slowly. Echo-Five noticed the man's reluctance to nod and asked, "Speak freely, soldier."

"I was just wondering where *my* men were, if these *Miners* made it out, sir," Geoff stated, asking a question without inflection.

Echo-Five looked at us, and everyone's head hung a bit lower. The answer was obvious just from that, but clearly Echo-Five wanted more because he commanded, "Explain!"

I took the opportunity since I may be the only one in the group aware of his *Truth-Seeking* Skill, which meant I could work around it. "They were all likely eaten by the White Goblins."

Geoff's face went red and his body shook. "Jack, Etien and Viccar wouldn't risk their lives for Miners!"

"You're right," I shrugged awkwardly with my hands still bound. "They didn't."

"Then, how in the hell did—"

The Guild Leader raised a hand, interrupting the Mining Leader.

"How were they eaten by White Goblins?" Echo-Five asked, his voice going hard again. Clearly upset not only on Geoff's behalf but also because some of his Guild members had been *eaten*.

"They were sent to scout ahead. We don't know how they were caught, but the Goblin's had their weapons…" I answered, being very careful to only tell the truth again.

"But you said they were *eaten*!" Echo-Five hissed. "How did you know they were eaten?"

"Well, I didn't actually check the cook pot, you understand. But with the way the creatures were acting, having their weapons, and based on the smell and the lack of bodies… I think it was pretty clear what had happened."

[Husk! Husk! Husk!] I repeated internally, not having realized my mistake. Internally, I was panicking, trying to stick to only facts that were true, but not incriminating. I was talking too fast and I knew it, but I also knew that the man's patience was coming to an end. I didn't have much time to think of something more to say—

"Boss!" someone shouted as he rushed into the room. Echo-Five glared at me but made a motion in the direction of the entrance, giving the runner permission to speak. "Police, Fire and Ambulance are here! They were told that a Portal was closed and there were injured!"

Echo-Five's eyes narrowed, and he turned to his guards. He loudly asked, "You took their phones as soon as they exited the closed Portal?"

The Guards nodded and looked at each other to ensure that their fellows hadn't *husked up*. The runner coughed politely and added, "They're right outside…"

Echo-Five punched his table.

* * *

Wednesday, May 1st, 2069

"Thank the lord you're okay!" my mother screeched as she entered the hospital room. Our entire group was in beds despite the fact that no one was hurt.

188

I'd Healed them all every day down in the caverns. Still, I felt like there was a dark cloud over the group. What would Echo have done if the Ambulances, Police and Fire Trucks hadn't arrived?

My mom firstly ran to my bed, but since I had no bandages and managed to squeeze her back during her hug, she immediately looked around and then hurried to my father. He, thankfully, was also awake and able to hug her back. She sank into his embrace, crying softly.

Everyone looked around at her entrance. I looked to Smegma, who was, in fact, the reason we were safe. He was clearly very happy ever since we'd discovered that the mural shards had become C-Ranked Crystals, "With the C-Ranked Crystals, you might be able to buy a decent Skill for yourself, *finally*."

[Not the time. Plus, I have to give a Skill to the guy you bribed!]

"Just let him use the Altar with Cores! I never promised him to supply the Cores, only one of the limited uses that the Altar had remaining. Then use the mC for yourself. Enough Gathering Skills!"

[Those Gathering Skills have saved all of our lives *and* unlocked Stats.]

"Whatever—" Smegma said and flew into a corner of the room to pout.

"—low Ranked Guilds. Never again! Do you hear me, Gary? Brodie?!" my mom shouted. My brain only caught the tail-end of whatever she had been lecturing my father about. Still, I didn't need more than that to understand her.

"Yes, Mom," I intoned, already thinking about what might come of the current situation. Surely, Mirage wouldn't just let this go—

"Brodie!" someone said from the doorway, and the tone startled me out of my thoughts. My head snapped up to find Mrs. Stovall breathing hard, a step inside the room. "The Courts are about to dismiss your case and rule in favor of Varnish!"

Her words made me perform an involuntary sit up and ask, "Right now?"

"Unless I can get you to the Judge's office before she signs the discretionary bench warrant!" Mrs. Stovall said breathlessly.

I looked at the clock on the wall.

Eight twenty-five. "What time does that happen?"

"Nine!"

I jumped out of the bed, scanning around the room in worry. "I'll get you checked out!" Mrs. Stovall said, even as she was walking back out of the room. Over her shoulder, she said, "I'll drop you at home after!"

CHAPTER 29: CHAPTER 81

Wednesday, May 1st, 2069

"You know Mirage isn't going to just let this go, right?" Mrs. Stovall said. We were currently in a small room waiting for the clock to strike ten. We'd confirmed with the Judge that I was in fact alive and ready to continue with the trial. So, she had forestalled signing a bench warrant for my arrest.

That had only taken five minutes, and I'd used the rest of the time to fill Mrs. Stovall in on what had happened in the Portal. I even told her most of the truth, too.

"The guy I made the deal with claimed they had been investing quite a bit of money to secure the park…" Smegma interjected from his place hiding below the table.

I sighed as I rubbed at my eyes with the palms of my hands. My mother and father were supposedly on their way here with a change of clothes for me—so I didn't enter the courtroom in a hospital gown over ripped and torn Miner's gear.

I just couldn't catch a break, could I? Eyes watering, I looked at Smegma before settling on Mrs. Stovall. "What am I supposed to do?"

"We could buy a Skill and kill them all?" Smegma suggested, which caused Mrs. Stovall to jerk in her chair and regard the 'monster under the bed' with a serious expression. "Kidding—what do you suggest?" His tone didn't exactly inspire confidence in me that he had actually been joking.

Plus, from my seat, I could see two of his three fingers crossed behind his back. Where had he even learned that?

"I suggest you get ahead of this. Maybe talk to Geneva and Kristen. Give enough of your story to make it clear without antagonizing Mirage. You need some way to protect yourself."

I blinked as pieces clicked into place. That was a really good plan. I pulled out my phone, realized it wasn't charged yet, and said, "Can you message them? I've got the camera with two days of footage for them."

"Does it have you getting trapped?" Mrs. Stovall asked, sounding excited despite the tragedy she was asking about.

I nodded, even as Smegma mumbled, "It might even have those shit stains abandoning you with the order to keep working."

Mrs. Stovall was already typing on her phone when I looked back up to her. She had placed a charger cable and battery pack in front of me. At my look, she explained, "When you're in court all day, it's super helpful to have access to power."

"In more ways than one," I snorted, thankful.

A man in a security uniform stuck his head in the door and said, "Mrs. Stovall, Mr. Flacarada, the Judge will be entering in five minutes."

"Thanks, Juan," Mrs. Stovall said as she put her phone back into her bag. I, on the other hand, plugged mine in and waited about thirty seconds for it to boot up—only so I could shut it off again. I'd watched enough TV to know better than to let the thing go off inside the courtroom.

A glance at Mrs. Stovall got me a nod of approval, which was confirmation enough that some things on TV were accurate.

* * *

"May it please the court?" Judge Dench gave a nod, and Mr. Varnish moved around the desk, nodding back to her. "Counsel, ladies and gentlemen of the jury, good morning. My name is Varnish, just Varnish, and I apologize for using my Hunter name, but it is simply what I'm used to nowadays. Plus, it's the best gift the people I protect ever gave me."

The jury shifted in their seats, a few of them looking moved by the man's words. The charismatic Hunter continued, and I fought to keep my face neutral. "You're going to learn in this case a lot about what it means to be a Hunter, a Skilled police officer, detective, and even private eye. As we take this journey together, you'll be made privy to some terms not often used."

Mr. Varnish walked back and forth in front of the jury box, addressing each person individually as he spoke. Meeting their eyes when they were willing, or simply passing his gaze over them if they weren't. "Terms like Cannibal and Snatcher. Terms that are known by the people I just mentioned but not the general public. Why is that?"

Mr. Varnish paused, as if waiting for a response from the jury. I thought a few even twitched like they wanted to raise a hand. Mr. Varnish answered his own question before it came to that. "It's because the terms are terrifying, beyond criminal, and should never have to be used. However, that's not the truth of the world we live in. As always, our society has had its light and dark—and for the remainder of this case, I'm going to ask you all to peel back that darkness with me. Can you do that?"

I blinked as many of the jury nodded along with Mr. Varnish. Wasn't there a time limit to these things?

"We'll start with the term Cannibal because that one is particularly important. You might ask why, and if you'll humor me, I'll get to that. Just like cannibals of the previous world, the word means to consume other humans. In this case, it means to consume the Skills of other humans—" Gasps sounded and Mr. Varnish raised his voice as he finished, "taking them for yourself."

A cry of alarm rang through the chamber. I glanced over my shoulder to see a relatively empty closed courtroom. Still, the cry of alarm had to have come from somewhere, right?

"Sorry," Smegma said from my shoulder. "I wanted to add something for dramatic effect."

[Stop husking around!] I ordered. Smegma rolled his eyes and began floating through the jurors as I fought my urge to glare at him. It definitely wouldn't look good to be seen angrily glaring at the people who would decide my verdict…

"—if you will. Now, a Snatcher is like a Cannibal but *far* rarer," Varnish explained, clearly having continued his opening statement as Smegma distracted me. "A Snatcher can take someone else's Skill and impart it to another. Usually, this is only possible when certain criteria are met."

Mr. Varnish used a hand to indicate me and Mrs. Stovall, along with John—her assistant, not her husband. "The defendant is going to try to convince you that Morgan Hallsbrad was a Snatcher, serial killer, and master criminal.

"And yet, I want you to think about the evidence that will be shown throughout this case. Think about those accusations and then on the situation Brodie Flacarada claims to have found himself in. A situation in which he faced off against not Morgan Hallsbrad, but some mythical, stone-cold Snatcher with a weapon and a body count. Let me ask you now—what are the odds that a young, F-Ranked Awakened college student would be the target of someone like that?"

Mr. Varnish returned his full attention to the Jurors. "All I ask is that you keep an open mind. Ask questions and wonder *why*. Why won't Brodie offer himself for a fully paid Awakening Scan? Why would Morgan Hallsbrad, accused of being a Snatcher for profit, target an F-Rank?"

He took another pregnant pause. "Or is there something else going on here? Something that I will do my best to uncover as we dive into this case."

With that, Mr. Varnish nodded to the jurors and the Judge before moving to his chair and table. His table, of course, was full with three people seated around it. I didn't see anyone I recognized from the 'settlement' meeting, but they all dressed similarly. Another five people in similar black Portal-material suits sat in the chairs behind the divider.

My breath stuttered as I observed the disparity and replayed the man's words. If I hadn't been there and experienced the moment, I might even be questioning it myself. The man was good.

Mrs. Stovall had a yellow legal pad in front of her. I hadn't noticed during Mr. Varnish's opening statement, but she clearly had been crossing out points and adding others in real time. I tilted my head to try to read what was on it—

"Mrs. Stovall, your opening statement?" Judge Dench asked. That took my attention off the legal pad. Mrs. Stovall gave me a confident smile, glanced at the pad one more time, and stood up.

"Thank you, Your Honor," Mrs. Stovall said as she moved out from the confines of her chair. She nodded respectfully to the Judge before walking around the desk and addressing the jurors. "Esteemed ladies and gentlemen of the jury, good morning. First, I'd like to take a moment to thank you for being here. Thank you for doing a duty that isn't always convenient. That, as you've just heard, isn't always savory or desirable.

"As Mr. Varnish said, you have learned some new terms—heard of new monsters in the night. Monsters that are far harder to discern than the ones on our television screens on a darkened Friday evening. Monsters that Hunters have trouble protecting us from. I know from my own experience that I slept better without that knowledge."

192

A few of the jurors shivered and Mrs. Stovall paused. She regarded each member of the jury with a slow, panning look. It was warm and motherly, in a way I couldn't quite describe. Maybe it carried some hint of pride? Like a mother encouraging a son or daughter to be brave.

"Knowing these Monsters exist is scary. Just like it was on the days those first Portals appeared. In those first days, humans proved something. They proved that we are brave and that we will fight to survive."

Mrs. Stovall motioned to me, somehow including me in the proud mothering vibe she was giving off. "Just like Brodie Flacarada did when he was confronted by one of those Monsters. A Snatcher—the rarest kind, as Mr. Varnish told you. In that moment, Brodie faced one such monster that wanted to take everything from him."

"However, Brodie wasn't in a Portal. He could never have expected a monster like Morgan Hallsbrad to show up on campus that day. A *serial killer* currently facing forty-two counts of murder in the first-degree—"

"Objection, Your Honor," Mr. Varnish said, standing up. "Prejudicial. Morgan Hallsbrad is innocent until proven guilty."

Mrs. Stovall turned slowly and addressed the Judge as well, "I'm simply stating a fact, Your Honor. He is on trial—"

"Sustained. I'm going to have to side with Mr. Varnish, Mrs. Stovall. The prosecution can claim the innocence of Morgan Hallsbrad because of jurisprudence and the rights of the accused. You, however, cannot do the opposite for the same reasons. Reporter, please strike that from the record."

Mrs. Stovall nodded to the Judge and then said, "Let me rephrase. Morgan Hallsbrad is currently on trial for forty-two counts of murder in the first-degree."

Mr. Varnish hadn't sat back down. "Objection, Your Honor. Prejudicial."

"Overruled. It is a simple statement of fact, Mr. Varnish," Judge Dench countered, this time seeming to side with Mrs. Stovall. John, the assistant beside me, wrote something on a paper and slid it to me to read.

'*It's bad form to object during opening statements. This is good.*'

Smegma read the note over my shoulder. Scoffing, he asked, "What sort of strange song and dance is this?"

[I have no idea,] I answered mentally.

Mrs. Stovall continued, and as she spoke, I saw the rapt attention and understanding from the jury that I'd feared when Mr. Varnish had created the same thing toward himself.

The court was dismissed for the day after the opening statements, reconvening for the first witness by the prosecutor tomorrow.

Mrs. Stovall looked happy with the way things had gone—which went a long way to making me feel confident as well. I could still feel a nervous pit in my stomach, but her smile and mood alleviated some of it.

It also helped that Varnish and his team of seven other suits rushed from the room. They didn't seem angry, but they certainly weren't as happy as Mrs. Stovall and John.

"Let's get you home," Mrs. Stovall said. "We've got some things to go over, and I think Geneva and Kristen are there waiting for us."

CHAPTER 30: CHAPTER 82

Wednesday, May 1st, 2069

"So, our goal is to create a video that shows the blue-collar aspects of Mining but also highlights the fact that Mirage saved your lives by clearing a Dungeon?" Kristen asked, sounding excited.

"I'm not sure that's the best course of action," Mrs. Stovall interjected. "It might be worth it to make two videos. Carrot and stick. We could put culpability pressure on them by showing they abandoned the Mining team—"

"That will only exacerbate the issue," Geneva explained, cutting across Mrs. Stovall. "First, no other teams would likely want to work with them in the future, which would put a final nail in the coffin in terms of creating a grudge, so to speak." Geneva gestured at me, almost to make that final idiom personal.

"Did she just threaten you?" Smegma asked, clearly not understanding the saying.

"No, no," Geneva laughed. "I'm just saying that Mirage would likely go belly up if they got a bad reputation—"

"Belly up?" Smegma asked.

"Stop interrupting, I'll explain those idioms later," I scolded and got a look of appreciation from Geneva.

"—which would force them to shut down the Guild," Geneva continued, after ensuring Smegma was in fact done asking questions. "That would likely make them act sooner. Instead, what we're going to try to do—is paint them out to be a Guild that would do anything to save trapped workers. That's what they were investing in, *don't you know?*"

At Geneva's final conspiratorial tone, I saw a look of dawning realization cross everyone's face. I assumed I had the same reaction—since I, too, had been a bit skeptical of the final plan. I even began nodding—wondering if some of the donations that I was getting might even go to them, or some of the C-Ranked Crystals I had. Would that help alleviate a financial burden or help return some of the perceived profits from Mirage's 'Permanent' Portal?

"Doubt that," Smegma said in answer to my thoughts. "Still, it's a good thought—if you can afford it. Maybe sell one or two of them?"

"Sell one or two of what?" a few people asked in near unison. The shit-eating grin that came onto my face couldn't be helped.

All day in court, my Necklace of Holding felt like it had been burning a hole in my sternum. I wanted nothing more than to empty it out and take stock!

Smegma started making a noise that stopped me short of emptying my Necklace. The sound was like a wailing keen that reminded me of the threat of torture we'd heard the night before. It was such a horrible sound that Dave incredulously asked, "What the husk are you doing?"

"Sounding the lament. We use it to emphasize when something amazing is going to happen. You guys don't have that?" Smegma answered, looking around the table. A few people had gone as far as to plug their ears at the strange keen.

"No, we don't!" Dave said.

"I'm thinking it's probably equivalent to our drumroll," I said as I moved out of the confines of my chair. "Maybe that has to do with the drums of war or something, which would make it even more similar…"

"Whatever," Dave said. "Just don't do it again, please."

The fact that no one laughed told me just how much it had bothered everyone else. I shrugged. It certainly hadn't been that bothersome to me.

Once in the center of our rather small living room, I emptied the Necklace of Holding. The vast majority of items were F-Rank Mana Crystals—but it was the streaks of vibrant indigo verging on purple, that I kept my eyes on. Those C-Ranked Crystals, the three metallic pieces with varying glowing hues, two Dragon Scales and a Heart Scale.

People gasped, and my shit-eating grin returned, only larger. I hurriedly snatched up one of the C-Rank Crystals and turned to Smegma. "How much can I get for one of these?"

"They're lacking in Mana, but the Crystal is pretty perfect. Probably because of the age or System conversion. So, I can only give you about twenty thousand mC for the Mana inside. But as much as another forty thousand for the Spent Crystal."

"Is that what I think it is?" Geneva asked, before I could complain. The D-Rank Crystals had sold for a hundred and twenty thousand.

[Those were mined by the System, not a bunch of unSkilled Miners with Enchanted Picks,] Smegma countered defensively. He clearly was just as upset about the lack of Mana as I was.

"If you think it's a C-Rank Mana Crystal, then yes!" I answered, adding false excitement back into my tone. It was still worth way more than F-Rank Crystals.

"What?!" Kristen, Jarred, and my mother all shouted.

Turning toward the table, I explained the situation to the people who had been in the caverns with a simple, "It's what the pieces of that metallic yellow mural turned into when we got out. For the rest of you, we found traces of an ancient Naga civilization down in the caverns. They'd used mid ranked Crystals to create lights—"

My happy mood fell when I recalled just how much of this Crystal we'd left down there. Each room in the complex had a light fixture, for husk's sake!

A few people around the kitchen table cursed openly as they made the same realization I just had. Geneva and Kristen looked around as they continued, a hint of confusion now in their voices.

"What?" Kristen asked.

Geneva didn't bother asking and just continued, "One of those can sell for a couple hundred thousand dollars at a minimum! How many do you have?"

"You're making it worse…" my father mumbled as his head fell. Geneva and Kristen squinted at him, but the others at the table had a similar reaction, even though they didn't voice it.

[How could they sell for so much when there is that little Mana in them?] Smegma mentally asked me.

[My guess is that they'll be purchased on the color and clarity. They won't know the amount of Mana inside…]

[Ahh, I see,] Smegma answered, sounding very excited about the prospect of tricking people. Which of course made me reconsider. Still, it wasn't like I was lying—they were C-Ranked Crystals.

I took a quick count, just for myself. That one mural had given us at least twenty full Crystals—no, twenty-two including the ones I'd put in the Mirage Bag of Holding. That meant we'd given at least four hundred thousand dollars to the Mirage Guild and left behind at least—I tried to do the math, but my brain stopped me. It was pointless to dwell in the past.

I won't say that the reminder didn't make me want to roll my eyes and shoot myself for being so 'wise.' But since it was internal, my only recourse was to scoff before answering, "Twenty." All the Shards had been put in the Mirage Bag, too.

My *Mental Fortitude* Skill chastised me again, and I reached up to tug my own hair in frustration. I now had a rather big decision to make. I could sell all twenty and get one million plus mC!

That would certainly buy me a Skill from *Demonic Vault*!

However, if I really wanted to get the monkey—the Mirage Guild—off my back, I needed to sell some of the Crystals and reimburse Mirage for their investment…

Plus, with the Spent Crystal holding most of the value I couldn't keep too many to identify Skills with.

I thought back on what I'd seen of the enclosure they'd been building last night but couldn't even begin to guess how much that had cost. Turning to Geneva, I asked, "How much do you think the Mirage Guild spent on that Portal?"

It was her turn to make a face—Kristen, too. I could tell that they thought that was why the others had been swearing, but I didn't bother explaining the misinterpretation. That didn't really matter. Their faces meant they had bad news—and I took a deep breath to prepare myself for it.

Kristen looked to Geneva, giving her permission to speak. Geneva's grimace grew before she whispered, "It isn't how much they spent—but what they could have made."

Sighing out my breath, I asked, "And that is?"

"The last low-rank Permanent Portal that sold in our area went for a little over two-million dollars," Kristen volunteered.

Everyone started cursing then. Me included.

"Surely, you don't have to pay them back all of that," Smegma stated. "Just give them a certain amount and claim it was the donations from followers. As a thank you for saving your lives or something?"

Geneva and Kristen nodded, as did Mrs. Stovall. Everyone else went quiet as they waited for the proverbial hammer to drop.

"I think they'd let it go for half of the amount, for sure—maybe as low as a quarter," Mrs. Stovall suggested.

Geneva and Kristen made motions with their hands to say that wasn't a sure thing. Geneva explained, "There's no guarantee. But it's probably safer to aim for half."

"So, sell enough of these to make a million, and we can't even keep any of it?" I looked around at the Miners in the group, surprised to find them nodding at my suggestion. None of them seemed upset with that decision.

Willa saw my look and chuckled. "Ya be payin' our wages, kid. Plus, you ain't the only one they be comin' after. So, why wouldn't we be okay with dat?"

"Plus, we all Awakened Skills because of you!" Dave added.

Kristen, Geneva, and Mrs. Stovall stared at Dave and then slowly turned on me.

"That is going to need some explanation," Mrs. Stovall said calmly but pointedly.

With the help of the rest of the group, I explained the whole story to those in the room. My mother only delayed the telling once by fainting.

* * *

"Tomorrow, Mr. Varnish will start calling witnesses. I have his list here," Mrs. Stovall said as she slid a page over to me. Geneva and Kristen had rushed out after the retelling of the events down in the caverns, claiming the faster they got started, the safer I'd be. "Do you recognize any of the names?"

I ran a finger down the page, reading through each name. The first ten to fifteen I didn't know, but somewhere around that fifteenth name, the list changed.

Ayla Moody, the woman who'd offered her card to me after *Demonic Vault* had ranked up for the first time. "I know this woman—well, I've met her. She saw me 'Awaken' in the car at the mall. I think she implied an invitation to her Guild, or maybe she's like someone who sources 'talent' for Guilds? I don't quite remember. She gave me her card and told me to reach out after I'd been Assessed..."

Mrs. Stovall raised an eyebrow, made some notes, and asked several follow-up questions. Then she made a motion to continue. The next name wasn't familiar to me, but my father, who was reading over my shoulder, said, "Larry was a member of P-Cubed's Mining Team. He was likely around when Brodie 'Awakened' his Skill after the Golem."

I felt my head want to fall to my chest but dutifully answered Mrs. Stovall's questions along with my father's help. The next name was another I knew. "Taz?" I asked. "The Guild Leader of Lynx?"

Mrs. Stovall nodded and this time didn't bother making notes. "The fact that he's willing to show up at a trial like this means that Mr. Varnish, and whoever is backing him, is spending huge amounts of money."

"But *why?*" I asked, throwing up my hands in exasperation. "Why do all this? Varnish? The trial, and now Taz? What are they getting out of this?"

I stopped fighting gravity and allowed my chin to fall onto my sternum. Right from the opening statements today, my stomach had started twisting, seeing Varnish work the jurors. Now, I was staring at a list of witnesses that made me acutely aware of the drastic difference between their side and mine.

Mrs. Stovall was certainly an excellent lawyer, but she wasn't a Hunter. She'd made a great opening, but what were we going to do after that? I guessed we'd call witnesses as well.

My mom rushed to my side, thanks to my hanging head. Kneeling, she hugged me. Dave, Willa and Jarred joined my father, reading over my shoulder as I took a moment to collect myself. Sure, *Mental Fortitude* was encouraging me to 'buck up,' but honestly, I needed to also come to terms with the situation—so I didn't rush it.

"Surely, Brodie has some witnesses too?" Dave asked. That got me to glance up, and I caught the tail end of Dave motioning to himself and the others.

"Certainly," Mrs. Stovall said and passed over another sheet.

This one made it worse. Mr. Varnish had about forty names on his sheet. I—no, *we*—had ten. Mrs. Stovall caught my eyes before my head could fall, though. "Brodie, their witnesses are also ours. It's called cross-examination. Plus, according to Sparkle Legion, you probably have a great many offers in your direct messages from other victims of the cases down south.

"We spent Saturday evening and most of Sunday consulting on that. Now that you're out, we should probably go through it all. Still, our witness list isn't due until after Mr. Varnish is finished with his. So, this number will definitely grow and isn't final."

I nodded and pulled out my phone for the first time in five days. Geneva and Kristen had assured me that they would give an update with the video, explaining why I had been absent to my growing following on SwiftGram. Still, seeing the notifications on the device was extremely anxiety inducing.

Three thousand on SwiftGram alone. Fourteen thousand on SmileBook, which admittedly, I had set to give push notifications for post likes. So hopefully it wasn't that bad. Then another twelve hundred emails. Thankfully, there were only about ten texts, all of which were from my mother, Sparkle Legion and Mrs. Stovall.

[I'm assuming you aren't going to be selling the remaining fifteen Crystals and looking through Skills again tonight?] Smegma complained.

I gave him a look that I hope conveyed my distaste of that question. There was nothing I'd rather be doing—that and discussing the Mana Batteries and what they'd do for our company. It would be great if I could afford a Skill for a million mC, which was the most I was going to get, including what I had left from inside the Portal. However, I doubted that amount would get me anything truly powerful.

Instead, those C-Ranked Crystals were going to have to be put in reserve. Some for mC as needed, and some for dollars—if my donations dried up.

"Fine!" Smegma said when he saw my look. Then he looked to Dave like a needy little brother. "Want to play with the Mana Batteries and your *Cut* Skill in the backyard?"

Dave perked up from behind my chair, but my mother slapped at him and—ineffectually—at Smegma. "You will *not* be destroying my backyard, thank you very much!"

Smegma's ears drooped and Dave hung his head sadly.

"Take it to the park," Mom said with a sigh.

"Yay!" Dave cheered, shooting out of the house and leaving me with my next great adventure.

"Husking hundred yard limit," Smegma complained as he stared longingly after Dave. "Why do I have to sit through this nonsense with you?"

I didn't feel bad for the Demon in the slightest. If I had to sit here bored out of my skull, feeling depressed, and worried—then so did he. Husking legal paperwork.

CHAPTER 31: CHAPTER 83

Thursday, May 2nd, 2069

To call myself tired would be an understatement. I was exhausted and wired from a great deal of coffee. Mrs. Stovall and I had finished going over witnesses around ten or eleven, at which point I had 'snuck' into my bedroom—trying to not wake Dave.

Dave, of course, had been wide awake and wanting to go over Skill options. What I was going to do with the Altar? How could he level *Cut* for Evolution? His excitement became infectious, and we'd spent a fruitless night looking through high ranked, unaffordable Skills in *Demonic Vault* and theorizing about how strong we might become one day.

We'd finally burned out sometime after four in the morning.

Thus, my exhaustion at—I glanced at the clock in the courtroom—eleven-thirty. The first few witnesses Mr. Varnish had called all spoke to Morgan Hallsbrad's character. Mr. Varnish seemed to be trying to establish Morgan Hallsbrad as a private eye—and a human, I supposed.

Admittedly, it was working. Mostly because Mrs. Stovall couldn't ask too many questions that would refute the man's job or humanity. I tuned back in as Mr. Varnish finished questioning Morgan Hallsbrad's old roommate in college. Turns out he'd studied criminology and forensic science.

That was pre-Portal, of course.

"Mr. Hanson," Mrs. Stovall said as she stood and rounded our table. "When was the last time you saw Morgan Hallsbrad?"

"At graduation, I guess?" Mr. Hanson answered. The man was a typical middle-aged father with a bit of a beer belly and a great deal of missing hair. He'd chosen to go with the eight-strand combover with what was left, and I couldn't help thinking he should probably just shave it off.

"Why didn't you stay in touch?" Mrs. Stovall asked, and I blinked, trying to understand where she was going. What did the TV shows call it? A line of questioning?

It was a game I'd been playing with the other witnesses, trying to figure out where Mr. Varnish or Mrs. Stovall were leading them. And believe me, both were definitely leading the witnesses somewhere. They were both excellent lawyers.

"I got a job in the Miami Vice Crime Lab right out of school. Morgan had to look for work elsewhere."

"You graduated in the same class, and he had better grades than you, correct?"

"That's right," Mr. Hanson answered.

"So, why did Mr. Hallsbrad have to look elsewhere for a job?"

"He had something on his record. So, the police were reluctant to hire him."

"Do you know what was on his record?"

"Nah, Morgan never opened up about it. I assumed it was something like drinking and driving. You know? Made a mistake when he was young and was still paying for it."

"So, he could have done anything? Murder—robbery—assault?"

"Come on, no way. He'd have served jail time if it was anything like that!"

"Are you claiming he told you he never served jail time, Mr. Hanson?" Mrs. Stovall asked.

"Well, no. But it couldn't have been that serious. Morgan was a quiet guy—never bothered anyone. Other than the teachers…"

Mr. Hanson's tone and joke caused a few jurors to chuckle. Mrs. Stovall even let a large smile come onto her face in clear amusement. Or what I thought was amusement until she turned and addressed Judge Dench. "I'd like to submit the Juvenile Detention Record for one Morgan Hallsbrad into evidence as J-forty-two."

She then picked up three pieces of paper from the top of her folder, handed one to Mr. Varnish, one to the judge, and the third to Mr. Hanson. She then returned to the podium slowly, giving Mr. Hanson the opportunity to read a bit.

As she turned back around, she asked, "Can you read a bit of the report to the court, Mr. Hanson?"

Mr. Hanson visibly swallowed and then looked up, his eyes seeming to vibrate and plead simultaneously.

Mr. Varnish stood up. "Objection, Your Honor. Relevance."

"Your Honor, I'm simply trying to establish the fact that Mr. Hanson didn't know Mr. Hallsbrad as well as his testimony implies."

"Your Honor, Mrs. Stovall is clearly trying to get a past arrest record into evidence. Prior crimes have no relevance to the current trial."

"They absolutely do, in fact," Mrs. Stovall countered. "Mr. Varnish here is trying to establish the character of Morgan Hallsbrad. I'm only trying to help him accomplish that. If prior crimes have no bearing on the character of a person, then what does?"

"Counsels, approach," Judge Dench said. Both Mrs. Stovall and Mr. Varnish approached the bench. A quiet deliberation occurred, and I watched gestures and facial expressions, trying to figure out what was going on. Of course, Smegma was hovering over the group of three, eating popcorn.

"They're coming to a compromise. The Judge agrees with Mrs. Stovall on her point of showing Mr. Hanson's lack of knowledge regarding the Shop. Yet, she wants her to go about it a different way."

Smegma paused then, and a great deal of chatting happened, making me curious as to why he'd stopped commentating. After all of that, Smegma simply stated, "They've reached a decision."

[What?]

"Just listen, idiot."

"The court will accept this piece of evidence into the case, but the jurors will only refer to it as something that shows that Mr. Hanson and other character witnesses didn't know Morgan Hallsbrad as well as they had thought, understood?" the Judge instructed.

Mr. Varnish returned to his seat, looking like he wanted to chew rocks.

"Mr. Hanson, I'll read it for you," Mrs. Stovall said, sounding like she was doing the man a favor. "Morgan Hallsbrad served a sentence of one year in the Miami Juvenile Detention Center for Breaking and Entering, along with Threatening Behavior. Sentence of three years remised due to community service and good behavior. Did I read that correctly, Mr. Hanson?"

The man swallowed and shakily answered, "Yes."

"So, is it safe to say you, and the other witnesses today, might not have known Mr. Hallsbrad as well as you claimed, Mr. Hanson?"

"Objection. Speculation."

"Sustained."

"Sorry, Your Honor. Is it safe to say that *you* didn't know Mr. Hallsbrad as well as you thought you did, Mr. Hanson?"

The man nodded, his face pale and his bald head sweaty.

"Let the record show that Mr. Hanson nodded in affirmation. No further questions, Your Honor."

Mrs. Stovall sat back down at our table, and I looked between her, Mr. Varnish and Mr. Hanson in confusion. Thankfully, Smegma took pity on me. "Mr. Hallsbrad hit an old man over the head with a crowbar, according to that report. The man had an unloaded gun, so instead of an assault charge, he got threatening behavior. Part of the agreement was to strike that portion of the report from evidence before the jury reviews it."

Mr. Varnish stood back up before Mr. Hanson was dismissed. "Mr. Hanson, if you had made a mistake like this—" Mr. Varnish held up the report. "—would you tell your college roommate about it?"

"Well, probably not, no," Mr. Hanson answered, his face regaining a bit of color as a bit of his faith in a friend was returned to him.

"So, did Mr. Hallsbrad not telling you have any impact on your friendship?"

"I guess not?" Mr. Hanson said, again getting a bit more color back. Then he shook his head, clearing the rest of his somber demeanor. "No, no, it didn't."

"Thank you, Your Honor, no further questions," Mr. Varnish said.

Mrs. Stovall was given an opportunity to cross examine, but she waived it, and I could see why. Without being able to discuss the beating, she couldn't counter Mr. Varnish's point. That seemed odd to me. Why would a past crime of this severity not be admissible as evidence?

Surely, I'd seen something like this on TV or the movies? Still, I couldn't point to an example off the top of my head. It just seemed broken. Wouldn't this be something like a pattern of bad behavior?

"Yeah, that *is* kind of stupid!" Smegma agreed from his current spot, sitting right on top of one of the jurors. I pointedly didn't look at him, even as I fought a shiver. It was quite a scene I could see in my peripherals—being judged by my peers, a terrifying black-and-red Demon with huge bat wings sitting atop them.

Of course, that shiver coincided with my first surprise of the trial. One I had known was possible but kind of expected to happen later.

"I'd like to call Detective Flair to the stand, Your Honor."

Detective Flair and Volt had their names on the list—both lists, actually. But in both cases, they were at the bottom. Mrs. Stovall had said that they could be brought in to testify about the scene or what they observed during the 'arrest.' But she had doubted that they'd be needed.

For Mr. Varnish to move one of the Detectives up in the order—not even move slightly forward, either…

"What's going on?" Smegma asked, floating over.

[I've got no idea.]

Detective Flair was sworn in and then took the stand and seat, after removing his hat and adjusting his stiff-looking dress uniform.

"Good afternoon, Detective Flair," Mr. Varnish greeted, making me realize it was now a little past noon. Meaning we'd likely get a lunch break after Mr. Varnish's questioning finished.

"That seems mighty convenient," Smegma said.

[Yeah…] I responded, trying to breathe normally.

"Could you please take us through the events of April 1st, 2069, starting from when you got the call regarding Mr. Flacarada's case."

"Certainly…" Detective Flair began and then continued to lay out the events.

I listened raptly, hearing some pieces of information and police radio jargon I didn't understand. Detective Flair clarified the terms with Mr. Varnish's prodding. That's when his story and my recollection of events began to overlap.

"—then me and my partner arrived on scene. The first on scene was a Skilled Officer who possesses a *Lightning Bolt* Skill in the upper D-Ranks. When we arrived, they described the scene they'd found. They claimed that they had begun Skill activation because they found Brodie Flacarada standing over Morgan Hallsbrad, wielding a gun."

"So, they found Mr. Flacarada with a weapon, and not Mr. Hallsbrad?"

"That's correct."

"And the Skilled Officer was prepared to stun or disable Mr. Flacarada because he was worried for Mr. Hallsbrad's safety?"

"Objection, Your Honor. Speculation," Mrs. Stovall said.

"Sustained. Mr. Varnish, please confine your questions to the thoughts and actions of the witness. If you would like the Skilled Officer to take the stand, you can call him up after adding him to your witness list." After her verbal reprimand, the Judge nodded for Varnish to continue.

"Apologies, Your Honor. This officer claimed to have pulled on his partners Mana Pool to activate his Skill?"

"That's correct," Detective Flair said.

"Thank you, please continue your retelling."

The Detective continued his timeline of events, meshing mostly with my own. The officers cuffing me for my own safety, calling paramedics, and then the many people examining the scene. Smegma floated in front of Mr. Varnish throughout most of the story, eyes narrowed. "What's he trying to do?"

[I think he's painting a picture of me as an assailant. His questions sure seem—]

"So, you bagged and tagged *all* evidence you found at the scene?" Mr. Varnish asked, interrupting the Detective's tale. My eyes narrowed. Hadn't Detective Flair been about to mention the book of names found on Morgan Hallsbrad?

"Once we arrived, me or my partner did, yes," Detective Flair answered. "It was our crime scene, as I mentioned."

"So, after you took the weapon from Mr. Flacarada, you immediately bagged it?"

"That's correct," Detective Flair answered while narrowing his eyes, seeming frustrated by what felt like a repeated question, even to me.

"I'd like to submit G-thirteen into evidence," Mr. Varnish said then moved through the same procedure as Mrs. Stovall. I held my breath again, sensing something was about to happen. "This is a report of fingerprint testing on the weapon in question. Can you tell me whose fingerprints are on the report, Detective Flair."

The Detective looked down at the paper and then back up at Mr. Varnish before answering, "Brodie Flacarada's."

"Is there any other name listed on the report?" Mr. Varnish asked.

"No, only Brodie's."

"Then Morgan Hallsbrad never touched this weapon?" Mr. Varnish asked quickly.

"No, we found two pairs of gloves on Mr. Hallsbrad. One latex and one pair of leather ones."

"But you bagged and tagged everything on the scene and put it into evidence?" Mr. Varnish asked as he spun and went to his desk.

"Again, Mr. Varnish, that is correct."

"Can you show me the gloves you mentioned on this Evidence Summary please, Detective Flair?" Mr. Varnish said. "I'm handing Detective Flair P-one, already submitted into evidence. It's a simple summation of all pieces of evidence found at the scene."

Detective Flair took the page, and Mrs. Stovall flipped in her binder to the 'P' section. It was the first item inside. There was only one page of items, but a quick scan immediately told me what Mr. Varnish was getting at.

There were no gloves listed. I blinked at the page—hadn't the Detective just confidently said they'd found *two* pairs of gloves on Morgan Hallsbrad?

"They aren't listed, are they, Detective Flair?" Mr. Varnish prodded.

"I can't find them on this list, no," Detective Flair answered, holding up the page.

"Did you or Detective Volt take the gloves off Morgan Hallsbrad before bagging and tagging them?" Mr. Varnish asked, following up quickly.

"I believe I did."

"Then, how are they not listed here, Detective Flair."

"I'm not sure—"

"So, you have testimony from the first responders, that they found Brodie Flacarada holding a weapon, and there is no evidence it was ever unholstered by Morgan Hallsbad first?"

"That's not what I've said—"

"Answer the question, please," Mr. Varnish asked.

"Objection, Your Honor. Argumentative. Detective Flair has already testified to there being gloves on Morgan Hallsbrad."

"Apologies, I'll retract my previous question, Your Honor. Let's move on from the missing gloves you *claim* were at the scene. How would you describe Brodie Flacarada at the scene and in the following days of questioning?"

My stomach sank as I knew exactly where this line of questioning was leading. I had just received *Mental Fortitude* without truly understanding what it was doing. I'd even noticed how others reacted to my seeming lack of reactions.

Detective Flair glanced at me for a moment before saying, "Brodie Flacarada was distant and cold at times, seeming to be in a state of shock—"

"Are you a doctor, Detective Flair?" Mr. Varnish asked.

"No—"

"Then, how do you know he was in shock?"

"Look, Prosecutor Varnish. You and I both know that officers of the law are considered expert witnesses when testifying on matters that fall within the scope of their law enforcement expertise. I've seen people shot, stabbed, poisoned, suicide attempts that survived and wished they hadn't, and even more things that I'd rather forget. Under the scope of that experiential expertise, Brodie Flacarada was showing symptoms that I would associate with other cases I've had where the victims were later given a medically confirmed diagnosis of shock. I've seen many victims in my time with the Windsor Police Department, and Brodie was exhibiting the same symptoms."

"So, what you're saying is that no—you have no doctor's diagnosis of shock or even a psychiatric evaluation of it?"

"No, just my *expert* opinion," Detective Flair answered.

"Why's that?"

"Why's what?"

"Sorry, why is there no doctor's evaluation of shock?"

"Because Brodie didn't have to go to the hospital," Detective Flair responded, sounding confused.

"Wait, you are saying that he was assaulted but didn't have to go to the hospital?"

"I said Brodie was assaulted. I never said he was battered. He was held at gunpoint—"

"Objection, Your Honor. Hearsay," Mr. Varnish intoned, objecting to his own witness's answer. "Didn't you just testify to finding Brodie Flacarada holding the gun, Detective Flair?"

"That's correct."

"So, where did the information come from that Morgan Hallsbrad was holding *Brodie* at gunpoint."

"From the victim."

"*Alleged* victim. The same cold and detached 'victim' you found holding the gun?" Mr. Varnish asked. I could see Mrs. Stovall, who'd been scribbling hurriedly, clench a fist at this question. I expected her to stand up and object but she didn't.

"Not the way I described it," Detective Flair responded.

"But you did say Brodie Flacarada was holding the weapon on arrival."

"Yes."

"And described him as cold and detached."

"Yes, but not at the scene."

"So, when was Brodie Flacarada cold and detached, Detective Flair?"

"When my partner and I visited him the next morning to inform him of Morgan Hallsbrad's death—"

It felt like someone had just hammered a nail into my heart.

"That's total bullshit!" Smegma shouted. "Mr. Varnish even knows you have *Mental Fortitude* 'cause of that Larvae bastard!"

"Allow me to restate your position, and correct me if I'm wrong," Varnish stated smoothly. "To the best of your *experiential* expertise, you'd say that Brodie Flacarada, the defendant, was 'cold and detached' after you informed him that his actions likely led to the death of another human being, is that correct?"

Detective Flair shifted awkwardly in his seat.

"Remember, you are under oath," Mr. Varnish pressed. "Yes or no, Detective. Did I fairly summarize your statement?"

Clearing his throat, the Detective leaned slightly toward the microphone.

"Yes."

CHAPTER 32: CHAPTER 84

Wednesday, May 1st, 2069

The dinner table was deathly quiet, and I could tell everyone was digesting the retelling of the information I'd just shared. I myself was still trying to digest just how frustrated and impotent the day had made me.

Every witness that was called to the stand had their words twisted by Mr. Varnish. Mrs. Stovall certainly did a good job of countering his points and fleshing out more of the story, but it felt like the seeds of doubt were being sowed. Mrs. Stovall had even told me that this would happen to an extent, but I just hadn't expected it to be this bad.

She also hadn't expected a key piece of evidence to have gone missing. This truly felt like a movie or court drama TV show—evidence didn't just go missing, right? Mrs. Stovall was talking to the Detectives tonight, and trying to get to the bottom of the 'missing' items.

The current theory from all parties involved was that it was simply left off the list. My gut told me something different though. It just felt like something Mr. Varnish hadn't stumbled onto. Or maybe I had watched too many of the aforementioned dramas.

"Trust Mrs. Stovall," my mother said, as she placed a hand atop my own. I gave her a weak smile, knowing she was right, but also not really in the best of moods to acknowledge it at the moment. "Geneva and Kristen have good news," my mom said with fake enthusiasm—clearly trying to change the subject.

I turned to the two women and caught the tail end of them both 'turning a frown upside down.' Kristen was the first to succeed, and with a wide, forced smile she said, "We've sold the five B-rank Crystals on your behalf, and we've finished editing the video. We brought it here for your review!"

Geneva began digging in her work bag beside her chair before Kristen was even half finished, and soon a tablet was on the table, ready to play. Part of me was excited to see the second video they'd made. I was especially curious after the first's wild success and yet it still took a moment for my brain to convince my heart to play it.

With a mood-changing sigh I stood up and pressed the play button on the black screen. Instantly, the sound of pickaxes on Crystal and ore could be heard as an image slowly came into focus. Somehow, the sounds of Miner's slowly began to morph into slow more recognizable swings on Crystals.

The video gained shades of a familiar green that was still fresh in everyone's mind. The Goblin Caverns! I'll admit that my mood increased by the second as the video continued, showing not only my skill as I quickly extracted full Crystals, but also the 'companies' capabilities. The women did a wonderful job of showing the Guild minder's shock at the speed and ability of our team, and even put in the section where my father left to renegotiate with Echo-Five.

I didn't recall it seeming so professional, and amazing in the moment, but Geneva and Kristen certainly made it out to be. Then, through carefully chosen clips they made it look like the Hunters who were sent deeper to scout had actually done so after the accidental cave-in to keep us safe.

It was brilliant. Untrue, to be sure, but it was genius editing that should appease Mirage. The deaths of the minders were shown to be tragic, and I even felt some outrage on their behalf as a line of text scrolled along the bottom of the video—saying they'd been eaten by the Monsters.

I was beyond impressed, but the video didn't end there.

Next, small snippets of famous Hunters and Guild Leader's were played. Snippets of them praising the hardworking people who toiled away in the Portals. Small conversations on podcasts and talk shows, where the dangers of the jobs for the lame Portal worker were discussed. The video ended with a beautiful shot of me and the group walking toward the Portal in the park, with picks in hand.

Words flew in and the sounds of Miner's picks resumed as it crashed into the center of the shot, and froze the video. The words read, 'Company Name.' The guffaw that escaped my lips, was joined by many others around the table.

The video and their small joke had effectively pulled me completely out of my mood. Not just because of the quality of this piece—but also because it was a great reminder. Information could be manipulated, and Mr. Varnish wasn't the only person capable of that. Here was a perfect example of the 'truth' being subjective. Geneva and Kristen were clearly good at their jobs to make such a compelling tale and narrative out of something that wasn't there.

Mr. Varnish was the same. Mrs. Stovall surely had that skill as well. I needed to remember, I'd surrounded myself with good and skilled people. I just needed to trust them to do their jobs.

And I needed to surround myself with more…

"No!" Smegma complained, breaking the jubilant mood around the table with his sudden outburst. Everyone looked at him in confusion, likely thinking he was talking about the video. "Not the video, idiots! I'm speaking to the biggest moron amongst you."

"*Yes*," I said, a smile still broad on my face.

"No!" Smegma shot back. "You and moron number two spent all night last night talking about what you would become in the future. Now what? You changed your mind on a stupid whim?"

"Smegma, this plan doesn't change that dream. It is an investment!"

"An investment into crappy Crafting!"

"Can someone explain?" my father queried pointedly. His voice wasn't upset but it carried the threat of going there if we didn't stop arguing and let the table in on the discussion.

"I want to use the Mana Coins to buy gear for other Portal Professions. Gardening Gear, Skinning Knives, and—"

"*And?*" Smegma shouted. "You don't have anyone who's a Skilled Cook, besides yourself, not to mention an Alchemist, Blacksmith or anything else!"

"We don't, *yet!*" I countered my grin only getting smaller as I pointed two thumbs at myself. "If I'm not mistaken I'll get a sub-Skill for each thanks to *Overflow*—" Smegma sucked on his teeth, making a noise that threatened interruption but I overrode it. "—Plus! I can change the target of *Overflow*, maybe get some others a Skill!"

"Oh, come on!" Smegma complained. "I've been wanting you to change its target to me forever!"

"And maybe I'll consider it if this works the way I hope for!"

Geneva, Kristen, my father, Dave and my mother looked at me and Smegma with mixed expressions. I could tell that Dave was disappointed I wasn't going to purchase a Skill from the Shop, but simultaneously excited to possibly become a target of *Overflow*, and get more Skills that way.

That was an experiment I'd need to run later, though. Mostly because I still had a great deal of stats and Skills to unlock. Plus, if it did work as intended, it would be extremely dangerous for me if it ever got out. Someone who could just grant Skills by entering a dungeon, was certainly valuable. Would I just become a government asset if discovered? Or worse, assassinated by people who wanted to keep others weak?

My parents both wore thoughtful expressions, clearly thinking about the business side of what I'd just suggested. Geneva and Kristen were unreadable but thankfully Geneva spoke up and excitedly snagged the tablet. "We can add a recruitment notice and explain the new parts to the business. It probably won't get you too many people applying, but it should get the interest of Guilds!"

I sighed and mentally shook myself of the dark thoughts from a moment before, even as the conversation continued.

"We'll handle the other recruits," my father said, looking at my mother. Then he followed up by asking, "How many Picks, Knives and Gardening Kits are you going to purchase?"

I didn't have an answer but I mentally opened the Shop windows for *Demonic Vault*, and checked the prices of those items. They were each just ten thousand mC and with the million plus Mana Coins they'd barely make a dent. I responded, "As many as we can recruit?"

My father nodded even as my mother winced before adding, "We don't know any other Trades, Brodie. Guilds usually take their materials directly to them. So, figuring out what it means to be an Alchemist, Cook and Blacksmith is going to be tough."

"That's okay, and not necessarily a bad thing. It means that the Guilds have had a monopoly on supplies for a while now. We might find that those materials are relatively cheap when considering what a Professional can do with them. We'll experiment a bit for now," I said and then canted my head before asking something I probably should have known before making this plan. "Does anyone know what things each Profession makes that is most in demand by Guilds?"

Smegma chuckled sadly and began rubbing the bridge of his nose. Then to my and everyone's surprise, he grumbled, "I might not know what you Human's want, but I know what was in demand by the Sects of Crendalar Five after five thousand plus years of battling the Portals."

210

As if his reluctant words were a call to action, everyone started moving.

"I'll make some calls!" my dad said.

"Me too," my mom quickly crowed right behind him.

"I'll help keep track of stuff," Dave said, sounding a bit lost, but rushing after them both. I shook my head and smiled, knowing he'd do a fantastic job but also be a bother.

"We'll edit this video, and post it—but we'll still need a company name!"

"Oh, right," I said, feeling my excitement wane a bit. How could the plan be so easy to come up with but a word or two be slightly terrifying?

Dave stuck his head back into the room. "Alonzo's Alloys?"

"We're going to be doing more than Mining," I pointed out.

"Mars' Mercantile?" Dave tried again. He cupped a hand over his mouth to call out down the hallway. "Gary! What rhymes with Flacarada? Alliteration is fine, too. The Flacarada Foundry? No? Well, couldn't you have picked a better last name?"

My mom and dad entered the doorway behind him.

Dad slapped Dave on the shoulder. "I'll be sure to let my grandfather's grandfather know about your criticisms of the family name."

I laughed at Dave's sheepish look and shook my head, not liking the suggestions either.

"Merchants of Mars?" Dave tried again. This one was admittedly closer to what I wanted.

"We aren't Merchants, though. Not really. We offer Portal Services, and Consumables…"

"Then go with something simple like that," Dave stated.

"Alonzo's Abyss: Portal Services and Consumables," Smegma suggested in a whisper.

I blinked and looked at the Demon. It only took that glance to realize how much the name Abyss meant to him. He'd even combined it with my online alias. I nodded.

"We'll get it done!" Geneva squeed, dancing in place and clearly excited to have a name settled.. "Shoot me a text with the spelling just in case."

I nodded, and everyone left the room again, leaving me and Smegma alone.

"Thanks," the Demon whispered.

CHAPTER 33: CHAPTER 85

Thursday, May 2nd, 2069

"Mrs. Moody, could you please explain for the court what it is you do?" Mr. Varnish asked the older woman.

"Certainly. My name is Ayla Moody and I'm a manager for Hunters. Normally, I discover talented individuals within the Hunter Track at Phoenix Academy or before they begin attending Phoenix Academy. Then I help get them sponsorships, scholarships, and funding to support them as they learn to become the best versions of themselves."

"So, it's safe to say that you're an expert on Skilled Hunters?" Mr. Varnish asked.

"I would never claim to be an *expert* on the subject, but I spend a great deal of time with and around them, certainly."

"How many Hunters do you manage, Mrs. Moody?" Mr. Varnish asked, seeming to be driving her and the jurors toward something. I assumed it was to make her testimony stand out more, or be weightier, but just like Ayla, I wasn't an expert in the court of law.

"Approximately…" She glanced up with her eyes thoughtfully, as if doing a rough count before answering. "Two hundred or so, I'd say."

"And how many of your Hunters are S-Rank?"

"Sixteen," Ayla answered again, her voice sounding proud. And admittedly, she had every right to be proud of that number.

Eight percent? That was huge!

"They all Awakened with S-Rank Skills?" Mr. Varnish asked.

Ayla shook her head. "No. Many Awakened with, and are even still using, lower ranked Skills but performing the duties of S-Ranked Hunters."

"How is that possible, Mrs. Moody?"

"A great deal of hard work, Mr. Varnish. I'm sure this isn't surprising news to you; you've met some of the top Hunters," Ayla answered, her voice growing frustrated for a reason I didn't understand.

Mr. Varnish laughed. "A different breed," he said between chuckles. "That's how I'd describe the S-Ranks I've met. Would you agree, Mrs. Moody?"

Ayla gave Mr. Varnish an evaluating stare but nodded. I could tell she was also trying to figure out the man's play here. He continued after verbalizing her nod to the court reporter. "So, would you say that every Hunter you've personally taken on made it to S-Rank solely through hard work?"

Ayla's eyes narrowed and she shook her head minutely. "I think you know quite well that many factor—"

"So, the answer would be a no?" Mr. Varnish interrupted her.

Ayla's eyes narrowed and she took a moment to work some tension out of her jaw before she said, "Yes, the answer would be no. There are multiple factors that contribute to and impact a Hunter's ranking."

"What are those factors?" Mr. Varnish asked, his voice sounding excited, like Ayla had arrived at his intended destination.

"Secondary Skill Awakenings? Is that the answer you're looking for?" Ayla asked. She blinked repeatedly as her face took on a disgusted sneer, directed at Mr. Varnish.

"I'm not looking for any specific answer. However, of the sixteen S-Rank Hunters you manage, how many of them have Awakened a third or fourth Skill during dire situations inside Portals?"

Ayla licked her lips and then took a deep breath. She looked to the Judge first, and then to the jurors, seeming to be looking for a way out. Her jaw began working, like she was chewing rocks. Finally, she whispered, "None of them."

What was going on? What about that answer made her reluctant to speak? I truly couldn't understand the direction Mr. Varnish was trying to take.

"And how many of them Awakened a new Skill during your training?"

Ayla's glare could have melted diamonds, and I felt my eyebrows raise as the pieces of the puzzle Mr. Varnish was weaving came together. Mr. Varnish seemed unmoved by the glare and even went as far as prompting Ayla by saying, "Mrs. Moody, please answer the question."

"Your Honor," Mrs. Moody said, turning to Judge Dench. "This is approaching a subject that infringes on my rights under the Hunter Protection Act of 2055. I refuse to answer any further questions in this vein."

My eyes and jaw were as wide open as they could be. I thought I understood what was happening but was doubting the conclusion I came to.

"Does she have a Hunter that increases Skill Acquisition?" Smegma said as he floated around Ayla Moody.

[That's what I was thinking,] I responded mentally, even as the Judge called for Mr. Varnish and Mrs. Stovall to approach the stand. Ayla never stopped glaring at the A-Rank Hunter, seeming to want to stab him on the spot.

They broke apart and Judge Dench addressed the court, "The jurors and reporter will strike the last line of questioning from the record. Mrs. Moody, I've directed the lawyers not to ask further questions about your business. Jurors, please treat Mrs. Ayla Moody's testimony as that of an expert in the field of Hunters. Understood?"

[That felt like it wasn't related to my case at all,] I mentally sent Smegma. He floated back to his usual seat in the jurors' box. Then, once he'd engulfed a young SwiftGrammer, he regarded me.

"What do you think it means?" Smegma asked.

"Mrs. Moody," Mr. Varnish said before I could mentally collect my thoughts enough to respond. "It's safe to say that you've witnessed more than your fair share of Skill Awakenings in your current career?"

Ayla took a deep breath, her eyes still throwing daggers at the man. "That's correct."

Mr. Varnish moved to his table, picked up a remote and clicked a button. As a white screen lowered from the court ceiling, he said, "Your Honor, this is video V-four—labeled as such in evidence."

There was a brief moment in which the courtroom all waited for the electrical motors of the projector screen to finish their hum. Then the projector itself booted up, producing a blue screen before going black.

For a brief instant, it showed an open folder of videos on Mr. Varnish's computer or tablet before he pushed a button on the remote and a file opened. Sure enough, the video showed me in the mall parking lot as the car glowed, and then Ayla came to my window. It was from fairly high up, perhaps with the camera mounted on either the side of a building or a light pole. You couldn't actually see me in my car, just a birds-eye view of my vehicle from up above.

Mr. Varnish paused it just after Ayla could be seen starting to approach the car. "Mrs. Moody, this is you in this video, correct?" Mr. Varnish asked, and Ayla nodded. "And who was in the car?"

"The boy there," Mrs. Moody said with a bit of reluctance and what appeared to be sympathy directed toward me.

"Let it be recorded that Mrs. Moody indicated Brodie Flacarada." Mr. Varnish looked to the reporter and got a thumbs up before he continued. "So, you witnessed Mr. Flacarada's Skill Awakening?"

Another nod.

"And you approached him?"

"Yes."

"Why?"

"To check if he was okay…" Mrs. Moody whispered, allowing her voice to fade out toward the end.

Mr. Varnish continued the video, which clearly showed her handing something through the car window.

"What did you hand Mr. Flacarada, Mrs. Moody?"

"My business card."

"Why would you hand him your business card?"

"In case he received a good Skill and needed an agent to represent him," Mrs. Moody said, some heat in her voice.

"Why would you think he Awakened a 'good' Skill?" Mr. Varnish asked, going as far as to use air quotes for the word 'good.'

"You saw the illumination his Awakening put off. There was a relatively 'good' chance that he Awakened a high-ranked Skill." Mrs. Moody returned Mr. Varnish's air quotes like they were a grenade. A few jurors chuckled.

"So, you believed that Mr. Flacarada had just Awakened?" Mr. Varnish asked.

Mrs. Moody furrowed her brow, glancing at me, and then back to Mr. Varnish. The latter clarified. "What if I told you that Brodie Flacarada is twenty-one years old?"

Mrs. Moody's eyes went comically wide before she transferred a very shocked gaze onto me. She did answer the question, though, "Then I'd have handed him my entire stack of business cards."

"Why the increase in the level of interest, Mrs. Moody?"

"Because Hunters that Awaken additional Skills often get a Skill that suits them—or should I say, suits their current lifestyle and initial Skills."

"You mentioned that you believed he'd Awakened a 'good' Skill based solely off the illumination the event created. In your experience, have you found a correlation between the strength or quality of an Awakened Skill and the power or strength of the light put off from such an event?"

Mrs. Moody paused then, as if considering her answer carefully. "In my experience… there does seem to be a connection between how bright or strong the light put off from an Awakening is, and either the strength or suitability of a Skill for the Awakened individual, yes."

"Thank you, Mrs. Moody. Now, about the specific location of said Awakening… You don't find it strange that Brodie Flacarada had a secondary Awakening in his car at a mall?"

Ayla Moody blinked, even as she smirked slightly. I watched her head tilt as she continued to regard me. After a time, her smirk morphed into a huge smile. "That certainly isn't where *I'd* expect it to happen, but we can never know another's life."

Mr. Varnish continued to question Ayla, clarifying a few points for the jury. Mainly that my Awakening a Skill in a mall parking lot was 'a bit odd.' Mostly reading statistics about how most Hunters who 're-Awakened' did so in Portals. Ayla simply confirmed his numbers were in line with what she knew. He then asked another question that I'd been expecting. "And what would be your response if I told you he Awakened another Skill a few weeks later, outside of a Portal, after a run-in with and the destruction of a Golem—by his hands with merely a Pickaxe?"

Ayla Moody's mouth fell open and she slowly turned to stare at me. "I'd want to have him enrolled in Phoenix Academy and signed with me as his agent. Immediately."

Another five minutes passed before questioning was passed to Mrs. Stovall. She stood up like Mr. Varnish's words were a starting gun. "Mrs. Moody, when you've seen other Hunters 're-Awaken'—is that the correct term?" Ayla nodded and Mrs. Stovall continued, "Did it always happen in the middle of a stressful situation?"

"Certainly not. There are no hard and fast rules for these sorts of things, you understand. However, with that said, re-Awakenings, in my experience, are *far more* likely to occur during, or in the wake of, a stressful, deadly, or threatening situation, yes."

"So, in your expert opinion, could an assault and near forced Mana Connection be stressful enough to cause an Awakening?"

"Objection, Your Honor. Hearsay," Mr. Varnish said.

"I have not accused Morgan Hallsbrad of these acts in my question, Your Honor. I am merely speaking in general terms here and trying to establish an example of a potentially stressful situation that might trigger a re-Awakening."

"Overruled," Judge Dench said. "But you are treading on thin ice here, Mrs. Stovall. There's no one here that doesn't understand what you're getting at with your chosen example. Make sure that you *are*, in fact, keeping everything to generalities."

"Thank you, Your Honor." Stovall nodded before turning back to the stand. "Would being held at gunpoint while being threatened with a forced Mana Connection be enough stress to force a re-Awakening, Mrs. Moody?"

"Certainly."

"If it didn't happen in the moment but occurred later, would you find it suspicious?"

"Possibly, but that depends on the individual."

"What do you mean?"

"Some Hunters have gone through a near-death experience, and only weeks later, when they'd come down from the stress of that situation, did they re-Awaken."

"Is that because those Hunters were in shock or something similar?"

"That's the most widely accepted theory, yes."

I fought to keep a smile off my face. That was very clever. Not only had Mrs. Stovall explained my numerous 'Awakenings' to the jurors but also established some groundwork to counteract Mr. Varnish's earlier accusations of my being distant and cold as some form of implied sociopathy instead of shock.

"In your expert opinion, would killing a man in self-defense also be traumatic enough to re-Awaken an individual?"

"Certainly. Sometimes even killing a humanoid Monster for the first time has caused Hunters to re-Awaken. However, as Mr. Varnish claimed with his statistics, re-Awakenings are pretty rare. So, we can't truly say if there are patterns or not."

"What about performing a Gathering Profession in the middle of an active Portal and being suddenly attacked by a Portal Monster and having to fight for your life?"

"I think that would be a textbook example of a situation that could lead to a re-Awakening." Moody nodded. "In fact, there *are* examples exactly like that in the actual textbooks at Phoenix Academy. A great many of those Hunters who have re-Awakened were once Gatherers or Mana Banks who were survivors of terrible situations inside of Portals."

"Thank you, Mrs. Moody. One final question. You quoted the Hunter Protection Act of 2055. What exactly is that Act and its purpose?"

"Generally?" Mrs. Moody asked, seeming to grow slightly concerned until Mrs. Stovall gave an affirmative nod. Mrs. Moody sighed in relief before saying, "Generally speaking, the Act is meant to protect Hunters and their Skills, both in description and acquisition. Outside some very specific situations, no government, person or authority can force a Hunter to reveal what Skills they've Awakened, or even what rank they are, nor how they potentially acquired them, if the Skill is the result of a re-Awakening."

"Thank you, Mrs. Moody." Stovall turned toward the Judge. "No further questions, Your Honor."

* * *

The remainder of the day was extremely monotonous. Mr. Varnish tried to paint a picture that I was somehow an unhinged monster who had premeditated murdering Morgan Hallsbrad to take his Skills. Or at least, that's the only logical place his argument could be leading.

Mrs. Stovall, on the other hand, simply refuted many of the points he tried to get to stick. I wouldn't say we were winning the case, but it certainly didn't feel like we were losing either. If I understood everything correctly—the only way for the prosecution to 'win' would be to prove that I had done something illegal 'beyond all reasonable doubt,' which seemed to be some kind of buzzword terminology. I felt like Mrs. Stovall had done a great job making sure there were still quite a few doubts.

"They can't prove you did anything intentionally," Dave said from his seat on my bed, agreeing with my train of thought.

"I know that, but I can't believe that it's even this cloudy in the first place!" I responded, thinking that it would be nice to have my family or Dave in the courtroom, but unfortunately everyone was barred. I assumed that was to keep the reporters from overhearing terms like Cannibal and Snatcher—but honestly, I also was happy that it would protect me and my family just a little bit more.

Sure, eventually people would put Alonzo Mars and Brodie Flacarada together, but not until the trial's results went public.

"You should just get a Skill to help. Like maybe something charismatic," Dave suggested thoughtfully.

"I'm pretty sure Mr. Varnish has something like that already. And I'm not going to be able to beat him at his own game."

"Fine, maybe just get a Skill to feel better?" Smegma suggested.

I laughed. Dave and Smegma were clearly on the same page in regards to my current spending of Mana Coins. They both wanted me to save and purchase known Skills and not waste my money on Crafting Gear or Gathering stuff. Still, I had my own reasons for sticking with buying as many Gathering items as I could, beyond just making money. "I already told you both. This might make it possible for me to unlock more Stats!" Dave opened his mouth to complain and I hurriedly added, "Maybe they can even unlock Stats for people I know!"

Dave closed his mouth and went into quiet introspection, clearly considering my words.

"And I'm telling you that if you get a whole bunch of Crafting and Profession Skills, you'll never become a Combat Hunter!" Smegma countered. "You already have too many!"

That of course reminded me that I wanted to check my current Skill list, using a Spent Mana Crystal. With the trial, it was easy to forget about my 'missing' Skill from inside the Portal—or maybe I had been intentionally trying to not think about it. The Skill planet vanishing in my Mental Universe had hit pretty hard.

I shrugged and pulled one of the C-Ranked Spent Crystals from my Necklace, lamenting at the Mana Coins I was losing by using it. Then, with a cheeky grin to Smegma, I said, "Let's see how many I have!"

Dave rushed to my side, excited despite me already telling him I'd lost the Skill. I gave him a look as I infused Mana into the nearly perfectly clear Crystal. While the C-Rank Crystals had looked impressive with Mana and light emanating from them, now that this one was spent, the imperfections and perhaps some of the reasons it had limited Mana were more apparent.

Small cracks and air bubbles were visible in its depths, even as the glow from my Mana infusion ramped up. As the five-minute mark approached, I held my breath. The Crystal began to morph into the Skill Cards, and I was greeted with the familiar back of *Mental Fortitude*.

I should have nine Skills in total. *Demonic Vault, Mental Fortitude, Recovery, Dragon Heart, Minor Heal, Weak Cleanse, Mining, Cooking, Fishing* and *Heat Sense*. I flipped through the Cards, not bothering to flip them over if I knew the backing already. *Mental Fortitude, Demonic Vault, Recovery, Mining*— flipping past them, I reached the first Card I didn't know.

I somewhat knew why I hadn't seen this Card before. Mostly because it was one of two that I could pull up information on without a Spent Crystal. The back had green backing with a woman leaning over a clearly injured man.

Minor Heal
(10)
Skill Type: Healing
Skill Rank: Peak F-Rank (Evolvable)

Minor Heal can only be used on others the Skill User is touching and Heals the individual's Health Pool at a rate of one Health per 0.99 Mana expended.

I could see the changes it had undergone since getting it with my Common Healer Class. It wasn't anything amazing, but it was now a Peak F-Rank and at level ten now instead of one, which saved me some Mana while using it. The next Card was also green and showed a man touching someone's forehead. The person was sweating profusely, and again, I knew what it was.

Weak Cleanse
(10)
Skill Type: Healing
Skill Rank: Peak F-Rank (Evolvable)

Weak Cleanse can only be used on others and removes contaminants, poisons, venoms and diseases from the individual. Limited to Common or Uncommon maladies.

Costs 9.99 Mana per use.

No change to functionality, but again some Mana savings. I pulled up my Skill windows for the two Skills and discovered the same descriptions. I couldn't pull up Skill windows for any other Skills yet, and I wondered if that was because they were all Crafting or Passive Skills? But there was one outlier in that consideration.

The next Card was *Heat Sense*, and it wasn't Passive. I needed to activate it, but admittedly, it didn't use Mana. Still, I had to wonder if I could only see 'Class' Skills with the windows.

The next unknown Card was clearly *Cooking* because the picture was of an Orc in a chef's hat adding quite a bit of salt to a recipe. It felt like the creature would go to war if I pointed out that amount was too much though.

Cooking
(10)
Skill Type: Crafting
Skill Rank: Peak F-Rank (Evolvable)

As you Cook, you slowly improve your understanding of ingredients, herbs and mixtures. As this Skill grows, this individual will notice improvements to all actions related to Cooking.
This Skill is amplified by the Dexterity Stat.

The next Card showed a fish jumping out of the water with a sun in the background? The colors almost made my eyes hurt to look at. At the shore there was a man Fishing.

Fishing
(10)
Skill Type: Gathering
Skill Rank: Peak F-Rank (Evolvable)

As you Fish, you slowly improve your understanding of techniques and creatures of the sea. As this Skill grows, this individual will notice improvements to all actions related to Fishing and reduced Mana costs.
This Skill is amplified by the Stamina Stat.

My count of Cards reached nine, but I could still feel another Card under *Fishing*. I looked over my shoulder at Dave, and then included Smegma in my excitement. He flew over.

Reptilian Body
(50)
Skill Type: Body Forging
Skill Rank: Peak E-Rank (Evolvable)

A Reptilian Body is one of the most versatile existences in the Multiverse, able to survive extreme temperatures and even grow strong scales to protect itself. A Reptilian Body is a highly sought after Body Forging Skill that can increase Stat effects by [Locked]%.

Reptilian Body's effects are amplified by [Strength], [Stamina] and [Locked] Stats.

Something about the *Reptilian Body* Card made me frown. What it was, I couldn't say. Thankfully, I had two others in the room with me.

"Holy shit, the color and back match *Dragon Heart*, don't they?"

"Not quite," Smegma answered, "but they're close enough that I'd have considered them part of a Set on Crendalar!"

I pulled out the Card for *Dragon Heart* and looked at it beside *Reptilian Body*. The colors matched perfectly, and even the way the Card was organized seemed very familiar. Still, that wasn't the strange feeling I was getting from the Card.

I reached into my Mental Universe and once again tried to find the Skill with no luck. Still, now knowing about the Skill, I could feel something—almost like a second static charge. One was my *Mana Pool*—but the other...

It was my actual body. It had been buzzing since the Portal, and I'd just thought it was the constant nerves. First, finishing the task for Nagina, and now the trial. But I realized now that wasn't it.

It had been my 'Body Forging' Skill teetering at the top of E-Rank. But why couldn't I find the Skill planet in my Mental Universe? "Smegma, help me find this Skill in my Mental Universe."

"Remember, you haven't found *Recovery* or *Mental Fortitude* yet, either," Smegma answered, but he did dive into the Universe and begin looking as well.

Dave left us alone after fifteen minutes of my muttering. After an hour, I was forced to give up.

I had court tomorrow.

CHAPTER 34: CHAPTER 86

Friday, May 3rd, 2069

"You've heard from a great deal of witnesses and experts over the last few days," Mr. Varnish intoned, his somber voice was serious and ingratiating. "Now, let me summarize what we've learned and lay out the events on the day in question."

Mr. Varnish already had a few pieces of equipment on the floor for his 'presentation' and the white screen to project onto was already down. He moved to his desk and pulled out a marker even as Smegma studied the pages and photos laid out on Mr. Varnish's desk.

"Honestly, it's just a bunch of pictures, and Private Investigator contracts," Smegma explained, sounding confused.

"On January 3rd, 2069, Mr. Morgan Hallsbrad was hired to investigate the murder of Lillianne Matthews, in Miami Florida." Mr. Varnish stuck a contract onto a rather large whiteboard, and handed it out to Mrs. Stovall and the Judge, entering it into evidence. "Lillianne Matthews' father Gerald hired him to assist in the Police Investigation."

More papers were entered into evidence and I read over Mrs. Stovall's shoulder as a rather convincing story took shape. The first page was the case file for Lillianne Matthews, and the second was a contract between her father Gerald and Morgan Hallsbrad.

Mr. Varnish continued his story, showing the investigation Morgan Hallsbrad took that led him into the morgues of the victims and explained the most glaring piece of evidence against him—the notebook. But most importantly—the DNA of the victims that was found inside of said notebook.

Mrs. Stovall and I had talked after each court session, and so I knew that the notebook was a rather big piece of evidence, and one that supported my side of events. To have it removed as evidence of Morgan's ill intent and potential culpability as the Heartless Killer murderer left only one glaring issue in Mr. Varnish's story.

If, as I suspected, Varnish wanted to try and paint me out to be the Heartless Killer, there was no way in hell that he could place me at the scene of any of the other murders. So, his original tale of Morgan Hallsbrad tracking the murders to me, made no sense. I wasn't—

"That brings us to why Mr. Hallsbrad was visiting Brodie Flacarada, on April 1st, 2069. Morgan Hallsbrad had tracked the killings through a link to a particular phenomenon. Something that at first, he believed was ludicrous. And yet—there was no other explanation."

Mr. Varnish put a picture up on the whiteboard and the magnet that snapped it in place sounded far louder than even the Judges gavel had earlier. The picture was so eerily familiar, that at first I assumed I'd seen it before—but the more I squinted, the more my stomach started to churn.

Mr. Varnish slowly walked the other two copies of the pictures to the Judge, and then to Mrs. Stovall. As he approached, he held the picture in front of his chest, his eyes fixed on me, while his face held a knowing smile. I blinked at the image and then up at Mr. Varnish, fighting my natural reaction of looking away—or looking to where I knew the individual represented in this picture was.

The closer the picture came, the more sure I was that it wasn't Smegma. It was a picture of a painting that looked almost exactly like the Felguard-Imp, but it could also have been something from the Catholic religion. Sure, it was eerily similar but because it was a painted piece—it also felt generalized.

I focused on that, even as Mr. Varnish studied my expression. Smegma floated behind me and also studied the picture. For once, he was deathly quiet, and I had the urge to mentally want to scream at him for an explanation, but managed to hold it in. I went as far as to tilt my head in confusion at the 'painting'.

"Morgan Hallsbrad believed that there was a Demonic Skill involved with the Heartless Killer murders," Mr. Varnish exclaimed as he spun to face the jurors. The gasps of alarm that followed his sudden motion and pronouncement were likely what he had been aiming for. "This 'Demonic Skill', he believed, had the ability to Cannibalize other Skills and grow stronger."

Mr. Varnish pulled out another page, which was handed again to the Judge. Mr. Varnish and then pinned a picture onto the board. "Here is a picture of a page in his notebook. I will read it.

"The Demon's Skill grows, the more it consumes. The more Mana it uses, but especially if it finds other powerful Skills… Then it powers up, growing in Rank."

Mr. Varnish paused, and relished the stillness in the courtroom. His tale had led everyone to a moment, balancing on the edge of our seats. Even myself and Mrs. Stovall weren't immune to his falsehoods. "Morgan Hallsbrad discovered that this Demonic Skill was so powerful it had, in fact, been shattered and Awakened in pieces and was still as powerful as his investigation indicated. The killer is one of these unfortunate souls who has a piece, and Morgan Hallsbrad suspected that Brodie Flacarada was another."

"Objection your honor. Hearsay," Mrs. Stovall said as she shot to her feet.

"Your honor, I am simply stating what Morgan Hallsbrad's notes indicated," Mr. Varnish said quickly. He held up a page, and the judge narrowed her eyes slightly.

"Counsels, approach," she ordered. Smegma obviously moved with them.

My mouth fell open, despite all of the warnings and training I'd gone through to not show emotion. I couldn't help it. Mr. Varnish's tale had no basis in reality, and yet how could I refute something that had no proof.

"Close your mouth you moron," Smegma scolded, and thanks to his demeaning tone I managed to recall where I was.

[How the husk am I supposed to prove that I don't have a Demonic Skill that consumes other Skills—when I do in fact have a Demonic Skill that doesn't consume other Skills, but a husking *Dragon Heart* Skill that *does?*]

Sure, my rant was a bit manic, and I knew that I didn't have to prove anything—other than my self-defense case, but this sure felt like an unrecoverable blow to our case. Somehow me and this *fictitious* killer had a 'piece' of the same Skill?

Wait—I turned to Judge Dench. She reportedly had a Truth Seeker Skill of some form. Still, she sat behind her bench, regarding Mr. Varnish, and Mrs. Stovall impassively. Surely, Mr. Varnish's accusations had been a lie though!

"It wasn't a lie. Not exactly," Smegma responded to my unsent thoughts instead of my rant. "It may be *wrong*, but it seems like he told only the truth about his understanding of Morgan Hallsbrad's notes on the *Demonic Vault* Skill. If he believes Morgan Hallsbrad's notes are true and that you're holding a piece of some type of Demonic Ability—that sort of thing doesn't trigger lie detection Skills. They operate based on belief, not on objective facts. Even if he doesn't believe the spirit of what he's saying, he may be skirting around things that might disprove his statements and sticking to only the things he believes are true. One way or another—whether he's being deceitful or honestly believes what he's saying, the wording is extremely well thought out, even while he's arguing with the judge here."

Mr. Varnish and Mrs. Stovall left the bench. Mrs. Stovall returned to her seat and Varnish to his board.

"I'll make it clear. That these notes are merely what led Morgan Hallsbrad to Brodie Flacarada. They are simply what's left behind by a great private investigator, on the last case he was on." Varnish looked to the judge and Mrs. Stovall when he was finished.

When the judge nodded in acceptance, I swear I saw Mrs. Stovall clench her jaw.

Mr. Varnish concluded his speech, reiterating all the points he had already gone over, not forgetting to ensure to paint a picture of Morgan Hallsbrad that made him out to be some sort of 'Dick Tracy-esque' private eye. It was a moving tale about a dedicated, selfless man who had been broken by the terrible and seemingly unsolvable relentless murders of the innocent. Living out of Motels, barely scraping by—all to find the next victim of a serial killer—only to find another Cannibal with a Demonic Skill.

Me.

"Since that's the end of Mr. Varnish's witnesses, and we're already past lunch break. We'll end it here for the week. Mr. Flacarada, I expect you to be here Monday morning. Another delay will be immediate grounds for me to ask the jury to deliberate, without Mrs. Stovall forming your defense. Understood?"

"Yes, your honor," Mrs. Stovall said on my behalf. We all stood as the Jury was dismissed, followed by the Judge. Then Mrs. Stovall and I quickly attempted to walk from the room as well.

"Mrs. Stovall, I think it's time for another quick settlement meeting, don't you?" Mr. Varnish said smugly.

Mrs. Stovall looked to me, and I was about to start shaking my head, when Smegma spoke up. "Take his meeting. I want to see what he thinks he knows—Or, more importantly, what his backer knows."

Trying not to give away the literal Demon on my shoulder, I slowly changed my intended motion into a nod. Mrs. Stovall raised an eyebrow but nodded toward Mr. Varnish. "I need to deliberate with my client. We'll arrive at your office in two hours."

* * *

This time my father arrived at the warehouse offices of Mr. Varnish. My dad made a face at the sheet-metal exterior. "If he's not from Windsor, is he renting this building?"

I blinked, not having considered that rather glaring insight on the last visit. If he was renting this space, and the inside looked the way it did—what the hell would his actual offices look like? My father's frown deepened when we rounded the corner and he saw the giant-sized double doors. He even went as far as to run his hand over it.

"This is Portal wood…" he mumbled to himself.

Mrs. Stovall gave him a stern look, and he composed himself before she knocked. The door swung open to reveal a small woman that couldn't be taller than five feet. The very fact that she had moved the massive doors was a testament to the oil on the hinges or their design.

"Please, come in. Mr. Varnish is just in the conference room. Can I get you a refreshment while you wait?"

Mrs. Stovall smiled. She'd predicted Mr. Varnish making us wait on arrival. She'd called it a power play. He likely was nearby observing—or at least that's what Smegma suggested.

I went over our discussion back at the house. All I needed to do was hear out Mr. Varnish's offer. Hear it out and not allow him to cast any doubt on the case. Mrs. Stovall claimed to still be confident in our victory—and so I just needed to believe in her.

I fiddled with my phone in my pocket. Sparkle Legion had posted the second video, and my desire to see the response was burning a hole in my pocket. Still, if Mr. Varnish was watching, that could make me look anxious, so I settled with just tapping the pocket to confirm I had my phone with me and as a promise that I'd get to watch it later.

That tap turned into a death grip as I shot to my feet. The door that led deeper into the offices of Mr. Varnish had opened, but despite my expectations of finding the smarmy A-ranked Lawyer framed in the doorway—I found Echo-Five. Echo-Five, as well as a glare that threatened severe pain that was directed at me and my father.

"What are *you* doing here?" I exclaimed, not managing to clamp my teeth shut before the words escaped.

"Ah, forgive me. The Mirage Guild is a new client of ours," Mr. Varnish said as he stepped into the waiting room behind Echo-Five. "Echo-Five here simply arrived to go over the facts about a new case they are preparing to bring to the courts. Have a wonderful evening Echo, we'll chat soon."

Echo-Five didn't immediately start moving toward the door. Instead, seemingly choosing to try to stab us with his stare. I couldn't speak for my father, but I certainly got goosebumps. There was only one 'case' that Mirage would be pursuing at this time. A case against the Miner's who'd closed their permanent Portal…

"Mr. Flacarada. Brodie. If you'll come this way," Mr. Varnish said, seeming to indicate that we should walk by Echo-Five and through the door. I looked at the holster on the Hunter's hip and then the knife that his other hand was twitching toward and simply stayed where I was. There was no way I was going to offer the man my back to stab…

Thankfully, Echo-Five scoffed and strode toward the exit an awkward moment later. Mr. Varnish's smile was a hair too large for the current moment, as he said, "Mrs. Stovall, we've set up to greet your party in the boardroom. Follow me."

I followed Mrs. Stovall while Smegma hovered behind me. Mr. Varnish stopped in the doorway, and asked, "Mr. Flacarada?"

At first I thought he was talking to me, but then saw his eyes were directed behind me, and with my father here he'd likely call me Brodie. I turned to see my father taking in the first sight through the doorway with a look of shocked reverence. Gary shook himself and took a few quick steps to catch up to us.

As he drew even with me, he whispered, "It's one thing to be told about all this and another thing to actually see it."

Soon enough we were back in the Crystal Glass Conference Room, and the same players as before were in the room. I looked directly at Aurome and Seleff, the two Larvae Guild members, refusing to break eye contact. I wanted them to know that I knew they were the ones who had wanted the last meeting. I also secretly hoped I'd catch the moment one of them used their Skill on me.

Instead, I got a shiver as the darker skinned man—who I believed was Aurome, smiled at me. He exuded a type of confidence that I'd seen in post-Portal interviews, and movies but had never experienced first-hand. His eyes made me feel like prey caught out in the open. Needless to say, I looked away first, even as my cheeks flushed red from embarrassment.

"So, my backers…" Mr. Varnish said, indicating Aurome and by association Seleff. "Would like to offer similar terms as last time. If Brodie is willing to be placed under Guild Arrest for two years, we are willing to drop this case. They simply would like to observe Brodie to ensure that he doesn't possess the Cannibalistic Demonic Skill that Morgan Hallsbrad identified."

Mrs. Stovall glanced at me before sighing angrily. "This is the same problem as last time. You have done nothing to prove that Brodie acted in anything but self defense on April 1st. As such, this is still a spurious offer—which, don't think I haven't noticed that you've now *doubled*, after you have already attempted to ruin my clients life."

"I assure you Mrs. Stovall, we have done nothing to ruin your client's life. We are simply presenting the facts of this case, as we know them. If there was some other way you could prove that Brodie doesn't possess the Skill in question—then we'd be amenable to that as well."

Mrs. Stovall didn't glance at me this time, even as she quickly retorted. "First of all, you cannot prove a negative. Second of all, any attempt to do so would be a violation of the Hunter Protection Act of twenty-fifty-five—"

"Not if Brodie agrees to be tested *and* share his results…" Ashley cut in. "The Larvae Guild is simply trying to see Morgan Hallsbrad's investigation through to the end."

"Morgan Hallsbrad's investigation? Don't you mean 'The Shop', who contacted all of the deceased victims on SwiftGram before the murders?" Mrs. Stovall countered.

"Ahh," Mr. Varnish said, as he held his hand out toward Ashley. She handed him a page which he slid across the table to Mrs. Stovall. "As you'll see Mrs. Stovall, 'The Shop' SwiftGram account is not owned by Morgan Hallsbrad, and has continued to be active after his death."

Mrs. Stovall frowned at the page and then looked at me. Her eyes carried a concern that hadn't been there earlier at the house. She blinked and it was gone, replaced by determination. "That does not mean the account wasn't used to gain access to the victims *for* Morgan," she said, emphasizing her point. "Plus, he's on the verge of being found Guilty in eight States…"

Mr. Varnish held out his hand again and Ashley placed another paper into it. He slid this across the table as well. This time, with no explanation. I leaned in to read with Mrs. Stovall and felt my blood stop as my heart seized in my chest.

'All Cases in Regard to the Heartless Killer Murders Have Been Suspended and Transferred to Supreme Court,' the title read. I looked at Mrs. Stovall and found her face also paling as she read on, clearly digging deeper into the page than I had. My brain remained calm, but frantic, as it tried to calculate what that meant for my trial.

I knew we'd be counting on Morgan Hallsbrad's connection to the Shop account, and the other forty-something cases of Murder. What else did we have?

"We have your version of events. We have their inability to confirm that you have the Skill they've claimed, and… we have what they really want," Smegma countered my racing thoughts.

I had been mentally with him until his last point, but he clarified when he heard my confusion. "The *Demonic Vault* Skill. It's clearly why they want you under them for two years. The rest is just bullshit."

[That doesn't change the fact that I'd be under *Guild Arrest*, in Europe, for *two years*!] I shouted mentally, while staring blindly at the page in Mrs. Stovall's hands.

Mrs. Stovall thankfully rallied on my behalf. "None of this changes the fact that my client acted in self defense. While you've woven a convincing tale and managed to get it on record. You and I both saw Judge Dench mark down a few notes that her Truth Seeker Skill picked out."

To my surprise, Mr. Varnish nodded, accepting that point. I hadn't noticed anything like that and so was slightly shocked at the news. That surely meant the jury would be told of the falsehoods Mr. Varnish had laid out. Didn't that mean I was fine?

"Ashley, please go get the member of Mirage," Mr. Varnish said, sounding nonplussed about the Judge possibly puncturing holes in his woven tale of falsehoods.

Ashley stood up and moved to the second set of doors our group hadn't entered through. She made a motion to someone outside and in walked a man in jeans and a stained white T-shirt. I narrowed my eyes, trying to understand what he was doing here.

"Oh husk!" Smegma cursed. I knew what he was going to say next before he even began. "That's the guy that called the cops and who I offered a Skill to!"

CHAPTER 35: CHAPTER 87

Friday, May 3rd, 2069

"This is Jesse Owens," Mr. Varnish said, introducing the man that Smegma had just told me could ruin everything. "He's a squad leader in the Mirage Guild. His team was one of the next to enter the Portal in the park when it unexpectedly closed. He has an interesting tale of being offered a Skill if he called the police. And you'll never guess where that offer came from? Jesse, would you care to tell them?"

"Uhh, the strange voice seemed to come from some sort of shadowy, Satanic being," Jesse said, sounding confused. I didn't blame him.

Mrs. Stovall's eyes narrowed in skepticism before she sarcastically repeated, "A *shadowy, Satanic* being? Are you sure you didn't smoke too much marijuana the night before?"

I pointedly looked at the man from Mirage and Mr. Varnish, trying my best to look confused. In my peripherals, I also watched Smegma, who was currently right beside Jesse.

Mr. Varnish nodded a few times. "Oh, I think you'll discover that Jesse is on the straight and narrow, Mrs. Stovall. Jesse, would you like to tell them the whole story of why you called the cops on Tuesday night?"

Jesse looked between Mr. Varnish and the others in the room before meeting my eyes. There seemed to be a moment of hesitation before he reluctantly began, "I was in my tent and was woken early due to the noise. Two of my squad mates came in and reported what had happened and how the Permanent Portal we were securing had suddenly closed."

He paused again and looked at my father, and then at Mrs. Stovall, as if trying to place them. After a moment, he shook his head and continued, "At first, people believed it was a strike-team sent from the Lynx or Snowbird Guilds—something to prevent our Mirage Guild from gaining traction or money. However, rumors began to spread that the people we caught were just the trapped Miners…

"Regardless, as I returned to my tent about half an hour later with no real explanation and only more questions—*something* spoke to me. Something sinister and powerful. It spoke out of the shadows in the corner of my tent—"

"I guess the shock and awe worked," Smegma commented from his spot beside Jesse. "I had hoped it would make him reluctant to speak up, until he reached out to you for that Skill, at least."

Smegma's words overrode Jesse's, but I still heard him relate the offer the 'extra-dark shadow' made to him. Smegma had just finished speaking as Jesse concluded as well, saying, "—I was told to find Alonzo Mars, and I'd be granted a Skill for my service."

"A Skill? This shadowed entity claimed he could offer you a Skill?" Mr. Varnish exclaimed, his voice filled with false surprise. "Goodness. How on Earth do you suppose he could do that?"

My eyes, however, weren't on Varnish's antics. They were drawn to the two Larvae Guild members. Aerome and Seleff both leaned forward in their seats, clearly more interested in this piece of information than any before it.

Smegma saw it, too. He hovered over to them and narrowed his eyes. "So… they *do* know about *Demonic Vault* and what my Abyss Sect offers!"

"Do you know who Alonzo Mars is?" Mr. Varnish asked after not getting a response to his first question.

Jesse Owens nodded, even as he scratched the back of his neck. "I found him on SwiftGram. When I realized it was just a kid, and a Miner at that, I realized I'd been fooled by a Skill, and well—now I'm here…"

"Thank you, Jesse," Mr. Varnish said quickly, seeming to want to cut off any further storytelling from the man.

Mrs. Stovall picked up on it, though. "Hold on one moment, Mr. Owens. Could you elaborate a bit further?" she asked sweetly. "You found Alonzo Mars on SwiftGram and discovered that you'd 'been fooled.' Why is that, exactly?"

"Well, I believed I was dealing with a powerful entity not of this world. Something with the ability to grant me a Skill. When I found out it was just a college-aged child—I realized he or someone in his group must have had a Skill that tricked me…"

"So, what did you do after discovering that this had nothing to do with this… 'shadowy *Satanic being?*'" Mrs. Stovall asked. She gave a smug look to Mr. Varnish, and the court reporter typed furiously on their tablet.

"Well, I was just trying to figure that out when Mr. Varnish here approached me."

"Is that so?" Stovall raised an eyebrow to Mr. Varnish. "He approached you? And what did he say to you?"

"He said he'd discovered who the anonymous caller was—and umm—encouraged me to tell him the story of that night."

"So, he already knew about your 'anonymous call' to the police before you ever even mentioned it to him? How *interesting*. Encouraged, how?" Mrs. Stovall said, looking very pointedly at Mr. Varnish, who was frowning deeply.

"He offered me safety from Echo-Five and told me he'd get me a spot in the Larvae Guild, which works overseas, after the trial."

"So, he convinced you that your life was at risk?" Mrs. Stovall asked, her voice neutral. My brain was whirring as I tried to process what was happening. I could tell there were a lot of underlying things going unsaid, but I couldn't quite understand what they were.

"He didn't need to do much convincing," Jesse responded, his voice small and squeaky. "Echo-Five was on a witch hunt after that night. I was already prepared to get out of Windsor, but Mr. Varnish just—umm—offered a better plan."

"So, there was no indication that he would reveal your identity to Echo-Five if you didn't testify?" Mrs. Stovall asked.

Jesse swallowed visibly but shook his head at the same time. "No, Echo-Five was already aware of my identity…"

"He was?" Mrs. Stovall said, looking pointedly at Mr. Varnish.

"He was," Mr. Varnish said. "He was the one who hired the investigator through my firm, Mrs. Stovall."

"So, you helped Echo find Jesse, even though he planned to kill him?"

"Come now, Mrs. Stovall," Mr. Varnish said, chastising her. "Jesse is right here and quite alright. Since Echo-Five hired the investigator through us, I was able to ensure his safety. He was never at any risk."

"So, why the offer of sanctuary overseas?"

"Jesse misunderstood. We simply offered him a position in another Guild—a *better* Guild." Mr. Varnish seemed a bit shaken, being called out on the holes in his story.

My eyes narrowed, studying the interplay between Mrs. Stovall, Jesse and Mr. Varnish. It would seem that there was a reason Jesse wasn't called to the stand to testify in open court in front of the Jury. What was it?

Was it these rather gaping holes in the story? The fact that Jesse hadn't seen Smegma? Was it the clear coercion that Mrs. Stovall was emphasizing?

"Jesse." Mrs. Stovall's voice was soft and concerned. She reached out and touched his arm. "Are you aware that Mr. Varnish here has done more than just hire an investigator for Echo-Five? He just recently took on Echo-Five and the Mirage Guild as clients."

Jesse's eyes widened as he turned toward Mr. Varnish. "Wha—What?!"

Knots stood out in Mr. Varnish's jawline at Mrs. Stovall's words. His teeth clenched as he breathed out through his nose and opened his mouth to speak. Before he could, however, Mrs. Stovall cut him off.

"Yes," Mrs. Stovall answered forcefully, her volume rising. "*We* only found out just a few moments ago when *we* passed Echo-Five in the lobby. Mr. Varnish here made sure that *we* knew he'd taken the man on as a client. In fact, *you* were nearly in the same room with Echo-Five, who you just said was on a witch hunt." She paused and shook her head sadly. "Jesse, I'm afraid Varnish may be playing both sides here. He's the same man Echo-Five used to hire the man who found the rat in his Guild. Then, when he did discover you, he brought you into this sham of a 'testimony' in a completely separate case. When he's finished with you here, do you think the offer from Larvae will still be good?"

As more and more of Mrs. Stovall's questions came out, they seemed to land on Jesse like hammer blows. He glared at Mr. Varnish. "Is she telling the truth? Are you just using me?"

Mr. Varnish's scowl disappeared as he calmly waved away Jesse's concern. "Nothing so diabolical or contrived, I assure you. In fact, Mrs. Stovall is correct in some of her points, but I'm afraid she's misconstrued the facts. I took on Mr. Five as a client in a separate case against Mr. Flacarada here." He gestured to me. "Who you know as Alonzo Mars. However, she seems to be implying that I need you to somehow win my current litigation case. There are a couple of reasons you are telling your story here and not in a courtroom, Mr. Owens. One of which is your safety. The other is that I already have more than enough *evidence* against Mr. Flacarada to win this case. Since I do have so much information on the man, it was only natural for the Mirage Guild to approach me to represent them against the same man I am currently prosecuting." He chuckled good-naturedly when he finished.

Jesse's heated glare cooled gradually.

"I'm… *so* sorry to interrupt. I just had one *more* question, Jesse," Mrs. Stovall gently butted into their conversation. "Aside from Mr. Varnish here refusing to grant you asylum overseas like you said he'd offered," Mrs. Stoval said, almost sheepishly. Her words drew another glare from Mr. Varnish, who clearly thought he'd side stepped that part of the conversation. She gestured toward Mr. Varnish and the Larvae Guild members. "Do you recall who first used the term '*Satanic* being'? Was that your description or… someone else's?"

"Umm, I'm not sure," Jesse stuttered, still looking hopefully at Mr. Varnish for direction. I could tell that Mr. Varnish, Seleff and Aurome were all pointedly trying not to give him any. Not seeing any signs, Jesse eventually added, "I think it was me?"

"You *think* it was you?" Mrs. Stovall asked. "It seems like a pretty big leap to take—you know, from a talking shadow, you may have imagined, to something Demonic."

"Well, umm, the voice claimed it was extremely powerful and lived for thousands of eons…"

I fought the urge to roll my eyes. I was somewhat excited to learn that Smegma hadn't claimed to be a Demon or a 'Satanic being' but also embarrassed on the Demon's behalf to learn he'd bragged about his age.

"And you reached the conclusion that must have meant it was Satanic in origin? Could it not have been a powerful Angel or Spirit that came from the System?"

"I mean—I guess it could have been?" Jesse answered, still looking desperately at Mr. Varnish.

"Okay, so you're saying—" Mrs. Stoval stopped, blinking rapidly as though a thought had just occurred to her. A brilliant smile showed on her face for a moment as she reached into her purse. Pulling out her phone, she swiped at it for a few quick seconds before turning it toward the man. As she did, I could see that it was an illustration that very closely resembled the painting Mr. Varnish had shown us in court. I wasn't sure if it was significant or not, but it looked like Smegma when I'd first met him—all thin and bony and much smaller than his current self. "I'm sorry, Jesse. Just one quick thing I want to clear up real fast. Does this painting look familiar to you?"

Jesse frowned, leaning in and looking at the phone closely. Mr. Varnish scowled behind him. Jesse blinked, looking around and scratched his head. "I don't know… I might've seen it in a horror movie or something? Some kind of renaissance thing, maybe? I can't be sure."

"Just so we're clear," Mrs. Stovall raised her voice, making a show of directing her attention to the court representative. "I am showing Jesse a picture I found online of a thin, emaciated Demonic figure, and I am also showing the members of this room." She turned the phone so that everyone could see and brought her attention back to the man. "Are you sure this isn't the 'shadowy

Satanic figure' that told you to call emergency services on the day of the closing of your Guild's Permanent Portal?"

Jesse chuckled. "What? No way. Whatever it was, it was *much* bigger than that. Don't get me wrong, I don't know what it actually looked like. It was super dark and sketchy, but whatever it was, was bigger and scarier than that little thing. Don't forget, ma'am. I'm a bona fide Hunter. I'd eat that little guy for breakfast."

"Fat chance, you gun-toting, little—" Smegma flew up to the man's head and started swinging his clawed fists through the man's skull.

[Dude!] My eyes rounded as I kept my neck unnaturally still, refusing to look around. [Knock it off! This guy's doing us a *favor*, idiot! Didn't you hear what he just said?]

Smegma stilled, but before he could do anything else, Mrs. Stovall continued.

"Super dark and 'sketchy,' you say? But you're sure this couldn't have been the creature that spoke to you. Is that correct?" At his nod, my attorney looked directly at Mr. Varnish. "*Fascinating.* Thank you *very much*, Jesse." Mrs. Stovall's smile was a sunbeam.

The man smiled back, seeming not only confused but also a little proud and oddly shy at her praise.

"That's enough," a deep, accented voice said, and all eyes turned to Aurome. "Everyone but the boy, out of the room. I'd like to have a little chat."

"That is highly inappropriate," Mrs. Stovall stated. "Any discussions regarding this case must be done in the presence of Mr. Flacarada's lawyer. Me!"

"I don't believe that Brodie will want this discussion on record, Mrs. Stovall," Aurome responded. "I have no issue with your presence if *he* doesn't…"

The man let that statement hang in the air, his eyes never leaving me. I looked to my father and Mrs. Stovall but pointedly ignored Smegma.

"I want to hear what he has to say!" Smegma said excitedly.

Slowly, I transferred my gaze to Aurome. After a time, I nodded, indicating that they could stay.

"As you wish," Aurome said, turning his steely gaze onto Mr. Varnish, the reporter and the other assistants of the lawyer. "Then I would ask that you give me the room for a moment."

Mr. Varnish bowed and began ushering Jesse out of the room. Jesse looked a bit lost but also happy to be getting out of the spotlight. The court reporter forced Mrs. Stovall to sign something before leaving, but I didn't get a good look at it.

"Good," Aurome intoned in his deep and accented voice once the room only had Seleff, himself and the three of us. Aurome's eyes seemed to glow with power as he focused back on me. "Let me be frank. That is the saying, correct?"

Smegma scratched his head, clearly confused.

[What now?] I asked.

"If he's going to be Frank, who are you supposed to be?"

The effort to not roll my eyes nearly sent me apoplectic, so it took me a moment to realize he was actually asking a question. Someone on my side must have nodded—that or he just continued without prompting.

"*Demonic Vault*," Aurome stated, that one word making my heartbeat sound like a bass drum in my ear. "You have it, and through it, offered a Skill to that man, yes?"

I began to shake my head, seeing what that whole play with Jesse Owens had been about. Clearly, Mr. Varnish hadn't wanted Jesse to testify in court, but Aurome, Varnish's backer, had needed him to—for this moment. I even opened my mouth, planning to deny having the Skill, when I remembered that Seleff may have a *Truth Seeking* Skill alongside his *Eye* Skill.

So, I snapped my mouth shut and began planning my words more carefully. "That isn't true. I can impart a Skill to Jesse Owens, though, yes," I said slowly, focusing on the last bit of Aurome's question. I hadn't been planning to give Jesse a Skill with *Demonic Vault*. This answer would hopefully help hide that I even had the Skill but also hint at something else that Aurome might want.

Seleff blinked at me and then nodded slowly. Aurome's face broke into a huge smile as he leaned forward further. The Portal Wood table creaked as he placed more of his weight on it. "So, you can impart Skills because you are a Snatcher like Mr. Varnish, and our leader, believes, then?"

"No, I am not a Snatcher," I responded simply. And I wasn't. My sub-Skill of *Dragon Heart* clearly said '*Skill Copy & Cannibalism.*' Seleff leaned forward this time, giving me a pointed look, but he still nodded after realizing I wasn't going to say anything more.

"So, you aren't a Snatcher, and you don't possess the *Demonic Vault* Skill?" Aurome asked. "But you have some way to communicate at a distance, create illusions, and still grant a Skill in another way?"

"Ooooh, this is an opportunity," Smegma crowed. "Because he asked multiple questions and even imposed a tense on the *Demonic Vault* one, a Truth Skill won't be able to distinguish between what you're answering."

[Okay, so I just focus on answering the final one in the affirmative? Won't it be a problem to seem to be claiming the other Skills?] I asked, trying to take the opportunity that Smegma saw.

[They have evidence of multiple re-Awakenings already…] The Demon said, then nodded encouragingly in answer to the first part, and I did exactly that.

"Yes, that's correct. I can reveal what my intentions for granting Jesse a Skill were, but those secrets are quite valuable. Can you guarantee you'll pay a fair price and that what I say next will remain confidential?" I asked, thinking of revealing the Skill Altar.

Aurome's smile grew broad, and he made some sort of motion toward Seleff. The man started to glow for a split second, and then a pulse of golden light shot out from his chest. It rushed past me and the others in the room before affixing itself to the Crystal Glass walls.

"Seleff has made it impossible to listen in on our conversation. You have my word that what you reveal will not be divulged to hurt you. We will pay an appropriate price, but we cannot negotiate without knowing this secret. I cannot guarantee more than that; it all depends on the information."

"Will you sign an agreement to that effect?" Mrs. Stovall asked. "An amended NDA for now—with promises of paying 'market value' to be discussed later." Mrs. Stovall looked at me when she finished. "We could do more, but I assume you'd like this conversation to continue today?"

"Are you okay with me revealing this?" I asked my father. He shrugged when my eyes moved to him. Clearly, he was leaving the decision in my hands.

"For the husking record, I'm not okay with revealing this!" Smegma shouted. "This is completely stupid. Why by the *Seven Deadly Trials* would you offer something like this to our enemies? The knowledge of Skill Altars has real husking value."

Closing my eyes, I pretended to be making a difficult decision. In truth, I realized that Smegma had good points but he was missing quite a bit as well.

[We are in a room with two men that are very high up in a very powerful Guild. If we try to go speak with Taz or some other *far lesser* group, we won't even be admitted. Then, there's the fact that they are the ones pressuring me and my family. So, with this secret, we can negotiate for them to back off. Likely even end this farce of a husking trial!]

"It's still stupid! You could just keep the information for yourself, use the fourteen Skill bestowals on you and the group, and then become a Hunter and collect more. Never telling anyone!" Smegma countered.

[Yeah, right! Smegma, don't take this the wrong way, but I'm starting to see why the Demons failed to Ascend.]

Smegma went deadly silent after that. I opened my eyes and glanced in his direction, where he floated behind the two men. He was blinking in stunned silence, and I got the feeling he realized I might be right. I took a deep breath and then turned back to the two men. "Sign what Mrs. Stovall suggested, and we'll negotiate afterwards."

The two men signed the hurriedly amended Non-Disclosure Agreement Mrs. Stovall pulled from her briefcase. She nodded to me when they finished.

With a deep breath, I began, "We were the ones who closed the Portal in the park. Not intentionally, mind you," I added quickly as I saw Aurome grow excited. "It was through the help of a Creature of immense power…"

I began telling an abridged version of our group's time in the caverns, leaving out a great deal, but highlighting the Snake's knowledge of the Skill Altar in the leader's stone hut. How triggering it had initiated the Dungeon closing, and how I had received a reward.

"—a 'low-ranked Skill Altar' was granted to me," I said as I made the small bird-fountain-like object appear on the desk. Eyebrows shot up as the Altar suddenly materialized. I saw both Seleff and Aurome's eyes flick to my Necklace.

Still, they dismissed the low-ranked spatial item rather quickly after discovering it. Aurome pointed to the Altar instead. "So, this object can impart Skills if you place nine Cores in it?"

I nodded, and he stood up as he indicated wanting to pick up the object.

"There are, however, only a limited number of uses," I added, wanting to drive up the value as much as possible.

"I see," Aurome replied. His small smile seemed to indicate he understood what I was doing. "May I?"

I nodded after a time, and Aurome moved around the table. I hadn't realized when he was sitting just how big Aurome was. He easily was six and a half feet tall, and his biceps were likely the size of my head. I may have been imagining it, but each step Aurome took seemed to be felt through vibrations in my feet.

I swallowed as he reached past me. Sitting down in the chair and having the huge, darkly-tanned, asian man reach over me felt terrifying. Like I was somehow feeling the weight of his power pressing me into the seat and floor below.

"Does he possess a Skill that can manipulate gravity?" Smegma surmised—which at least allowed my brain to focus elsewhere as Aurome took the Altar and moved to the head of the table where the court reporter had been sitting.

"What does your Skill say, Seleff?" Aurome asked.

Seleff looked at his fellow Guild member with a bit of disapproval on his face and then looked at the three of us, making it clear he didn't like having whatever his Skill was revealed. I looked at my father and Mrs. Stovall, and we all shrugged. It wasn't like we were going to reveal Seleff's Skill to anyone.

"Yutlq alayh esm mazbah' munkhafid al rutba, Aurome." Seleff said.

My eyes narrowed, and I blinked as I realized he must have spoken another language. Smegma, hearing my thoughts, said, "He just said, 'It calls it a low-rank Altar, Aurome.'"

[You can understand… umm… Arabic?] I asked, guessing at the spoken language from the tone and sound.

"The System translates languages for me, yes," Smegma responded. Still, Aurome's eyes on me made me return to acting like I didn't understand what was going on.

"My colleague says that it has something to do with Skills," Aurome stated. "But can you prove that it grants Skills?"

I shook my head, "I don't have any Cores—"

A pile of at least eighty Cores appeared on the table, cutting me off. I blinked at them and then looked to Mrs. Stovall and my father. I didn't want to get another Skill, but maybe one of them would want one?

"It only has fourteen uses left," I said slowly, waiting for Mrs. Stovall to meet my eyes. My father shook his head while indicating Mrs. Stovall with a slight jerk of a thumb. When Mrs. Stovall looked over, I nodded and said, "If you want?"

She stood up rather quickly and her voice was high as she asked, "How does it work?"

"I'm not an expert, but from my understanding, you need to use F to C-Rank Cores because this Altar can't accept higher ranked ones. I'm pretty sure that's what the 'low-ranked' part of the description I got from the System means. I think there are also affinities or Elements to consider. So, try to pick Cores that are similar or compliment each other. Once you slot them, you place your hand on the impression, and a window should pop up…"

"May I?" Mrs. Stovall asked as she pointed at the pile of Cores and the Altar.

Aurome stood back and nodded. It was slightly strange to watch three adults acting the way they all currently were. It was akin to seeing a video of a child and its parents on Christmas morning. It made me smile, even as Mrs. Stovall began sorting out the Cores that fit into the depression and were all white or brown in color.

That would probably be Light and Earth Elements? But without a label, her guess was as good as mine.

Once she had nine, she excitedly placed them in the slots and then put her hand on the impression. She made a small squeak of excitement when the screen appeared. Aurome placed a hand on her shoulder at this point and said, "One moment, if you please, Mrs. Stovall."

She reluctantly stepped back, removing her hand, and he placed his on the impression. The screen reappeared and he tilted his head. Looking at me, he asked, "So, what rank of Skill can this provide?"

"So far, only F and E-Ranked Skills," I answered.

"Do you believe that other Permanent Portals could contain these Skill Altars?" he followed up.

"I can't say," I responded.

"Does anyone else know about this?" Aurome asked, his voice excited but also deathly serious.

I frowned, not wanting to lie to the man—at least, not with Seleff in the room—but also not wanting to expose anyone. I didn't think the tone was a threat, per se, but I could tell that Aurome was extremely powerful. In fact, I was starting to question my decision to reveal this to him.

He must have seen my worry because he shook his head. "I'm sorry. I'm assessing the value of this information. Suffer to say, you haven't gone public with it yet?"

I could tell that he meant to say 'suffice' but let the slip pass. Instead, I simply nodded in affirmation. He motioned to Mrs. Stovall and indicated the Altar. She'd been completely occluded by Aurome's monstrously large bulk, but when I saw her face, I knew she had thought she wouldn't get a Skill with how everything was progressing.

Her face broke into a tentative smile before growing as she rushed forward to place her hand on the impression again.

"You do remember that everyone who got a Skill passed out, right?" Smegma said, reminding me of something I had indeed forgotten.

"Wait—" I began to say, even as the screen vanished and Mrs. Stovall's eyes rolled into the back of her head. Thankfully, Aurome caught her before she collapsed face first onto the table.

"What is this?" the big man asked, putting his fingers to her neck to feel for a pulse.

I scratched my neck in embarrassment. "Umm, I kind of forgot to mention that the Altar kind of knocks the person out when granting the Skill…"

Aurome narrowed his eyes but glanced at Seleff, who stood nearly atop him. Seleff's yellow eyes were wide with shock, and his mouth was partially open as he stared at Mrs. Stovall.

"'aelaa muharatiha alan hi salasil alhaqiqati, 'ayuha alqayid," Seleff whispered.

"Her highest Skill is now '*Chains of Truth*,' Chief," Smegma translated.

Aurome's reaction also made it very clear what Seleff had just said. The man's eyes widened, and he stared down at the Altar. "What do you want for this?"

I looked to my father, who blinked back at me. Then he coughed and turned to regard Aurome. "I don't think we should be making deals with the man who is trying to convict my son of a crime he didn't commit."

Aurome's eyes narrowed. "Your *son*. Is he not the one who kneed my Guild member in the face, causing his death?"

"Kneed your Guild member in the face, in self-defense, to protect his own life," my father countered, his voice growing aggravated on my behalf. "Are you telling me that you aren't aware of the crimes he was committing?"

"Morgan Hallsbrad was committing no crimes that I'm aware of. He truly was investigating the death of one of our members' daughters."

My brain froze. Even *Mental Fortitude* was unable to deal with the fallout of that statement. I didn't have a *Truth Seeking* Skill, but I could tell that Aurome's words were genuine. He truly believed that Morgan Hallsbrad was not a serial killer. Still, I was there. Hallsbrad had admitted it and had been in the process of stealing my Skill! My *Dragon Heart* Skill...

"What is going on?" Smegma asked, clearly as confused as I was. "Isn't he supposed to be the Guild Leader?"

The question gave my brain a direction to pursue, which helped me focus. What if Morgan had actually been living a double life? He was both 'Morgan Hallsbrad the serial killer' and 'Morgan Hallsbrad the private eye?'

"Still, someone had to have known. Someone was feeding him targets," Smegma said.

[So, if it wasn't the Larvae Guild, then who was it?] I asked. Smegma shrugged.

In a burst of sweat, I realized everyone was watching me. I'm sure my body had passed through multiple stages of emotional reactions to Aurome's words. I pointed to Seleff. "He has a Truth Skill of some sort, right?"

Aurome nodded, and I continued, my voice hard. "Morgan Hallsbrad was trying to kill me that night. Kill me and steal my Skill. He held me at gunpoint and forced a Mana Connection on me. He wasn't acting as a private investigator that night. I don't—no—I know he was there to kill me, all because of some Skill he had—" I almost said that I didn't know what he wanted from me but stopped myself because I realized that I actually did...

We'd already speculated that Morgan Hallsbrad had found out about *Dragon Heart*, or at the very least, that I'd possessed a Skill better than the low-quality UNMH Assessment indicated by listing me at F-Rank. I now knew that was because my Mana Pool, a part of my B-Ranked *Dragon Heart* Skill, had been at ten points, and that the equipment used could only check power that radiated from you. Since then, my Pool had grown but stalled at fifty. Smegma had speculated that my Pool would grow again when I reached an evolution for the Skill or something else that caused it to breakthrough.

The problem was that someone behind Morgan had fed him my name. They'd known my misidentification by UNMH but not fully informed Morgan of everything. I could clearly recall the serial murderer being surprised by my low Mana.

In that vein, Smegma had told me about Skills like Seleff's a while back. He'd given us the example of *Eyes of Truth* when we'd realized that someone must have been following Arnando's photoshoots to use it on Awakened people. The photographer dealt exclusively with helping young aspiring people get their foot in the door, mostly as Mana Banks. It was why I had been there, after all. I studied Seleff more closely. Could it have been him? I didn't remember seeing the man before our first initial introduction by Mr. Varnish, but still…

Seleff blinked at me, and then whispered something to Aurome. "He says you are telling the truth, or what you believe is the truth. Still, I personally knew Morgan Hallsbrad. So did Seleff. He could not have been this man you describe."

I blinked in confusion. But my father realized something long before I did. My dad pointed at Aurome and said, "Then why does your Guild want my son if you think he actually murdered one of your members?"

It was Aurome's turn to blink. He realized, in the middle of his confusion, that he was still cradling Mrs. Stovall and lowered her into a chair. Then he slowly returned to his own chair and silently sat down. His frown and introspective look were telling.

"I apologize, but this, I cannot answer. Let me call the boss," he said, after a quiet discussion with Seleff in Arabic.

Smegma summarized their conversation. "It's obvious they're both aware of *Demonic Vault's* Shop since they're the ones that brought it up, and they believe that's the reason the boss wants you in their Guild. However, they both also see the strangeness of the situation since you don't seem to possess it."

I put the Altar back in my Necklace at Aurome's direction, and Seleff dropped his Skill, evidenced by the golden light on the walls fading.

"We will be back after making a call," Aurome explained. Aurome and Seleff walked out of the conference room.

The door didn't even close before Ashley stuck her head inside. "Can I get you anything while you wait? Water? Coff—" She saw Mrs. Stovall slumped in the chair at the head of the table and rushed inside. "Oh my! Is she okay? What did they do?"

"She's okay," I explained. "She just was a little surprised by the conversation's direction," I lied.

My father gave me a look as he inhaled a deep breath. Ashley managed to get Mrs. Stovall out of the chair and onto the floor. "Should I call for a Healer?"

I knew from experience that Healing wouldn't wake Mrs. Stovall, as I'd already tried it on my family with previous Skill impartations, but in the present situation, I just nodded at Ashley's question. I wasn't going to be the one using *Minor Heal*. I'd already given away enough.

Smegma popped back into the space beside me, shaking his head. "They went into a room that, when I entered, sent me back here."

[Really? Enchantments, maybe?] I asked, surprised that this building had that much money spent on it. Wasn't this a rental building?

Smegma just shrugged. "That or the material used, maybe?"

Either way, that meant astronomical amounts of money were spent…

CHAPTER 36: CHAPTER 88

Friday, May 3rd, 2069

By the time Aurome and Seleff returned, Mrs. Stovall was awake but sporting a massive migraine—if her groans and swearing were anything to go by. Even as I watched on, the Healer attempted another Skill use, and Mrs. Stovall exclaimed, "Mother-husker, would you stop. It feels like you're shoving a husking hot poker up my nose!"

Aurome and Seleff raised eyebrows at her, but I could tell it wasn't from her language. At first, I thought it was because of her obvious pain, but after a whispered conversation, Smegma corrected me. "They wonder if more powerful Skills granted this way give worse 'hangovers.'"

I blinked.

That was an extremely relevant thought. Not one that I would ever have to worry about—or, well, I guess it was one I'd kind of experienced firsthand. If everyone went through the pain I did upon the mid-rank Altar's Skill Ceremony, and they didn't have *Recovery*—would they die? Would *I* die if I ever ran into a high-rank Skill Altar, even with *Recovery*?

I liked to pretend I had a high pain tolerance, but admittedly, there was no point of comparison. Plus, it wasn't like I was a Tank 'Class' Hunter, who literally took a beating for a living. So, I was probably just overestimating the pain I'd experienced.

"We've spoken to our backer. They're willing to pay for this information, all of what you've divulged, but you'll have to prove your innocence on your own," Aurome said after he motioned for the Healer to leave the room. Seleff barely got his golden bubble thing back in place before the words were spoken.

"What does that mean?" I asked, watching the door close behind the Healer. Had they heard that or did the bubble work regardless of physical barriers?

"If you are proven innocent in this trial, then not only will we pay you for the information, but we'll also sponsor you," Aurome answered, like the answer was self-explanatory. I looked at everyone in the room, forgetting for a moment that I was the only one who could see Smegma. Thankfully, he made a motion that quickly reminded me, and I scanned past him to Mrs. Stovall.

Mrs. Stovall groaned. "It means that they'll pay for you to attend a University or College that specializes in Hunter training. They'll also ensure you get the best treatment, and in most cases, specialized tutors and trainers where needed. A Guild that does this gets priority in the Hunter Draft—or can trade that person to another Guild for a higher spot in said Draft."

The Hunter Draft? Wait—Hunter College—like Phoenix Academy's Hunter Track? I shook myself and even bit the inside of my lip to make sure I wasn't dreaming. Sure, this wasn't as big of a deal as it once might have been—but I hadn't yet truly thought of it as a possibility.

Dave was going to crack a tooth if I told him.

Mental Fortitude was both a gift and a curse. Right now, it was the latter, reminding me pointedly that I had to prove my innocence before any of that. It was a more sobering thought than I wanted. It felt like cold water being poured over me.

My dad coughed politely and motioned around us. "You have to realize that *this*—" My father was motioning primarily at the offices of Varnish. "—is a bit excessive. It feels like your Guild is practically buying a guilty verdict."

Mrs. Stovall groaned again, and my father looked at her sheepishly. "Sorry, I wasn't implying that we weren't going to win—"

"Don't bother," Mrs. Stovall croaked. "This trial is like being crushed under the wallet of a giant—and I don't particularly like feeling like a bug."

"La yumkin iikhfaa' el haqiqa," Seleff exclaimed, and this time I didn't need Smegma to translate as I understood through context when Aurome spoke.

Aurome first motioned at Seleff to wait a moment and then began, "Mr. Varnish certainly commands a heavy retainer and fee, but it was important for Larvae that the facts of this case were told. We do not like the idea of our Guild Member being painted in such a poor light."

My frown was instant and deep. Most Guilds would distance themselves from this sort of bad publicity. Abandon the Hunter and save their reputation. So, Aurome and Seleff clearly believed that Morgan was not in the wrong—when I knew beyond a shadow of a doubt that he was exactly who the media had painted him as. Why the disparity?

And more importantly, why was the person higher up—someone who may have fed Morgan my name—still pursuing this?

"Having met my son," my father interjected, "do you truly believe he is as scheming and duplicitous as Mr. Varnish is making him out to be?"

Aurome frowned while looking at Seleff. Seleff shrugged, seeming to convey something unspoken. "We do not know what to believe. Having seen your boy and talked with him—we are even less sure. Still, if Morgan is truly the man Brodie claims, then we are even more unsure of our gut feelings. Seleff's Skill never triggered with him either. So, someone is telling a tale and is very good at it—but who is lying is yet to be seen."

Despite everything, that initial admission from Aurome did make me feel better. But it was a hollow contentment that faded just as quickly as it came. When the feeling was gone, I noticed that everyone, including Smegma, was looking at me. I simply shrugged.

"I know I'm telling the truth about what happened that night. I don't know how Morgan Hallsbrad fooled you both—well, specifically *you*." I motioned to Seleff. "But I do understand it a bit. You just want to believe the best of a man you thought you knew. I can't convince you otherwise, but could you at least ask Mr. Varnish to not use any underhanded tactics?"

"Hal taqsod ann'a ma faa'lahu hataa alaa'n laisa fouqa alshubha?" Seleff said.

"Seleff asks a good question," Aurome began. "Are you implying that what he has done so far isn't 'above board,' like in your courtroom dramas?"

I looked to Mrs. Stovall, who shook her head while wincing in pain. "It may only feel that way because the 'facts' he is presenting go against what you know. Still, there is the problem of the missing gloves. Maybe call him in here and ask?"

Aurome looked at Seleff for a moment and held up a hand—a gesture I didn't understand at first. "This information about the Altar is very valuable, and we must come to an agreement regarding it before we move on."

"What do you mean?" I asked, thinking we had already discussed the Altar and what I'd get for sharing the information, specifically the money and possible sponsorship.

"Our Larvae Guild will possess a very strong advantage if you keep this information hidden. We would like to have early access to the information and would offer a far higher price if you agree. We'd like to discuss *terms*."

"Who gives a flying husk what these jackasses want," Smegma shouted. "They are still willing to pursue a case against you, and in time, essentially make you a slave to their Guild! So, what does it matter how much money they give you now?"

"Selling this information to the UNMH may see this trial swept away, plus they'd probably sponsor me and pay me royalties or something similar," I answered incredulously, carefully wording my answer to combine my and Smegma's outrage while still responding to Aurome. "So, while I appreciate the attempt to get an advantage, you verbally agreed to pay a fair market price, and I think matching what the UNMH agrees to will be acceptable."

Aurome chuckled softly. "The UNMH can't offer you a deal until after this trial concludes. As a global entity, it is tightly controlled by statutes and laws written into its founding declaration. One of those laws forbids them from negotiating with criminals or citizens undergoing criminal trials in their home countries. So, while they *will* offer you everything you just said after this trial concludes—they will not be able to or willing to step in to 'sweep' Mr. Varnish and our Larvae Guild away."

"What he says is correct, Brodie," Mrs. Stovall said while rubbing her forehead. "However, that doesn't mean another Guild won't step in and pull some strings for this information. Or even the Canadian Government."

"Do you not find it odd that a lawyer from outside of the country is currently an acting Crown Counsel here?" Aurome asked.

"So, you made a deal with the Canadian Government?" Mrs. Stovall asked. The question sounded rhetorical, like she had known this must have been the case.

"That's correct," Aurome answered, despite Mrs. Stovall's tone. "We will be setting up a Guild headquarters here in Windsor, and in exchange, they granted our legal representative and members temporary citizenship and some positions in the local government." Aurome motioned at the building, giving me an answer to it's grandeur.

This wasn't a rental—it was a future Guild Headquarters.

"So, you're saying that they won't make a deal with Brodie for this?" Mrs. Stovall asked, her voice both pained and confused.

"That was part of the original negotiations," Aurome admitted.

"What about Paradox?" Mrs. Stovall said—too casually.

Aurome froze. Subtle waves of an unseen energy began to radiate off the man as he slowly stood. His eyes met Mrs. Stovall's with a level, deadly stare. "What did you just say?"

"The Paradox Guild," Mrs. Stovall enunciated slowly. "You should probably take your seat. This is a negotiation, not an arena, after all.

"I feel like Paradox might appreciate this information, particularly if we were to add that Larvae is seeking exclusive rights to it. They might even make things difficult enough for your Guild in enough ways that you won't have any choice but to back down from bullying a college student, wouldn't you say?"

"A negotiation," Aurome deadpanned.

He laughed then. It was loud, boisterous, and full of mirth as it echoed off the meeting room walls. After a time, the big man wiped a tear from his eye and took his seat. As the laughter faded, he turned a much more serious face back toward the attorney.

"So, you're now threatening the Larvae Guild? You've got balls, I'll give you that."

"In case you haven't been paying attention, you and your Guild have been both threatening my client and actively acting against him near constantly these past weeks." Mrs. Stovall's words were soft, completely contrasting the steel in her eyes. "You've looked into our affairs; is it any surprise that we've looked into yours? It seems like the Paradox Guild has had quite the animosity with Larvae over the years. In fact, your conflict seems to have its origin all the way back in the dawn of the Advent. What's keeping us from taking up the old adage that the enemy of our enemy..."

Aurome smiled then. That in itself made the hairs on the back of my neck stand on end. The big man leaned back in his chair and casually planted his boots with a heavy *thump* on the finely lacquered oak table in front of him as he pulled a flask from an inside pocket—*wait, did he have inside pockets?*—and brought it to his lips with an amused snort.

"You know," he said after a long pull. "It's cute that you think Larvae's been *serious* in coming after your boy here. In fact, I'm flattered. You see, we actually do care—to some extent—who's 'the bad guy' in this whole thing." He looked over at me, as if to check if I was paying attention. I nodded stiffly at him to indicate that I was. "If Morgan was a monster, I'll personally dance and piss on his grave, *Mrs.* Stovall. But if you think that the answer to our *very* reasonable and understandable conflict is to make things *personal* by involving genuine enemies of our Guild in our business? Well, I think that if you were to do that, then you will likely find out far too late just how reasonable we've been throughout this whole affair. Now, if you're done with the empty threats, I believe we can return to our very civil *negotiation*."

My stomach churned, and I instantly felt like I wanted to puke. *This is reasonable?*

Mrs. Stovall's face was pale, but she took a sharp breath, let it out, and nodded with the air of a professional. "Quite. I believe you were just telling us that the Canadian Government would be unlikely to make any deals in our favor in regard to this matter."

Aurome nodded. "They won't interfere in this case as long as everything is 'above board,' as you Americans say."

"We're Canadians, but the term still fits," Mrs. Stovall said. With clear agony, she managed to stand up from her chair and return to her original spot at the table. Once there, she opened a leather folder to reveal a yellow legal pad. The same ones that Mr. Stovall seemed so enamored by. "This sort of secret can benefit the whole world. How long of a head start is the Larvae Guild looking for?"

"Wait," Smegma interjected, which only I could hear. "How come she's even humoring a deal?"

Hurriedly, I repeated the question, "How are you even considering a deal with the people trying to prosecute me?"

"Benefits. In this scenario, you can essentially double-dip," Mrs. Stovall explained. "So, if we hold off on telling the UNMH or Canadian Government— we could make quite the profit. Win the case and then still sell the information to the highest bidder."

Mrs. Stovall gave me a look that held something more than what she said. It took me a moment to replay her words and catch up to the conversation with what she was leaving unsaid. It was true that the Skill Altar was something truly amazing, but finding it in the Goblin Dungeon didn't specifically mean it would exist in others, especially after the world had been interacting with Dungeons for dozens of years, and any discovery of the sort had never been found. Plus, I hadn't even considered revealing the information yet…

"We will allow the discoverer to make the reveal, of course—"

"Of course," Mrs. Stovall intoned.

Aurome smiled at her tone of certainty. I blinked some more. Was that not some sort of given?

"As I was saying, Brodie or Alonzo Mars can make the announcement. We are just hoping that you'd hold off for… half a year?"

"Six months? I doubt you can provide us anything that valuable. What are you offering?"

"This wasn't really part of our expectations today. So, we haven't prepared anything for this negotiation. However, if you have a proposal…?"

Mrs. Stovall looked at me and my father. Then back to Aurome and Seleff. After a moment, she asked for some privacy, and Seleff's Skill shrank to only encompass the three of us. Having it not affixed to the wall was even more bizarre, and I studied the golden bubble as it seemed to undulate around us.

I raised a hand without thinking and moved to touch it—but froze just shy, looking to Seleff for permission. Seleff smirked and nodded. I inched my fingers forward, and they passed through the bubble like it wasn't there. I continued until my whole hand was through and then noticed a subtle difference.

Outside the bubble, my hand could feel the circulating currents of the air conditioning. I glanced up at the vent and then moved my hand back inside. The cool sensation vanished, and I smiled childishly. This bubble also blocked outside elements? With a Skill like that—

"What do you two want me to push for? Money? Items? Try again to have them pull back on the trial?" Mrs. Stovall asked, interrupting my moment of wonder.

I shook myself and gave her my full attention. "I think they've made it clear the last one is off the table, but definitely give it a try. If not that, what if we got them to support us in some other way?"

"You mean our company?" my dad asked, and I nodded but held up a hand.

"That and definitely removing the holds on our current funds. Plus, pressuring Jagger? Sponsoring us with Lynx and Snowbird for Mining contracts, maybe? Something like that? Oh, and definitely interceding with Mirage!"

Mrs. Stovall took notes and began asking clarifying questions, digging into the thoughts. My father answered a good deal of these questions and even began texting my mother for clarification on certain parts of the business. To my childish delight, he was forced to place his phone outside of the golden bubble to get a signal.

Seleff noticed my excitement and tilted his head. I tried sending a text myself and then shoved the phone outside the bubble to see the reception return and send my 'test' message to Dave. Mrs. Stovall tried to smile but grimaced before closing her eyes tight and groaning. I stood up and stuck my head out of the bubble. "Could you grab some water and more ibuprofen, maybe?"

Aurome nodded and Seleff stuck his head out the door. The Healer returned with a glass of water and a Health Potion. I blinked at the clear display of both wealth and generosity. Perhaps we could really get them to pay us an astronomical amount for a few months of early access.

After my request, I'd ducked back into the bubble. The Healer came over and passed the Potion and water through to my father, who put them on the table in front of Mrs. Stovall.

Smegma suddenly zipped into the bubble, startling me. "Have you not been listening to me?"

I started drawing an even more curious look from Seleff and Aurome. I tried to pretend I hadn't jumped in my seat, even as my cheeks flushed crimson. [No, I didn't even know you were talking. Why are you screaming?]

"Oh? This bubble blocks out that much? I assumed because I was in a different phase—"

Seleff interrupted Smegma by promptly passing out, dropping his Skill.

I stared at Aurome and then Seleff, who was now cradled in his arms, just as Mrs. Stovall had been an hour before. Aurome looked at Seleff and then me. "What did you do?"

I shrugged as Smegma said, "Oh. My bad."

[What the husk, dude!] I mentally screamed at the Demon. [I'm already on thin ice here with these guys. What are you doing to me?]

"Yeah, sorry about that," Smegma said with a wince. "I think me being actually inside the smaller version was just too much overload on the Skill. I'm both here and not here—communicating and not communicating. He probably felt the oddity, and examined it. I don't think the Skill knew how to handle all that and just—" He drew his finger across his throat and rolled his eyes up, sticking his tongue out like a corpse.

"I'm sorry," Stovall said. "I tried touching my Mana Pool and using the Skill. That's what started all this. Then I drank the Healing Potion. I didn't know it would cause a problem…"

The Healer hurried back to Aurome and Seleff, and the discussions were put on hold for the night. We planned to meet up first thing in the morning to resume, and I meant *first* thing. We were still hoping to have a Guild to procure our company's services this weekend and wanted to keep ourselves open from nine in the morning onward.

Seleff watched me carefully as I left the room, clearly suspicious of me after his Skill went awry.

[You're sure he won't know about you from that?]

"Unless he felt it before, when Morgan Hallsbrad had *Demonic Vault*— then, yes, I'm sure. I'll stay behind and see what they say."

CHAPTER 37: CHAPTER 89

Saturday, May 4th, 2069

"We've purchased Portals, Portal's, Portalz," Mr. Varnish said distastefully. "These documents will transfer ownership to Brodie Flacarada, as well as its assets—including the Ores that were being disputed."

Mrs. Stovall began reading over the documents as Mr. Varnish slid them across the table. Mrs. Stovall looked up when Mr. Varnish continued, "I've also been instructed to release your accounts, and stop 'unduly' pressuring you during the trial, but otherwise to proceed as previously intended—unless I had done anything that would be deemed underhanded."

My inhalation became deeper and longer as I held my breath, hoping that he was about to admit to making up something that would prove my innocence.

He shook his head in absolute disgust as he continued, "I would never, and *have never*, manipulated evidence in a case to get a good result. I can assure you that whatever dealings you've made with the Larvae Guild won't change the facts of this case. Morgan Hallsbrad is a private investigator that worked with the Larvae Guild in London. He came over to America to find the killer of another member's daughter—those are the facts of this case, as I see them."

"What about the missing gloves?" Mrs. Stovall asked.

Mr. Varnish scoffed. "What gloves, Mrs. Stovall? My team happened upon that disparity in the case when reading over the Detectives' statements. As far as I can tell, Detective Flair is misremembering—"

"Misremembering *two pairs* of gloves?" Mrs. Stovall interjected angrily. "This isn't the man's first day on the job!"

"That part did strike my team and I as odd, but what other explanation is there?" Mr. Varnish asked, his tone admitting that he, too, was suspicious of that fact in the case.

"What about you being hired for this case in the first place?" Mrs. Stovall continued. "Don't you think it's a little strange that *you*, of all people, were called in to replace the normal Crown Counsel for a case against a college student with a background of *zero* issues with the law?"

"The reason that exemption was made has already been explained to you, Mrs. Stovall, and exactly how is it odd for a high-profile Guild to bring in their own Counsel for a case?"

I was glad to see that I wasn't the only one who stared at Mr. Varnish with narrowed eyes. After a moment, Mrs. Stovall sighed and returned to reading the papers. Clearly, Aurome's reasoning yesterday and Mr. Varnish's further insistence was enough for her. I was left studying the room.

This meeting wasn't taking place in Mr. Varnish's opulent warehouse. Instead, it was happening in the Portals, Portal's, Portalz offices—in what I could only assume was Jagger Vance's office.

I could even see spots on the desk and walls where paintings or degrees had once hung—now marked by slightly brighter paint, scuff marks and screws. I would never have called the office plain or cheap before being inside Mr. Varnish's 'warehouse,' but now it looked like a corner cubicle in comparison.

Jagger's desk was a large black square—made of Aluminum, if I was judging correctly. The chair behind it was certainly pricey but made of false leather. Even Mr. Varnish's compact frame made the identical chair he was in look small. Aurome, and the smaller Seleff beside him, made the things look beyond uncomfortable.

Smegma had stayed to listen in on conversations the previous night, but because Seleff had been regaining consciousness and put up a bubble again, he hadn't gotten much before the hundred-yard tether to me cut his espionage short. Seleff did supposedly describe the occurrence that caused his blackout as 'odd.' Like he'd examined a lost area of 'space' inside his Skill before he'd reformed it. When he'd tried to examine that spot further, he'd caused a… 'Mana Loop.' At least, that was Smegma's current assumption.

Supposedly, that was the Earth term used for something Smegma believed was what he'd known as Backlash—when a Skill essentially went out of control and caused the user to slip in their ability to manage a Skill, spilling the resource being used into their own bodies. From what we could tell, they didn't draw any conclusions toward Smegma and *Demonic Vault*, but we also couldn't stay in the lobby for long without drawing suspicion.

Mrs. Stovall tapped the last page of the document, and then motioned around at the building. "Everything seems to be in order—however, there needs to be one change. We would like ownership of the Company transferred to Gary and Clara Flacarada, instead of Brodie."

Mr. Varnish smirked. "That could be done, but due to your husbands case on ownership the Ores will need to stay in Brodie's name. Are you worried that he'll lose his assets when sentenced?"

Mrs. Stovall gave him a look with one raised eyebrow. "We'd simply like to have the company in Brodie's parents' names because he'll soon be attending a Hunter's Academy, thanks to the Larvae Guild sponsorship."

Mr. Varnish didn't roll his eyes, but he did glance at Aurome and Seleff. I smirked as my father clapped a hand onto my shoulder proudly. Still, there was one thing I'd promised to ask after. I turned to Aurome and Seleff as well. "Would we also be able to offer my friend Dave an opportunity to attend a Hunter Academy?"

"We do still have one item to negotiate over," Aurome answered, confusing me until he added, "The additional uses of the Skill Altar."

My flinch was somewhat involuntary as I looked pointedly at Mr. Varnish. Aurome began to chuckle. "Mr. Varnish is our exclusive lawyer. He has signed an NDA, and his team drew up the rough drafts for these contracts. He personally put the finishing touches on them once we shared the secret."

Mr. Varnish seemed proud as he smugly pulled out another document and slowly slid it to Mrs. Stovall. "We anticipated that change. However, we also cannot immediately transfer the ownership of the Ores, since the UNMH is involved." Mrs. Stovall nodded, she had already told me that would be the case. Still, once I got paid the money for the Ores. I could transfer it into Abyss. Mr. Varnish continued, "This contract should be acceptable in that case. As for the additional—" Mr Varnish looked at a notebook beside him. "Thirteen?" He glanced at me to confirm, and I nodded, so he continued, "Uses of the *low-rank* Skill Altar, the Larvae Guild could agree to Dave's sponsorship to a Hunter Academy—for the remaining uses, of course."

The silence that followed was loud. I hadn't planned to trade away *any* of those uses. In fact, with the Mirage Guild off our backs, I'd been planning to buy enough yellow Cores to provide my mother and some select others with Skills. Still, Mr. Varnish's statement, and his tone on 'low rank,' seemed to make it a final offer—but I doubted that.

"Four uses," I said and got the pleasure of seeing Mr. Varnish's smile falter. Aurome and Seleff looked at each other with a small smirk.

"Twelve," Mr. Varnish countered.

After that, Mrs. Stovall took over and a 'middle ground' was reached at nine—meaning I could give four people Skills. The number was actually perfect since my mother needed a skill, and Dave and my father could use a second. So, I'd have one left over.

"Nine and you'll provide thirty-six D-Rank Portal Cores," I quickly added before Mr. Varnish and Mrs. Stovall could shake on the completed deal. Mr. Varnish rolled his eyes and looked at Aurome.

"Acceptable, do you want any specific Element in the Portal Cores?" Aurome asked.

"I'll let the people pick for themselves, and send you the bill, if that's okay?"

"No point buying them from stores. Send us the choices and we'll drop off the Cores and Altar immediately," Aurome answered and I nodded.

With that, the documents were signed by all parties. The completed agreements included: P-Cubed purchase for over a hundred million dollars and its name change to 'Abyss: Portal Services and Consumables,' our agreement to keep the secret of the Altars for three months, Larvae Guild's full protection from Mirage, and Mr. Varnish dropping Echo-five as a client. There were also four Skill bestowals for us, with all needed Cores paid for by Larvae, and finally, sponsorship for Dave and myself to a Hunter Academy that we could get accepted to on our own merits—if I was proven innocent in the case.

Of course, I was going to be allowed to sell the secret again to the UNMH or other Guilds—after three months.

Just as everything was signed, Mr. Varnish looked at his watch and smiled. "You might want to get going, P-Cubed has a Portal contract with Lynx in the Detroit Field that leaves in forty minutes."

"What?!" my father exclaimed as he shot to his feet.

"Not to worry. It's just for a D-Rank Portal of one of their sub-teams. Missing today probably won't cause too many problems."

248

I got to my feet and smiled. That might be the best news I'd heard today! With Portals, Portal's, Portalz acquisition—Abyss didn't have to worry about hiring. That and I'd purchase some tools from Smegma on the drive over.

"We'll take our leave, then," I responded. "I trust you'll see yourself out?" I added, only indicating Mr. Varnish in that minor insult. The man took it in stride with a simple nod of acknowledgement as he began packing up his gear.

Aurome offered me a handshake as he stood. I was surprised but did quickly jump forward to accept. The monstrous mitt that engulfed my hand, forearm and almost elbow was fascinating, but I couldn't dwell on it because, in his deep baritone, Aurome said, "I hope what you've claimed is true. It would be wonderful to work with you in the future."

"Uhh—thanks!" I said and then motioned over my shoulder awkwardly. "I should get going."

Aurome nodded and let go of my 'hand.' "Yes, yes. Don't keep your employees waiting on you."

I smiled. "You mean my *father's* employees." I pulled out a gleaming Pickaxe from the inventory in my Necklace and casually swung it over my shoulder. "I'm just a regular ol' Miner."

* * *

We only had to make one call in the car, thanks to everyone waiting at my parents' place. After hanging up, I began purchasing a number of Skinning Knives, Mining Picks and Gardening Kits. The exact number of workers we had wasn't something my mother knew at the moment, but she was on her way to the P-Cubed building to find out.

Still, she estimated at least thirty of each. Our Ford Escort pulled into the parking lot with the multitude of ATVs just like we had in the past, and my father's eyes narrowed as we drove by an expensive car that was extremely out of place amongst the beaters.

"That's Jagger's car!" my dad said while trying to look through its tinted windows. As far as I could tell, no one was inside, which probably didn't bode well.

"What's that idiot doing?" Smegma asked, and I conveyed the question to my father.

"I'm not sure, but I can't imagine it's anything good."

Smegma flew up ahead, considering we didn't know what ATV we were assigned. My father and I did try asking a few people for directions, but the Demon found Jagger Vance first. My father and I jogged up to discover Jagger openly recruiting a group of Cleaners.

"—Specialists, so I could easily take all of you with me to my new, better company," Jagger said. We were too late to hear the exact number of Specialists that Jagger was claiming to possess, but Smegma filled me in with a simple 'ten.'

"Ahh, and here's your new owners—" Jagger motioned at me and my father. "They've got absolutely no experience in running a Portal Goods Company, and even worse, don't have any connections to keep you working with top-tier Guilds. Within a month, anyone who stays will be running with *low-ranked Guilds*."

A visible shudder went through the crowd. For a split second, I honestly was worried, but then I remembered what we were offering, thanks to *Mental Fortitude* instantly calming my emotions. Calmly, I met eyes with one of the group members who hadn't shuddered in revulsion at Jagger's words.

"Would you care to go grab the Miners and Gardeners? Like Jagger here, we have an offer—one that I believe is far better than anything he's willing to make."

Jagger scoffed and crossed his arms over his chest. "I've already got all the Specialists with me! What could you possibly give these workers?"

"I'd rather not repeat myself, but if you'll wait just a moment for the others to arrive, you'll be very happy you stayed."

"There's nothing you can offer. I still own all the Specialist Contracts and I have all the Bags of Holding for the runners!" Jagger guffawed. "This should be good."

We had three ATVs that were parked side by side, and so it only took a few minutes for the willing people to arrive. The total was probably just over a hundred and fifty, which made my earlier purchases of forty of each item a little lacking in at least one Professional category. But I would fix that later.

"I haven't gotten to speak to everyone yet," Jagger said first, raising his hands above his head to get everyone's attention. "However, I'll make the same offer to anyone who wishes it. I have ten Specialists in Gardening, Cleaning and Mining with my new company P-Squared—"

"Oh, the originality," Smegma interjected sarcastically.

"—the new owners of *Abyss*," Jagger sneered along with the emphasis on our new company's name. "Don't have a single *Skilled* Specialist in any of those three. Come with me, keep your current job, and I'll have new contracts with the top Windsor Guilds as early as today—go with *them* and you'll be working with the *low-ranked Guilds* by next month!"

I waited patiently, even as a few people in the crowd stepped forward to hurry to Jagger's side. Part of me wanted to interject and cut him off, but I figured it was better to have a smaller group of loyal people than a larger group of flaky ones.

Once the mass exodus was over, I was sad to see only sixty-odd faces not standing behind Jagger. Of those sixty, thirty of them were Miners who had likely stayed because they personally knew my father.

"Did you tell them about them all becoming Specialists?" Willa said as she jogged over to join the group. Dave and Jarred were with her since they'd all been having breakfast at my place.

A few people in the group behind Jagger perked up at that statement, but I shook my head. "Thank you for coming to hear what I have to say," I announced to the group that remained, instead of answering Willa. "Jagger may be offering you the same job you had with P-Cubed, over at P-Squared, but what I'm offering you is something more."

A few people behind Jagger who put two-and-two together attempted to cross back to the group, and I held up a hand in their direction. "We'll be taking applications if *you're* interested," I pointedly said to let the one who'd moved the quickest know that he was certainly not included in my offer. He froze, even as a few others slunk back into their place behind Jagger, clearly hoping they weren't noticed.

"What Abyss: Portal Services and Consumables offers is Enchanted equipment for anyone we employ, making them Specialists. That—along with each of your years of experience—is something truly valuable. We'll also be offering bonuses with higher caps *and*—" I was forced to stress the conjunction as Jagger attempted to cut me off.

"—better *benefits*!" I shouted the last word, knowing that my father and mother often complained about the coverage they'd had with P-Cubed.

"Come on!" Jagger shouted over the murmurs that broke out in both groups of workers. To my surprise, the better benefits were probably discussed more than the offer to purchase Enchanted tools for people. "You've all tried your hand at purchasing Enchanted gear and earning more in bonuses than you spent before it breaks. It doesn't work. Any company offering to supplement those costs will go bankrupt within a year! Don't be fooled."

His rant explained why the excitement of the crowd seemed focused on the benefits. I looked to my father, who stepped forward. We'd discussed what to say to the workers who waffled in this situation in the car—well, what *he'd* say.

But we clearly hadn't expected Jagger to oppose us directly…

"Maybe for someone who was keeping over fifty percent of the profit for himself, it would be difficult to keep a company running. What we're offering is partial ownership to all our employees. The company will still take a percentage— but only to cover the cost of equipment repairs, Healing, back of house, insurance and other such expenses. Some of you may not know me, but my name's Gary, and until recently, I was a simple Miner—one of you. I've already become a Specialist through the same process we're offering you. That rise has gotten me and mine a significant raise in wage and standard of living!"

Jagger scoffed but did glance over both shoulders, trying to catch people who might be persuaded. Not that I would have allowed them to cross over anyway. The lines had been drawn—for now—and I was okay working with this smaller number of *hopefully* trustworthy people.

Why?

Because I was going to reveal to them the prepared 'Equipment Repair Mark' tale. Not that it mattered much at this point, but I still wasn't comfortable with that knowledge being 'public.' Sure, it would eventually have to come out, but the longer I kept it hidden, the less questions I'd have to answer.

Especially in the courtroom.

"This is your final chance," Jagger shouted. "I'm going to take these workers with me and go discuss future Portal work with Taz—or maybe—I'll even get tacked onto this pathetic run."

Thankfully, Taz couldn't break the contract with P-Cubed, now Abyss: Portal Services and Consumables, without accruing a massive penalty. But admittedly, our skeleton crew of workers might put the man off.

And yet, we now only needed one ATV. And we'd all be Specialists. So, it might be a cost-effective trade-off. I wasn't aware what renting the ATVs cost—or the price of simply running them into the Detroit Field if Lynx owned them.

"Hopefully the latter," Smegma said. "Otherwise, Lynx already paid rental fees…"

I winced, looking at the three ATVs that had been assigned to P-Cubed. Still, it would be best to handle a few other problems that Jagger had highlighted. His group slowly began turning away to follow after the pompous man in his expensive suit.

Some seemed reluctant to go—and a few of the group that had stayed even rushed to my father to plead the cases of those individuals. Unfortunately, we also lost another five to ten, leaving our total at about fifty, which admittedly wasn't great—considering thirty of them were Miners, fifteen Cleaners and only five were Gardeners.

My father did allow the ones who were pleaded for by current 'members' to return, which upped our numbers slightly, bringing the total Cleaners to twenty-two and Gardeners to eight. It wasn't ideal, but with everyone working at the level of a Specialist, it might be enough.

Then again the Gardeners and Cleaners never had a repair issue… I thought.

"Well, they do. According to your mom and dad," Smegma interjected after my thought. "It's just far less than Miners. But I'm sure it still eats into their bonuses…"

Still, there was one other major problem that Jagger had highlighted, and I needed to solve it. Mentally, I sent Smegma, [We need Bags of Holding.]

"Yeah, the good news is that Bags of Holding are far cheaper than your Necklace—this one's probably best."

Bag of Medium Holding
Grade: High D

A Bag that has a space inside it of 300 cubic feet. Items can be summoned into and out of this space by mental command. This Bag is made with Dread Stallion Hide and can hold no further Enchantments.

Cost: 250,000 mC

Cheaper was a bit of a misnomer—considering that it cost half as much as my Necklace but held about a hundred and seventy-five cubic feet more. Still, I didn't really have an option. I turned to my father, "I'll head back to the car and get the gear."

He nodded, even as I asked Smegma, [What's my current mC total?]

"After the equipment earlier and the sale of the B-Rank Crystals for insurance against Mirage, which is now Abyss Company Capital? Eight hundred and ninety-five thousand Mana Coins and change."

Since I needed a Bag for each group, that meant I'd be down to a hundred and forty-five thousand pretty soon. There was one final consideration—

Would my purchase increase my contribution to *Demonic Vault* enough that I'd create a light show?

CHAPTER 38: CHAPTER 90

Saturday, May 4th, 2069

I made the purchase in the bathrooms, which were a permanent trailer installation, just in case. I held my breath as the Bags fell out of the coalescing Mana in the air, just like the Fishing Rods, Picks and other purchases always had.

I caught them and waited.

Nothing happened, making me sigh in relief. Losing Smegma today of all days wouldn't have been good.

My eyes moved to the Bags I'd just caught, and I couldn't help but marvel at the sleek look of them.

It reminded me of the time I'd held a friend's designer purse. The leather was practically glowing, and the stitching was done in some sort of golden accent. There wasn't an obvious mark on the Bags, like there would be on a designer purse, but they just *screamed* money.

"This could be a problem," I grumbled.

Smegma looked at me, and then the Bags, before scoffing. "It should just make it look like Abyss: Portal Services and Consumables has a lot of money to invest. Isn't that the image you're cultivating, moron?"

I raised my eyebrows and nodded in acknowledgment. Still, my guess was that they also had a Self-Repair or Cleaning Enchant on them—so, they wouldn't even get scuffed up over time, which was going to be mighty suspicious in a few months.

I shrugged. By then, we would have either succeeded with the company or have failed. I exited the bathroom, holding the three Bags, and literally almost ran into a cart of equipment. I blinked at the items inside the cart, trying to figure out what the cameras, booms, stabilizers, tablets and other expensive computers were needed for.

That was when Kristen and Geneva, pushing the cart from behind, came into view. The two women were so short they couldn't see ahead of themselves— thus, how I had almost become a 'casualty' of their efforts.

"Ladies, what are you doing here?" I called, getting a start from them both before their eyes found me. They must have realized they'd nearly run me over with the cart from my position pressed back up against the trailer.

"Oh, shoot! Sorry, Brodie," Geneva began. "This is a bit too heavy for one of us, but with both of us pushing, we can't see…"

I moved forward and shooed the women's hands off the cart, making it clear I would push the thing as I said, "That didn't answer my question."

"Well, I would think why we'd be here was pretty obvious!" Kristen exclaimed.

I gave her a canted head and a raised eyebrow, which conveyed my exasperation with that response.

She laughed and said, "Mrs. Stovall called us. She thought it would be good for us to start working with Abyss: Portal Services and Consumables—you know, managing your new company page!"

"We don't have a company page," I said as I began pushing the loaded cart under their direction.

"Oh, yes, you do!" Geneva answered, brandishing her phone, which was open to a SwiftGram page. She quickly flipped tabs on the device, and I saw that the women had somehow set up a page on every social media platform—and a website—in the time it had taken us to drive here and fend off Jagger.

"Wow," Smegma said. "Do these two women have a Skill for Internet Management?"

I repeated his words for the women, and they smiled widely as a slight blush crossed their faces. I watched the two women, realizing that they may benefit from a Skill from the Altar. If they could accomplish the things they had without System assistance, what could they do with it? Would it be better to gift them one, or a second to my father and Dave?

That decision didn't need to be made now. Right this moment, we needed to get on the ATV before it left. I'd steered the cart to a place near the Ford Escort and then pretended to rummage through the back as I transferred Skinning Knives, Gardening Kits, and Mining Picks from my Necklace to the Bags.

Seeing the items again made me acutely aware of just how lackluster what I was about to present to the Abyss workers appeared to be. The Gardening Kits were leather work-belts that looked like they were one stitch away from snapping and disgorging the Tools they carried onto the ground.

Worse—the fruit pruners, hand trowels, shears, multi-tools and hand rakes all looked like they'd break if they were dropped even the three-foot distance from a worker's hand to the ground. I knew they'd look better as the day progressed, but *damn* was handing them over going to be embarrassing.

The Skinning Knives might have been the worst. The metal edges were certainly sharper than the fileting Knives had been, but the metal felt both pliable and brittle. I hadn't held a Skinning Knife before and wasn't sure if the flexibility was intended or not. Then, of course, there was the 'handle,' or lack thereof. It was impossible to tell if the tang of the blade was wrapped in wood, leather, or twine because whatever it was looked rotten and mostly decomposed.

A lump began climbing my throat—

"Stop it, dumb-dumb," Smegma said, interrupting me. "First, you're going to tell them about your 'Repair Mark' in the ATV so no one can escape. Second, you have the newly-bought, rough-looking Mining Picks and the repaired ones to show them."

I nodded to myself and then moved back to the women and the cart. Motioning at the gear, I asked, "Would you two be okay if I put this gear in a Bag of Holding?"

I probably could have done so earlier and avoided having to push the cart, but I'd only just had the thought.

They of course nodded in relief, and I put the entire cart and equipment inside. The Bag did get noticeably heavier, and I'd have estimated it had increased by about a hundred pounds. I was impressed that it worked and even made sure I could summon it out as an entire unit. Just to be sure.

It worked.

I considered giving the Bag with the equipment to one of the ladies, but I needed all three for the Professions entering. I motioned to the Bag and said, "I'll get you one of these later if you're going to be coming into Portals with us more often."

They nodded, and we made our way to the ATV.

Thankfully, most of the workers had their own equipment, and Jagger had left behind the armor and loaner equipment as well. Whether he left the stuff by accident or because it was in the contract, I wasn't sure, but I was glad in either case. All thirty Miners, twenty-two Gardeners and eight Cleaners loaded into the ATV.

My father was already talking to a member of the Lynx Guild while indicating the other two ATVs intended for P-Cubed's use that Abyss no longer needed. The Lynx member didn't look happy and quickly rushed off.

"Arms up," Willa said as she helped Geneva into a spare set of Miner's gear. Kristen watched and attempted to climb into her own set, but Dave, seeing her struggle, rushed up to help.

As the two women got ready, I looked at the Bags of Holding. As soon as the doors closed, I'd reveal—

"That was a Squad Leader for Lynx, and he says there's no way a team of eight Cleaners is going to be enough. Especially as 'Equipment Specialists…'" my dad said as he climbed the loading ramp.

I was thankfully looking at Dave as he said that. Dave's *Cut* Skill was certainly more useful as a Cleaner than in the Mines. Plus, I could join that group as well, considering I'd likely get a Skill for it at some point, and *hopefully*, another unlocked Stat…

"We'll move Dave and myself to that group," I answered, looking around at each of the core group in turn.

My father grimaced, making it clear that he, too, thought that was just a stopgap. I nodded in acknowledgment. But there wasn't a lot we could do, so I shrugged and began planning what I would say to the workers.

Just as our ATV's doors began to close, I saw the Squad Leader who had been speaking with my father returning.

Beside him was Jagger Vance—in a suit of armor that looked out of place even with the Hunter who stood right beside him. It was like looking at a child playing dress up. Or like the Bags of Holding—

The gear Jagger wore was red leather with black accents. I swore I could hear the squeaking it made even over the motors of the loading ramp.

"Well that can't be good," Jarred said as he stepped up beside me to watch the P-Squared team return. Jagger had a smile on his face that seemed to suggest he'd already beaten us, which aggravated me and—from the clenched fists of my father, Willa, and Jarred—them too.

The door snicked shut, removing the infuriating piece of shit from my sight, and I spun—the aggravation of the man's smug smile motivating me in a way I hoped would transfer positively to the others who stayed with us.

"Look," I declared, pointing back over my shoulder. My tone and volume caused a great deal of people to start, but I definitely got their attention. "That piece of shit, Jagger Vance, is going to also be inside the Portal with his 'new' company. I don't think I need to go into detail about all the ways he's likely screwed you out of money over the years—do I?"

Almost every head in the ATV bobbed in acknowledgment. I smiled. "Well, today, we get the chance to do something about it. We may have fewer workers, but less can be more. Today, we will focus on quality over quantity!"

A few blinks and one muted cheer was the only answer I received to my call to arms. I didn't let it dissuade me and exclaimed, "Miners! Today, you'll focus on Mining whole Crystals. At the end of the day, each of you will pick one soft metal to extract as well. Understood?"

Thirty confused looks were my only answer, and again, I forced myself to move on. Thankfully, Smegma helped me with the rather large gap in my knowledge of the next two groups. 'Living Specimens' and 'Full Hides.'

"Gardeners!" I announced, turning to our second-largest group. "You'll work on cultivating live specimens when possible. I'll be starting with your group and show you some tricks to maintaining freshness of fruits, herbs and plants. Afterward, Dave and I will be with the Cleaners." My cheeks flushed bright red at saying I knew something about their jobs that they didn't, but Smegma assured me that he had a few helpful tidbits of information that weren't being used.

The Gardeners looked at each other with skepticism written clearly across their faces.

[Whelp, this is going wonderfully.]

"Shut up and keep going!" Smegma countered, sounding proud.

"Cleaners!" I croaked, trying to get over my embarrassment. "We will have the hardest disadvantage to overcome. With only ten of us, we'll need to work three to four times as hard. I know that's asking a lot, but if we focus on full Hides, we'll stand out. Plus, I'll get started on Cooking bite-sized meals that will keep you energized as you work."

Again, Smegma added that idea to my speech, and again, I flushed deeply with embarrassment. Sure, I could Cook some meals for them, but how that was going to help left me just as lost as they were.

"Don't worry—stupid man-child! If you're starting with the Gardener's, I have a plan," Smegma announced confidently.

The silence after my speech only made it worse. Not to mention when I got a punch in the arm from Geneva. "You could have given us back our recording equipment before you did that!"

"Maybe we can have him do it again, and all of you can even cheer after each pronouncement?" Kristen suggested.

Was it possible to die from mortification?

"How are we supposed to do that without Enchanted Gear?" one of the people in the seats of the ATV asked.

I closed my eyes, at an utter loss as to how things had gone so wrong. Sure, I hadn't expected my speech to be met with cheering as Kristen implied, but I hadn't expected the silence and that question to immediately follow it.

I took a deep breath, opened my eyes, and looked at Dave, Willa, Jarred and my father pleadingly. They were all smiling and holding back laughter. I could tell they were enjoying the moment—enjoying my awkwardness. I silently cursed at them.

"It isn't their fault that you're a totally useless public speaker," Smegma said between chuckles.

It seemed everyone was going to just let me hang myself. *Husking perfect!*

"Okay…" I began, trying to build up my courage for what came next. "So, about the equipment—"

"What, you don't have any?" someone called.

"He has it," my father shouted, his voice high pitched due to his clear mirth.

"Yeah, just be lettin' him speak," Willa shouted, openly laughing.

My fingers massaged the bridge of my nose as I let my chin touch my chest. I looked up after collecting myself and actually found a good deal of smiles greeting me. Clearly, my group's mirth was contagious because now the sixty-odd people were excited to be let in on the joke.

I personally didn't think this would end well—

The ATV lurched into motion, causing me to take a step forward to brace myself. Now I had a timer, too. I needed to finish my explanation before we were through the Gate...

"Okay!" I exclaimed, this time aiming the words at myself. "The equipment *I'm about to give you doesn't* look like much." I raised my volume to keep people's attention. "It's *very* second hand, and that's because I possess a Skill called Repair Mark." I glanced at the Lynx Hunters who were stationed in our ATV and saw them look at each other with raised eyebrows. "It only works on non-combat gear," I hedged, not wanting them to think I could somehow begin repairing their stuff. "So, what I've purchased is the best quality Enchanted Gear—in some of the worst states!"

Murmuring broke out as I pulled my father's Pickaxe from his hand. "This is a piece I purchased about three weeks ago. As you can see, it looks nearly brand new and will continue to repair itself as long as I mark it. This—" I began pulling out a 'new' worn and beaten Pickaxe. "—is what it looked like when I started."

"Bullshit!" someone called.

"It's truth!" someone else called, and I was surprised when it wasn't one of my immediate group members. I scanned the crowd for the voice, along with everyone else on the ATV. The person I found made me smile. Miguel was pointing at the Pickaxe that looked like it was a step above driftwood. "Saw kid bring *that* into Portal. I thought he stupid, but each day, it look better. Then we fight Golem, and *that* what three of Picks look like after."

Miguel's words seemed to do more to move the people in the ATV than mine would have alone. I was unsure if Willa, Jarred or my father would have had the same effect, but I nodded to the usually reserved Miguel in thanks all the same, before coughing and getting ready to continue.

"He's right," I said as calmly as I could. "My Pick was in just as bad condition as the ones you'll be getting today, and *this* is what it looks like now."

Mentally reaching into my Necklace, I pulled out my Miner's Pick. As it fell from thin air, my fist wrapped around the smooth, glossy handle that resembled a dark walnut. Three feet of pristine, textured wood ended at a gleaming crescent of elegantly blackened steel. The metal of the Pickaxe flowed and arched gracefully into a deadly blade on one end and an exquisitely crafted pick on the other.

I wasn't being completely genuine, due to the fact that the Pick had been Upgraded somehow after my fight with the Golem, but I didn't think anyone would begrudge me a little embellishment here. Plus, hadn't I seen Jarred's pick start to gain the same coloring? Either way, these people needed to know that their equipment was going to be significantly better and more reliable as time went on, and that was the truth I cared about. It was the other sets of gear that likely would be stuck at Peak-F-Rank till I found an Opportunity.

Eyes widened at the sight of my personal Pickaxe, and the crew finally seemed to be getting excited for the first time.

I also didn't fail to notice that one of the Lynx members' eyebrows seemed to be trying to crawl up into his scalp.

"So, when I hand you the equipment you'll be using today—don't get down on yourself. At first, it might not work the greatest and it definitely won't look great, but it will only get better throughout the day. That's a promise!"

I picked up the first Bag of Holding from near my feet and looked inside. Mining Picks.

"Jarred," I called—picking the only one of my group not still chuckling at my expense. "Could you hand out a Pick to each Miner onboard?"

Jarred took the Bag and began moving to distribute them.

As he did so, I raised a hand to get everyone's attention again. "Keep in mind that these need to come back to me at the end of the day so I can reapply the marks. Otherwise, they will act like any other piece of Enchanted Gear— wearing down and breaking."

The next Bag had the Skinning Knives and the media cart. I picked it up and then called, "Dave, can you hand the Knives out to the Cleaners, please?"

Dave came forward and accepted the Bag. As I let go, he squealed, overbalanced, and promptly collapsed to the ground with a loud crash. I looked at him in shock, even as he groaned in pain.

"What the hell was that?" Then, after a moment's thought, I added, "are you okay?"

"What do you mean? What the hell was *that*? This Bag probably weighs three-hundred pounds, jackass!" Dave grumbled as he rubbed his back with one hand and his face with the other. Thankfully, it looked like his head had hit the Bag—so other than some reddening from the impact, he was okay.

"Oh," I said, recalling the Bag gaining in weight from putting the video equipment inside earlier. I'd thought it had increased maybe a hundred pounds at most, but even if it did weigh that much, I probably should have warned my friend.

Seeing everyone chuckling at Dave's faceplant, and recalling his earlier giggles at my expense, I changed my thoughts on the matter. I reached down and mentally pulled out the media cart while chuckling.

"Don't laugh, jerk-face. That could have really hurt me."

That only startled more laughs out of the attentive audience. Geneva and Kristen rushed to their cart and quickly began loading themselves up with cameras and tablets.

Standing back up, I looked to the final group. "Gardeners?" I said, addressing them with a question. "Do you have someone who can act as a leader among you?"

Everyone turned to look at a skinny, brown-haired woman wearing glasses. She hadn't immediately raised a hand and even sighed when she realized everyone's looks. Reluctantly, she answered, "I guess I can do it."

"Perfect. Do you mind handing out the Gardening Kits to everyone?" I asked.

She nodded, and I handed her the final Bag of Holding. The muttering changed once everyone got a look at their 'equipment,' and I could tell that it wasn't in a good way.

I raised my hands once more and said, "I assure you all that they will look better after each task you perform. Look forward to it."

My words may have changed a few muttering conversations for a time, but I couldn't truly tell. Shrugging, I took a seat as Geneva and Kristen began capturing the moment.

Kristen in particular was recording but constantly looking back to me. Finally, she said, "Can you give the speech one more time?"

I began to roll my eyes as my cheeks grew hot. Then, to my utter horror, someone called, "Speech!"

My head spun on Dave so fast that I felt it twinge. My father joined the traitor. "Speech!"

Willa guffawed but caught the next call, "Speech!"

"Speech!" others began picking up the chant, and I truly considered crying.

CHAPTER 39: CHAPTER 91

Saturday, May 4th, 2069

"I'm saying I'll need an escort from the Gardeners to the Cleaners," I reiterated for the clearly dense Hunter.

As if to confirm my opinion of him, he stared at me with no comprehension on his face. Did he speak a different language maybe? It would be rare but—

"I cannot permit workers to move around in the Dungeon unescorted," he said slowly.

I blinked at him. Then I looked at the Gardeners behind me. We were just inside a Sective Agora Portal and about to split up to go to our separate areas to work. Thankfully, I saw a different Hunter behind me, with the Miners, and moved to him.

"Hello, my name is Brodie. I'm the foreman of the crews here today," I said by way of introduction. "I'm going to need to move from the Gardeners' group to the Cleaners after the first hour. Can you provide me with an escort to do so?"

This Hunter turned to look at me, then did a slow top to bottom, followed by the bottom to top assessment that spoke volumes. He was clearly questioning how I could be any sort of leader at my age. I knew I looked young, and on SwiftGram that helped me, I thought? But here, amongst adults—it was admittedly not a great look.

My dad stepped forward. "I'm the owner of Abyss: Portal Services and Consumables—he is, in fact, the foreman of the two other groups. Please do as he says."

The Hunter finished his appraisal of me and gave my father a skeptical look. "The owner of the company is inside the Dungeon with us? And I'm the Dragon King!"

My father's eyes narrowed, and he pointed across the field to Jagger in his far-too-expensive armor. "That's the owner of P-Squared, which is why I'm here to make sure we destroy them in Gathering."

"Oh?" the man said and studied Jagger Vance. He clearly looked the part more than my father or I did. He turned his judgmental gaze back to us and seemed to come to a conclusion. "He's just here to observe, and you're actually going to step up and work? I can respect that. Okay, give me a sec…"

The guard walked away to a gathering group of Hunters, and I sighed in relief. At least he had decided to get an escort for me. I looked at my father, and he could only give a chagrined shrug. It was clear that even the Hunter Guards of Lynx were already catering to Jagger and his group of workers.

Just watching the man preen in his armor made my blood boil. Abyss would kick his ass today!

"You do realize that he has almost double the numbers of all of the Gatherers here, except Mining—where you've got a slight advantage. Which surprises me—" Smegma began but I interjected mentally.

[Yeah, where did he get the extra Miners? Didn't they all join us?]

"As I was saying, he must have been hiring more Miners because of the ten Specialists he contracted. That means he could have as many as a hundred other workers, according to the ten to one rule he went by in P-Cubed."

[*Oh, shit!* So, those guys weren't there when I told them they'd all be Specialists…] I turned to my dad. "There are about twenty Miners who aren't Specialists with Jagger. See if you can't convince them to join our company."

"Oh, okay. When we take lunch, I'll try to chat with them." My father then whispered a question, "I assume we shouldn't tell them about the 'Repair Mark?'"

I nodded in confirmation as a group of five split off from the congregation of Hunters and moved in unison back toward us. The guard for the Miners was one of them, and the other four seemed to be made up of a Hunter and her Mana Banks. To my surprise, I recognized one of them—

Not the Hunters, but a dark-skinned beauty that was with them. Or what had been a stunning young woman last I saw her.

Eva walked along with the two other Banks, and she was nearly unrecognizable compared to when I'd met her in line at Arnando's photoshoot. She didn't even look at me or her surroundings as she sluggishly moved toward me.

I swallowed bile as it rose in my throat. When she'd won the 'picture of the day' at Armando's photoshoot, I'd been so jealous—but now… I looked at her. She almost looked like a zombie. Her skin was grayish, where it had once held a golden hue—her arms, once sculpted perfectly by a combination of muscle and grace, were now skeletally thin. And her hair! It looked like a rat's nest atop her head. Like she didn't even have the energy to run a comb through it.

I stepped forward, ready to—do something…

"Don't you dare, moron," Smegma practically shouted. "There is nothing you can do right at this moment. If you cause a scene right now—you'll not only accomplish nothing, but also hurt Abyss!"

Husk! I swore at myself, and the Demon, for good measure. He was right, but that didn't mean I had to like it. I was forced to swallow again as disgust at the decision I had to make tried to overturn my stomach. Another goal was added to my current list.

Get back at Mirage—Find the person behind Morgan—Save Eva!

"Save her from what, you idiot?" Smegma countered my internal thoughts once again. "For all you know, she just started with this Hunter and she's acclimatizing to it. Look at her other Banks, they are helping her and don't look to be suffering under the Hunter… Maybe she was injured doing something else, or working for someone else, and this person's taken her in and is helping her out. You need more information before you go around full-cocked like an Incubus at an orgy."

262

I finally tore my eyes away from Eva and studied the other Banks and then the Hunter. To my surprise, the Hunter was a female, as were the two Banks by Eva's side. Smegma was right—the two other Banks looked quite healthy, but that didn't mean he was right about her not needing saving…

The Hunter was clearly a caster of some sort. She wore loose-fitting armor and had both a wand and a large staff in hand. It actually looked a lot like the staff I'd had in the pictures taken by Arnando. It had a blue gem at its head and was made from some sort of blackened wood. The woman herself was beautiful in a way that was opposite to Eva's.

Where Eva was lithe and graceful, this woman was thick and sturdy. Short hair with shaved sides graced her head, and both arms were tattooed with half-sleeves that I couldn't make out from this distance. They arrived in front of us as I studied the dark, black lines of her tattoos—trying to understand what I was looking at.

The Hunter held out a hand, "Hi, my name is Alexus Fawn. I'm told you'll need an escort between our Gatherers?"

I tore my eyes away from the tattoos. Surely there was something I could do for Eva?

"Don't you dare!" Smegma scolded. "Plus, she'll be with you all day—at least husking confirm she's being mistreated first!"

[Fine!] I mentally shouted back and then turned a disapproving frown onto Alexus.

"That's right!" I accidentally exclaimed. I didn't bother correcting myself and just spun away from her to return to the Gardeners and the stupid Hunter that they had.

"What's his problem?" I heard one of the women behind me ask in a whisper. I tuned out any response, feeling my cheeks flush with both anger and a hint of embarrassment.

* * *

"What you need to find is a sapling tree, preferably Antikwa," Smegma explained as I stood in a field. The other Gardeners had already moved off to begin work as I prepared to show them some of the *tricks* I'd promised.

I scanned the forest, looking for Saplings in the heavy foliage. Alexus and the Mana Banks stood behind me. Three of the women looked skeptically at my back, with clear distaste for me after my earlier outburst. My fists clenched as I thought of the fourth. Eva, last I saw, still looked like she was barely able to stand on her own two feet.

[The *problem*, Smegma, is that the canopies of these larger Trees won't let Saplings grow.]

"Use your brain and check in the small gaps of sunlight, imbecile!" Smegma scolded.

I frowned and scanned for a patch of sunlight. Nearly right beside the first patch of bright yellow I found was indeed a Sapling. I wondered only for a moment why it wasn't *in* the sunshine, when Smegma scoffed. "You really aren't bright. Sunshine moves!"

[God dammit, Smegma!] I responded, not in the mood for his taunting at the moment. I knew what was distracting me. [What do I husking do with the thing?]

"Carefully dig it up, and then place it and some soil from around it into the Gardening box." I followed his instructions and wasn't the only one who was skeptical of his method. Small snickers and questions sounded out from the Mana Banks behind me, and I fought my urge to turn on them.

[Now, *what*?] I mentally asked Smegma, venting some of my frustration on him.

"Take it back to the Gardeners, idiot! Don't get all Changeling with me for stopping you from ruining your life and destroying your company all on its first day."

Standing up, I turned around and carried the box back to the Gardening area. The area was a clearing that was nearly a perfect circle. In fact, it was eerie in its symmetry, like it hadn't formed naturally but was somehow stamped by some godly creature in the heavens.

"That's 'cause it was created by the System. Just like the Mines and Monsters…" Smegma explained, his voice finally less scathing at my thoughts. Instead, he was introspective, like he once had asked the same questions.

The clearing had numerous Plants, Bushes, Vines and Grasses that were clearly not from Earth. While the trees of Secretive Agora could be mistaken for extremely large maples from the planet—these plants would be alien no matter what. Except for maybe on Pandora in that movie Advantor Fourteen: The Last Stand.

The Grass was five feet tall and ocean blue. The Vines were pink and had purple Flowers right beside yellow Fruits that could have been bananas if they didn't glow. The Bushes contained Fruits and Nuts both—and one Bush held every color of the rainbow. I shook off my returning marvel at the scene and hurried to the Bush area, as directed by Smegma.

"—shut that clap-trap of a mouth and get in them Bushes, soldier!" he shouted in my ear, causing me to jump and obey. Once I arrived, he continued in a slightly softer drill-sergeant-esque voice. "Now, get out the shears and cut exactly where I tell you and on the angle I confirm."

It took several minutes to change the angle of the shears and find the perfect spot along a stem—just in front of a purple bulb of what could maybe pass for overly large garlic.

"Cut slowly and with the same force the entire time."

I managed to follow his instructions thanks in large part to my Dexterity, or at least, I thought I did. I figured there was just no way one of my Stats wasn't helping my hand stay steady and slow. The shears weren't exactly 'sharp' but they managed.

"Move the other hand to catch the Grackle before it falls even a millimeter. But carefully time it for your hand to arrive as you finish the cut."

Again—I managed to follow his instructions. The 'Grackle' didn't fall at all, and I slowly brought it back to myself. The already fragrant air now hummed with what I could only describe as the smell of coconut-melon. It was a sweet smell but had a depth that spoke of vacation. I wasn't the only one who noticed this change, and a few nearby Gardeners stopped to sniff the air.

Following their noses, their eyes landed on me. They watched as I continued to follow Smegma's directions. Slowly, I brought the stem of the Grackle—which was cut at a steep, almost eighty-degree angle—to the Sapling. With the same precision as before, I sawed a mirroring notch, ten-degrees this time, in the thin Sapling's trunk and then cut off the backside of the Grackle's stem-bark to expose green cells beneath.

Smegma continued to direct me and I slid the Grackle inside the intended slot "Press the Sapling's bark firmly onto the Grackle and then stem-feed a tiny amount of Mana to it. Because this isn't an Antikwa Sapling, you'll need three drops of Mana or more."

To my shock, at five drops of Mana, the Sapling not only healed around the Grackle, but also grew about one centimeter wider, now easily supporting the Fruit's weight. The Fruit seemed to glow as well, maintaining the aroma in the air.

"What did you just do?" one of the Gardeners nearby exclaimed as they rushed over to check on the 'fruit.' I did my best to explain, having Smegma explain some of the process as I went. Unfortunately, none of the other Gardeners had any idea how to control their Mana yet, but Smegma assured me that the Tree would pull Mana from the air and have a high probability of accepting a transplant of more Grackles every five minutes.

When I was done, I showed the group currently tackling this Bush how to make the cuts to a Sapling, and the matching ones on the Grackle. Then, Smegma had me move onto what he called a KnuckleNut, which was also abundant on this Tree. As I moved to gather it, one of the Gardeners held up a hand above my shears.

"Don't bother. Those aren't worth much," he explained when I looked at him.

"Idiots! All of you humans are morons. KnuckleNuts can increase Demon's skin thickness and density over time. They only work up to the E-Rank, but they have a great deal of value!"

"Thanks for your advice, but if prepared properly, these Nuts can improve skin density and strength," I explained to the man. He lowered his hand, simultaneously giving me a stare that questioned my sanity.

I moved to bite my nail as I realized I had no way of explaining how I knew that. A glance at Alexus showed she was staring at me and intently listening to the interaction. It was too late now, so I doubled down and followed Smegma's instructions as I moved to cut clusters of the Nuts. This time, we didn't fix them to the Sapling and instead placed them in the soil around the Tree.

We also didn't have to make any specialized cuts, making the harvest of the Nuts far faster than the Grackle. I showed the Gardeners the method and explained that buried KnuckleNuts—

"They are called Farells. Are you sure you're thinking of the same Nut?" the same Gardener who'd nearly stopped me corrected my explanation.

"Yep. Yep. Sorry, I know them by a different name!" I blurted.

For the next thirty minutes, I moved around the clearing and showed Smegma's instructions to the workers. I was sure I was drawing a great deal of suspicion with each piece of knowledge I 'showed off,' but there was nothing I could do. Thankfully, Jagger's group had been brought to a different clearing.

I still had at least fourteen other visible Plants to address when Smegma vanished. I groaned, knowing what was happening. I had just picked up a new Skill—likely something to do with Gardening. A quick peek at my Mental Universe confirmed it.

After some deliberation, I announced, "That's all I have time to show you today. I'm going to go join the Cleaners now. Keep working as hard as you can. I'll send back some lunch later."

I placed my Sapling with the fused Grackle, Versail Leaves, Basilia, Ocean Grass, Eden Root, Witch Hazel, Wizard Bark, Yellow Gardle, and buried KnuckleNuts to the side for someone to collect, unwilling to walk around and find the Gardener with the Bag of Holding. I'd put it in my Necklace if it wouldn't kill the thing instantly. I then turned to Alexus and grumbled, "Could you take me to the Cleaners now."

Grumbling was the only way I could control my volume and somewhat keep my dislike of the woman out of my voice. Still, the two currently aware Mana Banks caught my tone and frowned at me.

"What's your problem?!" one of the two asked, no longer able to contain her frustration with my tone and where I was directing it.

"My problem?" I questioned right back, my tone now joined by volume. Unfortunately, we were right in the center of the clearing, so everyone heard. As if Smegma could somehow hear me husking up while making a Skill in my Mental Universe, he popped back into existence at my side.

"Kid, don't do this!" Smegma shouted in my ear, only taking a split second to put together the situation. But I ignored him.

"*My problem?*" I repeated, adding even more distaste to my words as I indicated Eva. "*She's* my problem. I met Eva at a photoshoot a few months ago! She was lively, energetic and healthy!"

I paused to suck in a breath. Eva seemed to rouse herself for a moment, looking at me with confusion in her eyes. Her lack of recognition only fueled my anger as it boiled over the controls *Mental Fortitude* put in place.

"Now look at her. She's a shell of her former self! You think I can just stand here while a Greed takes advantage of her?"

To my utter surprise, Alexus smiled sadly and moved to Eva. What she did next quelled my anger like a hot plate getting dunked into water. Alexus gently raised Eva's chin to meet her eyes and coaxed softly, "Eva, did you hear that? This man knows you. Do you remember him?"

I stood stock still, at an utter loss at the disparity between Eva's appearance and my assumptions and Alexus' words. What in the husk was going on?

Something hit me in the cheek, and because of the surprise, I tightened my neck muscles, not moving at all as one of the other Banks slapped me. It was the one who had spoken out, and she had tears in her eyes. In a whisper, she hissed, "Let's move away from here and not put my sister on display!"

The others, including Alexus, nodded, and the Hunter helped guide a still-confused Eva to follow. It took me several moments to even register the request and a few more long seconds to actually relax my tense muscles.

"I told you, kid. You should have left it alone. Now, you've got a horn in your mouth," Smegma said quietly.

[What is going on?] I asked, wanting an explanation.

"Follow them. You'll figure it out."

That got me finally moving, but thanks to Eva's slow speed while being guided, I didn't have to even jog to catch the four women. Once we were far enough away, the person leading the procession—the Mana Bank who'd slapped me—found a large, flat stone and we stopped.

Eva was lowered onto the rock by Alexus, and the Mana Bank spun on me.

"How *dare* you say that word in front of her without all the information. You stupid little boy! Eva was just getting better and now look at her."

Sure enough, Eva was shaking as Alexus held her. Any remaining spark of anger fled in that moment, and I felt like a cooling hot air balloon. I'd clearly misread the situation—and made it worse.

CHAPTER 40: CHAPTER 92

Saturday, May 4th, 2069

"Stop it, Dana!" Alexus said as the woman who'd just slapped me seemed to square up in preparation to fight me. I went as far as to purposefully place my hands in my pockets to show I wasn't going to fight back. I realized now that I had made some terrible assumptions.

And in this case, I'd really put the *ass* in the word.

"You can't fault him for caring for a friend. Wouldn't you want someone to speak up if they saw this situation?" Alexus continued. To my surprise, Dana's reddening face and wide, wild eyes vanished, almost like they'd never been there. Her shade even went slightly white.

"I'm sorry. She's right, but for you to accuse *Alex*," Dana whispered her apology but then regained a bit of heat as she explained herself.

"I realize now that I've made a terrible mistake," I said. "Still, I don't like seeing Eva like that. Can you explain what's happened?"

"Dana, come look after Eva," Alexus said, not letting the young, skeletal woman go until Dana followed her instructions and took her place. The other Mana Bank moved over and did the same.

Only then did Alexus stand up and move to stand with me. "I'm sorry for Dana, she's… very protective of me. You see, Eva isn't the only Mana Bank I've rehabbed from similar situations."

My anger flared again as my eyes grew wider. This had happened to others and Alexus was involved—

"Now, there you go assuming again," she said with a bit of a chuckle, and I shook off the rising surge in large parts because of her soft, understanding tone. "Sometimes, the first Mana Pull from a Bank can cause… issues," Alexus explained. "In Eva's case, she contracted with a member of Garneau in Toronto, and her Mana Pool cracked—"

"Ohhhh!" Smegma interrupted, and my head jerked to his position. He was studying the interactions between the three Mana Banks.

I was the only one who heard him, but my strange head jerk alarmed Alexus enough that she spun with a hand on her wand. She performed a thorough scan before asking over her shoulder, "What is it?"

"Uhh, my bad. I thought I heard something…" I lied—well, kind of—I *had* indeed heard something. I wanted nothing more than to interrogate Smegma since he seemed to know something more about Eva's condition, but instead, I let Alexus turn back to me and continue.

"As I was saying, when a Mana Pool cracks, it's like a fragile glass of water. It may leak, or it may not, but continued use will definitely make the problem worse. In Eva's case, the Mana is 'leaking,' causing her to feel physically ill. She has barely kept food down, and I had put her on an IV until recently. But the good news is that the Mana Leak has grown smaller now, and in time, like Dana and Lauren, it can heal."

"Uhh, what's this 'in time,' Felhound Feces? Is she just another example of how all you humans are idiots? You could fix her right now!" Smegma scoffed indignantly.

My heart began hammering in my chest as I sucked in a deep lungful of air. After a blink, I found Alexus looking at me like I was not reacting normally. I deliberated on what to do for a split second longer, before sighing out an exhalation. Revealing what Smegma had just told me could raise questions, but this was Eva.

"I think I can fix her," I whispered.

"*Fix her?*" Dana shouted, clearly being riled up again. "She's not a broken toy, asshole."

"No!" I raised my hands, shaking them back and forth. "That's not—I mean, not *her*. I meant—her Mana Pool."

"What?!" Lauren, the redheaded Mana Bank, exclaimed as she shot to her feet. Alexus' look had morphed into one of clear suspicion, and perhaps more telling—her hand had moved to her wand on her hip again. I scanned down to the wand and tried to figure out why she needed the wand and a staff.

Why was that important?

"A wand wielder will likely blast you to pieces, whereas a staff wielder will only bludgeon you to death," Smegma answered, and I gulped. What if she cast spells with both objects?

"Unlikely," Smegma began. "She probably has the staff to ward off Monsters if they come too close."

My reaction caused Alexus to realize what she was doing—and to a man who still had his hands in his pockets. She quickly let go of her *wand*. I refused to think of her blowing me to pieces after Smegma's words.

"I've visited thousands of the top Alchemists, Healers and other Experts in the past. Everyone said the only cure was *time*. So, you can excuse Lauren's and my reaction to your words. I know she is your friend, so, I'll let you take it back if you have some half-cocked idea. I'll also let you know that I'll kill you if your idea hurts her!"

Lauren and Dana were glaring at me from beside Eva, and Alexus was glaring *daggers* from a foot away. Mentally, I screamed at the Demon for not immediately offering me the method. I rather liked being alive and having all my limbs.

[Smegma!]

"What? I want to see if she'll actually blow you up," Smegma stated. "You know—for science." And he actually sounded like he meant it.

[If I die, don't you die, asshat?]

"Well, not exac—"

I mentally 'glared' at the Demon.

"Fine—fine. It isn't anything super special. First, you'll need to Cook her a meal with high calories, 'cause what we're about to do is going to take a lot out of her—"

[You do recall that she can barely keep food down?!]

"Oh really?" Smegma asked, his voice dripping with sarcasm. "I thought she just liked the anemic look. Now shut up and husking listen.

"Next, you'll need to mix the KnuckleNut and Sea Grass into a paste. For that, you'll need her *exact* weight—because too much or too little will cause… *issues*. And third, you'll need to apply constant *Healing* and *Cleansing* to deal with the slight poison that KnuckleNut and Sea Grass will create."

[You do realize that these three women aren't going to believe a word I say, right? How am I going to convince them to let me feed her an unknown mixture of Portal Herbs while claiming it's only *somewhat* poisonous.]

"You should probably say something to the women first. You've been silent for about thirty seconds, and I do think that's a *castrating wand* the more I look at it."

My paling face caused Smegma to howl with laughter.

I pulled a hand out of my pocket to scratch at the back of my neck. "I do have a method to heal her. I'm just trying to come up with a way to make it safer."

"Yeah, no!" Alexus exclaimed, her voice barbed. "Dana, Lauren, take care of Eva. Let's escort this *idiot* to the Cleaners."

With that, Alexus simply began walking away, and so did Dana and Lauren, with Eva supported between them. I stood still for a moment before deciding that I would follow from a distance that might make them feel like I wasn't about to try to force some sort of strange healing method onto one of their numbers.

I'd really messed this up.

"There *is* another option," Smegma said from near my shoulder.

[What's that?] I asked, truly curious.

"If you get an Alchemical Pill Cauldron, we can create a much better Pill by burning off the toxins and poison in the KnuckleNut and Sea Grass. However, since you have next to no experience in that—I doubt you'd succeed, which was why I offered the other alternative that could heal her today."

I had Smegma explain more about an Alchemical Pill Cauldron and how it worked as I walked behind my escorts. The way he described the process sounded highly theoretical, using generalized terms, which told me he didn't have any actual experience in the method. It brought into perspective a few things. Smegma had been a researcher with the Abyss Sect, and he had a great deal of knowledge—but it was mostly theoretical. He did say that he'd had real-world experience inside of Portals, but it seemed like the rest may be 'book smarts' at best.

For example—the Gardening tips I'd handed out and performed this morning. Smegma likely had never performed those tasks himself but had read about or studied them. Thinking about it that way caused me to shiver. Our time in the caverns negotiating with Nagina, the massive Universe-Eating-Snake-thing, had been him acting as a leader with minimal actual experience…

Just how badly that could have gone became apparent enough that I fixated on it until Smegma said, "Stop it, moron. Just because I learned things from a book doesn't mean I don't know it. Also, at least I've actually *learned* it— you have no clue!"

Any response I might have given fled as we exited the Trees into a clearing. Not a System-created clearing, like the Gardening one. This clearing was Hunter made. Well, Hunter and Monster made. I froze, staring first at the destruction of the massive Trees, which were reduced to splinters, kindling, and campfire-sized segments.

But then my eyes crossed over numerous mounds of flesh, and once my brain realized what I was looking at, I couldn't look away.

My eyes were frozen on a mound. It wasn't the largest mound I'd seen, but it was the only one that had the Monster's face pointed in my direction. I swallowed when I put together the hills of flesh with what they actually were. Some sort of Pig?

No, maybe a Porcupine?

Hedgehog?

Either way, they *stood* three meters tall with their legs broken and collapsed beneath them. There were sparse quills intermingled along their backs, and they seemed to have the heads of predatory canines. Not only did they have a mouthful of fangs, but they also had elongated snouts that were meant to rip and tear.

"Ahh, Gwyls," Smegma said. "I thought your people said this was a D-Rank Portal?"

"Uhh—what?" I answered, accidentally forgetting to keep my question internal.

"Porcu-hogs," Alexus said. "Frickin' pain to deal with. They shoot those quills out at high speed from range, before charging in to fight like wolves amongst the sheep. The only good news is that they have tough Hides and good-tasting Meat!"

"Yes on the Meat," Smegma retorted. "*Hell no* on being a pain to deal with. These are F-Ranked Gwyls. They bombard you from range and then charge in stupidly—fighting by themselves mostly. They have no tactics or pack dynamics and are relatively easy to deal with—other than a slightly high defense and strength."

My brain felt like it was short circuiting. Why would Smegma claim they were F-Rank, while Alexus was clearly describing the difficulties of the fight as a D-Rank Hunter? Plus, this was definitely classed as a D-Rank Portal by the UNMH. I thought back on that and nodded, recalling our first-semester classes discussing Porcu-hogs. They were low D-Rank but still D-Rank.

Smegma heard my thoughts and floated over to one creature. He began hovering around the body as he tapped talon to tooth. "Maybe the System upgraded them since my time?"

That simple explanation allowed my brain to stop frying itself with the worries I'd had. It would have been bad if humanity was fighting relatively low-ranked creatures and overestimating their strength…

Smegma's nearness to the corpse also unfroze my locked legs, and I began walking forward to examine it as well. Crossing over the sawdust and splinters eventually brought the nine Cleaners into view. They'd broken into three groups. Two of four, and Dave.

My eyes narrowed, thinking they'd excluded Dave because of his lack of experience. However, the three Cleaned skeletons of Porcu-hogs in his direction told the actual story. I smiled. *Cut* was revealing its worth.

I changed my course, moving toward Dave, who had seen me and was waving in my direction. I figured studying one corpse would be the same as another.

"This *Cut* Skill is husking epic, Bro!" Dave shouted in greeting. I winced, but he clearly didn't see it because he continued, "Thanks for giving it to me!"

Husking idiot!

"You were definitely lucky to *re-Awaken it*," I answered pointedly. Dave blinked for a moment and then saw the women that were eyeing him and me with a great deal of suspicion.

"Oh, right! Of course, that's what I meant. Like, getting stuck down in that cave may be the best thing that happened to us—ouch!" Dave said. His ending was because I punched him in the arm.

"So, how is the *Cleaning* going?" I asked, changing the subject.

"Good. Great, actually," Dave answered, holding up his clearly much-repaired Skinning Knife. "The others are working in groups to get the hang of it, but as you can see, they're moving faster and faster." With the Knife held up, it was clear what he was insinuating.

"Okay, well, who has the Bag?" I asked as a follow up. It would be a good idea to Cook some food for them before I joined. Plus, if I could Heal each one of them in a subtle way—that would relieve a great deal of fatigue and go a long way to helping us meet or exceed the quota.

"I do," Dave said and pointed to the Bag of Holding. "There're some really interesting cuts of Meat that come out of these big things. Still, I would say Cook the Loins or—"

"The Hearts," Smegma interjected. "If you Cook the Hearts with some minced Grackle, it will give everyone who eats it a great deal of Stamina."

[Not that I'm disagreeing, but you do remember humans don't have Stamina or Martial Power, right?]

"It should still do *something*," Smegma said. Dave had stopped talking at some point, recognizing my distracted look. When I blinked and looked back, he smiled.

"What are *you* planning to Cook?"

"The Hearts," I answered, and his smile grew even broader.

"Awesome—there's five in there, and they're each about the size of my head."

"You're planning to cook?" Alexus interjected into our conversation.

I nodded distractedly as I moved to the Bag.

"You do realize that a fire will attract Monsters if they're still out there, right?" she added, sounding very similar to my reminder to Smegma a moment before.

I blinked and then looked her way sheepishly. Her eyes narrowed slightly at my expression. It was probably clear I wasn't going to give up on cooking that easily. She sighed. "Okay, let me warn the guards, but you better give us some too!"

It was my turn to sigh but in relief. Food of this quality would help my workers keep working and hopefully beat out P-Squared. That and my Healing.

We needed to prove to Lynx that we could keep up—or Jagger would likely take any new contracts after our current backlog ran out and our reputation was put in the dirt.

Once I had the Bag of Holding, I used it and my Necklace of Holding to gather up sawdust, kindling and appropriate-sized logs. Then, using a simple lighter, I worked at the somewhat damp sawdust until it caught.

I'd chosen to build the fire in a pit that had either been where one of the Porcu-hogs had fallen or where one of the Lynx's Skills had carved out the underbrush and Trees to a depth of probably three feet. The crater was about ten feet wide, so whoever created it had impressive power.

I let the fire build and moved back to Dave. I needed to help the Cleaners as the fire built up some coals to cook on. Dave was knowledgeable on what he was doing—but unhelpful.

His *Cut* Skill just required him to envision where he wanted to slice, and then have Mana supplied, and it happened. Since he had one of our three Mana Batteries—he could make a single *Cut* and carve off the entire Hide.

I needed to understand how to work at the Hide in small sections. I was about to join the other Cleaners when Smegma said, "Go to that one over there. I'll help like I did with the Gardening."

My moment of hesitation was apparent, probably because he read my thoughts.

"Book knowledge is better than no knowledge. Now, get over to that one.

"Start by removing any remaining quills," Smegma began, and for the next hour, I worked under his direction. At some point he vanished for a few minutes and returned. When he popped back beside me, he simply answered, "New Skill, probably Skinning…"

It turned out that, once again, he was quite an adept teacher—and it was also apparent that my Stats and perhaps new Skill were immensely useful. When the hour finished, I had cut away one shoulder of the Porcu-hog, but I was simultaneously speeding up as the Knife gained sharpness and became denser while still maintaining flexibility.

Still, I took a quick break to add to the fire and check on the progress of the coals. I estimated another thirty to forty-five minutes would reduce the new logs and the remaining ones to coals, and then I could Cook.

That time passed in a near blink to me as I cleared the other half of my Porcu-hog's body. Part of me wanted to continue to see if I'd get guiding lines like Mining soon but I also needed to get to Cooking.

There was just one issue. I looked down at my hands, arms, and clothes. They were all covered in blood. Dave sidled up beside me and noticed my scrutiny. "Wash station is over there. You about to get Cooking?"

I nodded at him and he smiled.

"Good, I was getting husking hungry! I'll finish this hog up for you. Now, get your ass over there!"

My smile was short-lived because Dave made one single *Cut* and finished skinning the hog I'd been working on for the better part of two hours. I looked down to my much-improved Knife, my *Mental Fortitude* somewhat counteracting my jealousy by reminding me that my work had accomplished something.

My Skinning Knife was, of course, covered in blood like my hands. But it had also undergone a great deal of change. The most noticeable of which was the tang and hilt. It was something I hadn't been able to see when Dave had proffered his much-repaired Skinning Knife because of his holding it.

The leather or wooden wrapping had become what it likely was meant to be—a combination of the two. There was now a wooden handle, clearly carved to conform to a grip, and there was a leather wrap that kept the blade handle from slipping, even when drenched in blood.

The leather may have even been some sort of plant because it was porous and squishy in my fingers, allowing me to change its shape easily with my grip. The Knife was the first thing I cleaned when I got to the buckets of water. The station was comprised of a barrel-sized bucket of water and then two other buckets, one that was slightly red with blood already but clearly intended for an initial clean off before you used the second bucket to grab a portion from the large barrel.

The leather or twine grip of my knife didn't become distinguishable, even after a good cleaning, but the blade and edge sure shone now. After cleaning off my arms in the now very red water, I grabbed the other bucket, emptied the initial one, and refilled both.

Then I used the initial bucket for another secondary clean of my clothes and arms, before using the other one and a handful of grass to scrub away at any lingering stains. My clothes would never be the brown they'd started as, again, but I didn't care.

Once finished, I moved to the fire pit, which was now just a bed of coals. I pulled out the Frying Pans from my Necklace and the Grackle Fruit. Using the backside of a Frying Pan as a cutting board, I first harvested the Grackle and then broke it into bulbs—all under Smegma's directions.

"Skin the bulbs and set them aside. You'll want to dice and cook them as a side."

I did so.

"Mince the meat of the Fruit. Smaller and thinner. Good! Cut the Heart into half-inch or smaller sized shavings."

I gave him a confused look and Smegma added, "You're essentially looking to create bacon but like that odd-looking Canadian version."

I rolled my eyes. How had the Demon picked up on that sore spot of Canadian Back Bacon? Still, I did as instructed, having to cut the Heart into eight sections to be able to get my Knife to pass through it as intended. When I was finished, Smegma continued, "Sauté the skin first, until the smell of the Grackle goes from sweet to slightly tangy."

I inhaled deeply, not realizing just how much of a fragrant aroma my butchery of the Grackle Fruit had immersed the area in. The smell from the harvest and subsequent grafting paled in comparison. This was to that like a fairground's fresh cotton candy was to the bags opened from a store. There simply *was* no comparison.

274

Still, I added the sliced skins of the Grackle to the heated Huge Frying Pan, and thirty seconds after, I smelled the change. It was akin to the fragrant aroma of caramelized onions, only in reverse. Following Smegma's direction, I spread out the skins and then placed the Heart Meat atop it.

I only could fit about a quarter of the Meat into the Pan, but clearly Smegma didn't want me to cook on multiple Pans or he'd have directed me to split the skin.

"Add the minced fruit atop each piece and then flip them after five minutes."

My mouth began to water as the caramelized Grackle tang was joined by a rich aroma of pork fat. It was similar to bacon but also not. The exact aroma was difficult to describe because I'd never smelled something so wonderful before, but if I had to try—I'd say it was like a barbecued steak that was wrapped in sizzling bacon while a controlled fire sizzled from the drippings beneath.

I sucked in my drool as I flipped the pieces, causing the Pan to hiss and sizzle as the juices of the minced fruit attempted to cook to the metal but failed. The smell became mesmerizing, morphing from the best barbecue aroma to something only gods should smell.

My eyes were glued to the bubbling fats and juices beside the Meat, so when I heard a noise from the lip of the crater, I jumped. All of the Hunters and Cleaners had ringed the edge. A few wiped drool from their chins, which made me realize I, too, had some saliva to take care of.

[Thanks for warning me about the audience,] I said jokingly to Smegma to distract myself. When I got no response, I looked around and found my Demon missing. A quick peek in my Mental Universe found a newly forming planet—

Wait—that's not a single planet—and there's another beside the one that I had assumed was *Gardening*!

CHAPTER 41: CHAPTER 93

Saturday, May 4th, 2069

The mystery of my new Skills—possibly four of them in total—both intrigued and worried me. Intrigued, because if the Skills acted like *Mining, Cooking* or *Fishing,* I would unlock a new Stat—in this case, multiple Stats. That thought gave me pause. Surely these four wouldn't unlock my final four Locked Stats, right?

Meaning I would most likely be *doubling up* on some.

I shook off my tangent and returned to considering my worry. Why was I worried? For the obvious reason—Smegma claimed Skills inherently came with limits, and filling up on all these 'Blue-Collar' Skills wouldn't be good in the long run.

Warm drool leaking from my mouth reminded me of the cooking food, and I hurriedly removed it from the Pan. I then waited, letting it rest while I crossed my fingers and hoped Smegma would return before the Cleaners and Hunters ringing the crater decided they couldn't wait any longer.

I would totally understand that sentiment too. It felt like *Mental Fortitude* was the only reason I wasn't immediately devouring each piece of Porcu-hog Heart Bacon with sautéed Grackle!

"Uhh did you see the new—" Smegma said as he popped back into existence.

[Yep! If I get some privacy, I'll try to activate a Spent Mana Crystal, but right now, I need some instructions.]

Smegma scanned the ringed crater before turning back to me. "This isn't like the Mirror Fish. It isn't high in calories and isn't soporific. Still, the medicinal effect should occur even if people just have a small taste. Since we don't have any more Grackles without returning to the Gardeners—cut it up into eighty portions."

My eyes began making the cuts, and I frowned. [That will only leave about four ounces of Meat per person.]

"I know you've got to be thinking with your own stomach right now, dumbass. You can just Cook more *without* the Grackle to fill them up," Smegma retorted, his voice sounding almost jealous. "Right now, all you should be caring about is that everyone gets the buff from eating this recipe. You can fill up bellies later."

Maybe he remembers what this tastes like—

"Stop it, and just start portioning!" Smegma ordered.

Thankfully, my eyes met Dave's. He became the first one to break his drooling stupor to advance on the food. If *I* portioned this food, it would likely be uneven—but—

"Dave, can you turn this into eighty even portions, including the Grackle mince equally with each piece?"

My words caused him to start, and his unfocused eyes blinked a few times as he registered the words. I realized then that he had been intending to devour the food, as the aroma from the resting Meat only grew more succulent. He nodded, even as he clenched his jaw and wiped his chin.

His breathing was forced through clenched teeth in loud hisses. Seeing the impending disaster of the nearby observers and small portions, I began Cooking more of the Heart Bacon. Thanks to his *Cut* Skill, it didn't take longer than a few seconds to portion, which of course brought us to our next issue.

Dave was barely keeping himself back from devouring the entirety of the pork. How could I hand it out—

"Form a line!" Alexus shouted. "Food will be handed to each of you individually." Her words had a very small effect as the Hunters on guard began to move. Even Dana, Lauren, and Eva—her own Mana Banks—didn't budge. "*Hunters,*" she tried again, her voice firmer. "Get everyone in line!"

Alexus then followed her own orders and immediately began grabbing the people closest to her. The first two Cleaners she grabbed blinked and began moving as instructed, as if they'd woken from a pleasant daydream. The third, she had to forcibly manhandle.

Dana, Lauren, and Eva were thankfully of the first category of people. I turned to Dave. "Will it be more helpful to abstain from eating a piece or have one now?"

His jaw clenched tighter, and his hissing breath intensified, but he did manage to get out a head shake. That told me quite a bit and Smegma realized it too.

The Demon muttered, "Shoot, I didn't think this would have such a profound effect on people."

[Why would the Hunters be less affected?] I asked, already considering one possibility.

"What you're thinking right now is part of it—they've had training to overcome fear and other emotions in battle. However, the more prevalent part is likely they've had food of similar quality before. The Cleaners, Miners and Gardeners you brought likely haven't even been near Portal Food of this quality before."

[But humans eat Monster Meats on a daily basis?]

"Sure, you all eat F-Ranked Monster Meat, but not only is it the poorest cuts, from what I've seen your family eat—it also isn't prepared with a D-Rank Portal Fruit."

[So, I just spent a great deal of expensive Materials on one meal?] I asked.

"No clue. I can tell you that *Demonic Vault* and my Abyss Sect would have given you ten Mana Coins for the Grackle and a hundred for each Heart. What you humans would have paid is unknown to me."

I looked at Alexus, who was near the front of the line of Cleaners and Mana Banks. I motioned for her to come over and she misunderstood, bringing the first person in line with her. That first person was Eva though, which made me somewhat happy.

I quickly flipped the Heart Meat I was currently cooking in the Frying Pan, and was dexterous enough that I finished and met Alexus and Eva as they crossed the eight feet of crater to the coal pit. Then I stood there dumbly, wondering if I should let Eva take a portion for herself or hand her one.

It wasn't like I had thought to bring disposable plates or even napkins. Even Smegma didn't berate me with his usual snark. I guessed he couldn't, considering we'd come right from signing papers that had bought us P-Cubed.

Eva solved the problem by tentatively snatching herself a piece. It was in her mouth before anyone thought to react—but Alexus solved a further problem by physically escorting her away with the mouthful of food.

That then became the procedure for the next twenty people who came by to grab a bite. It gave me no time to ask Alexus my intended question about prices, until the twenty Cleaners and Mana Banks had each taken a portion. Only then did the five Hunters come forward to also have a much-earned piece.

The rich aroma had faded at that point, which allowed Dave to calmly take a piece and move off to join the other Cleaners and Banks with larger chunks of the Heart Bacon without the Grackle. He carried these pieces inside one of the smaller Pans that I'd acquired when we needed to cook the one hundred Mirror Fish or risk death.

Alexus eyed the food, and then me, not taking a portion for herself. A glance over at Eva told me why. She was thinking of giving a second helping to her Mana Bank. This, beyond everything else that had happened, made it even more clear to me just how much Alexus cared for her Mana Banks.

She was a true Selfless, which only made my earlier accusation of her being a Greed more embarrassing.

"Dave's handing out additional portions without the Grackle Fruit," I whispered, my cheeks red. I could barely meet her eyes as she regarded me once more.

"The what now?"

I motioned to the top of each of the Ham slices. She narrowed her eyes and took a piece for closer inspection. She looked at the minced pieces that had adhered to the Meat, and the caramelized skin that had been placed atop each portion. "The *Amaranthine Fruit?*"

"Yeah," I answered with a shrug—again realizing that my naming schemes were coming from a very unreliable source.

"Hey, I'm right here," Smegma said.

"I don't think I've ever seen that reaction to food before," Alexus admitted as she seemed to oscillate between eating the food and questioning me. She decided on the former and popped it into her mouth. A hum of appreciation came from her. "Mmmm. It melts on your tongue! You know, with skills like that, you could likely be a chef in a top restaurant, right?" She shook herself, seeming to get back on track, but then asked another question about the food. "What did you do to the Meat for the tenderizing effect?"

My brain was completely blank. I hadn't done anything to achieve that— not really. Not knowing what she meant, I suggested, "Maybe it's just the quality of the meat?"

"What did you use?"

278

"Porcu-hog Heart," I admitted sheepishly.

She scoffed loudly, and then started laughing. "Good one." I watched as her eyes narrowed in true suspicion. "Wait—was that the Tenderloin Medallions? You know each Hog only has a single portion of about two pounds. If you used that—"

I held up both hands and waved them furiously. I hurriedly said, "I didn't use the—*Tenderloin Medallions*—"

She looked at me pointedly even as I regarded her. Considering her reaction to my admission of using Heart Meat, I scanned up the crater to the people eating, or rather, choosing *not* to eat the second portion of Heart Meat that Dave offered. The only ones who were eating looked like they were chewing through shoe leather.

"Grackle has a tenderizing effect on certain Meats," Smegma explained, a bit too sagely, and definitely too late.

[You couldn't have said that earlier!]

"I'm unreliable, remember?"

Even as my muscles threatened to tense in frustration at the Demon, I motioned up at the people eating. "I can assure you it's Heart Meat. *Amaranthine Fruit* can tenderize tough Meats."

"No, it can't. Amaranthine Fruit is a great snack for anti-cramping and is often used in Alchemy to produce cures for Petrification—" it dawned on her, and me, the moment she started saying the Potion's name and Fruit's effects. Anti-cramping and Petrification Cures could both be considered softening of something hard or tough.

She undid her ponytail, finger-brushed it out, and then retied it, clearly thinking as she worked. Then, just to confirm what I said, she grabbed a portion of the cooked Heart Meat without the Grac—Amaranthine Fruit. Her jaw worked overtime to part the Meat, but she did force it down after some excessive chewing, which was more than I could say about the people behind her.

Still, her reaction answered one of my earlier unvoiced questions without meaning to. Clearly, Heart Meat wasn't the choicest of cut, at least not for humans. That didn't mean it was worthless, but at least I was less likely to cause problems using it. Unlike the Tenderloin Medallions, apparently…

I really hoped my crew was keeping those in peak quality.

My stomach unknotted, and I took a piece for myself. As soon as I placed it into my mouth, I felt the melting sensation she'd described. It wasn't actually melting, so much as my entire mouth was salivating to the extreme and my tongue pressing it into the roof of my mouth as it spasmed.

The combination was enough to separate the fibers of the Meat and turn it into a paste, drenched in my now highly flavorful saliva. I swallowed convulsively, eyeing the portions. I wanted to snatch four more pieces, but a red screen—that was now blocking the other portions from view—and *Mental Fortitude* stopped me.

You have consumed a Well-Cooked Meal made by a Professional. Your Stamina Stat has increased by 1 for eight hours. [Locked] will regenerate at an increased rate for eight hours.

My unfocused eyes, or what likely looked like unfocused eyes to others, caused Alexus to put a hand on my bicep. "Are you okay?"

I shook myself and nodded, glancing at Smegma as I scanned back to Alexus. He was smiling broadly. He smugly said, "Ask Alexus if she feels different?"

"How are you feeling?" I dutifully said.

"Good, why are you—huh—actually, now that you mention it, I feel *really* good. Almost like I didn't fight in this Portal the last few days!" she answered. Smegma's smile grew broader.

"That's what we're going for," Smegma crowed. "Now, hurry up and Heal all of your workers so we can go deliver this to the other groups, and kick Jagger's ass."

CHAPTER 42: CHAPTER 94

Saturday, May 4th, 2069

It definitely wasn't as simple as Smegma made it sound—to subtly *Heal* each Cleaner. Even excusing myself from the ongoing conversation with Alexus became impossible. She followed me as I moved away. Despite me carrying the still-hot Frying Pan, covering the portions. I then went to 'check on' each member of my company.

"What are you worried about?" she asked as I climbed the eight feet out of the crater.

"Well, we're trying to beat P-Squared, but we have less than half their numbers," I answered, looking back at the unattended portions of food. "Do you think you could keep an eye on the food? I'll be right back, and then I need to be escorted to the other groups again."

"Jorri, Masvidal, can you two come guard the leftover portions?" Alexus ordered and two of the guards jumped to follow her instructions. "Do you offer this kind of food to the workers every day?"

"We're a new company, so I can't say we offer it every day... Or rather, I suppose I *could* say that since it's only been the one day." I chuckled. "But I'm not sure I can always do so going forward. For jobs like this though, where we have an abundance of Materials and cuts of Meat that might otherwise get left in the Portal? I don't see why not." I answered as I motioned at Dave to come over.

"So, this is something that you're doing to motivate your employees to work harder?" Alexus assessed.

"Yeah, that's it," I said a bit too slowly, which caused Alexus to narrow her eyes. Thankfully, Dave's arrival saved further questions. I hurriedly grabbed his hand and gave it a shake. "I know you're doing a great deal of the work, so thank you. How are you *feeling*, though?"

Dave got my not-so-subtle hint. As did Alexus. Her eyes narrowed further, and she studied me and our handshake pointedly. Thankfully, my *Minor Heal,* which was being applied through our palms, wasn't very noticeable. Not with the sun so bright. The slight redness to my hand and Dave's from the glow hopefully just looked like increased blood flow.

"I'm good," Dave answered. I could keep at this all day. He shook my hand back as more of my Mana went into his body. "I should thank you for that meal. I'm sure all the others will do the same! Boy, was that good!"

I smiled broadly, partially at the compliment, but mostly at the Skill finishing after four drops of my Mana had been converted. "You're welcome. I'm going to run through here and check on everyone."

Dave nodded and then released my hand. My eyes found the closest Cleaner, and I moved to them. "Hey, just wanting to check in," I called with a wave. The woman turned to regard me with evident confusion in her eyes, but before she voiced it, I grabbed her hand in a forced shake. "I just want to thank you for joining our company instead of Jagger's. How are you finding the first day?"

"Umm—well—that food was certainly something I'd never have gotten with Jagger?" she said, seeming to question what answer would satisfy me and get her hand back. I felt my embarrassment at the forced handshake swell, before something changed. Her eyes lit up, and I forcibly stopped my hand from squeezing. This was going to get out eventually, anyway. "The equipment is repairing itself, just like you said it would! Look!"

She held up her Skinning Knife, and it was leagues better than it had been. There was even a hint of the point gaining a deadly look, the backside becoming serrated, and perhaps a hook forming below the handle. My *Minor Heal* finished, and I held out my hand as I asked, "May I see it?"

She hurried to hand it to me. "Absolutely. It's the company's, not mine!"

I chuckled to ease the worry I heard in her voice. "Not to worry, I just wanted to see its shape. Mine hasn't repaired anywhere near as much."

I showed her my Knife, which had a bit of the handle and blade repaired, as I turned her Knife over in my other palm. My peripherals tracked Alexus as she leaned forward, clearly interested.

Intelligence Increased by 1.
Intelligence Stat Unlocked.

Stats
Strength: 10
Locked.
Stamina: 10 (+1)
Intelligence: 2
Locked.
Dexterity: 10
Locked.

The Stat unlocking made me flinch and accidentally knick myself with the blade in my hand. I hissed and felt two hands from two different people suddenly on my forearm and another on my back.

Both women asked, "Are you okay?"

"Yep, I was just checking its sharpness," I said and quickly proffered the small cut in their direction before it could Heal from my passive *Recovery*. "Thanks…"

I faded off, not knowing the woman's name. She didn't get my hint, and instead of making it more awkward, I handed back the Knife and moved on.

[Smegma, why are my Stats not increasing past ten?]

"There's a bunch of reasons—but most likely?" Smegma asked rhetorically, even as I heard his talon start tapping his tooth. I reached the next Cleaner and performed the same song and dance while shaking his hand and

Healing. "Ten is the Card level between Peak-F and low E. So, I'm guessing you need to find a way to Evolve or breakthrough? How that will work, I don't know. However, it could be a unique encounter like the Golem…"

[Same with my Mana at fifty?] I asked.

"That one is strange. Since it's part of a Skill that is B-Rank. I've actually been wondering if Dragon Heart is a true Mana Pool…"

[What?!] I mentally exclaimed, even as I finished another awkward forced handshake and healed another Cleaner. That thought surprised me. How could it not be a Mana Pool? It gave me Mana, didn't it?

"It's just a thought, but would you, for example, be able to get yourself a second Mana Pool Skill? Normally, us Demons could only have a single 'Mana' Card in our Heart Decks. However, *Dragon Heart* has no Mana distinction in its name. It could theoretically be a secondary Pool."

[And what, getting an actual Mana Pool Skill could be the key to breaking through the fifty-point cap?] I confusedly recapped.

"No idea. I'm just throwing out theories. If Mana Pools weren't so expensive in the *Demonic Vault Shop*, I'd suggest trying it out."

That gave me a lot to think about as I continued my awkward handshakes. One of the Cleaners even saw what was happening to all the others, and seemed to desperately look for a way to escape before the owner's son shook his hand. Still, I managed to make it through the final five Cleaners. Each worker took about two Mana to 'wipe away fatigue,' as Smegma called the *Minor Healing* I was doing. Then I was ready to move on.

Smegma floated in front of me as I carried the double-stacked Frying Pans with the food inside. Alexus was eying me, as were her Mana Banks, and I could hear them whispering.

"How is he carrying those massive Pans so easily?" Dana asked Lauren.

"Look at his muscles bulging," Lauren answered, ignoring the question, or answering it, depending on who you asked.

Smegma guffawed. "These women can't keep their eyes off you, and you still think she's trying to explain how strong you must be with that comment? Honestly, Brodie, you really need help with women."

[I husking *do not*!] I retorted angrily. [Are you sure I can't put these in my Necklace of Holding?] I asked, wanting to stop being a spectacle.

Smegma shrugged. "You're welcome to, but remember the Mirror Fish? Your Necklace will freeze the food, and you'll need to defrost it for each group." I held back my groan even as the women continued to stare at me, clearly sensing that something was off about me—regardless of what Smegma thought, I was sure that was why they were staring.

[What do you think the Intelligence Stat does?] I asked Smegma, even as I saw another moon pop into existence around the planet the Stat was coming from and begin orbiting.

"No clue," Smegma admitted. "However, if it's anything like Strength, maybe I'll be able to stop calling you a dumbass." Smegma sniffed. "But I'm not getting my hopes up. Even System miracles can only go so far."

I wanted to roll my eyes, but he was a bit too spot on with that assessment. How could a person tell if they were getting smarter? *I don't feel like I suddenly know more…*

"Wouldn't be how that worked," Smegma answered my thoughts. "You can't just suddenly learn something new. If Intelligence is increasing your brain, it would be capacity and memory or something like that. The System can't create something from nothing. So, you'd just have a greater capacity for learning. You know, increased reading speed and comprehension. Better recall or something along those lines. Maybe all of the above. If you look at the definition of the word without System involvement, intelligence is basically how quickly you pick up and are able to apply information to a situation. So, maybe you have that to look forward to."

[I literally just asked you how it works and you gave me a sentence, but you had all those assumptions!] I complained.

"The problem with unproven theories is that they sometimes get relied on or become a 'fact.' Trying to define the limits and understanding of System-related aspects is dangerous. You'll inevitably find that your definition lacks the complete grasp of the thing, and if you try to use your limited, ignorant knowledge with the assumption that it's absolute truth, well… it usually limits your growth and blows up in your face like a suicide Demon." Smegma retorted, his voice sour and aggravated. There was clearly a story there, but the Demon waved his hand at me even as I thought to ask. He did at least give me something. "Yes, there's a story there. Suffice it to say something that gets put out can't get taken back."

Oh—This was sounding more and more like that story about the guy who hypothesized that wolves had an Alpha and then found out that he was wrong and spent the rest of his life trying to show people his initial hypothesis was inaccurate, but never succeeded. Smegma's groan told me I was very close, but also that I wouldn't be getting any more from him.

We arrived back at the Gardener's just as they were taking a break for lunch. Thankfully, this time the smell of Cooking Meat wasn't a problem, and the aroma from the food in the Frying Pans was just addictively fragrant, as opposed to drool inducing.

I placed them down and then shouted, "I've brought lunch for everyone. Please line up and come forward one at a time. I'd like to meet everyone and thank you all personally for joining Abyss."

A half hour later, I was done. Each Gardener was given two pieces of Heart Bacon—I'd decided to name it. One of the pieces was the Grackle-softened version and the other the shoe leather. Of course, I shook each person's hand and performed a quick session of fatigue wiping. This time, I didn't offer any of the food to the Hunters since there were twelve surrounding the clearing, and their Banks. It wasn't that I didn't want to, but that I couldn't. I had only thirty-three portions remaining.

And Abyss still had thirty Miners to feed.

* * *

"I can *see* that it's Fool's Gold!" my dad hissed, even as he took a portion of the Porcu-hog. I held out my hand with a bit more insistence as my eyes tried to warn him off that topic. Alexus was literally right—*there*.

Her suspicions—take your pick of which—were clearly only growing. My father didn't get either hint, as he popped the food into his mouth and instantly seemed to lose any semblance of caution. "First, my new *Mining* Skill, and now more food like the Mirror Fish!"

I snatched his hand and squeezed, startling him. Very pointedly, I growled, "Thank you for taking such good care of all the Miners here, *Dad*. How much Ore do you think you'll be able to Mine by the end of day?"

He looked to his hand, saw the slight change in color, which was slightly more visible down here in the caverns, and then scanned over to Alexus. I watched him put the pieces together and wince.

Sheepishly, he answered, "It's going well. Willa and Jarred haven't stopped Mining deposits since we got here. So, I'm assuming we'll get something like fifty to a hundred finished by the time we call it a day."

Just like Dave, Willa and Jarred both had a Mana Battery of absurdly good quality, meaning they could use their Skills without risk. Both of their Skills were excellent for Mining, which would reduce the wear on their Picks. Even though their Picks were of the 'best' quality we had. Willa's, in particular, being nearly as good as mine. Jarred's may even be starting to approach it.

Since we were in a D-Rank Portal, the cavern that Abyss was Mining was massive. Nowhere near the size of the one we'd gotten trapped within, but still large enough that we'd be working multiple days if it was just us.

But maybe not with the two crews...

"Why don't we hold off on using the new Miner's Equipment for today if we can, then? Since we likely won't need the single soft metal they *might* be able to handle after the Crystals," I suggested. "Any idea how much Jagger will get done?"

"I'm not sure. He's in the cavern further in. He has ten relatively high-grade Specialists working with him. So, if they can do five each—maybe fifty total?"

"Wait—" Alexus interjected pointedly. "You're claiming that ten Specialists will get fifty Ores done, and your two Specialists may get a hundred?"

"We have thirty Specialists," I answered, hoping she'd leave it be.

"Don't try that bullshit. You just said you can save their Equipment for today—as long as you're going to get more than the other group."

"That's not what he meant. Each Specialist will still be Mining a deposit today," my dad said, attempting to cover our combined mistake. "That was included in the one-hundred estimate."

"She can do math, imbeciles," Smegma guffawed.

"I can do math!" Alexus stated, almost seeming to have heard the Demon on my 'shoulder.' "That still means that two of your numbers, maybe three, if you're included—" She pointed at my father. "—are going to get seventy deposits on their own."

"We'll be tackling a great deal of deposits that others don't, though," I said as I began to sweat. Thankfully, I only had Willa and Jarred left to wipe free of fatigue, or this interruption would have meant we were holding up a line of hungry Miners.

"Okay, that's it. I've had enough—I've been watching you all day, kid. *Tell me* what the hell is going on," Alexus ordered. Dana and Lauren moved in beside her, looking ready to fight.

"They're going to fight you now?" Smegma asked, sounding a bit excited but also confused.

"No." I regarded the three women coolly. I gestured at their formation and stances. "Are you going to attack me for protecting the operational security and trade secrets of my dad's company? I thought you'd read the contract. Are you prepared to take responsibility for the lawsuit your questions and actions are about to bring down on your entire Guild?" I tapped the 360 degree camera that I'd gotten into the habit of wearing during my 'working hours' for emphasis.

Alexus looked at her two Banks and paled, realizing the picture she was painting. Dana and Lauren went bright red and began stammering words that clearly intended to convey that attacking wasn't their intention.

I didn't let them off the hook and kept regarding them with the same icy coolness I'd asked my earlier questions with. I didn't think it would do much, but maybe it would at least stop Alexus from sticking her nose into things I'd rather she didn't.

Agility Increased by 1.
Agility Stat Unlocked.

Stats
Strength: 10
Agility: 2
Stamina: 10 (+1)
Intelligence: 10
Locked.
Dexterity: 10
Locked.

The Screen popped up, changing my focus and making me start. Another stat had unlocked, which was great news but something on the screen made me feel like I had heartburn.

How did intelligence already reach ten?!

My jerk and feeling of un-comfortability only grew as I suddenly felt my chest tighten, followed quickly by my left arm going numb. My panic rose as I realized that I couldn't feel my heart rate increasing—like it normally would in a moment of life or husking death!

My right arm moved up and grasped my upper left biceps and chest, clutching hard. Was I having a heart attack? Alexus was at my side in a few moments, her mouth moving and her eyes filled with concern. My father was there too, and just as I felt my legs weaken, he caught me before I could collapse to a knee.

286

What in the hell was going on?

"Your Mental Universe is shaking! Oh, this is *big*. Something's happening!" Smegma exclaimed, his voice strangely warbled. Still, how could I hear him, when I couldn't hear anything else? Not even the background twangs of Pickaxes were audible. Plus, my eyes could clearly see my father shouting, and the same was true of Alexus.

Inherent Qi Pool Unlocked
Qi Pool Capacity: 32

A new screen popped up and the pain fled with it. I was just about to sigh in relief as the sounds of the world came back, but suddenly a pulse of blinding light shot through the cavern.

"Oh, *come on!*" I growled, even as I watched Smegma vanish.

"—Brodie! Can you hear me? Brodie!" My father was shouting, going as far as to shake me.

"Dad, I'm okay. Plus, I don't think shaking someone who might be injured is the best course of action," I answered.

Alexus, who was standing right behind my father, sighed in relief and immediately ran off, shouting for Dana and Lauren, who had apparently run off to get help—

With the small privacy that bought us, my dad asked, "Did you just Awaken a new Skill?"

I shook my head but grinned broadly. "I think it might be even bett—" Another couple of screens popped up all at once, cutting me off for a moment. "—er?" I finished slowly.

Class Awarding Feat Achieved!

Class Available:
Uncommon Rank: Martial Artist

You have unlocked three synergistic Stats and gained access to your inherent Qi.
You can now select the Martial Artist Class.

Martial Artists are granted two Skills:
Body Reinforcement (1) - F-Rank
Power Blow (1) - F-Rank

Agility and Strength Stats are unlocked and can be increased through the Martial Artist Class.

—

I blinked at the Screen, seeing the other three tabs behind it. Were they *all* Class options?

CHAPTER 43: CHAPTER 95

Saturday, May 4th, 2069

Class Awarding Feat Achieved!

Class Available:
Uncommon Rank: Spearman

You have unlocked three synergistic Stats and gained access to your inherent Qi.
You have killed a Monster in a Portal with a spear.
You can now select the Spearman Class.

Spearmen are granted two Skills:
Body Reinforcement (1) - E-Rank
Pierce (1) - F-Rank

Agility and Strength are unlocked and can be increased through the Spearman Class.
—
Class Awarding Feat Achieved!

Class Available:
Rare Rank: Battlefield Healer

You have unlocked three synergistic Stats and gained access to your inherent Qi.
You have unlocked the Common-Ranked Class: Healer.
You have additionally saved someone's life and killed a Monster in a Portal.
You can now select the Rare-Ranked Battlefield Healer Class.

Battlefield Healers are granted two Skills:
Heal (11) - E-Rank
Cleanse (11) - E-Rank

[Locked] and [Locked] are unlocked after choosing this Class and can be increased through the Battlefield Healer Class.
—
Class Awarding Feat Achieved!

**Class Available:
Rare Rank: Crafter**

**You have unlocked three synergistic Stats and gained access to your inherent Qi.
You have learned the Gathering Skills of *Mining, Harvesting, Gardening, Butchering,* and *Skinning.*
You can now select the Crafter Class.**

**Crafters are granted three Profession Skills:
Alchemy (1) - F-Rank
Leather Working (1) - F-Rank
Blacksmithing (1) - F-Rank**

[Locked] is unlocked after choosing this Class and can be increased through the Crafting Class.

My brain whirled, and I wished in that moment for Smegma to not be suddenly absent again. A quick check in on my Mental Universe showed me that I wasn't having new Skills formed, and his disappearance wasn't guaranteed to be short.

"Are you having a stroke? A heart attack? What is going on?!" my father practically shouted, breaking me out of my distracted musings.

His face was beyond worried and pale, but I saw him sigh slightly when my eyes refocused on him. It must have looked strange when I suddenly started reading something that hung in the air that was only visible to me.

"Sorry, I'll tell you about it tonight, yeah?"

My father clearly wasn't happy with that response, and I tried to brush him off so I could stand. He seemed to either resist or not move fast enough because I had to move his hands on my way to my feet, or risk knocking him over.

He gave me a look that answered that, though. What had just happened paired with my experience of my Strength Stat. Had Agility made me faster? It was only two points though, right? I still hadn't really gotten to test how much my Strength Stat had changed me, and I figured it was about time to start figuring out just what each of my unlocked Stats was doing.

I realized that everyone was looking at me as I scanned the cavern.

Right, the flash of light…

"What in the hell was that? Did me holding you bother you that much?" my dad asked, sounding confused and hurt.

Alexus hadn't gotten far in her run and was excitedly storming back toward me.

"I unlocked my Agility Stat!" I whispered right into my father's ear.

He jerked in surprise, mostly because I had just moved at a speed that I would have called urgent earlier that day—but now felt normal.

"You-you-you... You will give me an answer to my earlier question!" Alexus ordered, after stuttering over her starting point multiple times

I could tell that she was flustered and grasping for something to say, mostly due to her blotchy red face and jerky points with her finger—those soon would have poked me in my chest if I didn't lean out of the way.

She blinked in surprise when her finger passed through empty air. But then jabbed out the finger again, and I had no chance of 'dodging.' It wasn't like I had intended to move away from the first one; I kind of just saw it coming and flinched a bit too early.

"What is going on with you and your crew?" Alexus asked, each word accentuated with an absent-minded, overly excited jab of her finger. Each finger poke increased in strength as well. I winced away from each, more out of instinct than actual pain.

"Do we need to go over my earlier statement regarding operational security and trade secrets? Are you ready and prepared to negotiate on behalf of your Guild for proprietary information from my father's company? I'll warn you ahead of time—the negotiations will be *expensive*," I answered. She pulled back her finger menacingly, clearly intending to jab at me harder. Flinching, I hurried to add, "I awakened another Skill, obviously."

"Obviously!" Alexus exclaimed and jabbed me again, even as her cheeks flushed from the admonishment. "But what in the—no—*why* in the hells would you Awaken a Skill now?"

My dad regarded the interaction nervously. I could tell he wanted to help me in some way, but I forestalled him with a raised hand. People already knew about my last Awakening outside the Portal, when *Demonic Vault* had upgraded. So I weaved that into my lie. "It's happened before. In each case, I think I've Awakened a Skill associated with Mining."

"You have *multiple* Skills?" Alexus asked incredulously, her voice rising in octaves as she fought to contain her disbelief.

"Well—yes," I answered. "But they aren't very strong."

"What rank are they?" she asked. That question got a genuine wince from me, due to her rudeness. In her hyper-excitement, she misunderstood—in the worst way. "What? Wait—" Alexus continued, "don't tell me you haven't been tested?"

My wince became a grimace, because her words sounded a lot like Varnish's. I received another sporadic jab from Alexus' finger, even as her voice softened, "Why wouldn't you get tested again when you re-Awakened the first time?! The world needs Hunters!"

"Didn't you only have a Mana Pool?" a weak, tentative voice whispered. My eyes turned to find Eva standing nearby, looking at me with wide eyes that sparkled with unshed, happy tears.

She'd clearly remembered who I was, and our conversations while waiting in line for our photoshoot about my dream to re-Awaken a Skill in a Portal. It wasn't a hard dream to remember since she and about eight other people around us in line had similar aspirations.

"You're telling me, you've Awakened multiple Skills *and* have a Mana Pool?" Alexus asked, looking at Eva with soft eyes before realizing what she'd said, and spinning on me.

"Look," my father interjected. "This isn't the time or place for this discussion. We have work to do and you're interrupting it."

My mouth clenched shut as a sigh of relief attempted to escape. I probably should have thought of that reasoning a heck of a lot earlier, but I was just glad my father had pulled it out.

Alexus frowned at me and then looked over to Eva, her eyes softening and then lighting up with joy. She nodded to my father and moved to Eva's side, whispering, "I'm so glad to see you remembered him! How are you feeling?"

My father and I moved away from Alexus and Eva. My dad must have only just noticed the Miners who had stopped and were staring. "Get back to work! Do you want to beat Jagger or not?"

They all rushed back to working at the Crystals. I was pleasantly surprised to see full Crystals being pulled from the walls more times than not. I could tell by the clarity that these were a mix of F to E-Rank Crystals, which likely meant that their value was nearly the same as Shards, but I still thought it would help us stand out. Not to mention repairing the Picks.

My dad turned to me. "Any idea how we're doing against Jagger's teams in the other areas?"

I shook my head. "I'm guessing we're losing out in terms of quantity for both. I'm hoping we're going to stand out in quality, but—" I looked around myself and then whispered, "there are a lot of Herbs and Meats Smegma says are worth a lot, but others didn't seem to think so."

"So, we're Harvesting things that aren't valuable?" my dad asked, his voice sharp and extremely worried.

Again, I looked around and whispered, "I mean, along with other things. Plus, Smegma knows what they're good for—"

"It doesn't matter what value *you* think something has. Guilds will only care about how many Greenbacks we make them. Head back and make sure they're focusing on the expensive items!" my father responded hotly.

I grimaced, realizing that I had overstepped earlier with the Gardeners. The Cleaners were likely okay since they were already focused on full Hides—and they'd already harvested the Hearts without my direction. Surely they wouldn't have changed anything...

"I'll go back," I said urgently, already scanning for Alexus and her Mana Banks.

"Good! Quality is a good thing to focus on but only if it isn't hurting the bottom line, like with the full Crystals here. We aren't really slowing down to get them, not with the new constantly improving Picks," my father explained.

"I get it! We'll talk about this later *and* that food that you just ate, and you can tell me again *all* about how the stuff I asked them to focus on is worthless," I answered hotly, finding Alexus. "I'm going!"

* * *

We were halfway back to the entrance of the Mines on our way back to the Gardeners and had walked in awkward silence the entire way. Finally, Alexus coughed and asked a question. One I hadn't been expecting.

"Can you really cure Eva?" She whispered.

I'd turned to look at her and just blinked in confusion. Cure? Oh, right. I'd said I could Heal her because Smegma had said we could create a paste or a Pill…

Well, wasn't this just perfect!

"I can," I answered weakly. Not liking that it was a partial lie. I couldn't *right now*, not unless Smegma returned. I just didn't have the ability—

Wait.

Didn't I have a new Class that technically upgraded my *Minor Heal* to *Heal* and gave me an additional Skill? Would that be enough? More importantly, could I show that kind of capability to Alexus and the others?

I glanced at the three Mana Banks and found Eva looking at me with pleading eyes. Not just pleading eyes, but eyes that glowed with recognition and fondness. Maybe feeding her that Heart Meat had gotten her out of her shell? Perhaps it was the Stamina increase or the unknown regeneration at work?

Actually, it could be my Inherent Qi…

Either way, I'd try another piece of the Heart Meat later, right now I owed it to her to try…

Alexus let me come to whatever decision I was making. I assumed my emotions were clearly written across my face, and just as obviously, she had put some things together as well. The things I had been doing were not normal. I was clearly keeping secrets from her—and she likely understood that I was choosing whether to share them.

With a deep breath, I opened up the Class Selection tabs, and picked Battlefield Healer.

Wisdom Stat Unlocked.
Perception Stat Unlocked.
+1 to Wisdom and Perception from Heal and Cleanse Skill Level.

Stats
Strength: 10
Agility: 7
Stamina: 10
Intelligence: 10
Wisdom: 2
Dexterity: 10
Perception: 2

Wow, all the Gathering equipment must be funneling Stats fast… I thought, as I saw the Agility and Intelligence Stats.

I managed a single step in Eva's direction before the ground beneath me shook—no—it *vanished*. The only reason I made that startling realization was that I was suddenly experiencing a falling sensation as the four women grew taller around me.

Then my vision behind the screen went black, even as I continued to fall.

New screens began taking the place of the Stat-unlocking ones, and my left arm went numb once again as my heartbeat came to a standstill.

Magic Control Unlocked
Current Control: +6%
—
Inherent Soul Pool Unlocked
Soul Pool Capacity: 22

Congratulations! You've unlocked all available Stats and Pools.
This makes you eligible for a System Tutorial.
Upon entrance to a Portal, Brodie Flacarada will enter the Tutorial.

E-Rank Portal entered.

Tutorial Rank: E-Rank

"No husking way!" I shouted, trying and failing to find the hole I had just fallen through. Instead, my eyes only found black with no hint of light, no matter what 'direction' I turned in.

Perhaps the worst part was that I was still speeding up in my fall. Was I going to die once I reached this Tutorial? It seemed highly likely since I had absolutely no way of slowing my descent.

I began to scream. That screaming stopped for brief moments and idle thoughts of what colliding with the ground at this speed would feel like took their place. Then I screamed some more. Eventually Mental Fortitude gave me a momentary reprieve—I managed to examine the screens and notice that it had called the Portal I had been Gathering in E-Rank, despite everyone claiming it was D-Rank. Then I lost control and screamed again.

It must have been an hour later when my screaming and errant insane thoughts cut off—and that was only because it hurt my throat so badly that it snapped me out of my brain-paralyzing dread long enough for *Mental Fortitude* to regain a more permanent control.

How was I still speeding up?

In fact, by the sensation, I was likely moving faster than I ever had in the Ford Escort. Probably faster than any earthly plane. Just how fast was I traveling?

It was impossible to tell, even if I was good at math, I didn't know the laws that governed this strange, empty space I fell through.

Something in the distance made me twist my body and head around. After some effort, I managed to lock my head and eyes onto the growing blue spiral in the distance. It was about the size of a star in the night sky.

However, it grew at an alarming rate, becoming a marble, baseball, beach ball, full moon, and then uncomprehendingly large in seconds. Suddenly, it felt like I was heading straight toward an actual star in the sky—that's how big the strange swirl felt, and it was *still growing*.

I fought my descent, trying desperately to move myself off the current course, which was directly at the thing. I couldn't imagine a more painful way to die, than falling into a sun. It didn't work. There wasn't resistance or wind in this place that I could use. Instead, I just kept falling toward the left edge of the thing that was now so big I could no longer see the other edge.

Maybe the side will be less hot?

Then I began to slow. I wanted to start screaming again but focused on other sensations to stop myself.

My body didn't feel the friction against the air that I would have expected from such a high-speed descent, and I was apparently being controlled by another braking force. I didn't feel a single discomforting sensation as I quickly drew to a complete dead stop, hovering over a large, shimmering blue Portal—one that looked like the Portals we had on Earth but simultaneously nothing like them, due to the sheer *size*.

Then I was sucked in.

CHAPTER 44: CHAPTER 96

Monday, May 6th, 2069

"Your Honor, I can assure you that Brodie Flacarada has not run away," Shami Stovall assured Judge Dench. The Judge didn't bother looking at Mrs. Stovall and regarded Mr. Varnish with a level stare that clearly asked him what his opinion was. Shami would have thought this was bad news, even if it was just a few days ago.

Surely, before Saturday, Mr. Varnish would have asked for the maximum sentencing for a failure to appear. Even the fact that he hesitated was surprising. Still, his next move would likely depend on the Larvae Guild.

"Brodie Flacarada has failed to appear, for the second time. I'm sure Mrs. Stovall has another excuse prepared, but haven't we heard enough, Your Honor?"

"I'm going to agree with Mr. Varnish, Mrs. Stovall. Brodie Flacarada will pay the court a fine of—"

"If I may, Your Honor?" Mr. Varnish interjected, surprising Judge Dench, who was clearly about to begin fining Brodie for each day he'd missed. Mrs. Stovall raised an eyebrow in surprise at his interjection, which overwhelmed her capacity to keep a straight face. These things always started with fines and then escalated.

Then again, Mr. Varnish had never pushed for jail time…

"You may, Mr. Varnish, but in the future, make your suggestion during the time you have to speak, not by interrupting me."

"Yes, Judge Dench. Your Honor, I was simply going to suggest that instead of fines, arrest warrants or jail time—like *usual*—we court order Brodie to undergo a full Awakening Assessment."

"That is highly irregular, Your Honor," Mrs. Stovall stated.

"I agree, Mr. Varnish. To go against his Hunter Rights before they're removed upon criminal arrest would need a more significant reason than failing to appear."

"For the second time, Your Honor?" Mr. Varnish suggested.

"Even for the second time," Judge Dench stated flatly.

"Last time he missed multiple days, Your Honor," Mr. Varnish reminded the Judge.

"He was trapped in a Portal!" Mrs. Stovall reminded Mr. Varnish.

"And this time, Mrs. Stovall?" Mr. Varnish asked sweetly.

Shami wanted to sigh but managed to hold it back by adjusting her jacket. Instead of responding to Mr. Varnish, she looked to the Judge sitting behind her desk. She looked anything but imposing in her over-large chair, but the furniture itself—on the other hand—was the exact opposite.

Shami could picture it in the offices of a Prime Minister or President—maybe even the British Royal Family. The leather was a deep brown with hints of red that perfectly complimented it. It was simultaneously ostentatious and imposing. All of it was. The desk was dark amber and polished to a near mirror shine. Shami knew it was all from Portals—and could almost feel an aura coming from it. She shook herself. Ever since Brodie allowed her to use the Altar, she'd been having these moments. She hadn't yet used her new Skill, nor gotten an explanation of what exactly it did. Gary had claimed the man from Larvae had called it *Chains of Truth*, but that was all she knew.

Judge Dench blinked at her, reminding Shami that it had been a moment since Mr. Varnish asked his question. She gave a polite cough and answered, "I have eyewitnesses from the Lynx Guild who were present when Mr. Flacarada vanished. The leader of the team he was with was his escort as he moved between locations inside the Portal."

"What will this witness say?" Judge Dench asked, leaning forward slightly.

"That Brodie Flacarada fell into a hole that opened up beneath him on the ground, and he vanished, along with said hole, in the blink of an eye. She will also testify to the Lynx Guild delving deeply into the caverns, forests and valleys in search of Brodie, but finding nothing. They even closed the Portal and he didn't exit…"

"Your Honor, may I?" Mr. Varnish asked politely, which set Shami's hair on her neck to stand on end. She scratched at it as Judge Dench nodded. "This witness will also testify to Mr. Flacarada undergoing another Awakening, just before disappearing. There is no proof that this hole, which appeared and whisked him away, wasn't his new Skill activating."

"Why would he activate his new Skill and get left behind in a Portal, Your Honor?" Mrs. Stovall asked.

"Why else, Your Honor?" Mr. Varnish said, his voice derisive. "Brodie Flacarada is running from the outcome of this trial."

"He's a child who lives at home with his mother and father, Your Honor. We established early on that he wasn't a flight risk!" Shami countered.

"Since the incident on April first, Mrs. Stovall, how many re-Awakenings have occurred with Brodie that you know of?" Judge Dench asked, looking through some of her notes in a red-scaled leather folder.

With a sigh, Shami answered, "At least three."

"When I made that initial ruling, I believed I was dealing with a uni-Skilled F-Ranked Mana Pool Awakened," Judge Dench said with a nod of confirmation to Shami's answer. "I see where Mr. Varnish is taking us, but I do not agree with his conclusion. Still, I believe Brodie would rather have a forced Assessment of his new rank and his Skills than end up in jail for failure to appear, if only because they will Assess his rank and Skills anyway. Is that your intention, Mr. Varnish?"

Mrs. Stovall eyed the man. If this was his only intention, she'd eat her business jacket.

Sure enough, he gave a self-deprecating smile and answered, "That was my train of thought, yes. I'd never dream of illegally violating a person's rights; I was merely following events to their logical conclusion and attempting a peace offering toward a more equitable end. I'll admit that I'd also be interested in commuting any jail sentence to community service under the Larvae Guild as well—if you're looking for full-disclosure on my part."

Shami wanted to growl, but her hands were rather tied. Sure, she could fight for the length of time until Mr. Varnish's suggestion would be imposed. But in the end, community service in place of a jail sentence for Failure to Appear was an outcome she'd normally have to fight for. Mr. Varnish was giving her that olive branch, along with removing fines, fees, and possible arrest warrants from the table. She had to accept it, but that didn't mean she had to eat the whole pie.

"Placing an individual under Guild Arrest, under a Guild that blames him for the death of a member, would be near criminal, Your Honor. May I speak candidly?" Shami countered.

Judge Dench nodded, and Shami continued, "We are all of us in this room aware of the outcome of the vast majority of Guild Arrests, and as such, we can assume that putting Brodie under the control of a Guild that is not his fan is elevating those already abundant risks. With that in mind, I would like to accept Varnish's terms in parcels. Four months of failure to appear seems like a good timeline to re-assess the Guild Arrest, Your Honor. Don't you think?" Mrs. Stovall suggested.

Mr. Varnish's jaw clenched and Shami smiled.

"Certainly not, Your Honor. How long would a normal Failure to Appear take to move to arrest warrants and jail time?"

Shami knew that answer too. For a first-time offense, it would be a few weeks up to a month before the fines escalated. Judge Dench looked through her notes before responding.

"I think we can all agree, Mr. Varnish, that Brodie Flacarada doesn't appear to be a criminal mastermind?"

Mr. Varnish's jaw clenched further. "Yes, Your Honor," he answered through his clenched teeth. Shami almost smiled, even that one line from the Judge was a huge hit against Vanish's case.

"I'm willing to offer Mrs. Stovall sixty days to find her client and make him appear before this court before re-assessing and ruling *entirely* in favor of your suggestions. Is this an acceptable compromise for both parties?"

Shami clenched her jaw tight but nodded, she would have preferred to have gotten two timelines, one for the Assessment and one for the Guild Arrest. She turned to Mr. Varnish, watching him closely.

"With that length of time, we would have to restart all proceedings at the time Brodie reappears, Your Honor," Mr. Varnish countered.

"I cannot hold the jury in seclusion any longer than a week, Mr. Varnish, and I'm unwilling to sentence Mr. Flacarada to jail time for Failure to Appear in five days."

Mr. Varnish eventually nodded very reluctantly.

Judge Dench soon dismissed Shami and Varnish. Shami gave the man a look as soon as the door closed behind them. He got the message and they moved to one of the small side offices in the Court House. As soon as Varnish turned around and Shami had closed the door, she exclaimed, "What the hell? The

Larvae Guild purchased P-Cubed for Brodie—as payment for the information—but failed to check for non-compete clauses?!"

"I can assure you, Mrs. Stovall, that we are looking into that problem heavily. So far, we've uncovered that the non-competes that the Specialists signed for P-Cubed have a rather nefarious loophole in the contract. P-Cubed is synonymous with Jagger Vance in the original Corporation Documents. Thus, he was able to take his new and old Specialists with him."

"That can't be legal," Mrs. Stovall stated.

"That has yet to be determined—" Mr. Varnish began.

"And there's nothing your backers can do about that?" Mrs. Stovall stated angrily, recalling the threats from Aurome when she'd mentioned Paradox.

"Mrs. Stovall, I can assure you that Jagger in time will be in a world of problems. However, Larvae must operate within the confines of the law."

"Sure they do..." Shami muttered, thinking of the gloves and other oddities in the case against Brodie.

Mr. Varnish narrowed his eyes and then shook his head sadly. "Mrs. Stovall, rest assured that Larvae will make good on its promises. However, in no way does that promise impact the criminal case Brodie Flacarada is undergoing. Do you understand?"

Shami nodded and collapsed into one of the chairs. "You do realize that Brodie isn't running from this case, right?"

"I'm aware, Mrs. Stovall. I'm also aware of how odd my request in the Judge's office was. If the Larvae Guild truly wished to punish Mr. Flacarada, then jail time would surely be the obvious choice, wouldn't it?"

"Do you have any idea what's going on?" Shami asked as her neck jerked up in interest.

Mr. Varnish shrugged. "I've received no further instructions since before the beginning of the trial, *Shami*. So, no—I'm as lost as you."

* * *

"We have to head to the Portal, Mr. Flacarada," Dave encouraged. "The last thing Brodie would want is for Abyss to fail as a company because he's missing."

"That's my son you're talking about!" Mr. Flacarrada answered hotly.

"Exactly, and what do you think your son would want?" Dave asked, looking at the others in the small kitchen. Mrs. Flacarrada was glaring at him, but both Willa and Jarred were nodding in agreement. Geneva and Kristen had cameras out, which made him slightly uncomfortable—but they couldn't take another day off. Not if they wanted to earn future contracts with the top Guilds of Windsor.

"You expect my husband and I to work while our son is missing?" Mrs. Flacarrada asked, her eyes drilling holes into Dave's back.

"Whatever happened to Brodie, I think we can all agree—it wasn't normal." He looked around until he got nods of confirmation from everyone. "To me, it reeks of either System huskery, or something to do with a certain Demonic gargoyle... Husk knows that thing disappears whenever it feels like it. Either way,

I don't think it's helpful to act like Brodie's never coming back. So, shouldn't we all act like he *is*, and in that case... wouldn't we all want him to come back to a thriving company and not one that fell apart as soon as he was gone?"

Dave sighed and looked to the others in the room for support. No one met his eyes, or even coughed. He gave a polite throat-clearing and said, "Clara, Gary—Brodie isn't in that Portal. That we can say for certain, right?"

They both blinked at him, seeming to be asking how he arrived at that conclusion. Clicking his tongue, he answered the unspoken question. "If he was simply lost in the Portal, he would have popped out when it closed, which was last night. Lynx defeated the Boss and closed it—*we also*," Dave hurried to continue as Gary and Clara both began to look worried, "can assume he is alive—"

"Why is that?" Mr. Flacarrada asked, his voice pleading with Dave for a good solid reason.

"Well, this is just an assumption, but all of the gear, Bags of Holding, Mana Batteries and even *that* is still here," Dave answered—pointing at a small red Crystal that had appeared where Brodie had fallen through the floor. The light inside the Crystal pulsed, reminding him of a heartbeat.

"You know what that is?" Clara asked, also hopeful.

Dave shook his head and bluntly answered, "No idea, but I assume it's got some sort of link to Brodie, don't you all?"

Finally, Willa spoke up. "It *did be* showin' up on the spot that Brodie be vanishin'—"

"And only people close to Brodie could even see it!" Jarred added.

"That doesn't mean—" Gary began.

"You can either look at the negative side or the positive," Dave interjected. "No one else could even see this thing except us, Sparkle Legion, and Mrs. Stovall—we checked. So, either we get back to work and trust in Brodie, or we fold right now. But I know which one is going to upset Brodie more when he returns."

"Returns from where?!" Mrs. Flacarrada shouted.

It was Dave's turn to avoid eye contact. That was the part he hadn't worked out yet. He doubted he would ever work it out—not until Brodie returned and told them where the hole in the cavern had taken him.

Clara, seeing his reaction, sighed. "I'm sorry, Dave. I know you're only trying to help." She looked at the others in the room. "You're all just trying to help, and I think you're right—but I also don't think you can understand what we're going through right now."

Willa moved to give Clara a hug, but no one else moved. With a polite cough, Jarred said, "You're right, Clara. We can only imagine what this must feel like—but just because you two aren't working today—doesn't mean that Abyss can't."

"What do you mean?" Gary asked.

"We have contracts, and they invented leaves of absences for a reason. Let the kid take charge," Jarred suggested, gesturing at Dave, who blinked. He couldn't be impl—

"Yeah, we can be puttin' Dave in charge of da crew—I can be gettin' my husband to take some vacation and maybe even be workin' on hirin'. Jarred, can your wife be takin' any time off yet?"

"Maybe a few days," Jarred answered.

"That should be enough," Willa responded. "Let us be handlin' the logistics an' crews dis week, Clara," Willa continued, hugging the woman tightly. "We be tryin' ta give you as much time as ya be needin'."

Clara began to sob, which prompted Gary to stand and move in to hug her. Willa disentangled herself after a moment, and they all stood around awkwardly. Then Gary nodded—giving his approval—and they all sighed, except for Dave.

He couldn't take charge of the crews. He didn't know the first thing about how to organize them. A hand clapped him on the shoulder, and he turned to find Jarred looking him in the eye.

"Come on, kid, we'll help you get it set up this morning. You'll have a handle on it in no time!" Jarred said, his tone fatherly and proud.

* * *

Evelyn Treesong looked down at her unanswered text messages and then scanned to her computer screen one more time. It was certainly a handy device, and one of the few she might have taken back with her to Canopy, her original world—a world with numerous names depending on what Elf you asked—or what the Demons who had led them astray had called Sective Agora.

Evelyn was unsure if her multiple missed appointments and unanswered texts were a sign of a lazy-minded, young man with more important things on his mind—or if it was a sign of something more. He certainly had possessed the right aura to her senses when she'd first seen him. Still, was it worth contacting her people over?

It was quite the pain to send messages back to the Hive on Canopy. Pricey, too. There was also no guarantee her messenger would make it—and even less that the messengers would return to Earth. A good example was that she'd sent thirty-two messages, each with redundancies, to Canopy—but only received three responses.

Those responses were cryptic at best, and completely senseless at worst. Was she truly supposed to find a *savior*? Or were her people asking her to send them more trained humans to act as saviors to the Hive? Or was *she* meant to be the savior and start a refuge here on Gaia?

She'd prepared for each possibility and had created a Guild called Canopy in an out-of-the-way city. It was a place that was barely thought about in the minds of the general populace. Unless, of course, they lived nearby or had family living in the town called Windsor.

The Guild was somewhat well situated, with a few large towns nearby, and even had one of those abhorrent Fields right next door. If her people arrived en masse, she was prepared for any reaction from these humans.

Still, for her people to come here—to a planet that had only just begun its journey of Ascension—would be hasty. Humanity didn't even understand the

300

way the System was working yet. As far as she knew, and her people did have spies in many countries around the world, humans hadn't fully realized how to even acquire new Skills.

Not that she or her people knew the method yet, but they *did* know the System. There was always a way, and if she wasn't mistaken—this particular test was somehow highly personalized. Unlike her planet, and Crendalar—which had used Card Shards that needed to be collected, formed and traded—this planet seemed to have Monster, Portal and Elemental Cores as a central aspect to System function. What they were intended by the System to be used for, however, Evelyn had no idea. Still, the humans were certainly creative in finding their own highly inefficient uses for them, she supposed.

Her inherent Elven magic had yet to find how the Cores could be combined, but she was somewhat positive they could be. She'd actually sent a rather large number of the Cores back to Canopy and the Hive, hoping that the World Singers, Enchanters or Crafters could discover the method.

There was only one other thing she was certain of. If one of these Humans got too powerful or unlocked both of their inherent Pools, they were destroyed by the System. That or removed by it. Was that what the Demons and her race got wrong? Was the answer never about how many powerful Skills you got? Was the System trying to curb that?

Those were things that had been sent along with each of the thirty-two messengers. However, despite the return of three of them—they couldn't recall handing the Cores to the Hive, or if the Hive had a message regarding them.

Needless to say, something Draconic was going on.

CHAPTER 45: CHAPTER 97

Tutorial Day 1

"Interesting. I haven't heard of a new guy entering in months, and then one falls right into my lap!" a robotic sounding voice intoned.

A peculiar quality of the voice made it seem like someone was speaking from beside my shoulder. I was laying on my back, looking up at a sky filled with numerous suns. I had just started counting them, but the nearness of the voice and the sound of boots crushing leaves from farther away made me turn my head. A short man with dark hair, brown eyes, and smooth features looked down at me with a broad smile. He had a strange hunch to his body that didn't look like it was caused by age, but did seem to be due to pain, maybe? His face was too stoic to tell.

My slow study of the man brought my eyes to the Sword on his waist, and I jumped to my feet. The man held up one of his hands, keeping the other one braced on his stomach. He began moving the raised hand back and forth, even as his mouth opened and closed, but to my surprise, no sound came out—until approximately his third attempted word.

"I'm not going to hurt you. I was just out Hunting and returning through this Forest." Again, the voice sounded odd, mechanical—and far too close. It reminded me of my earlier assumption of having come from multiple people. I scanned my surroundings.

Quite a few Trees that looked like a mix of maples and evergreens surrounded me, but no other people. One of my new Skills highlighted some of the foliage with plaques that likely would give me the names of the Plants, and there were even a few dots and lines that were probably indicating how to Harvest them.

That makes sense since my Stats started increasing—all my new Skills must have Peaked...

My eyes returned to the man in confusion and found him already speaking again.

"There's translation magic here. Sounds strange, right? It will slowly get better the longer you stay. Still, we should get you back to Town. It's dangerous out here without a weapon. I'm Fong, what's your name?" Fong said. The gestures of his hand were deliberately slow and clearly meant not to startle me.

Slowly, I answered, "My name is Brodie. You said something about a Town?"

"Tutorial Town, follow me," Fong said, but I didn't hear it until he'd spun around and was already making a gesture over his shoulder for me to follow. His words brought back the memory of my final moments in the Portal with

Alexus. The System notices had claimed I was 'eligible for the Tutorial' and then sucked me through a portal to an *'E-Ranked Tutorial.'*

I wasn't an expert on games, not like Dave, but weren't Tutorials usually where you learned the buttons and functions of the game at a basic level? So, was this Fong not really a man but a Tutorial Guide? Also, I had to *pre-qualify* for the basics of a literal universe-altering change to my world and my life? How did that make any sense?

Coughing, I asked, "Are you a Guide, then?"

Fong laughed, which was highly disturbing, because instead of hearing a sound from what clearly was mirthful body language and laughter—I heard a delayed robotic evil 'ha-ha-ha-ha,' then the same robotic voice answered with no inflection, "I asked the same question when I first got here. But no, this Tutorial isn't what any of us expected. Basically, we're all trapped here."

Because of the lack of inflection, it took me a moment to register his last sentence and blurt out, "What?! Trapped here?"

"Don't worry about that yet. It's only your first day. Today, we'll get you signed up for a room and listed as a member of our Tribe. The boss will decide how best you can contribute."

That only brought up more questions, but I clamped my mouth shut, thanks in large part to *Mental Fortitude.* While I could tell I was still running high on adrenaline from the realization that I was in a 'Tutorial,' and 'trapped,' maybe even that absurdly long fall, I was thinking everything through. Fong was giving away a bit more than he might have intended. Instead of asking about the 'contribution,' which was my first thought, I chose a different route.

Fong motioned with his raised hand in a universal 'follow me' gesture again, then started walking. His walk was anything but healthy. His hunch became more exaggerated, and he shuffled his right foot along like it was somewhat lame. I swallowed my first thought of offering the man Healing. I just couldn't be sure if he was friendly.

"Is 'the boss' in charge of the Tutorial?" I asked, expecting that this boss was a human and not some sort of Tutorial Guide, or whatever games would lead me to expect.

"Nah, the boss has been here for many decades. He's the strongest of our Tribe and protects us from the other bosses."

There it was. The answer I was expecting but hadn't wanted to outright ask and alert Fong to my suspicions. The 'boss' was someone who was stronger than most other people here, and he used that power to control weaker Hunters, like myself. Not only that, but there seemed to be other people and groups with a similar hierarchy, which meant—conflict. My stomach began to knot, but I continued my casual questioning as I easily kept pace with the limping man.

"Your Tribe? Is that like a Guild?" I asked.

"Yep!" Fong began, his voice still robotic, but since he glanced over his shoulder at me when he answered, I could see that the movement of his mouth and the translation came faster. "Only difference is that you've got to join a Tribe in Tutorial Town or live outside of it."

"Why's that?" I asked, my heart hammering in my chest as my fears were confirmed.

Some of my thoughts must have shown on my face because Fong used the hand not clenching his stomach to 'wave away' something in the air. Likely meant to dispel my concern or worry. A moment after the gesture, the translation came through.

"Nothing sinister. The Town is owned by the Four Tribes, and the food, shops, supplies and Districts can only be accessed by Tribe members."

Some of my concern did melt away. It sounded like I wasn't about to be brought into Town and press-ganged into a Tribe against my will. "So, if you don't join a Tribe, you can live outside the Districts?"

"Yes, but I wouldn't suggest it. It's not so much living outside the Districts, as living outside the Town. Plus, you'd lose the protection being part of a Tribe gives. While our Tribe wouldn't attack those unaligned, others do," Fong said over his shoulder. Suddenly, he stopped and removed the hand holding his right side to place it on his Sword hilt. I stopped as well, trying to figure out if his actions were meant as a threat to me, or an indication of him sensing something I'd missed.

What surprised me most was that he didn't seem to have a visible injury under his hand. There was something odd to the image. Like his armor there was sunken in or 'dented,' but considering it was leather, I couldn't parse the dent. Maybe the man had taken a bludgeoning blow and was internally injured?

Then my distraction ended as I heard the breaking twigs and rustling branches. The smell in the air changed as well, going from the clean smell of pines to the rancid smell of a swamp. Fong pulled his Sword in a fluid motion despite his injury, and a moment later, words were translated into my ear.

"Stand back."

A mudslide undulated around a pine-like Tree at my eleven o'clock. For a moment, I wondered what Fong's Sword was going to do against the approaching natural disaster until he started swinging. His Sword glowed with blue light, and each swing parted a portion of the mud, revealing that it wasn't mud at all, but moving balls of… stuff. My brain gave me a name for creatures like this in video games.

Slimes. The two halves of some pulled themselves back together after Fong's Skill-infused slashes cut them apart, while others fell into pieces, becoming swampy, brown puddles. Now knowing what I was looking at, I made a quick count. Twenty, or twenty-five Slimes. It was tough to tell how many were still behind the tree, so there could be more of them.

Not only was Fong *fast*, but the Slimes moved slowly. Still, with each slash that didn't disable the lead Slimes, they seemed to speed up, forcing Fong to stumble back as he fought. To my eyes, many of Fong's movements were blurs, but even with all his speed and clear skill with a blade, he'd only actually disabled about three of the Slimes.

His back was only five feet in front of me when he did something that changed the light on his Sword from blue to white. His next slash also changed, becoming something of an exaggerated swing from hip to hip. Fong's face contorted in pain as he brought his Sword back and twisted his body—essentially coiling like a spring. Then he released the slash, but in a strange, deliberate sort of way. Where Fong's movements had been hard to follow before, this swing was easy for me to track.

In front of his swing, the Slimes segmented, almost looking like scalloped potatoes being cut by a master chef. The Skill *cleaved* through row upon row of the creatures and not even one of the Slimes caught by the ability pulled itself back together. Fong fell to his knee after the strike, his breathing heavy. I expected to see sweat pouring down his forehead to drip to the forest floor, but there was none.

Had the action only been hard because of the injury?

His right arm went back to the dent in his leather armor, clenching it tight. I stood frozen, staring at the Slimes, hoping they wouldn't reform because Fong likely couldn't take on another one. Not with the way his hand clenching his side was shaking.

Of course, I could still offer to Heal Fong, but again decided against it. While I didn't want to face Monsters without the man on my side—I still couldn't be sure he was truly *on my side*. So, for now, I'd keep everything to myself if I could.

I approached slowly and asked, "Are you okay?"

"I just… need a moment. Bottomed out my Qi," Fong explained through translation. Then he asked, "Could you go collect the twenty-five Cores while I recover?"

My body tensed. I wasn't thrilled with the idea of going toward the mud that could still be alive. And yet, could I refuse to do as the clearly powerful Fong 'suggested.' There hadn't been any indication that the man would react poorly if I refused, but simultaneously, there hadn't been any hint of his Skills in the moments leading up to the fight, either. He likely was a D-Rank Hunter, even injured as he was, and he could kill me without blinking. Or sweating, just like he had done with the Slimes…

Not to mention my pitiful Muay Thai Skills can't even hurt one of these Mud Slimes…

Eventually, I decided on the safest route—obedience—and slowly approached the mud puddles. If even a bubble formed on the surface of one, I planned to get behind Fong. No such disturbances occurred, however, and the round lump in the flat mud was easy to see. I reached the nearest puddle and pulled out a round, muddy sphere about the size of a softball. Then I looked for a place to put it and chose to begin tossing them in a pile outside of the puddles.

Sure, I could have used my Necklace, but then I'd be revealing to Fong I had it, and just like with the Healing, I wasn't sure how that would go. Bags of Holding were somewhat common on Earth, but I hadn't ever seen one in the form of a Necklace. Unless of course Varnish's Spatial item counted. I still thought that man had a ring. Then there was the fact that even a Bag of Holding could be beyond rare here.

I found twenty-eight of the Cores and while I considered stealing one, I thought better of it. Fong may be aware of the actual number of Slimes he'd killed and just said twenty-five as a test. I didn't want to chance it, not before I understood a bit more about this place and the others who were here. At the moment, Fong was the only bridge to others that I had.

Twenty minutes or so later, Fong got to his feet and shakily approached the pile. They vanished as he touched them, letting me know that he had some sort of Holding item. "Oh, there were twenty-eight, lucky, lucky," Fong said, making me wince. Maybe I could have gotten away with one to study.

They hadn't felt like normal *Monster* Cores, but the mud on them made it hard for me to tell. Still, Fong had seemed willing to answer my questions earlier, so as we started walking again, I asked, "Are those *Monster* Cores?"

"Not quite, but they're the equivalent of Monster Cores here, yes. You can sell them in Tutorial Town for Tutorial Points."

"Tutorial Points?" I asked, prodding Fong to continue his explanation.

"That's correct. You can spend Tutorial Points at the Shops in our District or on Learning. But be careful. The rent for rooms has a monthly fee. You also must pay for food, Healing or any other service provided by other Hunters. So don't go getting all spend-happy, no matter how many Points you started with."

"How many points? I started with?" I asked, unsure what he was talking about, or how to check the number.

"Just pull up your Status sheet," Fong said in his robotic monotone.

I did so and blinked at the blue System screen.

It had changed.

However, before I could really study it, the view behind the screen made me close it and stare.

We'd exited the forest and were standing on the top of a shelf that overlooked a valley. In the center of said valley, was a massive castle wall with a Town contained within. However, even more eye-catching was the massive yellow *arrow* and the signpost in the sky.

It read 'Tutorial Town' in bright purple cursive. A multitude of other languages other than English were clearly displayed on the massive sign board as well. The interior of the Town was split by the wall, which was evident from this vantage but likely wouldn't be anywhere else because the cross-shaped walls that segmented the interior circle were shorter. Inside each quadrant, there were wooden buildings of questionable construction and a few stone buildings of clearly superior make.

The only other noteworthy building in each District was a Tower. They each looked identical and rose higher than the walls.

Still hunched around his injury, Fong held out his one free hand theatrically and began speaking, followed a moment later by the translation, "Welcome to Tutorial Town."

CHAPTER 46: CHAPTER 98

Tutorial Day 1

Fong looked down the sheer cliff face leading off the steppe, and I joined him. It was probably a forty-foot drop to the rocky floor below. My eyes scanned for a path down but didn't find one. I soon found out why, when Fong simply leaped off the edge and landed with a non-robotic grunt. My mind argued with my eyes, seeming to question if I was seeing what I really thought I was.

Hadn't he been injured?

Was the drop less than forty feet? Maybe, but it was certainly higher than I wanted to free fall. Fong hunched around his side, looked back up, and found me staring down at him. I saw the confusion cross his face before he seemed to understand something. "What is your Strength Stat?"

"Uhh," I stuttered, unsure if I should tell someone else my Stats. Especially someone who was clearly stronger than me. Would he take advantage of my weakness? Still, it was obvious that I had a low Strength Stat from the very fact that I didn't jump. So, I said, "...Ten?"

"Gazi! I should have asked," Fong responded. The voice sounded slightly less robotic. He looked back up the rise. "Mine's nearing a hundred, but I still can't jump back up there. Follow me. There's a place to climb down about a mile this way."

I nodded and Fong started limping toward my right. I stayed close to the shelf-cliff, keeping a wary eye on the Forest edge, now on my right side, for Monsters. Still, if we were going to walk, it also gave me the chance to study the changes to my 'Status sheet,' as Fong had called it. I was glad my knowledge of gaming jargon would come in useful. So, with half an eye, I began looking at my Screen while keeping both the forest and Fong in my peripheral vision.

Status
Tutorial Name: [Enter Name]
Tutorial Points: 25,000
Skills: <u>Demonic Vault</u>, <u>Dragon Heart</u>, Reptilian Body, Heal, Cleanse
Role: Gatherer / Healer
Mana Pool:
50 / 50
Qi:
33 / 33
Soul:
11 / 11
Stats:

Strength: 10
Agility: 7
Stamina: 10
Intelligence: 10
Wisdom: 2
Dexterity: 10
Perception: 2

Obviously, the first thing I noticed was the Tutorial Points, and my ability to enter a name. I figured I could ask Fong about the name, but I'd likely have to wait till we got to Town to discover if twenty-five thousand points was a good or bad amount. Or I could of course risk asking the man—but that seemed dangerous. What if I was the Tutorial Town equivalent of a millionaire?

I wished Smegma was here, so I could bounce ideas off him. That, of course, made my stomach knot in worry. I didn't have any true idea of why he was absent this time. I returned to studying the Status page, so I didn't have to think about that.

The next oddity was staring me in the face. Skills. The first strange part was that they were listed at all, but also, I was missing about four that I'd seen Cards for—likely eight since I'd gained four new Profession Skills in the Portal. Still, the lines below *Dragon Heart*, and *Demonic Vault* made me smile. I had a feeling I knew what was going on. I mentally clicked on *Demonic Vault* first.

Demonic Vault Sub-Skills
Butchering
Classes
Cooking
Fishing
Gardening
Harvesting
Mining
Overdraft
Skinning

My smile grew larger.

This may be the answer I was looking for. I studied the title again. '*Demonic Vault* sub-Skills' and a wave of relief washed over me. It still wasn't certain, but it would appear that I only had five 'official' Skills at the moment, but a great many sub-Skills under the umbrella of two of my more powerful Skills. I clicked *Dragon Heart* next.

Dragon Heart Consumed-Skills
Heat Sense
Mental Fortitude
Recovery

The title of this one did make me a little less sure. I'd expected to see *Copy and Cannibalism* and my *Mana Pool*, but they weren't there. Instead, there was the list of the Skills I'd 'stolen.'

The list brought up another rather large question. I had received *Demonic Vault* right alongside *Mental Fortitude* and *Recovery*. So, why was it considered a Skill, while they were Consumed-Skills?

I didn't have an answer to that question. Nor did I truly think I'd be able to ask Smegma for confirmation. The Demon hadn't even mentioned a Tutorial before, which either meant his people hadn't had one, or perhaps it was just as difficult to enter and no one he knew had been able to do so? Or worse yet, been unable to leave in the *five thousand* years?

Then I had another thought. Was unlocking Stats that difficult?

Unlocking Stats had been relatively simple for me, but that didn't mean it was for everyone. For example, how had Fong unlocked his Stats to enter the Tutorial? How had the others in the Tutorial done so? What about the boss? Fong said his Strength was nearly one hundred. How had he grown it to such a degree? Those were certainly questions for later—right alongside the question of could my *Overflow* give other people Gathering Skills, and therefore Stats, like it had me? Would that question even matter if I couldn't make it back?

Either way, Smegma hadn't seemed to have been aware of the Tutorials existence, and the System certainly changed things between planet integrations, as evidenced by Nagina and other races that Smegma had described.

"Hey, you're passing the path down!" Fong shouted in his robotic voice.

I started and looked down, realizing I had failed in my original idea of keeping an eye out for Monsters or for Fong. I was about ten feet past a clear path down. It wasn't a walkway per se, but it was a pathway that I could use without needing to leap from the ledge and fall forty feet.

It was somewhat slow going, but not as slow as I might have feared, before I made it to the bottom and rejoined Fong.

"Alright, let's head into the Town," Fong instructed, and we began 'walking' together again. Fong was obviously still injured. I still had the Status Page open but decided to focus on pumping the man for information.

"Fong, how did you get here, if you don't mind me asking?"

"Not an issue," the robotic translator said in my ear. "Everyone has a story. If I'm honest, I can't recall mine. Hit on the head, I'm told. Still, someone from my party told me what happened. They said we all found Fruits in the Dungeon. It was purple with moving hues of every other color we could picture. We knew it was special. When we picked it, the scent made it irresistible, so we ate it. Then, here we are."

Again, Fong's movements were off compared to the timing of his voice. His gesture of the area around us was slightly early compared to his final statement. That and something else was off. Amnesia due to trauma to the head was beyond rare after the Portals Advent. Still, I wasn't willing to pull on that thread. So, instead, I asked, "Is that how most people end up here?"

"Some. Others find new ways to use Skills, unlock a new Stat, and keep exploring. They teach lessons now. Others are what we call Body-Awakened and have a Skill that ties them to Stats right away. Too many to list now, but everyone here can now grow."

I wanted to know more, but his final sentence stopped me from the proverbial 'I've got time' response. Instead, I said, "Now everyone can grow?"

"Yes, with Tutorial Points. You can buy items, train, or simply buy Stats, Evolve Skills and even learn new ones."

"There's no limit to that?" I asked, my voice likely sounding as surprised as I felt. Not that Fong would hear it.

"Limit? Yes, you can only raise Skills from F to E to D Rank in the Tutorial. Or do you mean Skill limit? Then, also yes. Ten to fifteen—depends on the person."

I blinked at his answer, but I realized that the second part was in line with what Smegma had always claimed. "Can you do more in other Tutorials?"

"I do not know if other Tutorials exist. But assume they must, because of the message we receive before coming here. Everyone that is here gets the same one."

I recalled the specific mention of 'E-Ranked Tutorial' and let that line of questioning drop. Should I return to the questions about other ways people got here? No, there were other more important things to ask before we arrived at the growing walls. "How many people are here?"

"There were about eight thousand, but now it's only about five and a half thousand."

"I thought you said people can't leave."

"They cannot. Well, that is not true. Some disappear, from time to time—so maybe they found the way. No, the majority of our loss of people is from war."

Fong didn't even look back as the mechanically robotic voice translated his words to me. He just kept shuffling toward the walls with his hand on his stomach.

There had been a war, and two thousand, five hundred or more people had died? That didn't seem like a lot until you realized that it was more than thirty percent of the previous population.

My voice froze in my throat, even as any further questions died on my tongue. This place was even more dangerous than I had originally thought. I was even less sure now that I wouldn't get press-ganged into some kind of future war.

The next five minutes passed in silence as I followed Fong. Then we moved closer to the gate and walls of Tutorial Town, and I was quiet for a whole different reason. The walls were lined with turrets, and the gate manned by guards that were definitely not humans. Giants maybe, but not humans.

Worse, I could see more of them up on the walls patrolling behind or in front of those turrets.

Fong took pity on me and said, "They are the Guards of Tutorial Town. As far as anyone knows, they have *almost* always been here. Even the boss says that there was never a time before the Guards. Do not cause harm to anyone inside the walls, or they will descend. We do not know how powerful they are, but even a man with an A-Rank Skill was forced to flee. Flee, or die."

"So, don't break any rules?" I asked to clarify, still staring at the ever-growing Giants in suits of full plate armor.

"That's the only rule..." Fong whispered.

CHAPTER 47: CHAPTER 99

Tutorial Day 1

The sight of the Guards made me tunnel visioned and I missed all the people coming and going from the open gate. The only thing that clued me into their presence was when someone shouted, "Hey Fong, got a new one?"

This voice was entirely normal to my ears, lacking the strange robotic quality of Fong's, causing me to look for the speaker. I found a lumberjack of a man with blonde hair covering his entire body. Sure, he had a quaffed bird's nest of a hairstyle on top of his head, but he also wore a massive beard that obscured most of his face from view. Then there were his arms, back and chest. While he was wearing a leather vest that obscured some of the latter two from sight, I could see curls of the same blonde hair trying to escape its confines. Had the man been a wooly mammoth in a previous life?

The closer he got to me, the larger he became, making me think for just a moment that he was the spawn of one of the Giant armored Guards.

Definitely a reincarnated wooly mammoth, I thought.

Fong put his hand on his Sword and faced the approaching man, making me step back into a ready position as well. Ready for what? I wasn't sure, but escape was at least a part of my current thoughts.

"Yes, Bear," Fong said, with a slight dip in his head. "This one just arrived, and I was bringing him to Maelstrom."

Bear—apparently, I had been slightly off on the man's heritage—eyed Fong's hand, which was off his stomach and back on his Sword, with wary eyes. He also seemed to take note of Fong's hunched posture and dented armor. The rest of his features were impossible for me to read before he transferred his gaze to me.

"What Skills you got, kid?"

"That is none of our business, Bear," Fong said, his voice still robotic. I heard a squeak of leather as his hand tightened around his hilt.

What were the chances, I wondered, *that killing each other in the doorway to Tutorial Town qualified as 'doing harm inside the walls?'*

I took a further step backward, eyeing both of the men and the massive Guards not a hundred yards away.

I guess we were outside of *the Town.* Still, I was sure I was missing something. Was Bear from one of the rival factions?

"Maelstrom was the one that told me to look for you, Fong," Bear answered, his eyes on the man's Sword again, even as his own went to the pair of Hatchets on his waist. I hadn't noticed the weapons on the massive man, at least not at first. Now I couldn't look away.

They were sinister looking things, with spikes on the back, and other such decorations that clearly made them worse for chopping wood and better for debilitating a man. Fong and Bear's interaction had gathered a crowd, and I could feel the press of the circle that was forming choose to include me inside it by about three feet.

I glanced back and found Hunters wearing all manner of Armor and Weapons. I also found representatives of many different races and ethnicities. The fact that Fong spoke a different language, and some of the cuts of clothing and armor in the group, confirmed that these people were from every corner of the globe. Not just Canada.

"Thank you for informing this humble one, Bear. This is fortuitous timing, *friend*—as I was on my way to see him," Fong responded, his voice still devoid of any emotion because of the translator. From his body language, he was still ready to fight, or perhaps defend himself from this man.

"See that you do, and get that useless kid inside before one of these onlookers chooses to take his Tutorial Points!" Bear commanded and then started laughing. Others in the circle joined his laughter, leaving me even more confused.

That hadn't been funny. A threat? Maybe. Especially if people could kill each other to steal Tutorial Points... Definitely not funny! So, was Bear so powerful that people laughed to kiss his ass, or was I missing something, and people had tried and failed to steal Tutorial Points in some humorous way?

Fong bowed, which was more of a slight dip of his head. He was already hunched over, so it looked like a full bow. Fong then began to take a slow, limping route around the massive Bear, his hand still on his Sword, but his second hand now holding his stomach again. Over his shoulder, he said, "Follow me, please."

The crowd dispersed with grumbles of disappointment and even a few catcalls at Fong, but the man ignored them. We crossed the final hundred yards of hard-packed earth and stone, each step bringing us closer to the Guards and the Gate. Before us was a clear line of delineation: inside and outside of a partition on the ground, and Fong was moving slowly but purposefully toward it.

Slate pavers exiting the Gate formed a semi-circle twenty feet forward, which both Guards stood upon. The edge of that paved semi-circle seemed to create a strange shimmer in the air. Fong stepped through it and a great deal of his tension left his body. Fong also took his hand off his Sword and returned the limb to holding his wounded side. Seeing that, I didn't hesitate and stepped through as well.

The change was noticeable to almost every sense my body possessed. First was the temperature. One step earlier the air had felt hot and muggy—causing me to sweat while merely walking. As for inside the stones, it felt like someone had set an air conditioner to a perfectly comfortable temperature and removed the humidity.

The light levels also changed—going from drab browns and muted, washed-out green foliage to near LED quality. I looked up to the sky and still found the several suns shining there, but where there had been clouds before, now only sparkling crystal-blue graced the heavens.

The next thing I noticed was the smell. Ever since the Mud Slimes, I hadn't been able to get the slight but persistent odor of swamp out of my nostrils.

Upon crossing the Tutorial Town threshold, the smell seemed to vanish. I raised a hand to my nose and sniffed, knowing that the swamp smell had lingered on my fingers from collecting the Cores. Nothing…

Finally, was the sound.

The catcalls and grumblings from the crowd were gone, changed to the constant hum of a mall. People conversed in groups as they moved through wide, paved streets. Others stood alone, shouting out wares and hints of strange desires I didn't fully understand. The closest one that I could hear had his voice translated robotically into my ear.

"Looking for four others to run a Tutorial's Dungeon Opportunity. Need Healing and three damage dealers," the translation intoned.

Fong looked at me with a small smirk on his face. His mouth moved and the translation said, "Strange, isn't it?"

Unsure which part he was talking about, I took his words to mean everything I was feeling. I nodded and his smirk grew to a smile. "Come with me. We're going to the North District."

With that, he limped straight up the wide street in front of us. Had his limp become less noticeable?

Once clear of the Gates, I noticed that the street was lined with the walls I'd seen from the top of the steppe. Each side of the street had one, making where we walked a strange, enclosed pathway between what felt like retaining walls. For just a moment, I wondered why the walls were here, but Fong opened his mouth, clearly anticipating that question.

"The walls and this street allow people to cross the city to the different Districts they want without having to enter others. They were purchased by the Tribes to keep people out of their zones of influence."

"Why would they want to keep people out of their Districts?" I asked, not understanding what was so important about the Districts.

"This is hard to explain in full. The simple answer is that each Tribe holds a building within its District. This building is where you can purchase Tutorial Items with Points. It also gives any member who gives tithe to the Altar within a boon."

"A boon?"

Fong stopped walking and looked at me with a strange expression. Then scratching his own neck, he said, "Translation is not perfect. A boon. A limited time increase to Stats or regeneration. Sometimes, it even increases comprehension."

"Oh, a buff?!" I exclaimed, and Fong nodded before returning to his purposeful walk. Knowing what he meant only brought up more questions. "Why would the Tribes wish to keep people from getting this buff?"

"My apologies," Fong answered. "It is not the 'buff' that is special—well, it *is* special and unique for each District. However, it is the Items inside that are what they most want to protect."

"The items inside?" I asked and then followed up with, "Do you mean the ones you can purchase?"

"Yes. Some are limited. Some items are only restocked once a month, others—once a year, and some only restock when the user dies. Items, also different. With descriptions. So, keeping out others keeps one safe. No exposed weakness, see?"

I was starting to get the picture. These 'buildings' provided a unique buff that the Tribes monopolized to a lesser extent. Then the Shops had items that had limited quantities, and descriptions of said items that would give information on what a given District had access to. There was one glaring issue with the whole thing.

"I thought you said you can't kill inside the city? I assumed that meant fighting as well, so how do you keep others out?"

"Limit entry points," Fong motioned at the walls and the translation came through a moment after. "If enemy comes, block entrance with bodies. If they push or attack standing Tribesmen, Guards come. Secrets safe, yes?"

The heads of people on top of the walls took on a bit of a different meaning. Still, to constantly have to patrol your walls and guard your entrance—that must take a lot of manpower. Then, on top of that, to block a building entrance with bodies? Were the people in these Tribes constantly on call?

I didn't bother asking that question, since the response was likely exactly what I was thinking. I even had a suspicion as to why Maelstrom was looking for Fong…

It took about five more minutes before we arrived at the place in the center of the Town where the four walls met. The central square wasn't 'square' in shape. Instead, it was an octagon with four diagonal entrances parallel to each other and the four walkways entering in between.

Outside, when Bear had confronted Fong, I might have seen fifty people. Here, in the central square, there were at least a hundred. Just like near the Town entrance, people called out for group members, but now that I was closer, a few other shouted requests could be heard. Some translated and some not.

"Need a Lava Ruby, will trade for two of any other gems."

"Looking for Devilsaur Leather, willing to trade forged equipment."

Other such requests were being made, and the people making them stood out to my casual inspection. They, unlike the people outside or even Fong right in front of me, didn't look like Hunters. They looked more similar to the employees of Abyss, or Crafting Fortune Five Hundreds.

Sure, they had Weapons and Armor—many even looked physically fit and were moving at speeds as they gestured that were far quicker than I could with my Agility—but the Armor I could see was too clean, the Weapons too ornamental. It was an assumption, certainly, but I believed that the people looking to trade for Items were Crafters of some kind.

I pointed to them and asked Fong about it, and he responded as expected, "Yes. They are all Crafters. They mostly stay inside the city, unless brought out by the Tribes for specific tasks under heavy guard."

"Do they get treated differently?" I asked, looking at Fong's serviceable but damaged Armor and the Crafter's pristine garments.

"All Skills get treated differently. Fighters—damage dealers, as they are often called, are the most common. Then Tanks—Hunters specialized in defense—and finally, Healers. Crafters are rarer than Fighters but more common than Tanks as a group, but specific Professions may be rarer than others. Understand?" Fong answered.

The translations for those particular roles were spot on. The terms 'DD,' 'glass cannon,' or more simply—DPS or 'deeps,' was well understood in online gaming. As were 'Tanks' and 'Healz.'

Fong had actually stopped to tell me this, and for the first time, I had the suspicion that Fong was answering my questions intentionally. At first, I believed the man was just talkative, but I was beginning to believe it was something else. The way he aggressively responded to Bear had been a major hint. Was Fong protecting and preparing me?

I still wasn't willing to tell him my Skills, but I pulled up the two I could see to check the changes myself.

Heal
(11)
Skill Type: Healing
Skill Rank: Low E-Rank (Evolvable)

Heal can only be used on others the Skill user is touching, and heals the individual's Health Pool at a rate of one health per half point of Mana expended. Additionally, it will stabilize injuries once Healing has begun, preventing nearly all Health Deteriorating Effects.

—

Cleanse
(11)
Skill Type: Healing
Skill Rank: Low E-Rank (Evolvable)

Cleanse can only be used on others and removes contaminants, poisons, venoms and diseases from the individual. Limited to Rare, Common or Uncommon maladies.
Costs 5 Mana per use.

Looking at them, I considered what I might be willing to reveal to this Maelstrom character. Disappointingly, Heal didn't allow me to cast it on people I wasn't touching. Still, if a Healer was the rarest Class here in the Tutorial, then I was certainly in an advantageous position, thanks to my Battlefield Healer Class. Healing was likely to be a very powerful negotiating chip. On the flip side, though, there was another worrisome possibility.

"Just how rare are Healers?" I asked, recalling the man at the front looking for one to join his group.

Fong nodded to the guards at the entrance to the gate across the square to our left as he shuffled through. He waited for about forty limping steps before he answered, "Rare enough that they are guarded resources with limited freedom in the Maelstrom Tribe."

I swallowed hard. My question had clearly, or at least potentially, tipped my hand to the Swordsman. Fong was definitely trying to help me out, and now that we were inside the District, I had limited time to figure out what I should be telling Maelstrom about my Skills. One thing was already certain—I'd be keeping my Healer Skills to myself.

"What about Gatherers?" I asked, recalling what the Status Page had called my other 'Role.'

"Gatherers are very important, and protected on Raids, Excursions and Dungeon runs. They often also become Crafters in this place," Fong answered as he turned down a street between buildings. The buildings inside this portion of the District were of shoddy construction, looking worse than the Goblin huts from the caverns. In some I could hear the sounds of people at work, letting me know that the ones nearest the entrance were likely in use by Crafters. Many others were nearly falling over, with doors wide open, and in serious disrepair.

"Why are these buildings so poorly made?" I asked, pointing them out to Fong.

"These are man-made and not purchased yet with Tutorial Points. You will see… difference as we approach… center," Fong answered.

"So… these Crafters are just… bad?"

Fong snorted a laugh, which sounded incredibly odd from the mechanical translator, not to mention letting me know that I'd accidentally said my thoughts out loud.

Sure enough, the further into the District we went, the more the buildings changed. It was almost like there was a line drawn. Suddenly they were brick constructions that began as one story and grew with each block we passed. The fact that the brick perfectly accentuated the gray tiles with the onyx and tan patterning made me realize what Fong meant by 'purchased.' It also became clear which building we were heading toward.

A tall tower-esque building, likely the one that had four identical ones in each district, was clearly visible. It reminded me of a clock tower in design and was still easily visible over the tops of the taller buildings near the center. At first, I hadn't noticed it due to the many other sights to take in. Now I wondered how I could have missed it as we walked through the Town. It was clearly of different quality than even the 'purchased' buildings we now walked between.

Instead of bricks, it was made from one seemingly solid piece of stone that resembled marble but shone like it was a polished piece in Go, a boardgame with white and black pieces. The other thing I noticed was just how many more people occupied the central section of the Districts. The buildings were a combination of shops, crafting halls and residences. I wondered if residency was based on seniority or contribution, or perhaps even through the simple expedience of wealth.

I opened my mouth to ask, but Fong held up a hand. "The escorts are here," he said.

I looked around confused until I saw the cloaked figures on the rooftops. *I guess question time is over.*

CHAPTER 48: CHAPTER 100

Tutorial Day 1

The cloaked guards on the rooftops followed us, or continued to multiply as we neared the onyx-marble clocktower. At first I had believed the structure to be of one solid coloring, but it actually was black and white. Having some sort of line down it's center, dividing it into a 'front' and 'back.' We'd been approaching from the black side, which I decided to call the front. The stories of the buildings we passed continued to increase, and I couldn't understand how the guards could be moving that fast and climbing higher.

Fong ignored them, and me to some degree, as he continued to slowly lead the way. I, in some ways, ignored him as well, too focused on the cloaked danger surrounding us. So when he suddenly wasn't in front of me anymore, it took me another five steps to notice.

A polite cough echoed off the brick walls, causing me to look around. I don't know what I expected to find. Perhaps a cloaked individual who had descended from the roofs, but I didn't expect to see Fong in the doorway of the last building before the central onyx-marble tower. The dividing line between white and black was right where the large arched tower doorway sat.

"Oh, shit," I mumbled as I rushed back to join him. He gave me a tight-lipped smile and then moved through the doorway into what looked like darkness beyond. I wasn't far behind him, but I did take a second to look back over my shoulder.

How many bodies would that huge doorway need to be totally blocked?

I didn't consider that question too long, and stepped through after Fong. I discovered that the darkness inside of this building was just in comparison to the multi-sun illumination outside. Inside, the building was lit by flickering candlelight—well, maybe not.

My eyes adjusted, and I discovered the light was coming from fixtures on the walls, but instead of fire, the interior of the sconces were filled with orange Crystals that flickered. Fong spoke up for the first time in minutes, "These are called Sunstones—it is how we determine night and day here."

He pointed back through the doorway, seeming to say, 'You know, with all those suns.'

"What do you mean?" I asked, truly confused by how a flickering stone could determine the night or day cycle.

"Six suns are blue; six suns are yellow. They take a long while to revolve. Likely ten to eleven days for each sun to rise as another disappears. These Sunstones go from a bright, constant light to flickering, and finally dark, before reversing in a twenty-four hour period.

"Right now, it is either early morning or evening."

"You don't know?" I asked, incredulous.

He gave me a strained smile, then a small shrug, before leading me down the hallway past staircases on both sides and a few doors. The doors at the end of the brick hallway were clearly different. Like Mr. Varnish's double doors. They were huge wooden things with inlaid metal bands holding together the planks. There were also metal spikes driven through that would likely injure people who attempted to batter their way in.

I wondered if that made them structurally stronger or not, but Fong reached a hand forward and knocked, cutting that question short. The sounds of scraping wood behind the door made me squint as I tried to understand what was going on. Only when I heard the scraping stop and something slide free in a swish, did I fully grasp the situation. The door was 'barred' in the literal sense.

A moment after the bar was taken out from the door, it swung open to reveal eight cloaked figures. In my distraction, I'd missed Fong unbuckling his Sword. Still holding his right side, he held it out with his other hand and the cloaked figures took it, before patting the man down thoroughly but not roughly.

I was next, and when they found no weapons, they checked again. I couldn't see anyone in the hoods, and I tried. Their hands also felt odd. More like a single wooden oar than an appendage with fingers that could act independently. Still, I could see five-fingered black gloves on the hands, so I shrugged the strange sensation away.

The eight figures surrounded us after the second pat-down check, and Fong limped forward again. I wondered why they hadn't taken Fong's Bag of Holding, and only his Sword. Surely, I could pull a Pick out of my Necklace if needed—and Fong likely had back up Swords, no?

The moment we passed through the doorway, something in the air changed. It was like gravity had increased, or perhaps—like my mind was aware of something that it couldn't quantify? The only way I could think to describe it was with an idiom I had never understood. The room felt *oppressive*. Like my clothing was pressing into my skin instead of sitting atop it. Like the oxygen in the air was fractionally harder to breathe.

My eyes scanned the room, looking for the cause of the change. They found nothing but more shadows and a man seated in an overly large wooden chair with red cushions. The fact that my eyes found hundreds of 'shadows' made me question something Fong had said earlier. How could there only be fifty-five hundred people total, when I'd seen at least two or three hundred of these cloaked figures already?

Was this Malestrom Tribe the strongest in the Tutorial and able to dedicate this many people to 'guard' the boss?

Fong sighed wearily, "Kai, you must leave this room from time to time. You will not discover an exit if you stay locked here and only send out your Shadows."

"Maybe I would leave more often, Fong, if you didn't vanish every time I turned around!" the man on the throne—clearly Kai—answered, his voice also robotic. Kai wore a black suit of leather Armor and a Crown made of the same onyx stone as the Tower outside. His features were eerily similar to Fong's.

"I told you that I refuse to be confined to Tutorial Town."

"Enough of this—you are my tool, and if I want you here, then that is where you should stay. Who is the boy?" Kai ordered, looking like he was angry with Fong, or perhaps frustrated by what he had said. It was tough to tell with an inflection-less voice. Still, why would Fong's wanting to leave Tutorial Town frustrate Kai?

Sure, Fong was strong, but with all these guards already here?

"Maelstrom, this is Brodie, yet to choose an alias. He is a new arrival."

"A new arrival? Fong, I told you that I don't want any others around who I can't trust. Why would you bring a possible spy into our Tribes' deepest sanctum?"

Fong sighed and motioned at the room around us. "This stupid room that you paid extra for because you feared assassins. You're calling it a sanctum now?"

"What do you know? You weren't the one *attacked* by those assassins. There are loopholes to the rules, and I almost died!"

"We've been here for *sixty years*, Kai," Fong responded. "Perhaps it is more risk that will grant us freedom."

The interplay between the two was strange. I couldn't be sure what it all meant, but I had a feeling that the war had started between the Tribes for nefarious reasons. One thing was abundantly clear the more they said—Fong and Kai had known each other since before the Tutorial. Maybe Kai was part of the party Fong had mentioned?

Only one other thing was strange. Fong wanted out. Why wouldn't Kai?

The other piece of information Fong had let slip was that the cloaked people surrounding us weren't people at all. They were 'shadows' and likely created by one of Kai's Skills. The two men stared at each other, making me feel like I should be sweating, especially in the room we were in.

"At least ask the boy what he does, Kai," Fong said.

"Why?" Kai answered. "I don't want any new members."

"And I do," Fong stated. The Shadows moved off the walls, getting into stances that seemed martial to my eyes.

The glaring resumed, and this time, I did begin to sweat. I could feel the line it traced down my spine. Maybe it would have been better to have been found by someone else? It was clear that this Maelstrom, whose real name was likely Kai, wasn't taking new members for his Tribe.

I crouched down myself, getting ready to at least protect myself if I had to. Still, when I went to reach for my Mana, I couldn't feel it. A lump of intense worry formed in my throat, and I almost stood back up but thought better of it. I pushed harder toward *Dragon Heart*, desperately needing to feel the Mana there.

I was just starting to feel the buzz of the electrified resource when Kai interrupted my focus.

"Fine!" Kai's mouth moved and the translation came through. He was still staring at Fong, looking worried when he asked, "Boy, what do you do?"

"I'm a Gatherer, but I think I could use my Skill for Crafting as well," I answered, my voice sounding unconvincing even to my own ears.

Fong looked at me with a raised eyebrow but gave no other reaction, even as Kai leaned forward in his seat. It was only then that I realized my tone likely wasn't coming through to them, if the translation worked the same way it did for me.

Kai's words a moment later confirmed it for me. "You have a Skill that you've used for multiple things already? Or are you unsure and just hoping you can figure it out?"

Drawing on what Fong had said on the way to Town, I slowly answered, "That's how I unlocked all my Stats, yes."

I saw Fong smirk. Even if someone had a Skill that could detect the truth—I wasn't lying, not exactly. So, why was Fong smirking?

Kai showed only an interested look as he leaned even further forward in his chair. "That is something few here can do now—and you're claiming that kind of Skill Mastery?" He made an appreciative noise and then leaned back in his chair. "What Crafting Skill do you think you'd be most suited for?"

That question was something I'd been thinking over in my head since Fong had become more withdrawn in the presence of the attending Shadows. There were really only three that I could claim—since they'd been on the System message when I'd unlocked the Crafter Class. Two of which were *Blacksmithing* or *Leather-working*, which I highly doubted I could pull off. Even with Smegma's help.

That left *Alchemy*, which I figured I might get away with. First, it was a rarer Profession on Earth, so the chances of someone having it here were lower. But second, and more importantly, I hadn't seen any in the cross-corridor that bisected the Districts or in the Central Square.

Fong had also claimed that many Gatherers became Crafters here—so if I claimed I thought my Skill could help me with a rarer Craft—all the better, right?

"*Alchemy*, I think?" I said and saw Fong flinch as his smirk vanished. His flinch caused him to redouble his effort on holding his stomach, which drew my gaze even more.

"Have you done any *Alchemy* before?" Kai asked, the translated voice not matching his expression.

I shook my head.

"Do you have any of the Equipment needed?"

His body language looked upset, and so I wanted to give a non-verbal response but realized I couldn't convey what I needed to say without an answer this time. "Not yet, but I believe I can make some in time."

"Have you worked around Alchemists on Earth?" Fong asked, his hand that wasn't holding his stomach twitching toward me, like he either wanted to place it on my shoulder or hit me. Since he'd only tried to help me on the way here, I chose the former and nodded while 'thinking' heavily about Smegma as an Alchemist. Fong turned to Kai.

Kai was studying me with narrowed eyes and a face that was beyond my capability to read for emotions. Something was going on, but what it was, I couldn't say.

"Maybe the kid could replace Miranda?" Fong suggested.

"You know the targets of the previous war as well as I do, Fong," Kai answered, and I blinked.

Targets? Of the war? So the war was between the Tribes, not with some outside force?!

Fong looked at me with a slight grimace. "I am assuming we can keep this one, or whichever Inheritor is chosen, better protected, then?"

Kai leaned forward and all of the Shadows even stepped up as well. "Fong, are you offering to personally watch over the child?"

Fong studied my face and then gave a world-weary sigh. "No, I will not. Perhaps in time, if he proves to be a potent Alchemist, but I must search outside the Town for the exit."

Fong's head fell and I thought for a moment it was in disappointment, or perhaps sadness at the words he'd just spoken. Instead, I saw his hand cradling a locket on his chest, holding it out just far enough that he could see it.

It was a locket that usually held pictures of precious people. Like wives, children or other family.

* * *

The door closed behind the newcomer. Kai turned back to his five Shadows in the room. Standing from his throne broke the illusion of hundreds of them, and suddenly the room changed, becoming more of a sitting room that one might find in an apartment.

Kai was in a corner of the room, and one of his Shadows occupied the chair that had been the throne. Kai glanced at the huge, ever-changing plaque on the wall. A board that was probably meant to be accessible to anyone in the Tutorial, but he'd monopolized.

Sure, part of it still popped up four times a year in the center of the Town, but that was only the overall Achievement Leaderboard for everyone in the Tutorial. This Leaderboard had more functionality.

"Is that really necessary?" Fong asked.

Kai narrowed his eyes at Fong as he stood up and pointed to the name currently at four hundred and eighty-sixth on the Tutorial Point section of the Northern District's Points Leaderboard. Brodie.

In one motion, Kai dashed behind Fong and touched the back of his neck. The wooden doll collapsed to the ground, illusion gone, and its 'wound' on clear display.

Something had clearly taken a bite out of his puppet's side. He shook his head and began pulling the Skill Orbs out of the indents in the wood that had been specifically designed to hold them. He was careful with only one of them—the modified Tutorial Core that Kai had created using his *Illustrious Illusions*. It acted as Fong's personality and memory center.

It also allowed his creation to touch Mana, Qi and Soul.

This puppet was made of a different material than the Shadows on display around him. His was a much more expensive and harder to find wood. Thankfully, he had back ups for these sorts of reasons.

"Bring me a spare," he called out, knowing that his other disguised puppet would obey. Unlike Fong, this other puppet was obedient.

Kai opened his locket and stroked the picture of his son and daughter. He was distracted enough that when the puppet that was the spitting image of his daughter dropped the Superior Puppet at his feet, he jumped. He transferred a narrow-eyed scrutiny onto her.

Was she beginning to act out like Fong?

"Why do you *let* brother Fong get away with so much? *It's unfair!*" she asked, her voice petulant and whiny. This was not acting out, but just how his daughter acted. She only truly went this far with family since she felt safe being her vapid self. She was also the only one of the group who could speak English fluently.

"None of your business," Kai responded and began slotting the Skill Orbs into the new puppet. "Take this one—" He motioned at the damaged puppet. "—and see if the Carver can do anything."

"Fine, Father, but like—this wouldn't happen if he stayed in Town," she said while still pouting from his earlier answer.

"Don't call me that!" Kai shouted. As the girl reached down to grab the broken Superior Puppet, Kai raised a hand to point at his door. "Keep an eye on that boy who just left as well. His story is too convenient. Also, I felt something earlier—like a pressure against the wards on this place."

"Surely you don't think that boy—"

"Of course not, but that doesn't mean that one of the other leaders didn't send him."

"Well, have your other spies watch him. I'm too busy. He'll be at the Alchemy Academy, anyway. Right? If he tries to join a Party, he'll like, only have one choice. So, I'll watch him then, *I guess.*"

Kai nodded before mentally diving into the Monster Core that acted as Fong's entire being. There was no memory that would increase Kai's suspicions toward Brodie—but there were a few moments where Fong had clearly guided Brodie. It seemed like Fong's acts of rebellion were growing. Could the child *Heal* also?

He'd tell his spies what to look out for.

Shaking his head, he modified those memories and then attempted to adjust the rebellious attitude but gave up when it threatened to destroy the modified Core. Finally, he placed the Core back in the puppet before he connected his Skill to the new Fong.

It instantly hopped to its feet, and Kai placed the image of his son atop it. As his daughter left, he told the new Fong about the boy waiting outside, and where he should bring him.

CHAPTER 49: CHAPTER 101

Tutorial Day 1

Four Shadows stood around me as I waited outside the large doors into the central room. With my exit came a profound sense of relief. The cloying pressure instantly dissipated, and while there were still threatening Shadows surrounding me, they clearly hadn't been the cause of the discomfort inside.

Almost as soon as the doors closed, I touched my Mana Pool and found it responding.

Fong and Maelstrom were clearly having a 'private' discussion, since I'd been *asked* to leave. I had a lot of questions I'd like answers to, but for now, could only speculate as to what had gone wrong with my choice of Crafting Professions.

How could an Alchemist cause a war? Poisons maybe? Or perhaps it was a very profitable career inside the Tutorial, so money or prestige had become heavily involved. On Earth, while Alchemists weren't the wealthiest of crafters, they did fall somewhere in the upper middle of the scale.

Then again, like Smiths, they relied heavily on what they could make. A Smith on average was near the bottom, but on the high end, they were likely one of the top earners. Plus, each was highly dependent on having a Skill that complimented their Craft. Or two, in many cases.

Still, the undisputed top Crafting Profession was Enchanting, which was why I hadn't even considered claiming it. That tangential thought brought me full circle. So why would an Alchemist be highly valued here in the Tutorial?

The only answer I could think of was that the last Alchemist had been a real monster. Someone who could create something extraordinary, or—could Alchemy be a key to leaving this place? I remembered that Fong had mentioned purchasing items that could help the people in the Tutorial grow their Stats, and even their Skill levels and Rankings. Was that the key? Could Alchemists make— what? Stat Potions? Skill Potions? My mind whirled as I continued to think of ever-more elaborate and convoluted possibilities.

Thankfully, Fong came out of the room at that moment, stopping my speculation. The look he gave me spoke volumes. He almost looked like he was seeing me for the first time, and I didn't need him to say anything to know I should wait to ask any questions I had.

Fong's mouth moved and the translation kicked in a moment later, "Follow me. I've been told to find you a room in one of the inner buildings. Also, I will introduce you to the guards, so you can access the Alchemy Academy's rooms with most of the stored Herbs. This way."

Fong began walking, and for the first time since I'd met him, he wasn't holding his side or limping. I hurried to catch up. He'd clearly gotten some Healing from Maelstrom or one of Maelstrom's people.

The Shadows, sadly, separated from their places on the hallway walls and followed, meaning I probably wasn't going to get a chance to ask any questions. Not yet, at least.

We left the building the same way we'd come in and crossed the street to the next building, directly across from Maelstrom's. The Shadows were following us, making me more nervous just by my sheer proximity—even if by proxy—to Kai, but also due to the man's words inside.

Fong eventually coughed politely to get my attention, which made me realize I was standing stock still just outside the entrance to the other building. He gave me a sad smile. "Do not worry overly much. Maelstrom may be a bit single-minded in his focus on the Tribe, but he will protect us all."

He mumbled something else that the translation didn't pick up. It only gave me a single word, 'made,' which left me more confused. Fong grimaced when he saw my expression and waved away my concern.

"Sorry, just my own musings. Since you are an Alchemist, you've somehow ended up exactly where you need to be," Fong continued, before turning around and walking into the building. "Perhaps it is providence."

There was something off in the way the man was speaking. Even though it was inflection-less due to the translator, it was still different—somehow. One thing I could point out was the fact that he had called Maelstrom 'Kai' up to this point, but had now reverted to Maelstrom. Had he been scolded after I left?

Then there was the lack of answers in what he had been saying. Like that statement. It only made me more confused. Still, at least his earlier words reassured me a little bit.

As soon as I walked into the building, I could tell it was different than the last one. It still had no windows, but the hallways were far wider, at least on the main floor we entered on. Another stark difference was the lighting. In here, the lights were closer to true sunlight, or at least, LEDs that could mimic it. The other building had been left almost intentionally dark, which seemed odd until I glanced at the four Shadows.

They looked truly miserable in the bright light. Not like it was hurting them, but it just highlighted all the oddities that made them clearly not human. In the building with Maelstrom, and on top of the roof, I could mistake them for living beings.

In here and likely outside as well? There was just no chance of that. The clothes looked almost see-through, gossamer and semi-real. I reached out to touch the dark cloak of one and had my hand grabbed by Fong. He shook his head with a soft smile. In truth, the Shadows looked like black, wooden puppets made from poor-quality wood.

The intimidation I felt from them reduced greatly with their appearance shift.

Right in front of the entrance was a staircase that went up a half story before ending in an atrium reminiscent of high school entryways. A quick glance inside an open door as we climbed those stairs further correlated this building with a school.

There were large rooms filled with desks and chalkboards, which admittedly were a bit outdated, but I definitely didn't think I was going to be able to get a tablet or laptop in here. So, I guessed blackboards and paper was going to have to suffice.

I did have my cell phone, and the lights above seemed to at least imply the existence of electricity. The only problem with that—I didn't have a charger. I wondered if anyone else in the Tutorial had brought one. It sure would be nice to be able to keep notes on something a bit more secure than paper notebooks.

My assumptions became dashed when I discovered that the desks in the rooms held only beakers, flasks, titration apparatuses, and other Alchemy equipment. I only grew more confused when I found two to three people working within each room.

I pointed to them and Fong shrugged. "You didn't think you would be the only Alchemist hopeful, did you?"

"Then how did the war start?" I asked. Fong gave me a look with a raised eyebrow then motioned at the 'Shadows.' I had no idea what any of that meant, but assumed I shouldn't ask about the war…

Fong approached two men in leather armor, and they snapped to attention. The man with blonde hair and blue eyes spoke, and a moment later, the words came through the translator. "Sergeant Fong! It's good that you're back. Our current teachers of the Sword—"

Fong cut him off with a raised hand. "I'm not back. This is Brodie, a newbie I picked up while outside Tutorial Town. He thinks he can use his Skill for Alchemy. I'm here to introduce him and get him settled."

"Another one for the Inheritance?" the blue-eyed man said, eyeing me up and down. "Is he going to study anything else?" he asked.

Fong looked at me, seeming to be expecting me to respond.

I stared back at him and gave a small shrug, trying to convey how lost I was. "I like to Cook…"

Fong shrugged and turned back to the guard. "Let's let him get settled and decide after his first week."

The man saluted Fong and then turned to the second guard. "Adam, since you can speak English, go get him settled."

"Yes, Erik!" Adam said with a salute. I was thankful to hear some actual emotions instead of the robotic tones of the translator. "What was your name, again?" Adam said, directing the question at me.

"Brodie," I answered quickly.

"Okay, Brodie—this way. We'll get you settled on the fourth floor. It's nearing night-time, according to the Sunstones, so probably best to find you a bed."

Adam marched off, hand on his sword, and I was left with the choice to follow after him or stay with the only man I felt I knew in this Tutorial, Fong. Fong was already walking toward the exit. He hadn't even waved. I felt abandoned for a split second but chased after the retreating Adam to assuage that emotion.

I sighed and matched Adam's pace once I caught up. The Shadows, thankfully, left with Fong—which made me realize that I probably wasn't their target from the very beginning. At least the Alchemy choice didn't appear to be *totally* the wrong one. Maybe.

As soon as we were in the stairwell and I had caught up to Adam a bit, I asked, "What's going on with the whole thing about Alchemist's causing a war?"

Adam looked at me over his shoulder. "Did you not know about that before you said your Skill could be useful in Alchemy?"

"Fong had said Gatherers often become Crafters in the Tutorial..." I mumbled.

"Well, shit, here I thought you were just another Inheritance chaser."

I blinked and Adam shrugged. "Back to your first question though. It wasn't 'Alchemistsss,'" Adam stressed the plural. "It was *one* Alchemist that caused the war. You see, in our Shop, we have a Skill for purchase that allows an Alchemist to *Mass Produce* Potions, Pills, Elixirs and Tonics. The last guy who had it was a bit of a monster and could create powerful items for Tribe use, and then replicate them. It was really giving us an edge for a while—so the other Tribes banded together to assassinate him.

"We protected him at first and then retaliated, of course, killing their Tribes' Inheritors. So each Tribe is kind of in the same boat."

"Wait," I said, even as I continued to climb flights of stairs. "I thought you couldn't fight in town?"

"You can't, as long as War isn't declared. Once War was declared, the Guards vanished. It became pretty bad for a while. Thankfully, after the Inheritors were killed, the War quickly came to a stop."

"Why would anyone want to become an Inheritor, then?" I asked.

Adam gave me a withering look that seemed to question my manhood. I let it slide off. Getting assassinated simply because people *knew* you had a Skill seemed like a really dumb decision. Adam looked away only long enough to open the stairway door and exit, followed closely by me.

"Risking your life to get such an amazing Skill will ensure you're set once you get out of this place," Adam answered.

It was my turn to give Adam a withering stare. "Do you know of a way out of here?"

Adam's jaw clenched and he didn't reply. In fact, he doubled his pace and arrived at a door with numbers on it far in advance of myself.

I called out after him. "Can't have a 'set' life if you're dead, right?"

I slowly walked up, reading the three numbers. Four hundred and twenty-one.

"This is your room," Adam stated and touched the door handle. "Guards have access to all rooms, and I've just activated the door to recognize the next Mana Signature to touch it. Push a bit of Mana into the handle and it will only allow you and the guards access, along with anyone you grant permission to."

I stepped closer, but Adam was already blowing by me, his parting words stiff and unpleasant. "Good day!"

I guess I said something wrong...

CHAPTER 50: CHAPTER 102

Tutorial Day 2

I'm unembarrassed to say that I passed out in the double bed as soon as I saw it. I didn't even bother looking around the rest of the room. The pillow and white linen sheets were just too inviting. Now, as I blearily opened my eyes and found myself in an alien room, many things were coming back to me, along with worries that my brain had dismissed yesterday.

I had been transported to a Tutorial World, or something like it. Literally vanishing from a Portal on Earth to arrive here. Vanishing from a Portal filled with workers and my *family*!

Any sluggishness I felt vanished as I sat bolt upright. What did my family think had happened to me? Kai's offhand comment about being here sixty years, as well as Fong's locket, took on a *whole*-nother meaning. First, that number was impossible. Humanity hadn't had the System that long. Still, what else could sixty years mean? But, even if he'd misspoke, if I had to spend twenty-four years here, like he likely had, what would my family think happened to me?

The answer was glaringly obvious—they would think I had died.

My infuriating *Mental Fortitude* Skill inserted a thought into my head. '*At least I left them in a good place.*' I picked up my pillow and attempted to tear it apart. I figured I would be able to with my Strength Stat of ten. The fabric proved itself to be stronger than I could have ever imagined.

What was it made of?

That tangent almost succeeded in pushing my worries from center stage in my brain, but I shook the considerations away with a few thumping punches into the offending pillow. There were still so many other issues. Smegma had vanished just before I was teleported here. That likely meant that he or his *Demonic Vault* Skill were undergoing an Evolution.

But it didn't have to mean that. What if the Demon was somehow locked out of this place? How could I possibly—

This time, *Mental Fortitude* was beyond helpful in stopping the toilet bowl of my negativity. I sighed. It was right; I hadn't even tried to access *Demonic Vault* this time—so I may still be able to.

Sending a bit of Mana into the large Sun that was the Skill in my Mental Universe did yield results.

Demonic Vault 4.3.4
Crendalar Five – Abyss Sect's Wares

Skills
Consumables

<Weapons>
Armor
Miscellaneous

Available Currency: 142,011 mC (Mana Coins)

I was unsure if that was a good or bad thing, if I was being honest. It ruled out the Skill going through an upgrade. Or at least I figured it did—since the last few had rendered the Skill unusable.

So then, where was Smegma?

My worry increased exponentially, thinking I might be trapped in a Tutorial Realm, Planet or Dimension without the Demon's knowledge of the System. Outdated or not…

Still, it wasn't something to worry about just yet. He'd always returned before, right?

I moved to the 'Miscellaneous' tab and began scrolling through options. Thankfully, Alchemy Equipment wasn't far into the list. Disappointingly, there were no Recipe Books or Instruction Manuals listed. Maybe I'd get one with the purchase? But based on the Miner's Pick, I doubted that.

Miscellaneous Professions Gear

Alchemy Pill Cauldron (1)
Low F-Rank
Durability: Unlimited

This Pill Cauldron consumes the user's Mana to maintain its internal fires at a desired temperature. The Cauldron will repair using Spilled Mana from ingredients and Evolves when the user crafts an appropriate Pill. It will also Funnel excess Mana to Brodie Flacarada's Overdraft Skill.

Cost: 100,000 mC

—

Miscellaneous Professions Gear

Alchemy Potion Making Set (1)
Low F-Rank
Durability: Unlimited

This Potion Making Set uses precise knowledge and measurements to create base liquids that can be infused with Endurance, Mana or Qi to realize their full effects. The set will repair and strengthen itself, making it unbreakable. The Potion Making Set will create better Elixirs, Potions and Flasks with more precise Magic Control.

It will also Funnel excess Mana to Brodie Flacarada's Overdraft Skill.

Cost: 1,000,000 mC

—

Miscellaneous Professions Gear

Alchemy Body Enhancement Tub (1)
Low F-Rank
Durability: Unlimited

This Tub is designed to contain and strengthen herbal mixtures designed to force body evolutions, the creation of which needs precise knowledge and measurements. The set will repair and strengthen itself from body run offs, making it unbreakable.

Cost: 100,000 mC

There were a few other items related to Alchemy that I didn't quite understand, so I skipped them. Of the three I wanted, the Potion Making Set was the one I wanted the most. The reason was simple: Potions, Elixirs and Flasks were by far the only items I'd heard of or seen on Earth. However, the price tag made it impossible in my current situation.

I'd never heard of a Body Enhancement Tub, and figured I'd like Smegma to explain that one to me before I purchased it. The Alchemy Pill Cauldron I had heard mentioned by Smegma already. It was what he had suggested I get to help heal Eva—another thing I'd left undone.

Strangely, when I was downstairs, I hadn't seen many Pill Cauldrons, if any. I couldn't recall them, at the very least. Maybe I could go out on a few excursions and collect Crystals, those strange *Tutorial* Cores or something similar to exchange for mC?

As long as the selling feature worked without Smegma…

I attempted to sell one of the Scales from my Necklace and discovered that it was functioning. I quickly canceled that transaction, still feeling like the Heart Scale and its smaller compatriots were needed.

This wasn't a decision I needed to make right now, anyway. First, I should explore my new room and this building. Maybe I could find some things with value that wouldn't be missed…

I got out of bed and found a set of blue clothes folded neatly atop a dresser that I hadn't made note of the previous night. Had someone come in and placed the clothes there when I slept? No, Adam had said that only people I gave access could enter. Well, and the guards.

Somewhat out of spite, I attempted to sell the blue robe and got no response from *Demonic Vault*. Figured.

This clothing must have already been there when I entered. Taking a look at myself highlighted just how badly I needed the robe. My clothes were about to fall off. All except for my Miner's Boots, which were held together by the thin metal that protected my feet. I chuckled and slid the rest of the way off the bed.

My laughter died as the lights turned on in the room and the bed glowed for a brief instant. I caught the glow from the corner of my eye and spun to find the bed made up behind me.

"Wow, my parents would have loved this!" I whispered and gave a low whistle. I stared at the bed for another minute—debating messing it up just to see it function again. However, I wasn't sure if it only worked once per day or something like that, so in the end, I left it alone—mostly due to not wanting to potentially create extra work for myself.

Instead, I spun and examined the rest of my room. There was a bedside table with a lamp on it. A lamp that wasn't lit, which led my gaze to the ceiling, where a massive overhead fixture was sunk. It was what provided the nearly blinding amounts of light.

After that I noted that I had two closets. One looked normal, with sliding doors, and another that literally looked like a floor to ceiling nook with no doors. I opened the closet first and found two other sets of clothes. One was a black set that consisted of a tight lycra T-shirt, pants, and a white robe that had a green leaf symbol over the left breast. I stared at it, marking it as odd.

It looked a bit like a doctor's uniform—which might mean it was meant for a Healer. So, either everyone got the same uniforms, this room had a previous owner who had left some clothes behind, or the room was able to analyze and take Roles into account…

I decided right then that no one would be coming into my room. Not until I knew more. I also placed the *Healer's* Robe in my Necklace for good measure.

Next, I went to check the cubby and felt that strange tingle run over my skin as soon as I walked into it. I froze, and then stepped back out, looking at myself. I ran my tongue over my teeth and felt a distinct lack of fuzziness that I associated with cleanliness. I stripped out of my defunct clothing and stepped back into the nook.

The same sensation washed over me, and I smiled. I could get used to a magic shower. It was certainly going to be a time saver. Maybe not great for my sanity—since I enjoyed long, scalding-hot showers when I needed time to collect myself—but then again, I'd been having those far less frequently thanks to *Mental Fortitude.*

I put on the blue robe, hoping it was something for Alchemists or Gatherers and then moved to my door. I opened it and found myself face to face with Adam, who had a hand raised to begin pounding on the exterior. He looked upset.

"I've been knocking for five husking minutes. Did you not change the settings to notify you?" he shouted.

I winced. Maybe he was supposed to say something like that to me after he told me to bind the door—but he'd left in a bit of a huff.

"Oops, can you show me how?" I mumbled and then spun, waiting for him to start explaining what he'd clearly failed to instruct me on the previous night.

"Oops?" Adam scoffed, but then he did instruct me on how to change the door's settings. Once he was finished, he sneeringly said, "You're lucky you opened the door now, otherwise you'd definitely have missed breakfast. The only reason I was sent up here was to inform you that you had twenty—now fifteen—minutes until the buffet closes and the classrooms return to Alchemy stalls!"

With that message delivered, Adam stormed away, clearly still unimpressed with me and my lack of discipline. Or at least I figured it was something along those lines.

I rushed down the stairs nearest my room, and thankfully did arrive on the ground floor while there was still a massive table of food set up in the center of the foyer. I rushed to grab a plate and then looked around to find a place to sit and eat. What I discovered explained what Adam had meant when he said the classrooms 'returned' to Alchemy stalls.

Many of the stalls were currently filled with groups of men and women wearing the same blue robe as me. I considered joining an existing group but thought better of it. I needed to eat quickly, and I'd likely have other opportunities to speak with the people here. However, I only had one such chance to eat before the Alchemy equipment might magically reappear.

I quickly grabbed a helping of some type of meat in gravy, a biscuit-like bread, some sautéed greens, and something that had the same fluffy consistency as eggs while clearly not being the Earthly eggs, or even Roc eggs, I knew of. Mostly because of the purple coloring.

I rushed to an empty table and began scarfing down my food, discovering that it was all delicious. I caught a few people giving me looks as I hurried to finish but ignored them for now—wanting to possibly go back for seconds.

The purple eggs were, in fact, the exact same consistency as normal scrambled eggs, and far better tasting than the bland Roc eggs, making them far more palatable—as long as you ignored the color. The meat tasted like pork but was more gamey. The 'vegetables' were the best part, but what they were, I couldn't tell.

I managed to get a second plate by skipping the biscuit for now. Thankfully, the table I sat at didn't magically refill with Alchemy Beakers, Flasks and other apparatuses. Instead, the people around me began to stand up and slowly clean up their areas before they themselves moved to gather Equipment from nearby glass cupboards that I had failed to notice.

The central buffet wasn't cleaned up, but there was a far more 'mundane' method for its removal. One of the guards approached and simply summoned the whole thing into a Spatial Bag. I briefly wondered what would happen to the heating elements if the Bag froze things like my Necklace, but dismissed it as unimportant.

A lady in her mid-thirties approached my table and coughed politely. "Do you mind if I start getting Alchemy Equipment out and placing it on one side of the table till you *finish*."

Mouth full of food, I nodded and gave her a universal thumbs up. She, thankfully, had spoken English and also understood my gestures. With a polite smile, she began moving to the nearest cupboard as I continued to stuff my face.

By the time she returned with her first load, I was left with only the biscuit and a mouth mostly empty. Carefully, I asked, "Where do I put the plates?"

She smiled and pointed to a table in the corner of the room, currently empty of all plates but with a guard standing by it, tapping his foot. I rushed over and the man snatched the plate out of my hand, making it vanish right after my fingers left it. "Next time, show up on time, newbie."

I shook my head, not happy with the treatment from the guards this morning, or last night for that matter. Slowly, I moved back to the table to see if the friendly girl was willing to chat. She was setting out equipment. I stopped a good five feet from her and said, "Hi, I'm Brodie. Thanks for your help."

She smiled at me and answered, "You're welcome, now kindly husk off. I've got work to do and don't like people hovering."

I blinked at her casual dismissal of me—with a smile, no less—and then stepped back when I realized she meant it. I looked around the room and discovered many groups and individuals in the same situation. Each group was clearly already getting to work, moving back and forth between cupboards that I'd also failed to notice and collecting Herbs.

I could overhear some conversations.

"We need the Gatherers to really start focusing less on Grasses and Herbs, and more on finding Fruits."

"You know as well as I do that the Fruits are often eaten in the field. Don't expect too much—since they spoil so quickly."

"Are we out of Blood Leaf again?"

"We had so much more resources before the War…"

I stood there, just listening to the scattered conversations, unsure if I should be attempting anything. Eventually, I made a decision and moved to the cupboards and drawers that I'd seen other individuals collecting materials from.

Mostly, I just wanted to check them out, but I was also hoping that my Skill would recognize a few. The containers had labels on them, but not a single name was something I'd heard of. The inside of the containers also didn't contain full herbs but ground powders and juices. It also wrote out the rank and 'efficacy' of the plants contained within.

After several minutes of searching, I had to admit that I was way out of my league in this room. I slowly left and checked the other classrooms.

My mood soured further each time I discovered new containers of Powders and Herbs with labels, that my Skill couldn't recognize. Finally, I entered the smallest and least frequented room and immediately knew something was different. Just looking at a few of the cupboards and shelves, I could see blue hovering plaques.

Fire Grass
Rank: Low F

I instantly recognized the red plaque since my *Mining* Skill had done something similar. Of course, then it had given me information on the vein as well as the rank and name, but I instantly felt better knowing that one of my two Gardener Skills would be able to help me—especially if I leveled it.

The fact that the label on the plastic container said Powdered Fire Grass, Rank F, with a eighty percent efficacy wasn't that important, surely. That extra information might not matter…

CHAPTER 51: CHAPTER 103

Tutorial Day 2

Purchase Powdered Fire Grass for 1 Tutorial Points a gram?
Yes | <No>
Price for entire eight-pound Container.
3632 Tp

I tried to take out the Container and study it but instantly selected no. After the purchase option, I didn't instantly go take stock of the rest of the shelves and instead returned to the foyer and the guards it held. Approaching one of them earned me a look of disdain, which spoke pretty loudly. It was clear that the guards didn't think too highly of Crafters.

Taking a deep breath, I steeled my nerves and asked, "I'm new here. Are the things on the shelves for us to use as we want?"

"As long as you're wearing that blue robe, and pay the fees asked to purchase them, then yes," the guard said, his voice strangely mocking. I knew he was attempting to be disparaging, and my brain worked overtime to find the hidden meanings, if there was more than one.

I could only find one. "Meaning that the robe can be taken away?"

The second guard gave a hint of a smile, which screamed the answer even though the other guard only shrugged. Instead of responding, I thanked them for answering my question and walked away.

As I left, I heard the second smiling guard whisper, "It's always so satisfying to throw them out!"

Now I only had one further question, and since there were more guards at the bottom of the half set of stairs from the entryway, I approached them. "If I choose to go Gather materials on a mission, will I lose my Alchemist Robes?"

They blinked at me, seeming confused by the question. They even looked at each other, not seeming to be confident in giving me an answer. Eventually one of the two took the lead and stumbled over his first words, "Ummm, well no. Alchemists only lose their designation if they remain in debt with the Tribe after each thirty-day cycle or have proven they can't Craft."

"Do they have to pay back that debt?" I asked, thinking I was understanding what the function of this place was. Not only would I have to pay for food and my stay, which I'd learned from Fong, but also any ingredients I used in Alchemy.

"Of course!" the guard answered, much more sure of this answer.

"Thank you," I said and then continued, "Where can I find Tribe members going out on missions?"

"Just before the District Gate is for our Tribe exclusively. If you don't find what you're looking for there, you can enter the Square and find a *random* group."

Again, the way the guard said 'random' set alarm bells off in my head. Either Maelstrom looked down on Tribe members joining others or joining random groups was dangerous. Regardless, I wasn't going to be making that mistake. Nodding to the men, I returned to my room and changed into the black lycra-like clothing, hoping it was what marked Gatherers. It was pleasantly tight on the arms and chest, while the pants were still somewhat baggy and cool.

I did wonder how they would feel once the sun hit them, but also put on my old Mining Gear over them, just to have some protection if Monsters attacked—which should also serve to keep a great deal of the punishment from the multiple suns off the black attire.

After I was changed, I left the Alchemist Building, which I had yet to discover a name for. Outside, I walked back up the main street of the District, back toward the Square. My mind was abuzz with thoughts as my body fully finished waking up after breakfast.

It was quite clear to me that the goods in that building belonged to the Tribe or people within it. Each one had a price, and as such, using them would incur that cost onto the Alchemist. If the Alchemist succeeded in making something of value, then it likely belonged to the Tribe in some way.

In that quasi-ownership, I wasn't yet sure of a few things.

Amongst those was if the Tribe paid the Alchemist in credit for usable products, if the Alchemist could sell the product as they saw fit, if those set Tribe prices were a fair value, or how much the Tribe charged Alchemists and other Crafters for the provided food I'd partaken in. Fong had made it clear that I would be charged for the room, and food, but not how much.

No matter the answer to those questions, the result was still the same. That building was most likely designed to put people into debt or at the very least force them to work continuously. It was better to go find my own supply of resources. At least until Smegma returned, or if the Demon truly was unable to be in the Tutorial—until I learned more.

The good news for me was that, as far as Gathering went, I had the ability to perform multiple roles—which hopefully would mean I could find a group.

Between one block and the next, I was into the 'poor' area of the District, which invoked further considerations. Were these people the ones who thought like me? The ones who chose to go it on their own, without the Tribe's '*full* support?'

Or were they just unfavorable Professions? Low Skill levels? UnSkilled Crafters? Some of the people exiting the wooden houses were also Combat Hunters, which gave me some hope. It was likely just cheaper to live out here. Maybe you wouldn't get breakfast, the strange magic shower, and constant guards, but you also wouldn't end up in debt to Maelstrom.

A thought I'd just had brought me up short. Why the 'unnecessary' guards? Surely if you couldn't harm others… then I realized. It was to settle disputes and prevent theft. I didn't know how that would work but decided it didn't matter at the moment. Nodding to myself, I continued my walk. I'd try to find out more from the group I joined. There was still the question of how the members of the District felt about the Tribe.

When I got to the entrance, I quickly discovered a complication. Many of the people that had been exiting houses simply walked directly to a group and then waited. There was no shouting of what groups would need. No, this was like a series of well-oiled machines that had been running efficiently from eight-to-five for years.

Even as I watched, groups collected final members and left. I wondered how many Maelstrom groups had already started their days. Swallowing the nervousness I felt, I rushed to speak to the nearest group.

"Do you need a Gatherer by any chance?" I hurried to say.

The members looked at me, taking in my Mining gear, and shook their heads in near unison. Thinking they might have assumed I could only Mine, due to the gear, I added, "I can collect Herbs, Skin, and Butcher as well."

A few of the individuals perked up a bit, but a man sitting near the middle sighed wearily. "Everyone here can Skin and Butcher, kid. It's not a hard thing to do, even without the Skill. Do you actually have a Skill that will help you Gather Herbs and maintain their freshness?"

"Well, I do have a Skill that will direct me to some extent up to high F-Rank, and I also have a Skill that will store cuttings and Fruits in a frozen state."

The lie about the Necklace of Holding was a bit spur of the moment, but I realized in a cold sweat that claiming to have a Bag of Holding might make me a target of thievery, same Tribe or not. Not to mention the Mammoth Bear's insinuation that people might just kill me for Points. The leader scratched his beard and looked at a few other Gatherers, who sat in a group of four inside the circle of eight Hunters.

They looked back at him with distaste clearly written on their faces. The man shook his head and answered, "Sorry, kid, we have all the Gatherers we need."

Nodding, I moved on. I could tell he would have taken me if it was his decision alone. My guess was that there was a contract of sorts between the Gatherers and Hunters—like it was back on Earth. So, disrupting that would take negotiations that he wasn't willing to deal with.

Four more groups had similar responses, and another five groups left before I could even get to them. Finally, I was left with three groups remaining in the Square. Two of which were large and looked like every other group that had already left or denied me. The final group had four members in what would be a stretch to call serviceable armor.

I had a feeling where I would end up, but stubbornly, I approached the two larger groups and was denied. The group of four was my final option, and I sighed. One of the reasons I hadn't approached them yet was the distinct lack of other Gatherers standing or sitting with them.

It didn't bode well. Nor did their attire and age. They were likely the same age as me, and even I could admit that I had no business leading a group. There was a decision to make, and with a few deep breaths, I made it.

Going back to the Alchemist Building and wasting resources could simply dig me into a hole. As would eating the food and simply staying there. The rejections wouldn't change from one day to the next, either.

"Husk, I wish Smegma was here," I grumbled under my breath. I knew that with him this wouldn't have even become a problem. I likely could have created a Pill with his help and the equipment available, or maybe even a Potion...

That thought showed me just how much I relied on the Demon, and that made up my mind. If I wanted to be a Hunter, I needed to take a risk. I walked up to the final group. The only good news was that they were far less threatening in appearance than most of the others.

One of them smiled at my approach and stepped forward to meet me. With an excited voice, he said, "I was wondering how long it would take for you to arrive at the same conclusion we all did. I'm London, what's your name?"

The young man had dirty blonde hair, brown eyes, and stood a whole foot shorter than me. However, where I was tall and slim, London was stocky. The Shield and Sword he carried looked like they'd seen a lot of use too. He even held out his hand to shake.

I grasped it and answered, "Brodie, I'm a Gatherer—I can—"

"We heard you with the other groups," a soft voice interjected. "We could really use your services if you'd be willing."

My gaze found the speaker, and I was somewhat surprised to see a young lady with two fencing-like Swords on her hip. I knew that style of blade had a name but couldn't recall it. London took pity on me and said, "She doesn't speak to just anyone, so she must already like something about you. This is Sarah."

Sarah was the only one of the group who was shorter than London. Her features were definitely feminine when standing this close, but since she wore a leather hood and tight-fitting armor, it hadn't been immediately apparent that she was a woman. Of her facial features, I could only see a small nose that was almost unpointed and light eyes that could have been green or blue.

"What do you guys usually do?" I asked, not wanting to commit to a group that entered those Dungeons, 'Challenges,' or 'Opportunities' I'd heard about yesterday. Not without understanding what that even meant.

"We've been going out and killing Monsters," another member of the group said. His tone was anything but excited, especially when compared to London's. "You can tell by our gear how well that's *going!*"

The speaker was a tall man with a long Sword resting on his metal-plated shoulder. His straw-colored hair was what I would normally describe as a bird's nest, and his face was freckled to such a high degree that one could almost call it a tan—if it hadn't been broken up by patches of pale white. His eyes, like London's, were brown.

"This is Gavin. Don't pay his tone much mind. He just wants to buy plate armor and can't afford it," London explained, his voice still exuberant. "However, if we finally have a Gatherer, that could change."

"Not if he's, like, useless!" the final member of the group whispered a bit too loudly to be called under their breath. She had an accent but spoke in English.

The last member was also a woman. But where Sarah was small and lithe, this woman was mildly tall and skinny. However, she was the only one not

338

wearing a sword or any visible weapon. She had dark black hair and wore an expression that made her seem to be smelling dog shit right under her nose. Her brown eyes didn't meet mine—telling me that she hadn't meant the comment to be confrontational.

She had pale skin, and looked a lot like Fong, actually. Then again, I'd thought Fong and Kai looked alike—so, it was probably that I couldn't distinguish key differences.

"I can't guarantee anything, since I just arrived," I admitted. "I was pretty good back on Earth, but that might just mean I'm the worst Gatherer in the Tutorial for all I know. Still, I'll be better than nothing."

"This is Jacky. She thinks of herself as a realist," London explained, and then in a low whisper, he added, "Most of the time people just call her a rude-witch."

I held my face neutral at the joke, even as Jacky's eyes came up to glare at London. "I don't have to hear what you say to know you just called me a name!"

London broke into laughter, simultaneously shrugging at Jacky. "Then maybe learn to actually mutter under your breath. Or stop 'keeping it real.'"

Jacky scrunched up her nose but let the retort go unchallenged. London smiled and then turned to me, "You game to give us a shot? We'd gladly give you a sixty-forty split."

"Eighty-twenty," I retorted, having been around Smegma enough to know that haggling was a necessity when you didn't know the actual value you had.

"Come on!" Jacky complained. "Sixty-forty was totally a deal. Those big groups do fifty-fifty at best."

London held up a hand. "We'll go seventy-thirty, but Equipment repairs come out of your cut. Deal?"

"Uhhh," I motioned at their current gear. "That seems a bit unfair."

London smiled. "Deal or no deal?"

"I'll pay for repairs within reason," I answered. "By 'within reason,' I mean if it exceeds ten percent, then the rest is on you, and not for anything that happened before I joined."

"Fine," London answered, his voice filled with false sadness, even as he winked and held out his hand.

Jacky's face soured further, which I hadn't thought possible, but the other three nodded. Sarah even went as far as to crack a half smile.

I didn't shake right away and instead asked, "Where do you usually Hunt?"

London's smile came back and he pointed in a vague direction. "We don't go out of sight of Tutorial Town. You know, the classic *Bunny* Hunters."

I laughed, knowing he was meaning it as a joke. It was a classic RPG trope that you usually had to hunt small creatures such as Bunnies to gain power early in a game.

Let's hope hunting Bunnies around Tutorial Town didn't require Holy Hand Grenades…

CHAPTER 52: CHAPTER 104

Tutorial Day 2

Leaving town made me more anxious than I thought it would. Due to *Mental Fortitude,* I had to truly concentrate on the feeling to know I was feeling it, but when I did—it was certainly there.

Especially when our group of young adults crossed through the milling crowd just outside the Gates. That step, from paving stones to hard-packed mud, was the hardest I'd taken since arriving in the Tutorial. I felt the cleaning magic pass over me again, making goosebumps rise.

And it wasn't just due to the change from 'air-conditioned' Town to sweltering humidity.

I almost held my breath. However, *Mental Fortitude* allowed my brain to counter my physical response with calm calculation.

I possessed a Skill that most people here probably did not. Plus, at this point, no one knew about it.

The calmness and logic inside my head simply pointed to a single Skill of mine to alleviate the chill. *Recovery.* I had it, and it would certainly increase my survivability.

I wasn't the only one in my group that was feeling the increased tension. A quick glance showed that the two women were holding their breath and the two men were breathing heavily, like they had been jogging here.

Did they go through this same 'gauntlet' each morning? Instantly, I had begun to sweat, as the perfect temperature of the city changed back to the humid heat that I vaguely recalled from yesterday.

I gained a newfound respect for the group—realizing that they were far braver than I'd originally known. I'd only been past this entrance once and somewhat forgotten about the milling crowd of people.

The eyes of the rabble followed the group. I could tell that a few were cataloging my presence with them. A few individuals made it more obvious, narrowing their eyes before rushing back inside. I was pretty sure the people manning the Gates in the Central Square would have already informed the other Tribes about me, but I guessed that there was a second layer of informants mixed in amongst these people.

Would Maelstrom be upset that I didn't immediately start working toward Alchemy? It had certainly seemed important to the man. Whatever the significance of that Inheritance was, it seemed it could either help him directly, or the Tribe. I hadn't gotten a good enough read on the leader to tell which yet.

My mind scolded me as I tried to begin speculating on what the other Tribes would do with the knowledge of a new Tutorial arrival. I had zero information on them. I figured I could fix that, and as soon as we were close to a mile from the gates, I turned to London.

"As you know, I just got here. First, and most importantly can those people kill us for our Tutorial Points? Also can you tell me about the other three Tribes?" I almost added a 'please,' but killed my inner Canadian. I didn't want to pander. Plus, London had seemed like a talker when we first met.

The group laughed, giving me something of an answer to the situation yesterday with Bear. The man wasn't that powerful to have panderers it seemed.

"Oh, not really on the first part. Supposedly, during the War you could— which is why it's not some kind of morbid joke. Like a boogie man. Watch out or I'll declare a war to steal Tutorial Points from you," London explained, coming out of his own anxiety-ridden state thanks to my question. I watched as he shook the remaining goosebumps off himself before smiling and regarding me seriously. "As for the second question, I'll explain the other Tribes, but don't go getting any ideas on trying to change Districts. I don't think anyone has survived that before."

That statement caused my relief over his first answer to vanish, and I frowned as I considered. What could London say that would make me want to switch Tribes?

"The Maelstrom Tribe is known as the Mage District. That's because the Skills that are offered inside its Tower are all Caster-based, that and Swords, but the Sword Skills are kind of weak—"

London cut off as Sarah gave him an elbow to his kidneys. The short woman had to make the gesture at about her head height to not hit him in the mid-thigh or hip. He looked at her, and somehow her scowl and impatient gesture at me conveyed something to him.

"Oh, right!" he exclaimed. "You're a Gatherer, so you likely would also want to know what Profession Skills the Tower has. Maelstrom is known for Alchemy. *Happy?*" He said the last pointedly to Sarah, who nodded.

"After Maelstrom in the North, is the Warrior District in the East. It's owned by the Hero Tribe. Its Tower supposedly offers Body Strengthening Skills and a good variety of Weapon Skills that are far more powerful than Maelstroms. For the Crafting side of things, it's known for Armor and Weapons—"

Jacky broke in, "Blacksmithing, you moron. They both fall under Blacksmithing."

London's face shaded slightly red as he tried to pointedly ignore Jacky and continue, "Then there's the South, which is known as the Assassin District. Its Tribe is called Shadow, and most of us can only conjecture what its Tower specifically offers. Definitely Skills that are based around sneaky shit." He caught another elbow from Sarah.

"Oh, umm yeah, no idea on the Crafting stuff either. It's speculation that they work with Leather, or Enchanting, since the other Districts don't have those. I've never spoken to a member of their Tribe, if I'm honest."

"How would you know if you did?" Gavin asked. "We never see anyone entering or exiting their District through the gate. You can only see the guards on duty at the gate, and the heads atop the walls. So if they got out and claimed they were from another Tribe, you'd simply have to take their word for it."

"Unless you have a Truth Skill," Jacky countered.

"Right, 'cause there's so many of those in here!" London responded a bit too hotly for what I felt the comment warranted, letting me know he was still upset over the name calling earlier.

Jacky stuck her tongue out and flipped him the bird as she pointedly turned away from him. It might have been amusing if this wasn't the group I was about to Hunt with. As it stood, their dynamic just made me nervous.

London continued, distracting me from that line of thinking. "The West District is kind of a catch-all. It's got Skills that don't focus on any one area. They are also the weakest of the Districts because of that. The Tribe is called the Hunter Tribe, and I guess they do produce more ranged fighters than any but the Maelstrom Tribe. They are also not known for any one Crafting Profession. I've personally seen members use Magic Traps, Formations, Skill Scrolls and other assorted items in combat."

London looked at me after he was finished. "Do any of those sound more appealing to you?"

Despite him not saying it, I instantly understood his implication from his tone of voice. I looked at the four members of this Hunting party. Only Jacky might have been a Mage, but they were all part of Maelstrom—a Tribe that offered Mage Skills primarily in its Tower.

London was projecting his feelings onto me. He wanted to join a different Tribe, and from the information he'd just offered, he'd likely fit better in the East Warrior District—the Hero Tribe. Next, I studied Sarah, who was small and thus used two Rapiers instead of more weighty weapons.

I could picture her with two daggers on her hips easily, and if the Southern Shadowy District really did specialize in Stealth, she'd likely be a better fit there.

Finally, there was Gavin, a man who wielded a large Sword, which might make him fit with Maelstrom—or it might not. He could also likely fit in the Hero Tribe, or maybe in the Hunters of the West…

I only had to look at my own situation to realize what had likely happened. I was found by someone in Maelstrom and was thus a member. If what London said was true, and people who left Tribes were often killed, then they were probably in the exact situation I was.

"Why do they kill people who try to leave?" I asked, not understanding that particular point. I could perhaps see why Shadow, who was largely secretive, might do so, but the Maelstrom and Hero Tribes seemed to be pretty well-known for what the Towers offered.

"We don't know," Gavin answered, causing me to look away from London, who I'd expected the answer from. "We think it's a hangup from the early days. But we've only been here for about five years. Some of the old-hats and the Tribe leaders have been around for forty or more years."

That wording made me stop walking, even as I suddenly recalled Fong's words about sixty years. I'd dismissed them because of everything going on. "Wait—the Advent was only twenty-four years ago. How can people have been here before that?"

"Oh," Sarah said as she stopped and spun to look at me. "That was one of my first questions. Maelstrom said it's total speculation, but he thinks there is a

Time Dilation on this place. He wouldn't give specifics, but he definitely arrived well after the Advent and is one of the ones who's been here for forty or more years."

Sixty years, actually…

The rest of the group had also stopped to look at me. I blinked as my brain turned that information over. So, as others arrived and were asked the year outside, the leaders of this place must have discovered the disparity. My hand rose to the nape of my neck as I began to scratch at the small, sweating hairs that were standing on end.

"Bet his next question is totally going to be about the severity of the Time Dilation," Jacky said haughtily.

"Now it will be," London growled. "Way to ruin it, Jacky!" The group started walking again as London called back, "It's approximately three to one. Or that's the best guess of the smartest people I've talked to."

My eyes widened. So, I was still in my first day in this place? At least as far as Earth's time was concerned. So, it could be Saturday night back home? Despite everything, that did make me feel slightly less worried for my family.

Surely, I could discover a way out of here before they pronounced me dead, right?

Mental Fortitude silenced that line of thinking, instantly pointing my attention to the start of another Forest and the hovering plaques I could already make out.

"Boar," Gavin called, stopping my smile before it managed to raise the edges of my mouth by more than a millimeter.

To my surprise, the group seemed to calm, in opposition to my slight tension. London moved forward first, his Shield swinging off his shoulder-carry position and onto his forearm. His Sword dangled toward the ground for a moment before it was flipped and held in a practiced grip.

Gavin stepped in on his right shoulder and Sarah on his left, forming a triangle around Jacky, who raised her hands before spinning her head to look at me. "You're with me. Get over here. Now!"

The fact that she didn't sling any names, and even had a commanding voice, made me instantly jump to her side. The three in front separated then. London moved forward while the other two moved on forty-five degree angles away from each other, but still toward the grazing boar Gavin had spotted. The thing wasn't difficult to 'spot' now that I was looking at it.

I could tell it would be alerted to London's presence first, since he was moving directly toward it. I took the moment to study the creature. It was nowhere near the size of the Porcu-hog, but it was sturdier looking.

It was easily six or seven feet at its shoulders and had two gleaming tusks protruding up past its bottom lip, which was clearly apparent with each bite of foliage it took. To my horror, I watched as a red Plant-plaque near its mouth vanished down its throat.

I scanned the Forest for the other plaques I could see. Knowing what to look for now, I could see Boars foraging through the Trees near a few of them.

Damn, so collecting Herbs wasn't going to be as easy as it looked on first approach. The thick mane of a mohawk on the Boar's back jumped as it stopped foraging and jerked its head up to stare at London.

A few loud grunts sounded out, followed by a squeal, making me unsure if it was angry or afraid. Either way, before I could blink, it leaped forward to begin a charge directly at London.

London raised his Shield, looking like he was getting ready to meet the couple tons of muscle head-on, and I couldn't help but wonder how much Strength the kid must possess to be willing to do that. I still hadn't tested my own limits with ten Strength, but I doubted I could even lift double what I used to in the gym.

If London was thinking of catching that thing with his legs planted—

Gavin and Sarah struck from the sides—Gavin with a slash of his great Sword at the creature's front legs, and Sarah with piercing strikes from her Rapier that glowed red. Even as her body closed the gap with the bulk of the beast, I saw her arms pumping back and forth in actions that were so quick I couldn't count them.

Needless to say, in that split second, she struck more than once but no more than ten times. The Boar squealed and crashed forward as Gavin's slash sheared through the leg muscles that supported it. London's Shield glowed then, and instead of the Boar charging *him*, the man was suddenly flying forward to charge against its skidding snout.

The Shield made contact, and the percussive sound was far louder than it had any right to be. It sounded like one of those ornamental tanggu drums that I'd often seen the Chinese use on TV. Light from beside me made my head turn to find Jacky weaving her hands and forming something between them.

At first, I watched on without understanding what I was seeing. My mind oscillated between Wind or Water—until I heard the strange crackle that only came from water freezing. She was forming an Ice Spear. Once the spell had become almost totally white around the blue core of the five-foot piece of ice, she shot her hands forward and it exploded outward.

I followed its trajectory, somewhat worried for London. The Spear passed by his right hip, skewering into the red eye of the Boar. Between one breath and the next, the Boar went limp.

The fight was over and I was left marveling at the coordination on display by the four in front of me. I might have had misgivings at first, but that teamwork had been beyond impressive. London looked back at me, seemingly unconcerned with how close the Ice Spear had been to his hip.

"You good to Skin and Butcher this guy?"

Blinking, I was about to nod when I remembered the foraging Boars, and the Herbs that were likely still far enough away from them that I could collect them. Unsure, I suggested, "I should probably collect the visible Herbs first, no?"

"We've never had a Gardener before. Do you think you can get them without pissing off another Boar? Jackie needs time to recharge her Mana…"

I pointed twice in quick succession, then added a third. "Those two for sure, that Sapling, probably. After that, I doubt it."

"Sapling?" Gavin asked, turning to look at the small Tree I motioned toward.

"What good is a Tree?" Jacky asked from right beside me, her volume and level of derision almost making me jump.

"It's a little trick I discovered in a Portal."

"Okay, we'll guard you just in case. Plus, we all help out with Butchering anyway. We just don't have Skills for Skinning, so we're often just left with scraps when we try."

"I'll be honest, I'm a bit slow on the Skinning myself, but I think I can get the Hide off in one piece."

I directed the group to the Sapling first, London moving in front of me and past it to ensure it was safe. One problem quickly became apparent. I had no bucket to place the thing in. Sarah solved it rather quickly, though, by handing me a bucket made of woven leaves. I wondered if this was something she already had on her, in a Storage item, or if she had made it that quickly. I was leaning toward the former, regardless of how fast her hands *could* move. Soon I had the thing dug out, thanks to my Gardening Tools, and we retreated to the two plaques I could see.

Without a pot to put the Sapling in, I first dug another hole outside of the forest and then prepared it for fusing as Smegma had instructed. Afterward, I returned to the nearest red plaque.

Witch Hazel
Rank: Low F
Quality: Good
Efficacy: 75%

The Plant itself was more of a Bush, with something I'd have called yellow Flowers adorning it. One of my two Gardening Skills, I assumed *Harvesting*, highlighted in blue where I should cut the Flowers off. Another line in purple highlighted where I could cut an entire branch off. Due to the angle and clear intention of the Skill that the instructed cuts were those needed to graft it to the Sapling behind me, I assumed this was the *Gardening* Skill that my Status Screen had mentioned.

In the same purple there was also a very large circle around the plant in case I wanted to dig it up.

First, I performed the branch trim with my Shears, and then I hurried it over to the Sapling before trimming away a thin branch and inserting the cut stem and some of my Mana into it. Once the wound on the Sapling closed over, I returned to the Bush and collected more of the Witch Hazel Flowers, following the clear instructions from *Harvesting*.

Sarah crouched beside me and began putting the Flowers into a Bag. I could tell it was magical because the yellow Witch Hazel vanished from her hand. Guess that answered where my 'leaf bucket' came from. At my glance, she explained, "This is a Bag of Holding meant to keep items fresh. It has a time dilation on it, but it isn't the most expensive. So, if we stay out here the whole day, things will probably lose half of their freshness."

After I had collected roughly a hundred Witch Hazel Flowers, I moved on, not wanting to collect the entire Bush if the Plant itself wasn't too valuable. Plus, leaving the Bush to grow more would surely mean I could come back in the future. Unless of course a Boar ate it whole…

The group protected me as I walked to the next plaque.

Earth Root
Rank: High F
Quality: Poor
Efficacy: 35%

This time, there was no purple line and only two blue ones. I followed the cutting 'instructions' and soon had a wriggling vine in my hand. It felt like a snake trying to escape. I hurriedly held it out to Sarah, who made it vanish.

The group gave me a look and I answered the unspoken question, "Probably not worth the risk to try to grab any other ones that are closer to the other Boars right now. We'll Skin and Butcher the first kill so we don't have to abandon it if we alert multiple Boars while going for the other Herbs out here that I recognize."

Sure, the 'recognize' part was a total lie, but I figured the group needed me to sound like I knew what I was doing instead of relying blindly on my Skill. Then again, for all I knew, they were used to others relying on similar Skills.

When I turned around and looked at the Boar corpse, I was shocked to find a plaque hovering above it. It was a bit far away to read, and I first wrote the thing off as being the Plant the thing had swallowed. I figured that perhaps the System was just letting me know I could get it from its belly.

However, the closer I came, the more the size and length of the plaque paired with the color of the lines floating on the Boar's skin, which began to stand out as different from the ones on the Herbs I'd collected.

When I finally got in range and saw the red plaque fully, I realized one other part that stood out. The final portion was orange, and while it clearly had something to do with my *Skinning* Skill, it also hinted at so much more.

Borker Skin
Difficulty Rank: Low E
Damage from Fight: Low
Quality: High
Skinning Rank: 10-30

Where had that final line been when *Harvesting* Witch Hazel or Earth Root? What did it mean?

At times like this, I wished I had Smegma hovering around, annoying me. Even if his knowledge of the current System had some gaps, he was still smart enough to theorize possibilities.

346

I certainly was smart enough too, but it would be nice for someone to confirm my current theory—was this Tutorial actually simply a place to level Skills, and maybe even Evolve them?

<u>BLOOPERS</u>

Desperately, I tried to school my face and not give away Smegma's plausible lie for the Mana Battery. In the end, I just looked at the floor in hopes that the Snake wouldn't notice.

The Snake pulled back, and the shadow receded—seeming to allude to a stay of execution. As it slowly returned to its spot deeper in the lake, it hissed, "I get nothing by granting thisss requessst."

"Excssept for the cooked Mirror Fisssh, Great One."

My head flew up to stare at Smegma. Why was he trying to talk like the Snake? The husking Demon winked at me.

"Are you making fun of me?" the Snake retorted, all three of its eyes narrowing.

"Are you making fun of me?" Smegma repeated, again doing a poor imitation of the Snake.

The other three people in the room all slowly turned to stare at the Demon, looks of terror painted on their faces.

"Ssstop that!" the Snake demanded.

"Ssstop. Don't make fun of me," Smegma said.

"What the hell are you doing?" I asked, my voice an urgent shout.

"Don't worry. Thisss Sssnake can't kill usss. We have plot armor!" Smegma said.

"What isss thisss plot armor you ssspeak of?" the Snake asked.

"Oh, just a little sssomething the God of thisss Universsse givesss usss and not you," Smegma said. "In fact, I bet we end up killing you if you do it!"

"Killing me?" the Snake asked and then started to glow.

"Anytime now, Ryan," Smegma said.

"Ryan?" I asked.

"That's his name. The one in control of all this."

"You mean all the bad shit that's been happening to me is this Ryan's fault?"

"Yea—" Smegma started to say, just before a wave of green liquid splashed over me and everyone on the shore.

Just as the pain hit, and I started to feel my skin burning off, everything seemed to stop and then reverse.

"Smegma, I've told you before not to antagonize things," a deep resonant voice said. "Now, all these words need to be thrown out."

"What about the bloopers, you idiotic, power-tripping God-wannabe…"

"Please tell me I'm not going to remember all this?" Dave pleaded, his skin slowly reattaching itself to his body.

A bright white flash went through the cavern.

* * *

Sure, I had seen something like a force wave expel outward after each impact. Well, those had started with that Black Hole, I think? That did explain how the impact waves could be darker than the blackness of space. Wait—that made no sense?

Whatever. The point I was trying to make—did I have a point?

Husk!

The rain seemed to bring the first new sensation I'd felt in millions of… years? Months? Days? Hours? Minutes! Surely it had only been minutes. The sensation of rain touching the superheated surface without evaporating above it— was like aloe vera on a terrible sunburn.

No, it was far better than even that. It was a drop of water hitting my tongue in the middle of a desert. Had I even been in a desert before? No, no, I hadn't.

The scene changed and scantily clad women with gold chains performed for me in the shade of a tent. I blinked as I looked around. The tent had no sides to it, but was extremely huge. I had to even swivel my neck from side to side to see each opening to the desert behind.

Wait swivel my neck? I arched my neck, and turned it, attempting to understand what was happening. The dancers nearby gasped and began to shimmy and shake harder than ever before. What in the world was going on?

I glimpsed my 'feet' and found only massive, webbed duck feet surrounding a throne. In a panic, and desperate I craned my neck over and stared at my body. It was feathered and white. I let out a large honk of indignation.

The Altar had said *Draconic Chosen*, but I was a massive fluffy tailed *Duck*. My shock gave way to anger.

"Is everything okay, Honkers?" a man on the throne beneath me asked.

I sat on him, and the people gasped all the louder. I would kill them all and Evolve into a Canada Goose…

* * *

"You need more information before you go around full-cocked like an Incubus at an orgy."

[A what?] I asked incredulously.

"An Incubus," Smegma enunciated. "Plus, I don't think you'd be welcome in Alexus Fawn's sex dungeon. She's clearly into Succubi."

[I'm so confused right now.]

"I'm saying she probably bats for the other team."

[No that part I get, but what's with the sudden topic switch to Incubi, Succubi and Sex Dungeons?]

"Oh, I know a guy named Arnold, he has a legendary sex dungeon. He's a farmer but totally gets off on that stuff ."

I blinked. Why did I know that name, and plot?

[Wait, are you just bringing up books you've read mixed with Demons?]

Smegma smiled. "At least you're not going to do anything stupid to *save* Eva…moron."

ROYAL ROAD

This story is also being posted to Royal Road. If you have a moment head on over and give it a follow, favorite and a rating. It would really help me out.

Royal Road

<u>LITRPG GROUP</u>

To learn more about LitRPG, talk to authors and just have an awesome time, please join the LitRPG Group.

GREAT LITRPG COMMUNITIES

If you love LitRPG, GameLit, or cultivation (Western Cultivation and Cultivation Novels) join these awesome communities on Facebook!

* * *

Or if you just want to be part of the community, try LitRPG Legion.

* * *

Finally, there is LitRPG + Gamelit Readers.

ABOUT THE AUTHOR

Follow Ryan DeBruyn, or join his Guardian's of The Grotto Facebook group to stay up to date on new releases. Click the images below for any other social media group.

ALSO BY RYAN DEBRUYN

Equalize - Book 1 of Ether Collapse Series
Excise - Book 2 of Ether Collapse Series
Earthdom - Book 3 of Ether Collapse Series
Equatorial - Book 4 of Ether Collapse Series

* * *

Tech Duinn - Book 1 of Ether Flows Series
Edda Gaia - Book 2 of Ether Flows Series

* * *

Starred Tower - System Misinterpret Book One
Endarkened Spire - System Misinterpret Book Two

TUTORIAL TOWN

Volume 3

By Ryan DeBryun

Discovering a Tutorial to help against the Monsters should be a good thing. But the Humans that came before Brodie had and have other plans.

Brodie must hope for the best for his burgeoning company as he is transported to a whole new world, with a strange new socioeconomic structure. If he and his family were middle class on Earth, he knows now that he's just a newb at the bottom of the Tutorial ladder.

There is a small glimmer of hope as he realizes just how much he can personally gain from the Tutorial. *Especially with Smegma's* help and knowledge of the System…

Can Brodie learn enough to return a true Hunter, or will he be stuck inside for decades…

Coming soon!

RISE OF MANKIND : AGE OF STONE

By Jez Cajiao

In all the games Matt has played, Dungeons are places to raid, places you dream of conquering, but when the world is stripped of electricity, and the first mana-twisted beasts start to prowl, the games all come to an end...

Matt's just an ordinary guy, but when he's beaten, robbed, and left for dead, bleeding out at the bottom of a gully, it all has to change as he grasps frantically at his only chance for survival, coming as it does in the form of a glowing, dangerously pulsing light.

With his reality forever altered, Matt must quickly find a suitable place to deploy the Dungeon Core, fighting his way through the hundreds of people between him and safety, because if he doesn't do it soon, a Core Detonation will solve all of his problems for him… permanently.

Welcome to the New World.

Experience a dark apocalyptic LitRPG Dungeon Core tale, Matt is a normal guy, pushed into terrible situations, and without anyone to hold his hand and explain the system. This is a weak-to-strong tale about doing what's right, not what's easy, in a nightmarish world. Fans of Dungeon Core stories, progression fantasy and strategy real time expansion games are sure to love it.

<u>Order Now!</u>

Ryan DeBruyn

WELCOME TO THE DARK AGES

Morgan and Merlins excellent Adventures
Book One
By
Malory

When Merlin needs a hero to save the world, he gets... well, me.

Fan-bloody-tastic.

I was supposed to be dead. Instead, I wake up face-down in Dark Age mud, possessing some poor bastard's body, while the ghost of history's most famous wizard rambles on about being murdered, cosmic energy and the end of all reality.

Just one tiny problem: I know about as much about cultivation as a pig knows about particle physics.

Now I'm fumbling with mystical energy that feels like juggling nitroglycerin, trying not to get shanked by everyone and their grandmother, and dealing with Merlin's constant "helpful" commentary.

Something dark is rising in Arthurian Britain.

Something that made even Merlin scared. They say fate has a sense of humour. Turns out it's the kind that laughs while setting your hair on fire.

Welcome to the Dark Ages, where cultivation meets chaos, and the only thing sharper than a sword is my questionable wit.

Read Now!

THEFT OF DECKS

By Lars Machmüller

When the deck is stacked against you? Change the game!

In the frontier town of Isarn, Chase will never be more than the lowly Darkborn thief he is. Banned from training, banned from acquiring better cards, if the Lightborn had their way, he'd be banned from life itself.

He's not alone though, and the one thing he and his friends have is determination. Losing a hand to a brutal punishment only fueled his obsession to get access to his own amazing, reality-bending cards.

That is the path to power and a future for them all. Nobody cares where you came from when you're rich enough. For now, though, they're facing both established powers, churches and age-old prejudices. It's time to get to work, and if the Lightborn won't share and play nice?

Sometimes the only way to get dealt a better hand is to steal the whole damn deck!

Buy on Amazon

QUEST ACADEMY

By Brian J. Nordon

A world infested by demons.
An Academy designed to train Heroes to save humanity from annihilation.
A new student's power could make all the difference.

Humans have been pushed to the brink of extinction by an ever-evolving demonic threat. Portals are opening faster than ever, Towers bursting into the skies and Dungeons being mined below the last safe havens of society. The demons are winning.

Quest Academy stands defiantly against them, as a place to train the next generation of Heroes. The Guild Association is holding the line, but are in dire need of new blood and the powerful abilities they could bring to the battlefront. To be the saviors that humanity needs, they need to surpass the limits of those that came before them.

In a war with everything on the line, every power matters. With an adaptive enemy, comes the need for a constant shift in tactics. A new age of strategy is emerging, with even the unlikeliest of Heroes making an impact.

Salvatore Argento has never seen a demon.
He has never aspired to become a Hero.
Yet his power might be the one to tip the odds in humanity's favor.

Buy on Amazon

WANDERING WARRIOR

By Michael Head

A divine quest to deliver justice.
One year to accomplish his mission.
After nineteen planets, there's something different about this one.

James Holden has reached the maximum level there is for a human. That's perfect, since he's the only one of his kind. A wandering warrior, without control of his destination, tossed between universes by gods who've failed to tell him why. James is the lone Judge on a new world in need of someone to balance the scales. He isn't afraid to do so with extreme prejudice. As the Chief Justice, he has to right the wrongs the innocent can't fix themselves.

As James quickly discovers, the roots of corruption run deep. Guilds choose to protect themselves rather than the people. Monsters roam the wilderness unchecked. Judgment is usually a decision between right and wrong, but nothing is ever that simple. This time, being the strongest human won't be enough to punish the guilty. James might have to recruit some new blood, even if he prefers to work alone.

On his twentieth world, he is going to win, no matter the cost. James will have to find a way to break past the limits of the system if he's going to have a chance at making a difference.

Buy on Amazon

KNIGHTS OF ETERNITY

By Rachel Ní Chuirc

When Zara awoke in chains she thought she'd gone mad.

She was Zara the Fury - mistress of flame and fear. Her name was whispered across the land, from ramshackle taverns to the royal court. Even the heroic Gilded Knights thought twice before crossing her path.
She was feared—*respected.*
Now she was curled up on a dirt floor on her fiancé's orders. Valerius, leader of the Gilded, mocks her cries for help. And the kingdom is on the brink of war over the missing Lady Eternity…
But that wasn't why Zara thought she had gone mad.
The reason why is that the last thing she remembered was blood, an arcade screen, and the gun that changed everything.

**But no chains can hold the Fury, and when she gets out?
The world is going to *burn*.**

Buy on Amazon

SCARLET CITADEL

By Jack Fields

Gormon Hughes is 19, thin as a broom, and has—not for the first time in his life—been swept into the path of trouble. Poor, recently heartbroken, and indebted to the sort of people who file their teeth into needle points and devour wriggling bloated spiders for fun, Hughes sets his sights on salvation.

That salvation is the Scarlet Citadel, a wealthy organization of pageant fighters, monster hunters, and secret keepers. With the aid of strange oracles, rare good fortune, and a unique power that bubbles like champagne in the core of Hughes' being, he must join the Citadel and advance himself.

But the ladder of progression is harsh and dark. The rungs are slippery.

And falling means disaster…

Buy on Amazon

LITRPG!

To learn more about LitRPG, talk to other authors including myself, and to just have an awesome time, please join the LitRPG Group

www.facebook.com/groups/LitRPGGroup

FACEBOOK

There's also a few really active Facebook groups I'd recommend you join, as you'll get to hear about great new books, new releases and interact with all your (new) favorite authors! (I may also be there, skulking at the back and enjoying the memes…)

https://www.facebook.com/groups/LitRPGlegion/

https://www.facebook.com/groups/GamelitSociety

https://www.facebook.com/groups/LitRPG.books

https://www.facebook.com/groups/LitRPGforum/

RYAN DEBRUYN
CREATIVE LITRPG FANTASY